WILSON B SMILLIE

A Wife Worth Dying For

Thanks for choosing my book, I hope you enjoy it
Wilson

First published by Bad Typewriter Publishing 2021

First edition

ISBN: 978-1-8383795-0-6

Editing by Abby Parsons
Cover art by Cherie Chapman
Advisor: C M Taylor
Illustration by Brian Wilson

This book was professionally typeset on Reedsy.
Find out more at reedsy.com

Contents

Preface

by C.M. Taylor

I was lucky enough to speed through the pages of Wilson Smillie's debut procedural noir, **A Wife Worth Dying For**, as it was being written. Quite apart from the pleasure I gained from a personal sentimental journey - I had lived in the City of Edinburgh, the book's setting, in my early 20s and was delighted to have it conjured back to my eye – I was also impressed by the tortured character gloweringly planted at the root of the novel.

The stony heart of Detective Lachlan Carter had opened once, to admit his wife, who he had then lost. But not before she had given him a son. Another tough break for a scarred cop. Mix into that his father-in-law, a Scottish judge with whom 'Leccy' has to routinely deal - and who, guess what – hates him for where he comes from. You'll get the picture: it's a challenging gig. The desperate life of Detective Carter, a man fighting to keep some semblance of normality in his existence, is the dark base on which Smillie builds his plot, as a series of crimes and a taunting antagonist make Leccy question everything he believed about his venerated, deceased beloved. Speeding through overdoses, comas and infidelity; taking in Vegas weddings, cold underground car parks and sealed envelopes, this is the noirest of noirs spreading its switchback plot across the bitter-but-gorgeous Capital city, as the last honest man in town tries everything he can to keep his heart beating.

It was a delight to have eyes on this novel as it came into being and I wish it, with its committed and modest author, and its beleaguered, tenacious detective all the best in seeing off the baddest of bad guys.

C M Taylor

Author of Premier Psycho. https://cmtaylorstory.com

Acknowledgement

For Boyd and Lexi

1

Dead of Night

Lachlan Carter gate-crashed his wife's funeral despite his father-in-law banning him from attending. Now hiding under bare winter trees in Old Calton Burial Ground, he peered through the low cloud settling over Edinburgh, contemplating the great, the good and the iffy assembled in the graveyard. The Old Town streetlights threw a shroud-like sodium glow over this entourage of questionable characters. Leading the party, Death lingered, eager to claim his prize.

Packed to the gunnels the cemetery was. Plus one.

Only a thin plastic mac defended Carter from the relentless January rain. His white hair had turned shades of grey, trickles of water had found their way down his back, causing him to shiver, but otherwise, he couldn't have cared less. These last weeks had been torment and, in his current state of grief, he endured rightful atonement. He'd stood by powerless, a horrified spectator, as Kelsa had wasted away before him, the illness consuming her body hour by callous hour.

A chorus of '*amen*' wafted up through the damp, heralding a new beginning for him and a final ending for her. He choked on his anguish as her coffin vanished deep into the rich east coast soil. Ceremony complete, her family and guests were ushered up onto Waterloo Place where the city's bars promised vibrant life.

He wiped the rain from his face, tasting bitter tears. Her moment had gone and his had come. In these ebbing minutes, she deserved to know his love would endure eternity. The downpour muffled the sound of his footsteps on the gravel path winding down to her grave. As he approached, a woman emerged from the deluge, stopping at the grave, quietly paying her respects.

He dodged behind a tomb and used the opportunity to check for lingering mourners in the ancient necropolis, studying her as she scanned the graveyard from under her umbrella. Unaware of his presence, she was of slender build, of his generation, her black hair cut in a bob, her pale neck featuring a distinctive St Christopher pendant.

Up at the cemetery gates Sheriff James Dunsmuir, his father-in-law, was glad-handing yet another senior judge. Turning back to the grave after a moment, the woman had gone.

Finally, alone with his wife, his knees buckled onto soft mud. He mumbled a prayer his grandparents had taught him. 'Protect her above all others. Saints, sinners, paupers, murderers and judges.'

Creeping shoes made a soft crunch on the wet gravel. He turned quickly, expecting to see the old bastard come to remonstrate with him for disobeying his command to stay away. Nothing there but rain falling like stair rods. Was he losing it? Was life to be defined by the death of his loved ones?

'You've found your peace, Kelsa. You showed me who I could be. Our life with Nathaniel promised so much, but where do we go from here?'

The crunch sounded again, softer and more cautious.

'Dunsmuir? Show yourself.' Carter stood up in anger, striding across the sodden grass to a marble obelisk with its head in the clouds. He searched its surrounds, finding no one. Back at his repentance, he wrapped up his amen on his knees.

'Until we meet again, darling.'

A shoe kicked him hard between the shoulder blades. He fell forwards, tumbling into infinity, embracing her in perpetual darkness. Landing hard on the coffin, breath escaped his chest. Soil poured down on him, smothering his face, penetrating his mouth, nose and eyes. The sodden earth continued to flow in, trapping him deeper under its avalanche. Thrashing desperately, he clawed for traction with hands and feet as the soaking walls collapsed inwards. He coughed mud from his mouth and cried out in panic.

For long moments rescue ignored him. Then, timely boots landed on the opposite end of the coffin.

'What the fuck are you doing, you stupid bastard?' Strong arms hauled him up by his lapels and pointed him towards life. Other hands, equally strong, reached down from above and dragged his flailing body over the muddy edge of her grave. The incessant rain washed his face as the diggers struggled to get him out.

Flapping on the ground like a beached whale, he lifted his face to the sky in gratitude and sucked on solid air. In the saturated atmosphere of the cemetery, he thought he heard someone singing: '*Bye-bye Kelsa baby, don't cha cry no more*'.

A few metres away, the woman looked on, mesmerised.

2

A Text from Hell

Carter arrived home many hours after the funeral. Somehow, his life with Kelsa had spiralled out of control these last ten months. Now, he'd been cut adrift to deal with her passing alone. To lose his parents early in life was unfortunate, but to lose his soulmate so soon in marriage was a fucking disaster. It was clear anyone who got close would pay the ultimate price. He was toxic, but even that insight didn't fully explain why his father-in-law had felt he had to inflict that despicable snub with no explanation. Dunsmuir's curt email before the funeral left no room for discussion.

The woman had vanished again before the grave rescue team had cleaned him off. In a stupor, he'd wandered the drenched streets of the city hoping to find her, intrigued as much by her identity as her ability to appear and disappear at will. After a wasted hour, he gave up and sunk a galleon-load of whisky at Captain's Bar in the Old Town. Later, he took the number 31 bus to Liberton, on Edinburgh's south side, where he lived. His profession as a detective sergeant in Edinburgh's Specialist Crime Division consumed all. How would that change now he had a baby son to care for? He knew mothers who juggled two or three kids and still held down a career. If they could do it, he could too. Nathaniel would never taste Kelsa's kisses again. Faded snapshots would be all he would know, supported by rose-tinted memories sung by his father – he parked coming to terms with single parenthood for yet another day.

While Kelsa had clung to life in hospital, her mother, Judith, had cared for Nathaniel to allow Carter to spend time with his wife. Now she was gone, contemplating chucking in his job to look after Nathaniel seemed impossible.

The extent of the night's plan had been to pick up Nathaniel from the Dunsmuir mansion, but he was in no fit state to drive. He tore off his dirty, sodden clothes, stumbled into the shower and allowed the hot water to cleanse him of his woes. Then, he scrambled under the duvet in the back bedroom to sleep it off.

He woke sometime later, disorientated by darkness and listless sobriety. The bedroom glowed softly. In his groggy state, it took him a minute to realise it was his phone. He retrieved it from the bedside table and fumbled to unlock it with his finger. There was no missed call or notification on the screen. He was about to turn over when a red dot flashing beside an unfamiliar icon invited him to tap.

It was like no text message he'd ever seen. In place of the sender's name was a sixteen-character code. Beneath the code was the date and time. Finally, there was the chilling payload.

[2019-01-14:0409] Did you kiss your baby bye-bye Leccy while

you were crying on her coffin? You have no idea who she really was. I've left you a calling card at Petite France. J

Now fully awake, Carter read and re-read the message but couldn't see how to reply or dismiss it. He sat up in bed. J knew his nickname – that he'd just buried Kelsa. A shiver ran down his spine, a single momentary image of his dead wife's scarlet-lipped smile. Was there a connection?

He got out of bed and dressed. Petite France was a short five-minute drive away. Gripping the phone like a priceless bar of gold, he went downstairs into the kitchen and unlocked the internal door to the garage. The text nagged at him. What was the '*calling card*'? He unlocked Kelsa's red-and-black Smart car, unplugged the charger, and folded himself inside the tiny motor. The garage door opened slowly. While he waited, he unlocked the phone to re-read the message.

But the app and the message had gone as if neither had ever existed.

3

Days Without Kelsa

Only just 8 a.m. Day One of life after Kelsa and Carter's future promised to be full of bleak mornings and driving rain that would depress the happiest of resilient people.

Officially, he was on bereavement leave. But his choices were stark: stay at home weeping over pictures of Kelsa holding Nathaniel, get pished on the Balvenie – or take his mind off both by working. He'd called the Dunsmuir household first thing to say he'd collect Nathaniel later in the day. A maid said she'd relay the message.

'Morning, Tam,' Carter said, breezing past the front desk of St Leonard's Police Station, dressed in his Crombie coat over a suit and tie.

'Eh, Leccy—' Sergeant Tam Watson was caught off-guard, stumbling out his words before his brain engaged first gear. 'Sergeant Carter. You're no' supposed to be in today. I mean, it was only yesterday you buried that bonny lass o' yours.'

'I can't cry over her every day, Tam.'

'Aye, well, but – listen, the boss wanted to know if you

came in.'

'Sympathy from Chief Inspector Cheryl, is it?'

'Aye, she's in her den.'

Tam disappeared into the booking office while Carter loitered at the desk like a thug with a headache.

'Go straight up.'

DCI Cheryl McKinlay met him at the door of her office. Retirement was catching up on her fast, and she had amassed all the grey hair and worry lines necessary for membership. Crow's feet were firmly established in the corners of her eyes, but the baby blues still sparkled. Serious Crime for Edinburgh City was her remit, however; rumour had it she practically ran E Division single-handedly, leaving Chief Superintendent Goodwin to implement her jottings at leisure.

'Leccy, our thoughts have been with you these past weeks,' she consoled him.

'Thank you, ma'am.'

Tea arrived, and McKinlay leaned back in her chair. 'How are you coping?'

'I want to get back to work.'

'Nice girl Kelsa was, down to earth too, considering her parentage. We need you back. But I need to know you're ready, eh?'

'Ma'am?'

'You're the only one with no caseload at the moment,' she said. 'Get over to the Royal Infirmary. Bilston Glen took a call from A & E at 2.13 a.m. An ambulance crew admitted a woman; they thought she was a hit-and-run. There's no ID. The Glen downgraded it because she's in care, but a couple of PCs wandered over first thing, and they've asked for brains at the bedside. We dinnae have any, so you'll do, eh?'

Edinburgh Royal Infirmary at Petite France. He'd gone there in the wee small hours, despite the disappearance of the text from his phone. There had been no '*calling card*' for him, and the night reception staff didn't have a clue what he was talking about.

'Sure, ma'am,' he replied cheerily, glad of something constructive to do.

'Counselling is the latest initiative from Big Boy Towers,' McKinlay carried on. 'We're required to cherish our staff and massage their mental health if they've been subjected to trauma at work or home. The Chief Super worries that coppers with deranged minds like yours might batter a deserving bampot into mince just for the sport. He doesn't like the style of TV news interviews and wants to keep his job.'

'Ma'am?' queried Carter, trying to keep up.

'Bereavement therapy. At Fettes Operations Centre. She'll assess your state of mind, probe your inner man and turn your boxers outside in to check for unhealthy stains.'

McKinlay stood up, extending her hand. 'I want you back on the job, soon as.'

4

Call an Ambulance

Twenty minutes later, courtesy of the number 8 bus, he was standing in a corridor deep inside Edinburgh Royal Infirmary chatting with two PCs from Dalkeith. Next to them was a private room with an NHS window in its NHS door. Inside the room, a woman lay on a bed with wires and tubes running everywhere, orchestrated by NHS monitors.

To Carter's eyes, the woman was younger than Kelsa; perhaps in her twenties. She had blonde hair, her face was puffy with purple bruises and covered in staples. A brace was around her neck, and a traction kit supported her stookie-covered legs.

'She's serious but stable,' said PC Dewar, consulting his notes.

'She's a mess.' Carter stared through the glass. 'Scarred for life. If she lives. Where was she found?'

'West Approach Road,' said Dewar. 'The slip road at Henderson Terrace, you know, opposite the Athletic Arms pub.'

'The Diggers,' Carter corrected him. 'It's not your part of the world.' He gazed through the door window again as Dewar carried on with his briefing.

'Ambulance crew said they heard a bang but didn't see her on the road. They stopped and attended; she was lying on the verge. Both her legs are broken, with damage to her spine, neck, and face, so they brought her here straight away. Saved her life, but she might never smile again.'

A doctor arrived outside the room with a pair of nurses in tow.

'DS Carter, St Leonard's,' he introduced himself.

'Dr Angela Murray, orthopaedic trauma. Lucky it was an ambulance, she'd have been dead otherwise.'

'I'm sure she's giving thanks for it,' Carter replied. 'You handing me the crew for dangerous driving?'

Dr Murray coughed a sound of disgust and swept a stray hair away from her freckled face. 'Hardly. She's got severe injuries caused by the vehicle and other injuries I can't associate with being hit by a van.'

'Oh, aye?'

Dr Murray opened the door of the private room. The troops swarmed in, taking up pre-planned positions, checking vitals and adjusting the liquid drips. Dewar motioned for his mate to stand guard outside the room while he stayed within earshot.

Loosening the brace around the woman's neck, Dr Murray drew Carter's attention to the purple-coloured skin beneath. 'Look at this bruising, it's too regular to be caused by an impact. That's the marking of a ligature. Once I saw that I carried out a more thorough examination. There's dirt under her fingernails and extensive bruising on her arms, also bruising to the upper parts of the inner thighs. The inside of her mouth is cut and bleeding, and she's lost some teeth, hard to tell—'

'She's been attacked.' Carter ran all the way with the doctor's line of reasoning but braked before the end.

'More than that,' said Dr Murray. 'She's been brutally raped.'

5

Approach Road

'Who is she?' Carter asked.

'I thought you'd know,' Dr Murray replied.

'I want to interview the crew,' Carter instructed PC Dewar. 'At St Leonard's this afternoon.'

Was this J's calling card?

He caught the number 8 bus going towards town and alighted at Liberton High School a few minutes later. After a five-minute walk to his home in Malbet Crescent, he threw the Crombie on the back seat of the electric Smart car, unplugged it and drove back towards town.

His mood was brighter now he had a puzzle to solve. What did J want with him? Who was the mystery woman in the graveyard? How did this woman get on the roadway? Outside, the sun was hoovering up the clouds, painting a bright blue across the sky to tease the natives into leaving shelter.

After twenty minutes of stop-start city driving, he joined the Approach Road from the west end at Lothian Road. It was a poorly maintained stretch of tarmac, only half a mile long but stubbornly potholed. He slowed down to survey the setting, taking in the daytime scenery of grubby winter verges and the dirty hulk of the Fountain Park entertainment complex on his left. Residential flats crouched gloomily on his right. Up ahead, a bridge loomed. As he came to it, the road split like an eagle's talon, syphoning most traffic away towards Murrayfield. He kept left and passed underneath the bridge.

There was nowhere to stop here, no hard shoulder, no pedestrian footpath, only steeply sloping verges covered by wild bushes and hardy trees. The Smart car scooted up the exit ramp and arrowed straight through the crossroads onto Henderson Terrace. He parked in an impossible space next to the Diggers pub, got out, shrugged on the Crombie and walked up the gentle slope of Dundee Street.

Old Dalry Burial Ground was on his left side, the black iron gate wedged permanently open. He stepped inside for a quick look. Overgrown and semi-derelict, untended bushes grew everywhere and headstones had been knocked over. The grass hadn't been cut recently. Human detritus scattered around the place. It was a jakey's paradise that screamed, '*rape me in here*'. Directly across the road from the cemetery gates, furtive steps led up to an iron footbridge obscured by trees.

He turned around and walked back down the slope to the traffic lights, crossed the road and faced the traffic coming up the West Approach Road. The footbridge was thirty meters away. He stumbled along the verges, ignoring the looks from drivers who considered him not in possession of the full ten quid note. For five minutes, he scoured the windblown verges, discovering nothing of interest. Then he spotted something hanging from the branch of a tree, just out of reach of the footbridge. He snapped it on his phone and called DCI McKinlay.

'Ma'am, get the Crime Scene Examiners down to Dalry Cemetery at the Approach Road. They'll need a cherry picker.'

6

Bondage

On his return to St Leonard's, Carter was called into DCI McKinlay's office.

'Good work with the handbag, Leccy,' she said. 'I've set up the investigation team with you as SIO, reporting to Nick Mason. I know there's been friction between you in the past but put it away. He's a DI now so you'll need to learn to love his Weegie ways.'

Carter inwardly groaned at mention of Mason. They'd worked on the McCalman case two years ago, both as sergeants, nearly coming to blows over the reliability of witnesses. 'Does this mean I'm officially back at work and can ditch the counselling?'

'You need a case to take your mind off your dead wife. The good Dr Flowers has rearranged her schedule. So, after your kissy-kiss chat with Nick, you get your sad arse on her couch. And get a decent coffee on your way, 'cos the free stuff in Fettes is recycled from local sheep farms.'

'Yes, ma'am.'

They walked along a short corridor and McKinlay knocked

on a door. DI Mason was sat behind his desk but stood up when she entered. Mason was tall with dark hair combed up and eyes set back in his head, giving him the shady, Jack-the-Lad look that Carter found difficult to trust. The jacket of a grey suit hung over his chair. His white shirt sported a blue tie that suggested loyalty to a particular Glasgow football team. Two women sat on chairs in the room and both stood up to respect DCI McKinlay's rank.

'Nick,' said McKinlay to DI Mason, 'you'll support Sergeant Carter in his role as Senior Investigating Officer.' She'd clearly arranged everything while Carter was travelling back to the station.

'You know DC Ellen Podolski, Leccy. She's all yours when she's got time away from Victim Support. DC Charlotte Garcia is a new recruit to our merry little band. She's on her first ever investigation, so treat her gently, eh? Right, I'll leave you to get on.'

As the door closed, Mason sat down and leaned back in his chair with a smug grin on his face. 'So, Leccy, our paths cross again. What do you know about this woman in hospital, and what do you want from us?'

Yep, this was the Nick Mason he'd remembered: arrogant and full of himself. He wondered what Mason had achieved to deserve the accolade of Detective Inspector. He was sure the man would tell him soon enough.

'The victim is in a coma in hospital,' Carter said. 'Apart from the injuries inflicted by the ambulance, she's also been raped. At the moment she's stable, and the doctor will keep us up to date.'

'So we just hang around and wait for her to live or die, is that it?' Mason's Glasgow accent felt like needles stabbing into Carter's eardrums.

'Nothing for you yet – sir,' he kept it formal. 'DC Garcia,' he turned to the younger, dark-haired woman. 'Ensure ICRS is up to date with the statements collected by PC Dewar from the hospital staff. The CSEs in Fettes will process the contents of the handbag once they retrieve it from the tree. Assuming it's hers, we might have some ID soon. Ellen,' Carter turned to his other colleague, a more familiar face, 'you might have to visit some rellies, so keep yourself available. I'm off to another appointment.'

He closed the door on his way out and sighed with relief to be out of Mason's presence. He needed more time to get used to his new DI's boisterous approach.

7

Inner Workings

At ten minutes past midday, Carter nursed a treble-shot, full-fat latte in a third-floor office at Fettes that reeked of sacked brass. Fettes Operations Centre had been touted in 2013 as the global headquarters for the all-new Police Scotland. Still, the Big Boys were concerned about favouring east over west, so moved the HQ to Tulliallan Castle, thereby pissing off Edinburgh and Glasgow.

FOC Fettes was in Stockbridge, north of the New Town, in a lamentably featureless landscape on Comely Bank Road between the Waitrose supermarket and the gothic Fettes College, an institution whose contributions to British culture included the education of Tony Blair and the inspiration for Hogwarts School.

The office was cold and narrow with rudimentary furniture, the deserted burrow of a senior officer that no one dared occupy, fearing infection, and for that Carter was thankful. Had the place been bright and glowing and busy and gay, he would have screamed. The single impressive feature of the room was a picture window which occupied his attention while he waited for his therapist to start the game. Outside, the sun cowered behind the clouds and God's power washer was in full flow, sweeping pedestrians off their feet and scouring paint off cars. It seemed winter was a permanent fixture around here, despite the brief respite of earlier, its thick grey atmosphere fitting his mood like a coffin.

His phone pinged: a text message.

[2019-01-14:1212] You should know, Carter, I'm going to kill you. You'll soon know why. She begged me not to do it but she's not here right now. Are you afraid? You should be. J.

Before he could react to it, the message disappeared.

He slid the phone into his pocket and tried to concentrate on the woman sitting in the chair, inwardly confused why J would want to kill him. Separated by a social class or three, the ray of blonde sunshine finished preparing her paperwork and instruments of torture. Her style was sharper than anyone he'd seen on the force, and he guessed she was a consultant from the alternative reality, brought in at high excess to check his tear ducts were working.

Dr Lisa Flowers, PhD, looked up and changed down into empathy mode.

'I'm sorry for your loss, Sergeant Carter. DCI McKinlay asked me to assess your fitness for duty, given your recent bereavement. Do I have your consent?'

'Will I take my clothes off?'

'No.'

'That's a pity.'

'Lachlan Carter, thirty-three, born in Edinburgh,' she read

from a sheaf of white copy paper. 'At three, you survived a car accident that killed your parents. No siblings. Raised by grandparents in the mining village of Gorebridge, you joined Police Scotland at twenty-five as a uniformed constable and have spent all your career at St Leonard's.'

'Key skill, reading,' replied the subject of interest.

'Promoted to detective at twenty-nine, since when you've been involved in four murder cases, the last two as SIO, and in those, you got convictions. It's an impressive record.'

'You would know, of course.'

'Don't you think it is?' Her accent sounded like it came with the education.

'It's the job.'

'I think it's your vocation.'

'What's this got to do with Kelsa?' Carter snarled suddenly. 'You're jumping to conclusions already.'

'Death is something that comes to us all, Sergeant Carter.'

'Really?' Her reply was too textbook for him. 'Do you practice lines in the mirror?'

Lisa Flowers sat back in her chair and regarded him carefully for a moment. 'It affects each person differently.' She leaned forward again, re-engaging. 'How did she die?'

Carter sipped from his latte, simmering. He made eye contact, keeping it for a decent few seconds to clarify that he didn't see the point in this line of chat. But McKinlay had insisted; otherwise, he'd have given the experience a body-swerve. Therapy was for sick people. 'In hospital,' he answered. 'Giving birth to our baby, Nathaniel.'

'That's tragic,' Dr Flowers replied sympathetically. 'Death in childbirth is uncommon these days. Did she have underlying health issues?'

'Anorexia nervosa complicated by depression. By the end, she was just skin and bone.'

'When was she diagnosed?'

'I don't know,' said Carter, not really wanting to explore it. 'I'm a policeman, not a doctor. She went into hospital in October last year.'

'Was she forced to eat in the hospital? For the health of the baby?' Flowers persisted.

'I wasn't there every day.' Carter could feel his voice rising as he recounted those difficult times. 'Maybe I should have been there more often, but sometimes I just couldn't do it. She wanted to die, but I don't know why.'

'How do you feel now she's gone?'

'Relieved. Guilty, because it must've been me that drove her to be like that.'

Dr Flowers made some notes on her pad. 'Are you able to come here every day and talk about it?'

'Do I have a choice?'

'Can I call you Lachlan?'

'Can I call you Petal?'

'Doctor Flowers, please,' she admonished him with a long stare. 'Nine o'clock every day, until I feel you're ready for work.'

'The boss wants me back soon-ish.' Better not tell her he had a job on.

'Until I say so, you're off duty.'

'Can we do more hours every day? There's not much private life for me to go home to.'

'Tomorrow. Sergeant Carter.'

Carter turned his head and gazed through the window. The Holy power-washer continued to clean up the city and, he wondered whether he'd still have a job by the time this nonsense stopped.

8

Flying Lesson

Back at St Leonard's a few hours later, Sergeant Tam Watson called Carter to say the ambulance crew were in reception.

'Did they bring the wagon?' Carter asked. Sergeant Watson confirmed they did.

'I'll be right down.' He rounded up DC Podolski and DC Garcia. DI Mason said he'd give it a miss.

The crew waited in the station's rear yard; a younger man and an older woman dressed in green overalls. His badge said Dorman, hers said McMahon. Carter introduced himself.

'You said you didn't see the woman on the road?' Carter recalled, assuming one of the pair would do the talking. 'How did you know you'd hit her?'

'There was a bang, and the wagon swerved to the left, but it came out of nowhere,' Dorman said. 'I stopped. She was lying on the verge seriously injured, so we strapped her up for a run to the Royal.'

'Any cars in front of you as you were driving along the Approach Road?'

'Aye, quite busy at night.'

'What time?

'We recorded the hit at ten minutes after midnight, told control we were heading for A & E.'

'None of the cars stopped to let a woman out on the verge?'

'No, we would have seen that.'

'And behind you?' DC Garcia chimed in.

'We were blocking the exit ramp to Dundee Street. Once drivers saw what was going on, they all reversed back onto the Murrayfield spur.'

'You didn't call the police for help?' asked Carter.

'Too busy,' Dorman replied. 'By the time they arrived, she might have been dead.'

'Number plates of the cars behind you?'

'Seriously?' said Dorman, shaking his head. 'We had other things to do.'

Carter walked to the ambulance's front, a specially built snub-nose Mercedes kitted out in white paint with green-and-yellow reflective panels on the sides. Its blues-and-twos were above the driver's cab, but only its regular hazard lights were flashing now.

'Right side?' he asked.

'Right,' McMahon confirmed.

'No damage,' Carter examined the driver's side front wing. 'If you hit her here, it would have crumpled and smashed the light cluster. Any chance it was repaired overnight?'

Dorman snorted, 'You're joking, right?'

Carter walked around the vehicle. Behind him, at the rear entrance to the police station, Tam Watson and two coppers appeared, carrying a set of extendable ladders.

'Which bridge was it?' Carter asked Dorman.

'Eh?'

'Two bridges span that short stretch of road, very close together. The second one is a footbridge.'

'If you say so,' Dorman nodded, watching Tam Watson place the ladders at the back of the van, where the patient access doors were closed and locked. The two coppers held it safely while Carter climbed up. After a moment or two, he climbed back down.

'We're keeping this van. Ellen, arrange for the Scene Examiners to go over it. Tam, give our two friends here a lift back to Ambulance HQ once we have their statements.'

'You can't do that,' whined Dorman.

'It's a crime scene, I do what I need to do.'

'But we never saw her, it was an accident.'

'No, it was deliberate,' stated Carter flatly. 'You didn't see her on the road because she was never there. She was up on the footbridge as you approached. Probably with the someone who pushed her off the bridge. That was the thud you heard: she's dented your roof. When you swerved, she was thrown off the top of the ambulance onto the road, then you ran over her.'

'Christ,' said Dorman, impressed.

'Her handbag was hanging in a tree on the north side of the footbridge, and there was no evidence of broken lights on the tarmac. When she went over the ledge, either her handbag left her hands, or she had the presence of mind to throw it into the tree while falling.

'She'd been raped and beaten before you hit her,' Carter told them. 'Quite viciously. I think that happened in Dalry Burial Ground. There are steps leading to the footbridge across from the cemetery exit on Dundee Street. But I don't know why he'd drag her from the cemetery just to push her off the bridge.'

DC Garcia added a new theory. 'Maybe she jumped on her own?'

'It was attempted murder,' Carter replied, convinced by his own thinking. 'You don't bring your handbag with you if you intend to kill yourself.'

9

I AM

Detective Inspector Nick Mason was waiting for them when Carter and the two DCs arrived back in the detectives' room after they'd supervised the CSEs work on the ambulance.

'Alice Deacon,' he said triumphantly. 'Aged thirty-two. Her driving licence gives us an address in Shandon. House keys were in her handbag recovered from the tree. PCs are on their way there now.'

'What else?' Carter asked. 'Did she have a phone?'

DI Mason ran his finger down the list of contents. 'A Samsung Galaxy S9, in purple.'

Carter looked at his watch. 'About fourteen hours since she was admitted, add three or four hours to when she last used it,' he verbalised his thoughts. 'Have they tried to get into it yet? Would she have pictures?'

'Of him?' Mason wondered.

'Of her dog. Are you really stupid?'

'You're a sarcastic arse, Carter,' Mason said, rising like a salmon. 'This isn't one of your comedy gigs. I'm not impressed by your pish patter. You think we're all idiots, don't you? I want a detailed update, including next steps, so I can brief the boss.'

DC Garcia looked on open-mouthed as her senior officers traded verbal blows.

'And you two,' Mason pointed to Podolski and Garcia. 'Don't you have other work to do?'

'C'mon,' said Ellen Podolski to DC Garcia. 'Let's have a cup of tea, till they sort themselves out.'

'Choose your words carefully,' Mason cautioned Carter after the two constables had left the room. 'The phone is at FOC Fettes, along with the contents of her handbag. Shall I ask the question again, Sergeant?'

'The phone has a fingerprint sensor,' Carter set it out, standing nearly toe-to-toe with his senior officer. 'And pictures of her attacker would help.'

'You said the bag was the priority.'

'Priorities shift,' Carter replied. 'We've got limited time before the phone will prompt for a password. She probably works in an office in town.'

'Maybe she's got a rich daddy and runs around all day in an expensive Smart car. You're drawing this out Carter, and I'm totally pissed off with it,' Mason stepped back, running his fingers through his black hair in frustration.

'Fingerprint ID on Samsung phones,' Carter explained. 'If she doesn't use the phone regularly, it'll prompt for a passcode as well. I've got a Samsung too.'

Mason fished his phone from his pocket. His cheap Nokia didn't have a fingerprint sensor. 'So you take the phone to the hospital and use her fingerprint to unlock it. Sometimes, Leccy, getting to the point gets you points.'

'She was pushed or thrown off the bridge after being raped,' Carter laid out his thoughts. 'She landed on the ambulance, bounced off it, and it ran over her. A suicide attempt is feasible, but until she comes out of the coma, we should treat it as attempted murder.'

'OK, I'll inform the boss.' Mason calmed down.

Carter left the detectives' room and found DC Podolski and DC Garcia drinking tea in the small kitchen.

'Ellen, go to Alice's flat and supervise the search. Find out if she's got family.' He turned to DC Garcia, 'Charlotte, you come with me. We're going back to see Alice.'

'I am Charli. With an "i",' she said. 'I will call you Leccy.'

'Whatever. Everybody else does.'

They found their way to Carter's Smart car, parked on the street rather than in the car park. It had acquired a ticket. Carter searched fruitlessly for the culprit. 'Sixty quid,' he muttered. 'Robbin' bastards.'

An hour later, after signing out her Samsung S9 from FOC Fettes, Carter and Garcia stood outside the private room in the Royal Infirmary, gazing through the window at the newly named Alice. A nurse passed them, and Carter asked for Dr Murray. A few minutes later, she stood beside him. He introduced Garcia.

'She's stable, but still in a coma,' Dr Murray began recounting the diagnosis before he asked. 'We're preparing her for a series of scans, to see what else is going on, what other damage there might be.'

'Do you ever go home?' asked Carter, eyes front, staring through the window.

'Do you?' Dr Murray countered.

'Nothing there for me.' He felt Dr Murray's eyes on him.

'Have you always had white hair?' she asked.

'This I want to know too,' Garcia jumped into the social chat.

'Most men have hair,' he felt cornered. 'What's your problem?'

'White hair is unusual, at your age,' said Dr Murray.

'You colour it, yes?' Garcia had made up her mind.

'No,' he said exasperated. 'Can we focus on the job?'

The women shared a glance.

'Why is she in a private room? Aren't these reserved for insurance jobs?' Carter asked Dr Murray, feeling the banter between them had made something in him click.

'My discretion, after I saw the rape injuries. She's been violated by some sick arsehole. No need to add insult to that by putting her in a general ward. She would upset the other patients anyway, the condition she's in.'

Carter nodded. 'Alice Deacon. She's thirty-two. Lives in Shandon.' He gave Dr Murray her full address.

'Thanks,' she said. 'We'll track down her medical records now.'

'I need a favour,' Carter asked before she left. 'I want to use her fingerprint to open her phone, and I need a witness. It'll be quicker than waiting for police techs to do it. It might be a breach of privacy and – if she recovers – she might be upset if she was of a mind. Do you think her injuries could be caused by consensual sex? Some like it rough—'

Dr Murray wasn't fazed by the question. 'It's always possible – but who consents to be thrown from a bridge?'

They entered the room. Carter handed his own Samsung phone to Garcia. Then he and Dr Murray stood at Alice's right-hand side. The video started. Dr Murray introduced herself,

Carter spoke into the lens, recounting the date, time, and circumstances, and he identified DC Garcia.

Carter wore latex gloves. He removed Alice's phone from its protective packaging, preserving the evidence chain by showing the camera the inventory ID label. Dr Murray removed the pulse sensor from Alice's finger, causing the monitor to respond with a highly pitched alarm. She silenced it.

Carter held Alice's phone and pressed the side button. The screen came alive, requesting its owner's confirmation of identity. Gently he lifted her hand, noticing the delicacy of her fingers. He turned her thumb so only the outside edge would present, as it would if she used the phone one-handed. Her thumb touched the sensor. Nothing happened. He tried again, still nothing. Turning her thumb around, he pressed harder, this time getting an error message: *Not recognised*'.

He spoke into the video, recording his failures. 'I don't know how many attempts I'll have, but I'm going for three. If it doesn't work, we'll have to try something else.'

He released her hand, then picked it up again. 'Right forefinger,' he said to the video. 'Two-handed method, holding the phone in her left hand.' Her finger touched the sensor. *Not recognised*, the phone repeated. Gently, Carter laid her hand down on the bedcovers.

'One more chance,' he said to Dr Murray, who nodded her agreement silently. 'I'm assuming she wouldn't use her other fingers on that hand, so that leaves two more choices.'

Carter and Murray walked around the bed to Alice's left side. Garcia followed them with the video camera.

'Maybe she's left-handed,' he said, carefully handling her bandaged and stookied left arm. She'd broken her wrist and forearm in two places when she landed on the ambulance or when she'd rolled off onto the road. Her thumb, forefinger and middle finger protruded, the other two were encased in plaster.

This time he pressed the phone onto her thumb and held it there.

The screen flickered and displayed some familiar multi-coloured icons.

'Now what?' said Dr Murray, clearly relieved that Carter wasn't going to subject her patient to more gruelling exercises. They both stood gazing reverentially at the unconscious Alice, giving silent thanks. The video kept rolling.

Carter placed Alice's phone on the bed and removed one glove from his hand. 'I'm going to reset her phone's security.' He picked up the Samsung and went over to Garcia, recording his actions in the video. Once complete, he placed the Samsung back in its evidence bag and sealed it.

'Show's over,' he said, taking possession of his own phone from Garcia and saving the video clip.

'Gracias, Dr Murray,' said Garcia. 'Thank you, Alice, too. You have helped us more than you know.'

Carter left without saying goodbye.

10

Crime Scene

In the privacy of the car, Carter removed Alice's Samsung from the evidence bag and scanned her call log. Garcia was keen to know what he was doing.

'There was a call at seven-fifteen yesterday evening to a cab company, Uptown Cabs,' he told her while switching into Alice's calendar. 'Look, there's an appointment last night at seven-thirty. It doesn't say where, but she's meeting someone called "J".' He skimmed through the calendar. 'There are quite a few meetings with "J", going back a few months.'

'The forensic tech guys can make location data from the phone to find where she was?' Garcia asked.

'Yep,' he nodded as he skimmed through her pictures. Mostly they were of groups of attractive girls in bars, but none was taken last night.

'Look, she's got a dog,' he smiled. 'Single Shandon girl, living with a dog.'

For the next ten minutes, he reviewed every calendar event over the previous two months. 'Going by the calendar entries in the daytime, she's a self-employed PR consultant,' Carter said, then added, 'as confirmed by her Twitter bio. She also has WhatsApp, and Facebook Messenger installed on the phone.'

He opened WhatsApp, scanning the conversations and contacts. 'She's got a boyfriend called Hamish. Facebook seems to be for friends and Twitter is clients only.'

He scrolled through two pages of apps and sat up stiffly. Garcia spotted the change in body language.

'What is it, Leccy?'

'Give me a minute.'

They sat in silence while Carter flicked through screens. After two minutes he still hadn't said anything but was staring through the windscreen, his thoughts a long way from the present.

'Leccy, what can I do?'

He came out of his reverie and handed Garcia the phone.

She looked at the screen, where a message was displayed in a format she didn't recognise. Above the message were the date stamp and sixteen-character code.

[2019-01-14:0015] Now I've got your attention, Leccy, was my calling card what you expected? What secrets will Alice tell you and how will they help you? There's more to come. J.

'What does this mean?' Garcia asked.

'He planted it on her phone while the ambulance crew battled to save her life. He was there, watching. The timestamp confirms it.'

'Who is J?'

He told her about the two texts he'd already received.

'There are more messages here,' he pointed to Alice's phone. 'History,' he said, troubled. 'Alice has responded to them, but it doesn't look like she's mentioned his name and all his texts have got different sixteen-character codes.'

'What do the codes mean?'

'I don't know. We have to get this phone to the techs as soon as we can.'

He replaced the phone in its evidence bag. They drove to Uptown Cabs at the West End and asked for the supervisor. Procedures existed for getting information from cabbies, and Carter followed them. Within a few minutes, he was given the destination, the cab number and the driver's name. 'One passenger, officially,' said the supervisor. 'You'll have to ask Billy to be sure, eh?'

Within a few moments, Carter spoke to the driver, who confirmed one passenger dropped on George Street, close to the Dome. 'How did she seem? Happy, upset, nervous?'

'Played wi' her phone, only spoke when she got in and when she got out.'

'Did you see where she went?'

'Nah, got another fare an' drove off.'

The supervisor confirmed Billy's assertion with a nod and cancelled the line. 'She paid by card.'

'Any other jobs within twenty-four hours back to her home address?'

'Not from us,' said Supervisor. 'You'll have to check the other radio taxis yourself.'

As they walked away, Carter turned to Garcia. 'Charli, find out which businesses around George Street have CCTV. We need to know where Alice went after the taxi dropped her off.'

'Sure,' she said. 'As soon as we get back to the station.'

Once they were back in the car, Carter dutifully called DI Mason, keeping quiet about the messaging app for now. However, he recommended that the phone's contents be downloaded and analysed as soon as possible.

'Ellen has arranged for Alice's dog to go to kennels,' said Mason. Carter smiled, noting no irony in his superior's tone of voice. 'She's expecting family information to bubble up, but I guess you'll leave that to her. Too touchy-feely, for you, eh?'

'Given my state of mind,' Carter said, 'you've no idea what I might say to them.'

'The Big Boys think you're still on compassionate leave under the care of Dr Flowers. She'll get reamed if they discover you're running loose on the streets. Go home.'

'Once I drop DC Garcia at the station.'

First, they detoured to Dalry Burial Ground. Officers had found the spot where Alice had been raped and protected it with a white tent. It was fifty metres up a slope on the left-hand side, not far from a rough path that led to the black iron gates that exited onto Dalry Road. Crime tape segregated off a section of ground, full of tombs, memorials and mature trees. Two uniformed coppers strolled around, looking bored; visible policing after the event to reassure the TV-watching public that Police Scotland was on the job. Carter didn't think the residents of the graveyard worried too much.

The Crime Scene Manager was an old hand. She told Carter and Garcia they'd recovered knickers and tights and they might get DNA from them. 'Won't help us if this is his first time, though.'

'Because he's not in the Forensic Science Lab database?' Carter confirmed.

'Aye.'

'Any ideas on how she got here?' he asked. 'There are only two entrances, and I don't see her scrambling over ten-foot-high walls.'

'We've not found anything outside the tape that provides a trail,' she said, still wearing her paper suit. 'There's plenty of discarded stuff about – clothes, shoes, cans and bottles. It's a microcosm of the city, but it's all been here a long time. Her knickers looked clean, even if they were torn and ripped.'

'You think she came here willingly?' asked Carter.

'We have evidence proving she was here, but none of it says how she arrived or how she left. But look around yourself,' she replied. 'This graveyard is semi-derelict; it's not open for business unless your family bought a plot here last century. There's been a recent burial on the west side, less than six months ago, I'd say. These days most go to the burny fire at Mortonhall. This place is overgrown, it's rough ground. Headstones have been pushed over everywhere; some cut grass, decent hard paths, evidence of people visiting graves. And the usual homeless and gormless using it as a bar, toilet and bedroom. The scene is at least fifty metres away from the top entrance, and yet there's no evidence she was dragged down here against her will.'

'Can you find the rapist?' Garcia asked. 'Any evidence?'

'Not that we can see. We're still processing the tests taken from her at the hospital. If we assume there's been DNA transfer from him to her, we still won't know until we get comparisons.'

'A johnny?' proposed Carter.

'We didn't find one. No semen either. He cleared up afterwards.'

'Right,' Carter summed up. 'There are two theories, as I read it. One, they came here together; the other, they came here separately. I know she took a taxi into town, but how did she get from there to here? We'll have to check the other cabs to confirm if she used one, but you're speculating that she might have come here willingly. On her own, to be raped by a stranger in a dark graveyard.'

11

Dalry Burial Ground

Leaving the CSEs to their work, Carter and Garcia strolled around the graveyard.

For Carter, the feel of Dalry Burial Ground wasn't the same as Old Calton, where Kelsa rested. While both were decrepit, Calton Burial Ground had history, the famous names, the eye of the Council, and those like his father-in-law to keep the city honest. There'd be no pauper's grave for the likes of Dunsmuir. Dalry, on the other hand, fell into an outside-tourism orbit and was left to police itself.

'What reason would he choose to attack her here?' Garcia asked him, noticing that he seemed content to wander through the graveyard in silence.

'Convenience, maybe.'

This cemetery was on three levels: a top section cosying up to Dundee Street and a bottom section slowly sinking onto Dalry Road. The middle tier boasted an impressive neo-Gothic terrace, dug into the hill's slope, decaying with grandeur equal to that of ancient royalty. Carter was no expert on architecture, but it had clearly been built to last because everything else around it was crumbling. Its centrepiece was a zigzag set of double sandstone steps, damp with lichen and used as a canvas by spray artists. Left and right, Gothic arches protruded, of the kind found in churches. Dual entrances to Hades, now blocked by black railings, as if to prevent a mass escape of the undead. Unfortunately, as the first defence against the zombie apocalypse, it failed, as significant quantities of human detritus scattered inside the railings attested.

Carter grasped the irons like a prisoner and shook them, scanning the interior of discarded cans, beer bottles and food wrappings for signs of current occupancy. Collapsed stone inside spelt danger, but some light filtered down from above.

'Why are we still here?' Garcia tried again to reach him. 'Is there something else we could do? Taking her phone to the techs?'

'I know,' he said, but followed up, 'I'm trying to get a feel for him. He knows things about me he shouldn't know. He's targeting me and I'd like to know why.'

'You think you'll find the answer here?' she said.

'No.'

They tramped up the damp steps of the mid-tier and surveyed the graveyard from the whole length of the terrace. An abundance of mature trees; chestnut, elm, sycamore and plain, with pine bushes filling in the gaps. Bramble and thicket, lush in summer, provided ground foliage, sucking up the rich nutrients provided by the decaying human corpses deep in the soil.

'We can trace him from the message he sent to Alice's phone, yes?' she asked. 'With phones, this is possible, surely?'

'If it was that easy, he'd be arrested already. He's using a messaging app I've never seen before. We have to wait until he tells us more – and he will. In the meantime, all we have to work with is Alice, and she's not saying much. But if we could find out where she's been, we might find traces of him too.'

Some gravestones stood out; two-foot-high rectangles hewn and polished from grey granite: the resting places of soldiers killed in the Great War. Whoever had pushed over the hundreds of other stones had the respect to leave these ones untouched. In this garden of weeping angels, it was peaceful. At the same time, outside the high walls, heavy traffic rumbled through an ambivalent world.

'Is there a "J" in your life?' she mused. 'You mentioned "Johnny" earlier?'

Carter laughed. 'You're Spanish, right?'

'My mother was English.' Her dark eyes were full of Iberian tension. 'But I was born and raised in *Andalucía*.' She felt Carter was dissing her.

'It's Scottish slang term for a condom. One of many.'

'Ha. A *goma*.' Garcia didn't seem embarrassed by the mistake. It broke the ice between them, and she laughed with him.

Daylight was fading and being here reminded Carter too much of Kelsa's funeral. Across on the east side, the CSEs were packing up. The white tent was gone already, leaving crime-scene tape behind as a pathetic deterrent.

'I think it's time we left,' he replied, pulling the collar of his Crombie around his neck.

They exited upwards, onto Dundee Street, crossing the busy arterial road, taking the steps up to the footbridge. Made from post-war iron painted industrial grey, with large round-headed rivets, its splashes of red primer paint reminded him of weeping sores. The bridge was another spray canvas for street gangs. The graffiti was another kind of deterrent, more frightening and vicious than the flimsy blue tape Police Scotland's accountants preferred.

'Alice fell from this bridge into the traffic below,' Carter described it for Garcia. 'Was she pushed or did she jump? If she jumped, what motivated her to do it? Climbing over this barrier is more difficult than it looks. I felt the delicacy of her hand when I held it in the hospital, there was no evidence of metal or paint flakes on her skin. She's petite, and for a big man, throwing her over the parapet might be possible. But why would she let him do it?'

He took out his phone and tapped her postcode into Google Maps.

'Her flat is about half a mile away,' he squinted at the phone in the semi-darkness. 'Crossing this bridge could be a shortcut for her if she'd been in a bar or restaurant in Gorgie or Dalry. The missing hours between seven-thirty p.m. and two a.m. should tell us how she got here.'

'Where did she meet this Johnny?'

Garcia had voiced what Carter was thinking.

12

Babysitter

Carter drove back to St Leonard's station and dropped DC Garcia off just after 6 p.m.

'I'll see you tomorrow. Get Alice's phone into the hands of our techs,' he said, driving off without waiting for her acknowledgement.

It was no more than a ten-minute drive to Hermitage of Braid on the city's south side. Hermitage Drive was wider than most residential streets in the capital and was populated by expensive mansions. He parked across the road from his in-laws home, an early twentieth-century pile with pencil towers and elongated windows designed and built in the Glasgow Style. Ivy covered its walls, adding thousands to the market price. He walked up the broad pathway, rang the big bell push and hammered on the solid-wood double doors with his fist.

The door was opened by the maid who'd answered his phone call in the morning. Nathaniel was asleep, she said, inviting him in. She led him through a small maze of corridors, opened the door of a chilly room and asked him to sit while she fetched Sheriff Dunsmuir.

Five minutes passed, then a man in his sixties entered, sporting a hawk nose and bald head with thinning grey hair at the side. Wearing a classic grey suit and patterned country shirt with a New Club tie, he was bent slightly at the shoulders, making him six inches shorter than Carter. But his chiselled jaw was set, and his grey eyes were blazing with indignation at the intrusion.

'What do you want, Lachlan?'

'I'm here to collect Nathaniel,' Carter replied, angered by his father-in-law's tone.

'That won't be possible. He's asleep,' snapped James Dunsmuir.

'He'll be in his Moses basket. He won't wake.'

James Dunsmuir paused for breath as if considering some flawed logic put forward by a witness in his court.

'Wait here,' he said, walking out of the room.

He returned quicker than Carter expected – without Nathaniel.

'I have papers for you,' he said, coming over all business-like. 'Drawn up by our family lawyer. Kelsa took legal advice in the months before she died. Obviously, I couldn't act for her.'

'She said nothing to me about a lawyer,' Carter was puzzled. 'Why did she need advice?'

'He drew up her will and represented her in court,' Dunsmuir said, ignoring Carter's point, 'once she was no longer able to attend herself.'

'Court?'

'She knew she was dying and wanted arrangements put in place, of course.'

'Arrangements?' Carter sat forwards, feeling unbalanced by the conversation.

'For after death. She expressed a wish that Nathaniel be brought up by us, in a safe and stable—'

'What?' Carter leapt to his feet. 'She can't do that. I'm his father. He stays with me.'

'I'm afraid not,' insisted Dunsmuir, waving a bound folder as his defence. 'I have here a temporary residence order issued by Sheriff Robertson four weeks ago. We are now the guardians of Nathaniel James Dunsmuir and will bring him up as we see fit.'

'Jesus Christ.' Carter stared at his father-in-law in disbelief. 'We'd agreed that I'd pick him up after the funeral. But you never felt it important to mention this residency order then, did you? What does Judith have to say about this?'

'Indeed,' Dunsmuir replied calmly, ignoring Carter's question about his wife. 'It wasn't appropriate then. It is now.'

Carter circled the room, unable to comprehend what was happening. Slowly, it sunk in that he was being stitched up. He rushed towards Dunsmuir in anger and grabbed him by the lapels of his jacket. 'Just a fucking minute.' His spittle peppered the old man's face. 'You're telling me that Kelsa consulted you behind my back, to plan the future of our son? Your dead hand is all over this.'

Dunsmuir's eyes threatened to pop from their sockets. 'Release me this instant, Lachlan, or I'll call the police.'

'I am the fucking police!'

'You won't be for much longer if you don't let me go.'

'I have paternal rights,' Carter said, releasing the old man after a decent few seconds. 'Why wasn't I consulted?'

'Scots law allows for exceptional circumstances, and they

were put before the court. Kelsa was dying but confirmed she was of sound mind. In the matter of parental rights, she attested that the father expressed no interest in the child and could not be trusted. Sheriff Robertson accepted that the wishes articulated in her will overcame all objections then issued a judgement that the order could proceed.'

'What?' Carter stopped in his tracks, holding his hands out wide. 'She said I couldn't be trusted?'

'It would appear so.'

'And when were you planning to inform me of these "wishes"?' The shock had started to wear off.

'You are hearing them now. The formal reading of her will is soon. Before that event can happen, she left instructions that you receive her share of your joint home. Plus, a cash sum of two hundred thousand pounds and various personal items. Conditional on you not contesting the order.'

'You're bribing me to disown my son?'

'Of course, you are free to seek legal advice and challenge the residency at court. However, I advise you to think carefully about that.'

'Why?'

'Perhaps, if he was older when she died, things might have been different. But Nathaniel should grow up believing we are his blood parents. Just as you did, Lachlan. But unlike yours, his education will be first-class.'

'Fuck you, Dunsmuir.'

James Dunsmuir ignored the jibe, knowing he'd won the argument. He opened the folder one last time and presented Carter with an envelope. 'She asked me to give you this letter after her internment.'

Carter handled the envelope as if it was poison. Kelsa's

scrawl was clear on the front.

'Open only when you understand.'

The back was sealed with her scarlet kiss. His anger flared again. 'You might have residency, but I want access to my son.'

'Out of the question,' said the older man.

Carter turned on his heel and stormed out of the small room, pulling the door open so hard the handle dented the solid wall.

'I advise you not to come back, Lachlan. There is nothing here for you.'

Carter stumbled through the dim corridors trying to find his way out. A well-dressed elderly gentleman holding a glass of whisky veered into his path. Carter barged through, causing Old Boy to crumple against a wall. Reaching the front door, he wrenched it open, then turned to Dunsmuir who was helping Old Boy back to his feet.

'At her funeral yesterday. A dark-haired woman wearing a St Christopher pendant was there, about my age,' Carter said. 'Who was she?'

Dunsmuir didn't even look at him. 'There was no such woman.'

'She hung back at the end after you'd all gone.'

'You're mistaken. And you were not to attend—'

But Carter had already disappeared into the night.

13

Action Man

Carter sat in his lounge for hours with his Xbox turned on, staring at the screen. The game was paused as he slowly exhausted the Balvenie Doublewood. Eventually, he abandoned the game and dragged himself upstairs, trying to douse the embers of his frustration. Despite the large intake of whisky in its purest legal form, images of Kelsa, with her full dark hair and scarlet lips, nudged him awake whenever his eyes drooped. At 1.58 a.m. – at least six hours until his next scheduled appointment with a living human, he got out of bed. An endurance test he knew he'd pass, but the waiting would tick over with agonising slowness.

Liberton had been their chosen suburb on the southern outskirts of Edinburgh: a community of families with children, nurseries, schools, parks, a golf club and a smattering of shops. Town was only thirty minutes away by bus, the Royal Infirmary a few minutes' drive east. They'd bought a newish three-bed detached house with an integral garage. The front and back gardens were of a decent, child-rearing size, and inside the partitions were painted job-lot cream. An 'executive villa', touted the brochure when they'd pooled their resources fifteen months ago; the perfect place to start a new family. Kelsa had had a list of requirements to tick off. He'd had only one: a view of Arthur's Seat and Castle Rock from at least one window.

Their new home was far removed from the tiny miner's cottage in Gorebridge where Carter had been raised, but so soon his dream had become a nightmare. The Liberton house reeked of her. The stench of Calvin Klein's Obsession permeated the walls, and she stalked him nightly, hiding in cupboards and in other unexpected places like a tenant ghost. Their bedroom, now her exclusive lair, was off-limits since she'd passed. Instead, his nights were spent semi-comatose in the back bedroom. He'd sell in the spring. She would always be in his heart, but he couldn't clear her out just yet.

Casting off the bedsheets – approaching the fourth week without a change – he started to dress. Such scumminess would never be allowed if she was here. One week tops and sheets always changed after sex. Despite his attempts to limit her presence in the house, many reminders remained. Pictures of them in Las Vegas, taken at their wedding, punctuated the walls, upstairs and down. Professional images of her photogenic gaze and long dark hair that changed the shape of her face if she wore it curled or straight. As he finished dressing in old clothes, he stared at each picture in turn. She wore sunglasses in some; in others, her dark eyes dominated the frame. She was serious, funny, happy, sad, pensive and brooding, in both colour and monochrome. 'Enigmatic' summed her up. Carter was in most shots too, standing just behind her as if he'd photobombed a celebrity.

Unless he could find a way forward in the coming weeks, he'd be imprisoned in Room 101 with his ultimate nightmare for a long time.

Nathaniel's room was full of baby stuff: an empty crib, packs of nappies, baby clothes, toys and teddies, a pram, a mobile hanging from the ceiling – all stilled. Both mum and baby had vanished, leaving him behind to soak up the aftermath. He had no idea how to stem the subtle flow of grief that infected him. Downstairs, he buttoned his Crombie coat over a cable-knit jumper and jeans and climbed into the Smart car, knowing he was well over the drink-driving limit, but the hell with it.

He drove back to the home of his in-laws and parked the car on Hermitage Drive in almost exactly the same spot he'd parked a few hours ago. He was convinced of his mission – that the Dunsmuirs would have no choice but to concede to his plan to save their public face. His breath froze in the cold air as he got out of the car. He crossed the street, pushed back the wrought-iron gate, strode up the pathway with purpose and confronted the black doors that had earlier allowed him entry. His fist hammered on the ancient wood.

'Dunsmuir, you old bastard, I demand to see my son.' His slurred shouty voice echoed back at him from the cold walls. He kicked the door with the sole of his boot and kept kicking when there was no answer. 'Nathaniel, I'm your father.' Carter pummelled the doors again with his fists, then stood back, looking up at the ivy-clad windows. 'Dunsmuir, you have no right to keep my boy from me.' The mansion's door remained resolutely shut, so he slumped on the cold steps, his voice falling low, justifying his actions to himself. 'I just want to see him. It's not a crime, is it? I just want to see my beautiful boy.'

He sat there, defeated, head on his knees until the tears flowed. Half an hour later, the doors stood just as firm and uncaring. Carter picked himself up.

'I gave you a chance to right this wrong. You ignored me, so I'm leaving, but it doesn't end here. You can't keep him forever.'

He stumbled back to the car, unlocked it and squeezed himself into the back seat. He locked the doors from the inside and turned the heater on, wrapping his coat around himself, resting at an uncomfortable angle until he succumbed to whisky-ravaged demons.

Sometime later, he woke. His phone had buzzed. Slightly more sober, he registered the Dunsmuir house across the darkened street while he unlocked the phone. The messaging app had reappeared, inviting him to tap.

[2019-01-15:0422] Feeling totally alone, Leccy? She never really loved you. While you sit outside nothing is what it seems to be. The boy is safe now so we will go mano-a-mano J.

How did J know about Nathaniel? Carter oozed himself out of the back seat and stood in the darkened road, looking around. His watch read 4.22 a.m.

'Fuck yez all,' he shouted, sliding into the driver's seat and driving off.

14

Bring Me Flowers

Carter rocked up at Fettes next morning looking better than he felt. Wearing his Crombie coat, jeans, collared shirt and tan brogues, he'd even stuck some gel in his white hair and combed it up to pretend he was confident and in total control. Holding his treble-shot latte, the coat kept the chill of the office at bay while he waited impatiently for Dr Flowers to begin. The previous evening's discussion with his father-in-law was still raw.

She sat behind the table wearing a powder-blue suit with a skirt that rose up over her fine knees. At the end of her shapely legs, killer stilettos matched the colour of her outfit. He lounged over the chair, his arms folded, watching her prepare for the interrogation. Her blonde ponytail was perfectly intact as if she'd just teleported from a fashion runway. Where was home for her? The south – perhaps London, or of that ilk? She'd be staying locally while consulting. The Grosvenor or the Caley, maybe. Definitely not the Balmoral. Police Scotland wouldn't pay that kind of dosh to sort out the petty niggles of his wretched soul.

'Good morning, Lachlan. Are you making a fashion statement this chilly morning?' Dr Lisa Flowers opened the morning's session, nodding towards Carter's Crombie, still firmly in place.

'It's cold in here,' he shrugged.

'How is your mood today?'

'You really want to know? I'm feeling angry.'

'And why is that?' she scribbled quickly on her notepad as if this was an undesirable turn of events.

'My in-laws have taken out a court order, allowing them to have residency of my son. It appears Kelsa testified in court months ago, while she was still able, that I wasn't a suitable father. She kept that little nugget from me.'

'She should have told you she was planning to do it,' Dr Flowers responded, as devil's advocate. 'So, what can you do about it?' She stared at him.

'Apart from digging her up to ask why? Old Dunsmuir dared me not to challenge the court order, so I'm going to get a lawyer. Someone who will totally fuck him off.' He pointed his finger at her. 'Take down a note in your pad, Petal. "Definitely not a suicide risk."'

'So, tell me about meeting Kelsa for the first time.'

She wanted to get on with her plans, but he had more steam to vent on the current topic. 'What will that achieve?' he responded.

'Humour me. Was it love at first sight?'

'It was big love if that's what you want to hear. I'd finished my stand-up gig at the Stand, and a few of us comics went to the Dome on George Street. She and her girlfriends had seen my slot and she came over to say hello. We chatted, dated, fell in love and married. We got pregnant, she handed off my son, abandoned me and died. The circle of life, what else is there?'

'You're a stand-up comedian?' Dr Flowers seemed dumbfounded.

'As a career, it has more prospects than an axe murderer.'

'I guess,' she smiled nervously, wondering if she should reboot the morning.

'Knocked you off your stride, Petal?' Carter teased. 'You came in here to be all serious and psyched up, and now you've stalled.'

'A bit,' she blushed. 'I wasn't ready for that.' She shuffled some papers about nervously. 'Nobody mentioned it during my research. And don't call me Petal.'

'It's still one-nil to me.'

She ran her fingers through her hair and took a deep breath. 'Did Kelsa feel the same about you?'

'Yes.' His grin went from one ear to the other. 'We just clicked. The fire hose to the face kind of love. You know, *boom.* She was the woman I was going to spend my life with because she wanted to spend hers with me.'

'You'd dated before, I assume?' Her composure was coming back.

He chewed on his answer, wondering if he could noise her up some more. 'Has this ever happened to you before? Patients knocking you off-course?'

'I've sat in front of killers and child molesters and made them weep, but nobody has blamed stand-up comedy as a reason for taking up life as a serial killer. Maybe you'll be the first.'

He decided to temporarily let her off his hook. 'I've had my fair share of dating, but not serious. One wanted the full wife-and-kids package, but she wouldn't move to the city. I'll be honest and say that wouldn't have worked for either of us.'

'What about Kelsa?' Dr Flowers asked, back online again and scribbling furiously in her notepad. 'How did she feel about family?'

'The same. We never talked about our exes. There didn't seem to be any point; we'd found each other, no one who came before mattered.'

'How long before you married?'

'We went on our first holiday to Las Vegas. While we were there, we just did it. Eighth of December 2017,' Carter counted back the time. 'About eight months after we met.'

'Something is bothering me,' Flowers said, the slightest of dimples appearing as she smiled. 'Do you dye your hair?'

'Are we finished now?' He felt that the ice between them had melted a bit.

'Not till you tell me about your hair.'

'My gran said it turned white after the accident.'

Her smiled faltered. 'Has the grief hit you yet?'

'Some,' he said. 'But it's only been days since her burial.'

'I mean your parents.'

Her left-hook caught him by surprise.

'What do you remember of them?' She followed up with a right.

'Nothing,' he whispered, groggy, annoyed at what she'd done just when it was going well. He spun away from her, not towards the exit but to the picture window, to gaze outside at life and the things that everyday people do. The kids at Fettes College were playing football and hockey.

'Who cared for you as a child?' He heard her voice from a

million miles away.

'I don't want to talk about this anymore.' He buttoned up the Crombie, turned and walked to the door.

'That's a shame,' she said. 'I'll see you tomorrow.'

15

Rocketman

Mary Brooks saw Carter coming down the stairs after his session with Dr Flowers and plotted an intercept course.

'Don't,' he said, striding past her, his face set tightly. 'I don't want to know.'

'OK,' she called to his disappearing back. 'Shall I tell Rocketman you're packing it all in for the stage?'

Carter pulled up and did a U-turn. 'What does he want?'

'He wouldn't tell me,' she replied, betraying a lifetime of disappointment in the man who would never tell her what she wanted to hear.

'Basement Two?' asked Carter.

'Where else?'

Carter took the stairs rather than the lift. The forensic labs for the south-east of Scotland were underground at FOC Fettes, the hideout of Chief Technical Officer Davey 'Rocketman' Johnstone, a man who held the same rank and stature as DCI McKinlay and had been around just as long. He and McKinlay had joined the force together, it was rumoured, and he knew where McKinlay's bodies were buried, it was whispered whenever new recruits were indoctrinated.

Basement Two was light and airy and spread beyond the visible footprint of the FOC building above like weeds spread roots. It shared its accommodation with Forensics and Firearms. There was a vehicle garage with a secure entry that from the outside looked like a fire station. The forensic suite was state of the art. It was suspected a long-departed Chief Constable had conceded to all of Rocketman's equipment demands based on a real promise to exhume some of those putrefied bodies.

Carter arrived at a frosted glass door that spanned the corridor's width, pressed the visitor's button to announce his arrival and waited. He imagined sensors scanning every millimetre of his body to check he was a fit and proper person to be granted entry to the Lothian kirk of criminal science. The door relented with a click and he was admitted into a reception area that could have graced Holyrood Palace. With one hand suspiciously hidden under the table, a young receptionist smiled at him and told him to sit while she informed CTO Johnstone.

Moments later, Johnstone himself appeared in a doorway further down the corridor. 'Sergeant Carter,' he commanded.

Carter stood and walked towards him, his footsteps making no sound on the rubberised floor, musing that Rocketman didn't look anything like the lead guitarist of Elton John's band. They only shared the same name and city as a home-town. Johnstone was small for a man, dark-haired with quick eyes and a faster mind, who could and did detective work if pressed. However, he drew the line at playing 'Saturday Night's Alright for Fighting' on the streets of Niddrie.

Carter entered a laboratory full of white-coated young people busily doing stuff on impressive machines usually only seen by mortals on television. Rocketman got straight to the point.

'The girl in hospital, Alice Deacon. We've got some news, but how much of it is useful, I think you'll decide. First—' Rocketman launched straight into an analysis of clothing and cell transfer and soil samples and DNA testing. Carter waited a full five minutes until he finished.

'You didn't call on Mary to catch me just to tell me the soil on Alice's clothes came from an old graveyard. What else?'

'That what I like about you, Sergeant Carter, you cut to the chase. So first, there are her shoes.'

'What about them?'

'She wasn't wearing any. We checked with the ambulance crew and Dr Murray and the nursing staff. Coat, dress, underwear, tights, gloves: all accounted for. Handbag in a tree. As you found the scene, I'm assuming you didn't lift her shoes off the verge as a souvenir?'

Carter thought back to his search of the scene at the bridge.

'Nobody goes on a night out in winter in stocking feet,' Rocketman carried on with his assessment. 'So, a serial rapist who takes keepsakes. One step away from a serial killer.'

'That's a leap of faith.'

'We can't find enough DNA from her clothes and skin to get a reliable sample. Either we've been unlucky this time, or he's forensically aware. Gloves, facemask, a prophylactic, wet wipes, etcetera. That takes me nicely to my main course.'

'Which is?' asked Carter.

'Drug-facilitated sexual assault, our American colleagues call it.'

Carter hadn't seen this coming. 'Which drug?'

'There're many to choose from, and all are hand-boiled. We're running the blood, hair and skin tests. Scoop is the leader in the clubhouse.' Rocketman smiled, waiting to see if his allegedly smarter colleague could decipher his chemist's code. 'The street names constantly change, because no batch is ever quite the same. GHB and GBH, goop, scoop, soap, liquid X and Mad Max are just some of the monikers.'

'Rohypnol?' Carter guessed.

'No, that's flunitrazepam, known as Roofie in some circles and Rope in others. This is hyoscine, a derivative of the nightshade plant, probably prepared as *scopolamine hydrobromide.* Known as Scoop, Burundanga, or the more cultish Devil's Breath. Common in the UK because the base is legal – but prescription-only. Most base drugs are mixed with other drugs and excipients to get more potent effects. A few years ago, GHB was the fashion amongst the unfashionable. But Leith Drug Squad got the dealers by the balls, and the girls learned to finish their drinks before going to the loo. Ms Deacon would've been staggering all over the place, so your man would have had to hold her up.'

'It explains how he was able to rape her in the cemetery,' Carter ran with it. 'She'd look like she was blootered and he was taking care of her. And it explains how he was able to get her over the bridge parapet.'

'It's not for me to plant ideas in your head, Leccy, but I don't think this is an opportunist rape. This drug is easy to buy, but not easy to dose. Too little of it and your victim will fight back. Too much of it and she's a ragdoll; maybe even a dead-doll. I'm guessing he's experimented before – or he's been lucky. But I think we've just discovered a small piece of a much bigger picture.'

'He's done this to other women?'

Rocketman nodded. 'Maybe Alice was his first murder attempt, but it's likely he's built himself up to it. If he was a chemist, he could make it himself. That would narrow down your search. How many sexual assaults in the city last year?'

Carter pondered the quiz question. 'I don't know. You'd be better placed to answer that.'

'Ten murders. Not many by some cities; Glasgow had sixty-five, London was one-hundred-and-thirty-two. In Edinburgh and surrounds, close on a thousand sex crimes, all told.'

'Bloody hell,' Carter blew out his cheeks.

'I'll tell Cheryl, but I think you'll need a bigger team. You've got a lot of digging to do, and I do hope that's only a metaphor.'

16

Team Meeting

After leaving the forensic suite, Carter took out his phone, opened the Police Scotland ICRS case management app, found his team icon and sent them a secure text message. '*Diary Buster*'.

At 10.30 a.m. DI Mason, DC Podolski and DC Garcia were in a meeting room in St Leonard's. Carter brought them up to speed about the date-rape drug.

'Nick, have you authorised the analysis of Alice's phone?' Carter asked.

'It was couriered to Helen Street in Glasgow last night,' Mason replied. 'Our Kiosk is out-of-bounds. Check ICRS yourself and see if Roy's team have started work on it.'

'Alice has messages on her phone,' said Carter, 'assumed to be from the man responsible for her flight over the footbridge.'

'How do you come to that conclusion, Leccy?' Mason asked.

Carter fiddled with ICRS on the desktop computer, struggling to find the evidence he was looking for.

'Leccy's name was in the text on her phone,' DC Garcia said, filling the void in the room while the tech played up.

'Thanks, Charli, I can explain it,' Carter admonished her, finding what he was looking for at last. An image of the text message appeared on the electronic whiteboard.

[019-01-14:0015] Now I've got your attention, Leccy, you know I am serious. Was my calling card what you expected? What secrets will Alice tell you and will you ever find me? J.

'How does he know you, Leccy?' Mason asked, ready to pounce.

'I don't know, but there's more here. This sixteen-character code seems to change every time he sends a message,' said Carter.

'So what?' Mason said.

'There are more texts. Her messages have her name, his have these random numbers instead of a name. And I've received messages to my own phone in the last two nights, direct from him.'

'Why haven't you told us this before?' Mason saw leverage. 'Are you holding back evidence?'

'The texts were erased from my phone. There's no evidence they ever existed.'

'So, there's a link between Alice, J and you,' Mason concluded. 'It must be someone else you know.'

The tension in the room tightened. The junior officers held their breath, waiting for the next revelation. Carter knew he had to share his fear with Mason sometime but was now the moment? He thought not.

'J knows Kelsa died, and he knows about Nathaniel.'

'That's awful, Leccy,' DC Podolski said.

'Come clean, Carter,' said Mason. 'You're holding back.'

'You'd like that, eh?' Carter snapped at Mason's lure.

'You're involved, somehow,' Mason said. 'It would be a dereliction of duty not to look into your background. I'll propose it to the boss – right now – see if she agrees.' He got up from his chair.

'Is it really necessary? We should focus on this app, see if the techs can shed light on it.'

Mason ignored his plea and left the room.

'Ellen, any luck with Alice's family?' Carter felt he should get on with the rest of the briefing.

'Yes. We contacted her boyfriend, Hamish. He gave us the address of her parents. They're shocked, as you'd expect, but knew nothing about anyone who could be J. Alice seemed to compartmentalise her life. They went to the hospital last night to see her.'

'CCTV, Charli?'

'Two cameras on George Street show someone getting out of a taxi and going into the Dome. The timing suggests it's her, but the street was busy, and the resolution isn't great.'

'Follow up with the Dome, they might have private CCTV inside.'

The door opened. DI Mason accompanied DCI McKinlay. She sat down in Mason's chair.

'Nick has explained the complication, Leccy,' McKinlay summarised. 'You've received two messages from Alice's rapist, but they've been deleted from your phone?'

'Not by me, ma'am. I don't know how they were deleted.'

'And you're mentioned in a message he sent to Alice?' She looked at the whiteboard.

He nodded. 'He also knows about Kelsa and my son.'

'Somethin' strange going on,' she said, pondering. 'Nick wants to give you a latex finger, but I'm not keen – it could be a distraction. Your privacy trumps your role as a policeman in today's environment, and you cannae investigate yourself. I'm assumin' if he's sent you two messages, he'll send more. I'll authorise Gavin Roy's team to poke deep into Alice's phone, maybe we can identify him from there, eh?' she said, explaining her reasoning.

She looked at DI Mason and shook her head. 'My call, my responsibility. If you get another message, Leccy, tell us straight away.'

17

Upwardly Mobile

Scoop took the investigation up a level, Leccy felt. But it spawned a whole new puzzle. Leith was a hotbed for narcotics in Edinburgh, but it wasn't the only suburb where dealers dealt. Any of the council schemes that pockmarked the city had a drugs market if you knew where to look – or who to call.

Carter called Andrew MacIntosh in Drylaw, a needle's-length from the Pilton and Muirhouse housing experiments in the north of the city.

'Mac, it's Leccy,' Carter said.

'Aye, this won't be a social call then, unless you're calling in that beer I owe you.'

'Forget the beer if you can tell me who does scoop around your way.'

'What's the gig?' asked MacIntosh, suspicious as always that he might be kept out of something big. 'Does Cheryl know you're calling me? She wasn't too chuffed when you came over to review the evidence we had on McCalman's rackets last year.'

'She doesn't know I'm calling you – yet.' Carter said. 'A girl's been thrown off a bridge and is in a coma in hospital. She'd been raped too.'

'Easier than a goodnight kiss, eh?'

'Anyone making it on your patch?'

'Around Drylaw?' MacIntosh was incredulous. 'You're kidding. It's not like growing cannabis. You need special equipment and the knowledge of a chemist. You can cook it between the soup and the tatties, though.'

'Anyone trading?'

'It's the kind of thing McCalman was into, but he's in HMP Saughton and won't see daylight for a decade. But you know what they say about vacuums, eh? You want me to sniff around?'

'Aye. Where would the goods originate?'

'Livingston – Bathgate, maybe. More likely Glasgow or Dundee, or from down south. Birmingham, Manchester, London.'

After agreeing that Mac would look into it, Carter ended the call. The drug markets were invisible; many operated on the dark web, and big onshore busts were rare for drugs like hyoscine. Cocaine had to be imported, but legal organic drugs could be just as profitable, have similar effects, and be manufactured easily if you had the knowledge, resources and motivation.

Back at his desk, he opened his computer and turned his attention to Alice's mobile phone. The case records on ICRS said she was eight months into a two-year mobile contract with InterMide. The record also indicated they'd tracked her locations on the night she'd been attacked. He called the Operational Services Department at Helen Street in Glasgow.

Gavin Roy's Cybercrime Investigation Team was colloquially known as OCD. It was responsible for liaison with mobile phone network operators, internet service providers and the big tech companies, amongst other darker arts.

'Gavin, DS Carter from St Leonard's. The Alice Deacon case.'

'That's the one DCI McKinlay authorised?'

Carter gave Gavin the ICRS reference number and Alice's phone number. He asked for the location data on a map overlay.

'Sending it to you now,' said Roy. 'It's interactive, all the data is in a pivot table, so you can slice and dice your way to heaven. An interesting approach to messaging on this phone. I can see why your boss wants a deep dive done on it.'

'You seen anything like it before?' Carter asked him.

'Total identity cloaking and bleeding-edge tech altogether. In phones, an app is usually pre-installed to enable SMS messages and consumes about fifty megabytes of storage. On this one, the app and its message are one and the same. It's a nano-app – meaning microscopic – and it consumes only two-point-five kilobytes of storage per message so it can be sent over low-speed networks. It's Cold War spy tech in digital form, using a one-time, unbreakable, 160-character cypher. The 160-character message is coded using the cypher then sent with a random, sixteen-character origin code all wrapped up in TLS encryption. When she responds, the origin code and cypher are never used again. He's the controller and could erase all the messages on her phone in one click. But he's not done it.'

'Why wouldn't he erase them?' Carter asked. 'Would he get an app like that from Google Play or the App Store?'

Roy sniggered the way an adult would to a child who thinks farting is funny. 'This is dark-web stuff. He must have skills, he'd have to side-load the app on his own phone first. If he used WhatsApp and a smart-arsed copper like you gets hold of an unlocked phone, he'd be fucked. But not erasing the messages tells me he's been lazy.'

'There's another angle,' Carter said. 'He's messaged my phone twice. Each time the message was erased.'

'Oh. So, he doesn't want those messages being read by anyone except you,' Roy mused. 'Maybe he's not that lazy after all. But why go to all the bother?'

'Keeping things from a wife?' Carter proposed.

'You, me and everyone else would stick with WhatsApp, smart-arsed coppers not assumed.'

'Thanks, Gavin.'

Carter opened the email Gavin sent him and saved the files in the case's shared location. Opening the Excel data file, he ran the program that overlaid Alice's movements in a twelve-hour timeframe, six hours before and six hours immediately after the rape. The time data-points were overlaid on a Google Map of Edinburgh. They appeared as irregular lines, coloured red, green and blue. The lines slithered their way through the hotspots of the city, like a kid who'd drawn a demonic railway track. Blue were GPS coordinates, mobile phone masts were red. They combined to green when both technologies agreed exactly where the phone was. Both gave him spot times in Universal Coordinated Time.

With this granularity of data he didn't really need the CCTV from the City Council; he could trace every step she took on the night just by following the coloured lines. He scrolled the map and zoomed in until he located Dalry Cemetery, then he checked the data in the Excel file. Her phone arrived at the crime scene at 23:34:06 UTC. She was on the bridge at 00:09:48 UTC. The ambulance crew had recorded hitting her at ten minutes after midnight. Half an hour later they were on their way to the Royal Infirmary A & E, via the city by-pass, arriving just before 1 a.m. After that, it all got a bit blurry.

He scrolled up through the data looking for 23:00:00 but couldn't see it. 22:21:02 was the closest time. Phone mast data said her phone left that location sixty-nine minutes later. He traced the reference backwards on the map, looking to find the most likely place where she could've been drugged.

The Reverend bar on Dalry Road. Less than fifty metres from the entrance to Dalry Burial Ground.

18

Brief Encounter

After lunch, Carter got pulled into a one-to-one meeting with DCI McKinlay. She'd had her hair done, but all that did was make her look more like his gran. He kept that insight to himself.

'You knew Alice Deacon was in the Royal before I sent you there.' She got to the point before he sat down. 'Why didn't you say?

'I got a message from him. He said he'd left a calling card at Petite France. He didn't mention Alice at all.'

'Do you know this "J"? If he turns out to be your best mate, I'll be pushed off the fourth-floor roof in a wheelie. But you'll be washed-up at thirty-three and reduced to spitting out one-liners on the streets for coin.'

'He knows things about me, but I haven't got a clue about him. Honest, ma'am.'

'Soon as you know more, you tell us. OK?'

'OK.'

'How're you getting on with Dr Flowers?'

'She's said I should be off-duty, but you haven't.'

'Operationally, it's my call. Don't be open all hours and remember to delegate. And don't wind up Nick, he's got talents that others dinnae have.'

'Thank you, ma'am.' Carter wasn't sure he liked the last bit.

'Now, go home an' relax. That's an order.'

So, Carter caught the bus to Leith.

Tommy McGregor's practice was on Great Junction Street, sandwiched between a Syrian tailor and a payday shark called Dosher's Loans. The windows and door of McGregor's surgery were reinforced with metal shutters. Above them, the sign screamed 'Criminal Defence Lawyers – We'll Get You Off'.

When Sheriff Dunsmuir discovered Kelsa had used Tommy McGregor's services to buy the Liberton house, he'd nearly had an aneurysm. But that was Kelsa – she knew how to poke her father.

Carter was on the fence about McGregor being the right choice for this task. They'd shared court time in the past, resulting in an honourable draw. McGregor dressed down for the part, oozing charm and professionalism, and Carter admitted to himself the reason he had come here was that McGregor took no prisoners.

The brief's secretary had gotten them coffee and Tommy McGregor wanted to establish the ground rules. 'So, who am I talking to? Detective or husband?'

'How many policemen do you have as clients?'

McGregor shook his head slightly. 'What can I do for you, Leccy?'

Carter smiled. 'Stenhouse Dunsmuir LLP.'

'Ah,' McGregor relaxed into his black leather chair. 'Your father-in-law's crew.' His office was basic but colourful. Green and white walls, with photographs of smiling children and an attractive blonde woman that Carter assumed was McGregor's family and wife. A signed Hibernian football strip. Framed certificates of law, Glasgow prominent in the crests.

'Ever met them in court?' Carter tried not to appear desperate.

'A bit too upmarket for my clients. What's your point?'

'It's no secret that Kelsa was— unwell.'

'Why me?' McGregor queried. 'I'm flattered, but Edinburgh isn't short of briefs.'

Cut a deal with the devil. Hope not to see you in court again.

'You're hurting.' McGregor filled the void when Carter said nothing. 'But you're not stupid enough just to put one over on Dunsmuir. What's happened?'

'Temporary residency for Nathaniel with his grandparents,' Carter handed over the papers to McGregor. 'That seems right, given my situation. I'm struggling at the moment, and Dunsmuir knows it. Whatever the future holds, I'm not ready to give full-time care to a vulnerable baby and still work as a detective. Maybe later. But Kelsa's last testament says if I challenge the residency, I'm cut out of her will.'

'First question – and don't take this the wrong way – are you the father?'

'Yes.' *Wrong way taken, you fucking shark.*

'Nathaniel's birth certificate?' McGregor asked.

'Not with me,' Carter replied. 'Dunsmuir registered the birth because I was stuck at court. A witness for the prosecution – you know: the day job. Kelsa couldn't do it, obviously.'

'I'll get a copy from the Registrar. When were you married?' McGregor scribbled notes on a pad without looking up.

'Las Vegas, eighth of December 2017. I have a copy of the Vegas licence at home.'

'That must've pleased the Sheriff.' McGregor looked up and grinned. 'Did the family attend the wedding?'

'A snap decision. We'd flown there for a holiday. Her father wanted Cramond Kirk on a summer's day.'

'As Nathaniel's father, your parental rights trump any residency instruments. We can challenge the provision of access when you want and can petition to contest her will.'

Carter hesitated. 'I don't know if I'm the best person for him to be with right now.'

'He's your son.'

'He's seven weeks old, he needs his mother more than his father.'

'He doesn't have that choice, and neither do you,' McGregor said, with finality.

Carter stood up. 'Maybe this was a bad idea.' McGregor's reception room was stacked with a microcosm of the Leith underworld – nobody Carter recognised, but he was sure they all knew him.

Following him out, McGregor held the door to the street. 'Goodbye, Sergeant Carter,' he said, blowing Carter's cover wide open.

Once outside, the coldness of the season hit him. He pulled the collar of the Crombie up around his neck. He had no scarf, hat or gloves so stuck his hands in his pockets, enduring the tingling cold in his ears. Darkness came early in January; already, it felt like the freezing depths of endless night, and it was only 5.30 p.m.

Having McGregor lay the legal facts on the table had brought home to him just how little he knew of Kelsa and her family. The blindness of love at first sight. Was J another blind spot?

Carter walked to the bus stop at the Kirkgate Centre where the number 7 would take him past Captain's Bar. The number 10 would force him into Sandy Bell's folk pub.

After five minutes of feet-stamping and finger-blowing, the number 10 made up his mind. Inside the bus wasn't much warmer than outside. Condensation rolled down windows, and everyone sat ignoring everyone else. But buses were a childhood comfort, reminding him of Gorebridge. Papa Carter had taught him to look after himself: if it's too far to walk, get the bus. And with climate change threatening, he felt by taking the bus he was doing his bit.

He glanced at the faces around him; the trodden-on classes, money worries ingrained in their manner and bearing; a mix of pensioners and the under-employed: school children chattering away about phones, boys or girls or football or computer games. He was of them, but not with them.

After a twenty-minute ride, he alighted at Princes Street, walked breathlessly up the Mound, crossed the Royal Mile and hurried along George IV Bridge. He dodged pedestrians and selfie-snappers at the Elephant House, finally arriving at Sandy Bell's on Forrest Road. Once inside, he stood at the bar and ordered his favourite Balvenie. Feeling the rich warmth find his stomach, a glow rose to his face, and its punch revived his heart. Sandy Bell's was a venue of tall tales and live music – fiddlers, guitarists and whistlers of a folk bent – but it was early yet with an empty bench. He'd once gigged here as a young comedian but wasn't invited back and never knew why.

After more drams and a bit of chat with the worthies, he was tempted to settle in, but resisted. He'd fall to maudlin over Kelsa, twisting himself into drunken knots, then harangue some poor sod whose only crime was to listen.

Left alone, anything could happen – except the return of his lover from the dead.

He deserted the pub and headed home, catching the number 31 at Surgeons' Hall, across from the Festival Theatre. At the Malbet Park stop on Lasswade Road, he walked for ten minutes through the residential streets until his darkened home in Malbet Crescent came into view.

Mail lay on the carpet when he opened the door. He hung up his coat, switched on the lights and gathered the post. Calvin's Obsession endlessly reminded him she wasn't here anymore.

The house was warm. The central heating was on a timer cycle, much like he was. Eat, drink, sleep, wash, eat, sleep, leave, return. Grieve.

One envelope was addressed to him in handwriting. First-class, locally posted and thick. The others were bills and junk. The envelope contained a card. A black dahlia motif was embossed on the front, with '*Deepest Sympathies*' as text. Hand-written inside the card was a list of names, colleagues of Kelsa's, he assumed.

From: Raymond Henderson, Sam Dingle, Jonathan Gordon-Davies, Ken Barlow, Roy Johnson and Stan Butler.

Underneath was a signature written large in confident, swirly script.

J.

19

Comedy Rehab

Ten miles south of Edinburgh, the village of Gorebridge sat in the black mine fields of Midlothian. Its coalpits, the Emily and Gore, had closed in the sixties. Work had still been plentiful for hundreds of miners at the Lady Victoria Colliery in the neighbouring village of Newtongrange until 1984 when the coal mining world changed forever. For two long years, the miners battled a suicide mission against the Thatcher ideology's scorched-earth policies. Somehow, despite the decimation of the communities that followed, the village survived.

The bowling club sat at the centre of the old village, in Hunter Square, up the steep brae from the railway station with its direct link to Edinburgh's financial heart. The club was open for business all day, every day, because what else was there?

Men dominated the bar, drinking cheap lager and cheaper whisky, their ages ranging from red-faced teenager to proto-corpse. January was a dead zone between the New Year and the Champions League second half in February. The club had stand-ups on stage all year round, but now was a perfect time to mine the depths of performers' material.

For Leccy Carter, detective by day and stand-up comedian by night, the experience was priceless. It was another step towards his holy grail of a month's gig at the Edinburgh Fringe in August. The Scottish comedy circuit was still unthinkable. Mainstream TV was light-years away, but he had promise. All he had to do was get out there and make the right people laugh.

He wondered what Dr Flowers would say if she knew about tonight's alternative therapy. He stood at the side of a creaking stage that had suffered over the years, behind drawn curtains that had seen better days. Peeking through a slit, he watched his audience tank up. There were about eighty punters tonight. He even recognised a few folks from Gorebridge's Siamese-twin village of Arniston. He was big-game nervous. Butterflies exercised themselves in his gut. He'd grown up with these people and they knew him. No quarter would be given.

The gig was as compere; ten minutes upfront. He'd earned that right over the last years, and the spot was his any time he wanted it. There were six acts tonight, and he'd punctuate a few minutes between each to allow them time to sort their back-line if they had one. After ninety minutes he'd close if they didn't overrun.

It was his first gig for six months, what with work and Kelsa's illness. A step towards reclaiming his future. Half of him wanted the adulation, the other half wanted him to die in front of his mates. These boys and girls he'd grown up with, who'd played with him, fought with him and dragged his bruised arse home for his gran to clean up afterwards. For all that knowledge, all that history, all that background that could never be erased, he hated them.

For one night only.

Inwardly bricking himself, outwardly confident, he shrugged on his stagecraft, expecting a thumbs-down after the first punchline. This audience held power of life and death over him. As a stand-up gladiator, his routine was all the armour he had.

A disembodied voice squeezed through the speakers, announcing the entertainment would begin. 'Ladies and gentlemen, please give it up for our own local hero – Leccy Carter!'

The curtains pulled back and, for a split second, he was naked. He bounded into the centre of the small stage and grabbed the mic from its stand. 'Boolers of Gorebridge, I salute you.'

'Where you been, Leccy? We thought you were deid and buried.' A snigger rippled its way through the audience.

'Bad comedians never die,' he parried, knowing the gig would turn on the riposte. 'They just pay to heckle.'

They liked it: he'd bought himself another gag.

'So, you all know I'm a detective in Edinburgh, but I also do a little moonlighting on the side. Cash in hand, no questions asked. Just like you Jimmy Wilson – I mean, who else here does patios at nine o'clock at night, eh? So – a wummin in the New Town asks me to follow her husband. Thinks he's seeing another woman. I track him to the Caley hotel and watch for an hour, then he goes to the George for another hour, then the Balmoral. Finally, he goes home. I tell her all this, and she asks me, "Is that grounds for divorce?" I told her, "Sure, he was following you."'

Things were warming up. He paced back and forward along

the stage, dropping into one-liners. 'You know, a woman will never date a man that lives with his mother, but she'll always date a man who lives with his wife.' And then, 'My wife doesn't trust me. That's one thing she has in common with my mistress.'

He kept the lines going for another few minutes, before getting a signal that the first act was ready. 'Ladies, it's been spankin' for me, and I don't care how it was for you. So, put your hands together for up-and-coming tribute band, One Distraction!'

He dashed off stage; one round down. 'Good effort, Leccy,' said the old stage manager, who seemed to live in the place.

But over the next hour, his time on stage shrank. He had a problem with the material and his belief in it. A massive bubble of doubt was growing in his heart, a bubble he couldn't burst. He couldn't run through material about wives, sex and adultery as if he was a parrot. The audience knew he'd buried Kelsa only days ago. Besides, his soul wasn't ready for material like this. He contemplated not showing for the final slot, but that was taboo. The show goes on. Send them home laughing ... or crying.

The curtain rolled back for the final time. 'Nice one, Leccy,' someone encouraged him from the darkness. A lone spotlight picked him out, all other lights dimmed, the punters in the room merging into a solid black shape. Only the first row of faces looked up at him. He knew them and named them.

'Billy MacDonald, you bit me on the arm when I was seven.' Billy smiled, holding a half-empty pint, but he said nothing. He knew what was coming. 'Jimmy Wilson, you tried to teach me to play football. You always put me in goal, 'cos I was crap in any other position, and you, Andy Stone, I knocked your teeth out at school, remember? We've been besties ever since. Slider, you pushed me out of a tree at Harvieston. I broke my arm on the fall, you sick bastard. All of you – you've all been there for me. Without your help, I wouldn't be the prick I am today.

'I want to tell you about the girl that broke my heart. She died ten days ago, six weeks after giving birth to our son. She'd been ill for months, wouldn't eat, took only enough to sustain the baby. Anorexia said the doctors. She refused all help, would accept no medicines, but was determined to give birth to a healthy boy. Once born, she cuddled him and kissed and cooed at him for a few hours. I took loads of pictures of them both before they fell asleep. But the next day, she just gave in to the illness and let herself drift. I pleaded with her, but once Kelsa made up her mind, there was no going back.'

Was this therapy? It didn't feel like it, it felt more like he was baring his soul, speaking of things that men dare not talk about. Cutting open his breast and exposing his heart, dripping red raw. He, Leccy Carter, the snotty-nosed bairn who ran around the village with skinned knees and dirty clothes, was capable of high love and was prepared to admit it.

'The woman who died in my arms wasn't the woman I fell in love with. Two years ago, she was vivacious and beautiful, tall and elegant, with long dark hair and a wicked tease of a smile. She walked on water. I watched men drool when she sailed past them. Honestly, I saw it with my own eyes. The sway of her hips was like a finely tuned Jag purring past. I met her after a gig at the Stand. I was pretty drunk when she came over to me. She'd been in the audience with her girlfriends, and they were quaffing champagne. She came over, said my patter was great. I tried out some new ones on her.

'I wanted her phone number.' Carter sank to his knees on stage, his voice trembling with emotion. The room was totally silent. A hometown comedian was dying on-stage for their entertainment. It would live long in the village memory. 'She ripped my shirt open and wrote her number on my chest in big red numbers with her lipstick, then she walked away.'

Tears flowed as he recounted the moment. This was his confession, his absolution, his blood-letting. He was of their ilk, and if penance were required afterwards, it would be pint-shaped and lager-flavoured, topped off with intravenous shots of Clan Macpherson whisky.

'Next morning, going into the shower, I realised what was on my chest. Her number had smudged. I looked in the mirror and tried to write it on paper but kept getting it wrong. I panicked – was nearly in tears. I might never see her again. I called three different phones, including a bloke who was keen to hook up, but eventually, I got the right number.

'Within a year, we married in Vegas. I'd never been so happy.' He coughed, wiping his nose with his arm. He'd nearly unloaded it all but wasn't quite finished.

'Everything was great, until one weekend she went on a night out and didn't come home for two days. Everything began to change then, and I still don't know why.'

Carter sobbed into his knees. Nobody breathed and silence took over. A man at the back started sniggering, quietly. 'That's the best one of the evenin'.' He clapped softly, then harder, encouraging others to take it up. A few turned to see who it was. More joined in, soon the whole room was taking it up, louder and louder as hand met hand, resonating around the venue till it deafened. Whistling started, the floor shook like an earthquake, with shouts like 'Aw right man', 'Leccy yer a star'. The mass of the audience converged on the stage to help him, everyone wanted to be next to him, the whole club proclaiming the crowning of a king of their own making.

One man skipped the coronation, quietly slipping into the darkness.

20

Anger Therapy

At nine o'clock the next morning, Carter arrived at Fettes somewhat hungover.

'Morning, Mary,' he said breezily to the keeper of the gates of Hades. 'Nice day today, isn't it?'

Her glower spoke volumes about the state of him.

In her usual place, Dr Flowers was wearing a grey high-necked woollen dress with a black belt around her waist and black heels with thick black tights.

'Good morning, Sergeant Carter,' she eventually looked up at him. 'You're looking tired today. Had a sleepless night?'

'It's amazing what alcohol can do,' he replied wearily.

'We need to make progress today. I expect your cooperation.'

'Sense of humour failure?'

'I've heard you're working a case after I explicitly said you were not to return to duties.'

'Take it up with DCI McKinlay,' he said flatly.

'Really?' Sarcasm suited her. 'The Chief Superintendent is right behind this initiative you know, and he's just looking for reasons to push more old nags out to pasture. Know what I mean, Lachlan? A change of the guard at St Leonard's would suit him fine and to do that all I need to say is "subject is uncooperative".'

'I have a question,' he interjected. Turning the table on her felt good. 'Do you truly think I'm unfit for duty? Do you think I'd recover quicker staring at the walls of my home for hours or going back to live with my grandparents?'

'Tell me about living with your grandparents.'

He knew what she was doing but was too tired to put up a fight. 'What is there to say? They brought me up.'

'What about your mother's parents? In North Berwick. Do you ever see them?'

'I've only met them once when I was fifteen, and only my grandmother. I looked up the name. Telephone directories still existed then. Only five McKenzies in the town. When I arrived at the house, I recognised her as soon as I saw her, but she didn't invite me in—'

'Why do you think she behaved that way?' Flowers was motoring now, scribbling away on her pad as each answer was given.

'It doesn't matter,' he shrugged. 'My real grandparents care about me. I don't waste effort on people who don't.'

'Why did you join the police?'

'I don't know.' The change of context allowed him latitude. 'It seemed exciting, chasing bad guys. More exciting than drafting engineering drawings for the mines.'

Dr Flowers leaned forward on her desk and scribbled much more. Minutes passed as if he wasn't there. She consulted some notes from open books beside her, then scribbled yet more into her pad, then read more notes, flicking over pages.

'Why don't you use an iPad or a laptop?' he said finally, feeling ignored and realising how lonely it was. She maintained her silence, letting his loneliness grow, eventually giving him the attention he craved.

'It helps me concentrate. Typing is distracting during sessions.'

'You're not very good at interviewing either,' said Carter, understanding he had as much right to control the discussion as she had. 'So, what's next, Lisa? Do you know where you're going with all this? Because it seems to me, you're playing at it.'

'Being superficial, you mean? Like you. You're hiding behind yourself. People you love abandon you, so you're not going to invest time in them, and you won't invest time in yourself either. You're behaving like a machine. A cyborg that switches on then off when you're done. That's why you're such a good detective. You wipe all emotions away until only the intellectual puzzle is left.'

'So what? That's the job description.'

His phone pinged: an incoming text message, but not of the regular type.

[2019-01-16:0930] Lipstick in the Dome was it? You were her plaything Carter. Remember the Sick Kids. You don't know what I'm talking about do you? You will find out very soon. J

Something snapped inside him when he read the message. Rage forced him out of his chair. This time it tumbled over, and he turned and kicked at it hard. It bounced along the floor to the opposite side of the room. He made straight for her desk, a rumble of thunder clouds clear and visible on his face.

'You have no idea what it's like to deal with what I see every day,' he raised his voice. 'Look at this.' He pushed his phone across the desk. 'Give me your professional opinion on this, doctor.'

She sat forward, read the text, but said nothing.

'Write the words down, Petal. It's actual evidence.'

She scribbled the message on the pad, then looked up. 'Why don't you just grab the screen?'

He felt his face redden; he hadn't thought to do that with the other messages? He snapped it on his phone.

'This is what I'm investigating,' he explained. 'The raping bastard must've been there last night, in the audience. My wife is dead, and my child has been taken away from me. And today, you want to know how I feel about growing up without parents?' He leaned over the desktop and swept all her things off it. Her pen shot across the room like a bullet, bouncing off the picture window. The writing pad crumbled into a heap on the carpeted floor. The books she'd consulted during their session bounced on their spines and settled into the carpet like shot pheasant.

Dr Flowers just sat there, unsure whether or not to call the cops.

'You just don't understand,' he shouted at her this time, in case she couldn't hear him from all of four feet away. 'He knows Kelsa's dead. He wants to own me. He's said he's going to kill me. I don't know why, and I don't know when.'

'What do you expect me to say?' She defended her approach resolutely. 'This is your working life. My working life is to help you achieve mindfulness and balance and come to terms with what's happened to you.'

'You're so just like him, doctor.' Carter wanted her to get

angry. 'You're a licenced manipulator, a fixer, mediator and negotiator. You're the judge, the jury, the executioner and the fucking undertaker. You push pigeons into holes according to the rules of your high-minded psycho-babble profession. And you're wasting the time of this fucking useless copper who'd better get out there and start doing his job.'

He picked up the books and the writing pad and placed them back where they belonged. He found the spent rage of his anger cosying up to the spent bullet of her pen and laid both neatly on her pad. He collected his chair from the corner it cowered in, turned it upright, then marched towards the office door.

'Tomorrow, at nine,' she said as if all her therapy sessions ended this way.

He left the door open so she could watch him walk away.

21

Victim Support

Back at St Leonard's, he walked up two flights of stairs and negotiated the narrow corridor to find Victim Support at the far end. A team exclusively made up of women, there was no chatter from the other departments about a lack of gender equality here. The room was quiet and empty except for Ellen Podolski.

'Leccy,' Ellen stood up from her desk and hugged him like the mother-of-three teens she was. 'This is the first chance we've had to talk freely. I'm so sorry for you. Kelsa was such a beacon of a girl, we're all poorer without her. I've wanted to ask you, how are you coping with the baby?'

'Fine,' he said, perhaps too jovially. 'Raising kids? It's a doddle.'

'Oh, aye? Wish I'd had more.' She threw him a quizzical look.

'What did Alice's parents tell you about her?' he changed the subject.

'Don't change the subject, I'm not daft. You'll need help. I'll come round, help you bathing him and make you a decent meal. Who looks after him while you're at work?'

'The in-laws. Judith supervises, but she's got staff doing the dirty work.'

'You're using formula at night, of course. Feeding him every two hours, you won't get much sleep?'

'I'm coping, Ellen, really,' he smiled at her to reassure her everything was alright. 'What did Alice's parents say?'

'Mum and Dad are now at her bedside. They weren't aware of her ordeal until we told them. She's an independent girl, and the boyfriend confirmed that too.'

'Where was Boyfriend when this happened?' Carter asked. 'How long have they been together?'

'Name of Hamish Kier. He was at home watching football with some mates. His alibi checks out.'

'Any of his other mates have a forename or surname beginning with "J"?'

Helen checked her notes. 'No. Apart from the "J" in Alice's calendar, have you found any other references?'

Something important tugged at Leccy's subconscious, in response to her question, but it kept out of reach. He let it go.

'Not unless we believe everyone with a name starting with "J" are suspects. Did you get some background on her?'

Ellen nodded. 'An only child, she went to St George's and was the wild teenager. Had a revolving door of boyfriends and fell pregnant at twenty. Mum convinced her to terminate, but afterwards, Alice distanced herself from them. She had multiple jobs in the city, but she'd started seeing her parents again in the last years. Still, they didn't delve into her private life in case they got cut off.'

'Are you tracking down her girlfriends?'

'You're the one with all the constables,' Ellen said. 'Do you know what "Victim Support" means?'

'Rocketman thinks he might have done this before,' Carter said. 'Her blood showed evidence of Scoop. Does that ring any bells with you? Other cases?'

'Not immediately, but I know people at Leith and Livingston. I'll ask around.' She glanced up at him. 'I can come and cook you a good meal every other day if you want?'

'Ellen, I'm not helpless, and you've got Marcus and those three boys to look after.'

Ellen smiled. 'There's a couple of lassies in here who'd throw themselves at you to help, in fact, Joanna—'

'Stop. I'll see you at our team meeting later.'

Carter walked away. While Ellen's concern was a comfort, the conversation was turning a bit too raw for him. She'd known him since he was a rookie detective and could tell when he was bullshitting, but if he broke down in tears in public, he'd be carrion for someone like J. The gents' toilet in the corridor was empty. He chose a stall and locked the door, collapsing onto the seat for a moment's peace and quiet. Last night's lager therapy had helped, but he wasn't fixed yet. What got to him was how emotional he'd become, for a man who'd never been emotional before. Kelsa had set out to change that. She'd showed him what love could be, and he'd dived into the deep end.

Tears had touched his eyes when Ellen asked him about Nathaniel. Now they returned, stripping back his veneer of invincibility. He couldn't possibly explain to Ellen what had happened, with Kelsa's father waving Nathaniel's residency order at him. He sat with his head in his hands and cried softly, pondering how long he could keep up the pretence that he had a son waiting for him at home: six months, but likely sooner.

There would have to be a wappenschaw.

When he was a gadge, Papa had regularly attended wappenschaws at the booling green. A parade showing off the quality of his bools. During the light nights and after the games with his booler cronies in tow, he'd arrive home very late, completely, happily pished. The memory dried the tears as he remembered Gran standing in the kitchen, berating the old fool for his transgressions. At the same time, Papa had tried to sweep away his drunkenness with the one-liners, like a broken record stuck in the groove. It always made her laugh. Then he'd try to kiss her – 'No' in front o' the boy,' she'd say. 'Away wi' ye Deek Carter, ye daft auld bugger.'

Good memories, good times. It was because of those nights, he was sure that he'd wanted to be a comedian. To make his gran laugh at his jokes.

Would he now be denied a wappenschaw for Nathaniel when it was time? If he couldn't show the boy off in good order, the older witches would mark him, and the younger apprentices would shun him as damaged goods. He swept those evil thoughts away and replaced them with a fresh batch. Flowers already thought he was damaged goods simply because his parents died when he was a toddler – and that automatically meant mental health issues, right? He wasn't the first orphan to walk the planet and have a dead partner too. Worse things happened in the mines.

If growing up with grandparents was good enough for him, it was good enough for Nathaniel. The boy would be fine and Judith would love him to bits. He'd always got on well with his mother-in-law even though Kelsa's relationship with her was tepid. On the other hand, he could never imagine Sheriff Dunsmuir bouncing Nathaniel on his knee and telling him long tales about his father's crime-fighting exploits. Emotion and old man Dunsmuir were continents apart, that was for sure. Though they didn't speak much about her childhood, by all intents it was a miracle Kelsa hadn't murdered her father years ago. But right now, Carter reluctantly admitted, it had to be the best place for Nathaniel to be.

Footsteps entering the toilet area brought him back to the here-and-now, and tissues wiped away the dregs of his tears. There would be more of this navel-gazing to come, of that he was sure. Dr Flowers had punched some holes in his dyke and, like the Dutch myth, his pent-up emotions were slowly leaking through. He only had so many fingers to stop it from bursting.

What would be the consequences once the dyke broke and he was swept downstream? Drowning in white water and clawing for air, desperate for any raft to grab on to.

Who'd catch J then?

22

Bear's Den

The rest of the day was consumed by discussing the evening's activity. The Reverend bar on Dalry Road was a suspected haunt of one of Edinburgh's gangland bosses. It had been identified by mobile phone tracking as the most likely pub where Alice Deacon had been drugged. DI Mason had pulled rank and insisted on a bit of preparation. Ellen had been excused, it not being her kind of evening.

At 9 p.m. Carter sat in an unmarked Police Scotland Astra, parked just off Dalry Road, a hundred metres from the Reverend. One other vehicle was in the car park, a dark Mercedes four-by-four. Carter had briefly considered coming here alone, just to check out it was what they thought it was. But, a DS flying solo would have stirred a corporate hornets' nest at St Leonard's. McKinlay ran a tight ship, picking the brightest and sharpest from wherever she could find them, including Mason's hometown of Glasgow. Supersmart coppers don't walk into a suspected criminal bar in Dalry on their lonesome. Not if they treasured the lifelong use of both legs, because

McKinlay's team wasn't wheelchair friendly.

'If he's there, we want a chat, that's all,' DI Mason had reminded them.

Outside the Astra, the air was chilly. On the other side of Dalry Road, two smokers in long coats chewed the freezing fat at the entrance to the underworld.

'What do you think?' Carter asked Mason, who'd been silent in the passenger's seat since they'd arrived.

'Those two haven't moved since we got here,' mused Mason. 'Must be something going on inside.'

'Should we come back tomorrow?' Carter gave his senior officer his place.

'It's Jimmy Logan's HQ,' Mason replied. 'Allegedly.'

'Who is Jimmy Logan?' Charli Garcia asked from the back seat.

'Brilliant comedian, Jimmy Logan was,' Carter played to his audience. 'Scotland's Bob Monkhouse.'

'Very good, Leccy,' Mason snorted. 'Might come and watch your gig next time I'm sleepy.'

The thought of Mason in his audience filled Carter with horror.

'Are we arresting a comedian?' said Garcia, confused by the chat.

'How many pubs does Logan own?' Carter asked.

'Officially six, but he controls more,' Mason informed them. 'Then there's snooker and pool halls, a couple of George Street clubs—'

'Ha, Logan is a crime boss,' Garcia caught up.

'Don't say that in front of him, if he's there,' Mason warned. 'Remember the plan. You can stay in the car, Charli, if you want, this being your first time and all that.'

'So – are we just going to sit here and watch these goons freeze to death?'

'You know, Leccy, you're just too gung-ho at times.' Mason pushed open the Astra's door but struggled to extricate his lanky frame from the small car. 'Jesus, bring back the Vectras.'

Garcia jumped out too. Carter locked the car with the remote. The bright flashers told everybody in Dalry the police were coming.

'Sentinels have gone inside,' said Mason as the three of them walked down the sloping pathway towards Dalry Road. A wooden fence concealed their approach from anyone loitering at the bar entrance. 'Either the show's over, or they've gone for a piss together. Maybe holding each other's cocks as we speak, eh, Leccy?'

Despite Mason's boldness, Carter was anxious about what might happen next. He'd come up against some of McCalman's henchmen in the past, but Mason's apprenticeship on the streets of *No Mean City* gave him a shield Carter hadn't yet earned. He just hoped he wouldn't crumble in front of his superior.

He whispered to Garcia, 'This might get rough.'

'And so?' she asked.

They crossed Dalry Road disguised as three plain-clothes coppers on a mission, complete with heavy coats to bulk themselves up. The outside of the bar was old school, painted dark brown to achieve the authentic '*criminal haunt*' look. The window frames hoped to see glass again someday. Mason pushed through a set of saloon doors inside the heavy storm doors with a copper's swagger. Carter and Garcia hung back for just a moment, so they didn't get smacked in the face.

The bar was warm and busy, and the football was on TV: Serie-A. Juventus were toying with AS Roma. The Hearts hadn't seen Europe since the post-season holidays. Celtic had bowed out of the Europa League before Christmas, so no one was getting over-excited. Some customers standing at the counter turned and recognised the arrivals for who they were. Their expressions predicted that a career-defining, knee-high tackle on DI Mason would see them promoted to the Premier League.

'Evening, Mr Mason. Lemonade?'

Nick reached the counter. 'Jake Malone, haven't seen you in a while.'

'I don't want trouble, sir. We're all just minding our own business here.'

'DS Carter,' Mason introduced his trailing colleagues, flicking his chin sideways, 'and DC Garcia. We're investigating the rape of a young woman in Dalry Cemetery last Sunday night. We've reason to believe she was in here after eleven p.m., possibly with her attacker. Did you see her, Jake?'

'My night off.'

Carter stepped forward and described Alice Deacon. Jake shook his head again.

Mason addressed a couple of men standing at the bar, asking them if they'd been in on Sunday and seen anything. The men were young, in their twenties, lanky and tense, lean firecrackers smouldering for action. One had a snake tattoo on his neck, slithering up from inside his tight white T-shirt, its fangs threatening to strike at the cortex on his buzz-cut head. The other had football tattoos climbing both arms, with the Heart of Midlothian shield prominent. Dobermen. Paid experts in the profession of violence. When they shook their heads and turned away, Mason knew something juicy was going down. He turned to Carter and whispered, 'Stay close.'

Garcia had wandered around the bar's inner perimeter and was picking up attention for the long Spanish looks she was giving some of the punters.

'Charli,' Carter said meaningfully. She came back into close quarters with her colleagues.

Carter surveyed the room: only two women in the bar, sitting together on a comfortable bench seat a few metres away, both mid-forties with stony faces. Mason asked the question. They looked at him like he was an alien in paradise, their glassy eyes full to the brim with vodka. His blood began to run in his veins, and his throat became tinder-dry, matching the tension in the bar. Then somebody sparked the match.

He detected movement: two men in scrubby clothes came at Mason from his right quarter. Mason turned and ducked like a boxer, just as a fist whistled into dead space, its owner's balance following it. Mason diverted a kick from the second man, grazing his knee. He stumbled backwards but stayed on his feet.

'Get intae them!'

A table fell with a crash, drinks spilt, glasses smashed on the floor. Suddenly, there was a melee of men shouting and wrestling and pushing and punching and kicking. They all ignored Garcia until she broke a punter's jaw with a straight right that knocked him flying across the floor.

Carter got in close beside Mason, and Garcia stayed close behind both men, kicking and punching like a UFC fighter. Carter threw a right hook that connected with a face. An older man with lank grey hair crumpled, spilling his broken false teeth on the floor like a burst tin of sweetcorn. The saloon doors opened, and the two gorillas appeared to prevent anyone from leaving. The Dobermen protected the entrance to the snug. The TV kept playing while all the other men in the main bar piled into the coppers.

Carter kept on Mason's left. The DI was confident and relaxed and elbowed someone in the nose, spattering blood on a picture of the Hearts football team hanging on the wall. The notorious crew who lost the Scottish Premier League Championship on the last day of the 1986 season. Carter felt a punch land on his ribs. He grabbed the arm of a man wearing a Hearts football strip, leaned in and head-butted him in the face. More blood sprayed over the walls and gallons of cheap lager sloshed around the floor.

Carter's ire was up. Kelsa and Alice were put aside; this was more like proper therapy. He pushed a man to the floor, grabbed a second by his long hair, pictured Sheriff Dunsmuir in his mind and sank his knee hard into the bowed face. The man groaned and sooked lager off the wooden floor. On his right, Garcia rang a bloke's bells with her left knee.

Carter felt exhilarated like he'd been fired from a cannon and was flying at the speed of sound. A scar-faced man in front of him produced a chib, waving it under Carter's nose. Carter laughed, goading the leering man to come closer. 'Take me, fuckwit. If you think you're hard enough.'

'Enough!' commanded a gravelly voice from the snug. The man-mountain owning it appeared in the bar moments later. Over six feet tall with a shock of orange hair balding at the front, Jimmy Logan was as imposing as his rep implied. With his barrel chest and powerful arms, he swung a hammer fist at the closest man and caught his ear. The man collapsed onto the floor and stayed there. Time in the Reverend stood still as everyone looked to Logan.

Carter grabbed a bottle from the floor. At this moment, his memory of Kelsa dying was fuelling his desire to rip someone's face off. All he cared about was slicing Chib-Man's throat to avenge the death of his wife. He smashed the bottle on a tabletop and was left holding the neck. He wielded it from hand to hand, advancing towards his intended victim.

A hand reached out slowly and took the razor-sharp glass from Carter's hand. 'That'll do, Sergeant.' Carter turned and saw DI Mason standing tall with not a single mark on him.

The Dobermen stepped into the midst of the carnage, protecting the three detectives. With their mobile phones, they snapped pictures of Mason, Carter and Garcia before they could object.

'Everybody out,' directed Jimmy Logan. The over-used term 'businessman' fitted him as well as the fine-cut grey suit he was wearing. His polished brown shoes and white shirt with blue tie topped off the neo-criminal dress code. Clearly, Logan could handle himself in a brawl. 'And if I hear about this wee spat on the streets, you'll answer directly to me.'

The gorillas threw out everyone still capable of walking, leaving the defeated and humiliated lying on the wet floor to compose themselves. History would record a six–nil result to Police Scotland.

'You three – in here.' Logan retreated to the snug, leaving the Dobermen to do his bidding. Three other men in suits with half-finished drinks sat in the small room behind the bar. No names were offered. The detectives sat down, and the door closed.

Logan spoke to Nick Mason. 'You're Cheryl McKinlay's crew?'

Mason stayed silent, so Logan kept talking.

'Cheryl and I go way back. We have – an understanding. I'm concerned, though. This rape – you say the girl was in here on Sunday night with a guy. You think he did it, eh? Do you have a description?'

'No,' Carter leapt in before the angels got organised. 'But we think he drugged her in here.'

'What are you implying, son?' Logan stiffened. 'Nobody does drugs in my pub.'

'He didn't mean anything, he was speculating.' Mason tried to keep everyone calm.

'You're Nick Mason,' Logan took control. 'An Inspector now. Jake knows you from his time in Shettleston. Do you have a photo of this girl?'

Mason looked at Carter and Carter pulled Alice's picture from his inside pocket. He handed it to Logan along with his business card.

'I'll find out,' said Logan. 'It'll be quicker than leaving it to you three.'

'Do you know where he'd get Scoop around here?' Carter pushed his luck.

One of the suits sitting next to Logan choked on his drink and coughed Amstel over the big man's suit, before folding over into a fit.

'Oh, for Christ's sake,' said Logan in disgust. 'You three get the fuck out of here before I change my mind.'

23

Young Fathers

Back at the station, Mason held quick wash-up. 'You've not been honest with us, Miss Garcia,' he said.

'Charli,' she replied defiantly.

'If you want to work with the A-team again, honesty is all,' Mason demanded.

'Muay Thai. I was gold at the Sevilla championships in 2010,' she replied. 'It is my sport. I train most nights.'

Carter looked at his constable with new respect.

'Can I go home now?' she asked. 'I am tired and need to shower.'

'Don't take what Logan says at face value,' said Mason, once they'd let her go. 'If he sees a way to get leverage, he'll take it.'

'Do McKinlay and Logan really have an understanding?' Carter asked. 'What did you think of that?'

'I don't know, but the boss is clean. Now, this wee joust didn't take place. Are you hurt?'

'I took one in the ribs, but just bruising.'

'Asking Logan about Scoop ... Jesus Christ, what a stupid move that was. He tries for old school, and he's been known to hand out cash to keep his rep up. His companies are all legit. He pays taxes and keeps his nose clean.'

'So, what's his game?' Carter asked.

'Drugs, people, prostitutes. Online gambling, reset – but all rumours, and we can't get anyone to tell us anything. Word is he's behind phishing scams, porn exploitation and aggressive cyber intrusion. He's always looking for leverage. And since we put McCalman away, he's stepped into the vacuum – he creates a crisis, then rides to the rescue to keep things from imploding – officially. But he takes the profits.'

'His fingerprints aren't on any papers, right?'

'Right,' said Mason. 'Leave the boss to me, but if she asks you, Logan was in the snug and invited us in. Say he was keen to help because a rape was bad for business.'

Back at home, Carter couldn't sleep in his cold bedroom. The fight in the pub kept buzzing at him. At half-past midnight, his restless mind forced him awake. He dressed in jeans and a jumper and went downstairs and through the lounge. Around him hung more pictures of Las Vegas. Kelsa was laughing at the camera in one, the Mirage Hotel pool behind her. On a lamp table stood a picture of Kelsa nursing Nathaniel in hospital that Carter had snapped and printed himself. Taken a year apart, it was hard to recognise the two photos as the same woman; in the more recent she was gaunt, only skin and bone, nothing more.

Poisoned memories.

He went through the kitchen and into the garage. The Smart car sat expectantly in the glare of the strip lighting.

However, he ignored it, going instead to the Master Lock safe bolted to the exterior garage wall. He kept their passports, birth certificates, the Las Vegas marriage licence, Kelsa's phone, and their laptops in the safe.

He keyed in the safe combination, opened it and removed the envelope his father-in-law had given him.

Open only when you understand.

It wasn't bulky. He turned it over in his hand, wondering when he would understand . . . just what, exactly? Why she let herself die when she had so much to live for?

Should he open it there and then? He tried to force his finger in the gap, as with the ordinary post, but it wouldn't tear, almost as if she'd anticipated his clumsy attempt. He thought of the knives in the kitchen but stopped half-way, conflicted. If it were another half-clue, that would drive him mad, but when would he understand? Whether he opened it now or never, she'd never know.

Committed, the paring knife dealt with the envelope and he extracted a single sheet of paper. Written on it, in her scrawl, was:

8 2 6 4 2 8 9 5
Licence to thrill, M
Zip up a dress, Joe

Frustrated at her conundrum, Carter deflated. This was no time for puzzles. All he wanted was a straight answer: why did she die instead of living? Why did she always have to be so cryptic? He returned the paper to the safe, beside her Apple MacBook Air and iPhone.

After locking the safe, he shrugged on his Crombie coat, and a few minutes later was driving through the empty city streets towards Shandon. He stopped at an all-night convenience store in Wester Hailes, then, ten minutes later, parked the car outside Alice Deacon's address.

The block of development flats was decades old but in good repair, with white paint only peeling here and there on woodwork. The streets were freezing quiet, and parked cars huddled together along the kerbs, many already encased in ice. She lived on the third floor and breaking and entering was not his plan. He turned away and began walking the half-mile along the silence of Dundee Terrace towards the cemetery.

At the bridge of Alice's flying lesson, Carter stopped to listen to the night. No vehicles travelled on the road underneath. It was eerily quiet, but the silence was pregnant. As if an army of Armageddon's nuclear babies would explode from the tenements and attack him at any moment. He crossed the bridge, leaning over the iron parapet again, trying to force the scene with Alice and J out of its icy history into this frozen moment. But it wouldn't come, so he kept walking, crossing the main road, entering Dalry Burial Ground again.

He repeated the tour of the middle tier of the graveyard he'd carried out with Charli Garcia two days earlier, reaching the neo-Gothic terrace with its pair of arches. He noted that the detritus was still there.

'Hello?' he called into the darkness of the vault. 'I'm Leccy. I've a half-bottle of Clan Macpherson for you.' He reached through the iron bars and stood the bottle on a ledge, then shone his torchlight on it. 'You'll have to come and get it, though.'

He sat on a stone for five minutes, until his arse cheeks

were solid ice. He considered taking a walk to get his blood going but held off. After another five minutes, his fingers were turning white. He was regretting not bringing gloves when he heard a noise from inside the vault. He shone the torch into the darkness, towards the source of the sound.

'Hello? I just want to talk.'

Too late, his sixth sense warned him of danger. He collapsed onto the hard ground, knocked unconscious.

24

Buddies in Crime

'Sit down, Sergeant Carter. Time for a heart-to-heart before this morning's session.' Dr Flowers' office was its usual mirthless self. Across the desk, her writing pad and pen were in their familiar places.

'You're late this morning.' Her tone was ominous. 'Where were you?'

Carter couldn't read her face, so he allowed dread to settle in his gut like a stone. The implications of her failure to remediate his grief slowly occurred to him. If he couldn't convince her that he should continue working, then it could be a black mark against him. It might lead to disciplinary proceedings and, at best, he could be stuck on the DS rung forever. At worst? Civvy.

'I was working overnight and slept late.' He acknowledged her right to a truthful answer – with wriggle room. 'And I've got a terrible headache.'

Since Kelsa's death, he'd expected that bereavement would give him some licence with colleagues; that he deserved sympathy and they would indulge him. McKinlay, in her gruff

Gorgie way, was handling him gently. DI Mason's approach reflected the Glasgow man's tough love, although he doubted Mason would put it in such terms. But now, in this instant, his failure to respond to Dr Flowers' reasonable question could be interpreted as a refusal to engage with due process. A determination to go his own way, whatever the consequences.

'Right.' Lisa Flowers really did do sarcasm well. 'Did you even think I might be sitting here waiting for you? Did it ever occur to you I might have other people to see? Is your phone broken? You, Sergeant Carter, are selfish and wilfully refuse to acknowledge your grief's psychological impact on others. You are a serious risk to yourself and your colleagues. Police Scotland could be accused of breaking their own codes of conduct by allowing you to walk the streets. I'm seriously considering pulling you from this programme by telling the Chief you're unfit for duty.'

So, there it was; the elephant in the room had finally trumpeted. He was emotionally shattered. His wife was dead, his son had been snatched from his hands, his career was disappearing down the pan at pace and catching up quickly with his morning dump. While he took him seconds to contemplate his approach to life and death, Dr Flowers sat back in her chair and waited for a reaction.

He shifted uncomfortably on the seat, which now felt like it had sharp nails growing out of it. He turned away from her disenchanted stare to gaze again at the picture window, wondering if she'd deliberately chosen this office for their sessions, and concluded she had. The picture window was a go-to relief, a Shangri-La with a rolling aspect; a daily feature film of Edinburgh life, complete with scudding weather and rollicking actors.

It was a deliberate reminder that life went on, regardless of how he felt about it. He may be grieving the loss of his lover, but outside, no more than a few hundred metres away, the rest of the world was ignorant of his pain, would never know its source and cared less. He thought of walking out to the world, of strolling over to the young boys playing hockey in the fields of Fettes College. He'd tell them about Kelsa, about Nathaniel, about growing up after his parents' death, about how he just put it all away. He'd tell them about his grandparents, about going to school and everything that happened there. What would they say?

'You're a fucking weirdo!'

He was thirty-three years old. Papa Carter was eighty-eight and still going. Carter's generation's life expectancy meant he had a higher chance than ever of living beyond one hundred years. If he celebrated that birthday, it would be sixty-eight years after Kelsa's death – and he'd still have white hair. Was he to live in suspended animation until then? Right now, those coming years were filled with indefinable activities – with new lovers, discarded lovers, more children and even grandchildren. How could he make it all happen? He had no choice but to travel on the train. But right now, he was messing around on the station platform, refusing to release the brakes holding him back. He had living family that loved him deeply but had childishly ignored their help.

'I'm sorry,' he said.

'What for?' Dr Flowers queried from the other universe. 'Be specific, Leccy.'

That was a hard question. It wasn't fair to ask him something like that so quickly when he'd only just allowed the rest of his life to pile on the power.

'For disrespecting your attempts to help me with my grief,' he stated, warming slowly to these new concepts. 'For believing I was the only one who'd ever had to cope with the death of his parents and wife. For not calling you to say I'd be late.'

'Good,' she sat forward. 'How do you feel?'

'Liberated.' He could do sarcasm too.

'It will help you become a more rounded man.' A smile lit up her face, 'And it won't do your comedy any harm either.'

'So, what's next?' he asked. 'Learning to fly?'

'Despite my recommendation that you shouldn't be at work,' she began, 'I'm re-thinking that approach. Tell me about this case you're working on.'

Carter smiled at her gifted victory. 'I'm not sure I can. Privacy and confidentiality, you see. You might blab about it to your Metropolitan friends over a bottle of Pinot Grigio. Then we'd both get fired.'

'You don't have to worry about that,' she smiled confidently. 'I'm joining your team.'

'Cheryl McKinlay will never agree to that, she hates interference in her cases.'

Flowers glanced at her watch. 'I guess the Chief Super has just finished briefing DCI McKinlay by telephone. As of now, I'm your buddy on this case, whether she likes it or not.'

25

Served with Relish

After leaving Dr Flowers, Carter descended the stairs into the main reception area of FOC Fettes. His phone pinged with an incoming message. His on-the-nose bet would be DCI McKinlay recalling him to St Leonard's to 'Please explain Dr Flowers' new status'. And McKinlay would no doubt heap choice words on him for lashing a civilian to the team. Blame would be slapped on him like a black spot, and everyone would know it before tea.

But it wasn't McKinlay. Gavin Roy's Castlemilk accent had left a voicemail asking him to 'Gie us a call'.

'I've got the mobile operator analysis authorised by DI Mason,' said Roy when Carter called. 'All connected mobile phones within a three-cell triangular pattern, either side of when you said she was on the bridge. InterMide, O2, EE, BT, giffgaff, blah, blah. Also includes GPS coordinates harvested from the operators' data feeds.'

'Did you run an initial analysis?'

'Yep. The case notes say the Reverend bar on Dalry Road was the source, so I filtered out all the mobiles that never went near the bar or were in vehicles travellin' past and those around the bar going away from the cemetery and bridge. We can bring them back in later if you want a different result.'

'Good work, Gavin.' Carter needed a computer.

Dr Flowers had told him she had other matters to tidy up, that she'd join him at the next team meeting and introduce herself. She'd also inadvertently offered him snippets about her private life. 'I have to change,' she'd said about her patterned dress and black stilettos. 'These aren't suitable for fieldwork.'

'Where are you staying?' he'd asked.

'During the week, Prestonfield House.'

'And on weekends?'

'Yes, OK – I live in London. North Hampstead actually, but my family is from Kent.'

Carter smiled. 'A southern softie, eh?'

'What you've seen of me, Sergeant Carter, is as soft as it gets.'

Carter approached Mary Brooks' reception area, planning to ask if there was a room with a computer he could use. 'Sergeant Carter,' she said neutrally as he approached. 'There are two gentlemen in Meeting Room Four waiting for you.' The look on her face demanded to take the minutes if trouble was brewing.

Carter walked into the meeting room and immediately knew trouble had brewed. Two bulldozers of men stood with their backs to the wall and their hands visible. Each wore a smile that suggested a long-desired experience was about to take place.

On the desk in front of them, a thin buff folder awaited its reveal.

Before Carter could ask, one stepped forward, keeping his clasped hands close to his groin for protection. 'Detective Sergeant Lachlan Carter?' He reeled off Carter's home address in Liberton. 'We represent Bentley McNaughton, Sheriff Officers for the Sheriffdom of Lothian. Please, sit down, sir.'

'What's this about?' Carter asked.

'An interdict has been granted against you by Sheriff John Robertson, QC, on behalf of Sheriff James Dunsmuir, QC. We're here to serve papers and ensure justice.'

'Really?' Carter mumbled, dumbfounded. 'I doubt you understand what justice means in this case. So, the vindictive old bastard—'

'Sir, please refrain from swearing. We get upset at profane language, and you wouldn't want us to get upset now, would you? An unfortunate incident took place at Sheriff Dunsmuir's residence, on Hermitage Drive, Edinburgh, in the early hours of Tuesday, which the complainant considers a breach of the peace. Luckily, he has agreed not to press charges, provided you abide by the terms of the interdict.'

He opened the folder, removed the papers and handed them to Carter. Carter hesitated, smiled wryly and took them. 'Papers served,' the man said. 'In summary, sir, you are to maintain a minimum distance of one hundred metres from any property where Sheriff Dunsmuir or his family are resident or present. For example, in case of an accidental breach, you are in a restaurant, and a member of the Dunsmuir family should appear, you must leave immediately, without attempting contact, else you could be arrested. I don't think that would be good for you, sir. Would it?'

'No,' said Carter.

'Goodbye, sir,' the man said. 'Have a great day.'

Both men left the room, leaving Carter to contemplate his options. It wasn't long before Mary Brooks appeared, closed the door and sat down beside him. 'Not paid your TV licence, son?'

'Worse than that,' Carter managed a response. 'To do with my son, if you must know. That's all I can say. Now, I really need to use this computer.'

Mary Brooks patted his knee. 'Your secret's safe with me. You can have this room for an hour. There's a senior management meeting at twelve o'clock – you'd better be out long before then.'

The screen powered up, he logged onto his virtual desktop and opened his email. Gavin had sent him a link directly to the files. Otherwise, he'd have had to dig through mountains of competing records on the ICRS case management system to find it. If it did hold crucial evidence, it would rise to the top of the system, like cream. But for now, it was just another data point.

In a few seconds, a map of Edinburgh's West End appeared on the screen. The software put the Reverend bar at the centre, then paused. Waiting, like a theatre stage anticipating the start of Act Two.

26

Data and Information

Mary interrupted him. Carter had five minutes to leave before the Chief arrived with his executive committee. He logged off, but his confidence required a reboot. Suppose he believed the data and Alice had really been in the graveyard alone. In that case, McKinlay might downgrade the case to attempted suicide and send him home to get his head together.

Unless Alice miraculously woke up and ID'd her attacker.

But he felt the data wasn't telling him the whole story. Raw data can only take you so far. Knowing who really was in the Reverend at the critical times was the key to it all.

Outside it was a typical January day, tetchy clouds threatening and sudden salvos of rain keeping the natives honest. He'd taken the bus to work because he couldn't justify driving the short distance to St Leonard's. Now he pulled his Crombie's collar around his neck and walked down Fettes Avenue to the stop heading into town. While standing in the shelter, he felt the phone in his pocket vibrate. He looked at it.

[2019-01-17:1243] I shot him when I was 7 years old. Didn't need him anymore. Been many more since then. I know everything you think and feel, Carter. Look around and fear me. J.

The number 29 took him south through Stockbridge, across Princes Street and onto North Bridge. His hands shook as he grabbed the screen. He felt helpless to do anything to stop these texts. He pushed a message out on ICRS: a team meeting. He texted Dr Flowers, giving her the time and location. The number 29 continued south on Nicholson Street to St Patrick Square. He alighted and stood in the shelter to compose himself. After a time he walked leadenly along Rankeillor Street onto St Leonard's Street. Twenty-five minutes was all it took for him to go from policeman to prey.

While he waited for the team to come together, he opened the data plot on his computer and tried not to think about his phone. He delved deeper into the plot, researching names and addresses gleaned from the data. He cross-referenced them against the Scottish Criminal History database of convictions, finding a few names with minor form. A sex offender whose phone had been in the bar when Alice was present seemed like the best lead.

An hour later, they were all in the detectives' room.

'We have an addition to the team,' said Carter evenly. 'Dr Lisa Flowers, a psychologist with interests in psychopaths and crimes against women.'

'Is that why you've been spending your mornings with her, Leccy?' Mason asked, attempting levity. 'Is there something you want to tell us?'

'Nick,' Ellen interrupted him angrily. 'You're out of order. He was getting grief counselling. If you started acting the DI you're supposed to be, we might make progress.'

'Don't lecture me, Constable Podolski. There's a connection between Carter and "J". How well up to speed are you, Dr Flowers, about these mythical text messages your *"patient"* claims he's been receiving?'

Lisa Flowers opened her writing pad and flicked through it. 'I wrote this one down yesterday. It came in during our session.' She passed the pad around so they could all read it for themselves.

'Have you added this to ICRS, Leccy?' Mason refused to back off. 'What does *"remember the Sick Kids"* mean?'

'I don't know,' Carter said. 'But here's another text he sent today.' He showed them the screengrab of the message and waited for their reaction.

'Oh, my God.' Ellen exclaimed. 'He's going to kill you, Leccy.'

'Maybe Dr Flowers should investigate your background.' Mason said. 'I've had threats worse than this in Glasgow. Your man here is all mouth, trust me.'

Carter switched on the whiteboard and ignored Mason's comment. He wasn't the one in J's sights. 'This is the data you authorised, Nick. From the mobile operators and UK tech companies. Signed-off and approved by DCI McKinlay. Every mobile device in the area around the Reverend and Dalry Burial Ground. Names and addresses of bill-payers and minute-by-minute locations. It's been pre-filtered by Gavin Roy. I've spent time on it too.'

'OK,' said Mason grudgingly. 'What do you want to do?'

'The analysis is inconclusive on its own, but somewhere in here "J" hides. I've identified twenty-eight people to be interviewed,' Carter said. 'Names and addresses are in your inboxes. Most are local, five are from Glasgow, three from Livingston and one from London. All are priority.'

'No surprises there, then,' said Mason. 'You'll want to doorstep them?'

'I'll interview the shortlist if uniform finds any good candidates. Last night, I returned to the graveyard and found a down-and-out who sleeps there, Duggie McLean. He saw the rape, but can't give a clear description, and won't make a statement because he's scared.'

'We're police officers, we'll drag him to the station if necessary,' said Mason. 'What is there to be frightened of?'

'Jimmy Logan.'

'He saw Logan rape Alice?' Mason replied, astonished.

'The description he gave me matches Logan's build. I think you need to take that to the boss, see what she says.'

'I know what she'll say.'

Carter's phone rang. He looked at the screen, then at his watch. 'I have to go.'

'Wait, Carter,' Mason said. 'No secrets. Who's on the phone?'

Carter hesitated. 'It's an informer.'

27

Delia's Kitchen

Carter got off the number 41 bus in Cramond, at the north-western edge of the city, where it touched the Forth Estuary's golden sands. He crossed the street and walked down Cramond Glebe, a narrow thoroughfare that forced cars to squeeze past each other like jousters. Stone-built walls hemmed him in on both sides, hundreds of years old, punctuated by expensive gates that protected private driveways. Tall, leafless trees hibernated inside these walls, awaiting spring. The Glebe curved steeply downwards, its slope telling on his knees. He hoped for a lift back up.

Half-way down on his right side was the entrance to Cramond Kirk, where old man Dunsmuir had wished his daughter to marry. Kelsa, however, had other ideas. Carter stood at the churchyard gate, gazing in. It was beautiful, even in winter. An English-style church with a crenellated bell-tower, a manicured graveyard of weathered Roman tombstones, and a chocolate box picture of what *Midsomer* implied all Englanders had at the bottom of their Cotswold acreage.

Despite Dunsmuir's wishes, spontaneity and passion had overtaken them on a pre-Christmas holiday – they tied the knot in the desert heat of Las Vegas. She wanted to have a second ceremony right here in spring, but Dunsmuir wouldn't hear of it. Spitting in the face of God, he'd said. It was one of the few arguments with her father she lost. Carter didn't mind; her soul was his, no matter what God's view was. No tears consumed him here. He accepted the sadness and realised it would always be this way whenever he stumbled across a place that had meaning for them. He was coming to terms, nothing more. He moved on.

Cramond Village would give the East Neuk of Fife a run for the cutest village-on-the-coast title because every village needs an inn. The Cramond Inn was a weel-kent place, hidden away on a tidal beach that offered a haven for pleasure craft. It promised warmth, good food and a hearty welcome. But he walked past these adjectives towards the beer garden, where an indistinctive man sat at a weathered picnic table nursing a distinctive Edinburgh pint.

'Lenny Yule?'

'Carter?' Yule replied, in the voice of a fully qualified drinker, bored and hoping someone would turn up and buy his next pint.

Carter sat down, feeling the dampness from the wooden bench seep into the seat of his trousers. An offshore breeze made it chilly enough for him to snap up the collar of his Crombie. The tide was out, and the causeway to Cramond Island saw a few brave souls crossing before the tide reverted. Yule poured the remainder of his beer down his neck, then dumped it decisively on the table. Carter stood up and lifted the empty. 'Innis and Gunn IPA?'

'Aye.'

He came back minutes later with the pint for Yule and a Coke with ice for himself.

'Hope that's a voddy,' said Yule derisively.

'Do you make your own?' Carter replied in a level voice. DS MacIntosh had said Yule was flighty.

'As a student at Strathclyde Uni, aye, I did. Way beyond legal proofs, one shot and you were legless. We got ourselves a wee customer base, and things looked rosy. Called it Goldfish, because you forgot your name within five seconds of a swally. Then someone shopped us to your lot.'

'Busted?' asked Carter, smiling.

'Naw, got off with a slap on the chops. They were going to confiscate the equipment until I told them we had an unlimited supply and they'd get a bill from the university, new for old.'

'And now you're here. Where did it all go wrong?'

'I could just fuck off. Then what would you do?'

'Call MacIntosh. What would you do?'

Carter stared at Yule, and he stared back. It could go either way, one of those moments where the blink of an eye made an enemy or a friend. Yule was forty-something, dark-haired, had an easy way with words, probably attracted more women than he could handle and hung in there swinging. His clothes were decent, old and frayed, but Carter concluded he regretted past sins while content with them at the same time. He stank of alcohol-laced depression. In ten years, Carter could be Yule Mark II if he let himself go.

Carter lifted his Coke and tipped it towards Yule's half-consumed IPA. Yule acknowledged homage and nodded.

'Shoot.'

'Scoop,' said Carter.

'Method, ingredients, supply, toxicity, distribution? You've got your own people, you know?'

'What's on the street just now?'

'I'm strictly Delia and my kitchen's clean. Are you religious?'

'Eh?' Carter queried.

'A doubled-edged death in the Middle Ages, religion was. A wrong word in the wrong ear at the wrong time could see a man up at the Inquisition, know what I mean?'

'A girl was drugged, raped and thrown from a bridge. Word is it's difficult to dose, with a reputation like your Goldfish. We think the rapist has experience.'

Yule swallowed more beer while Carter spoke, listening carefully. He placed his emptying glass carefully on the weathered table. 'I'm not 118 118. What do you want from me?'

'Can you ask around?' asked Carter.

Yule laughed uproariously. 'Aye, no problem, there's a conference next week. I'll ask when I'm at the bar.' He stood up to leave. 'You haven't got a clue, Carter.'

Carter stood up too. 'Wait,' he said. 'I don't know this stuff. Educate me. He could do this again.'

'I'm not your teacher.' Yule walked away through the garden hedge, crossing the grass, heading for the promenade to join a brace of dog walkers making for Granton.

'McCalman or Logan,' shouted Carter to Yule's disappearing back. Yule stopped but didn't turn around. Carter thought he heard a word blown in the breeze that sounded like '*fuck*'.

Still, Yule stood, clearly wrestling with loyalties. Carter's shot in the dark had inflicted a flesh wound that might putrefy if not cauterised. Yule spun around and marched back over, collapsing defiantly onto the bench. 'You getting another round in?'

'You going to be here when I get back?'

'Hurry up, the nuts are freezing.'

Carter returned with the drinks and Yule gulped at his like he'd been drouthy for months.

'A first-year chem student could make Scoop, or just about any other psychotic drug. All you need is excipients, heat and distillation. It's a recipe, so imagine baking a cake when you've got a fabulous picture in *Delia's Winter Cookbook* to go by. Does your cake come out of the oven like that? Probably not. Same problem with Scoop. It looks OK, but you won't know till you taste it.'

'I get it,' said Carter. 'So, what's the solution?'

'Smart cunt, eh?'

'Some would say.'

'Practise and feed it to your kids. Or go down the supermarkets and get a professionally made one. Most take option two 'cos it's easier, but you need big coin. Even then, dosing is problematic; big girls, small girls, heavy or light, there's still an element of luck in what happens. The big drug companies test, test, test and test. The crims don't test.'

'And around here?' asked Carter, wanting to know the answer to his question.

Yule stared at him. 'Bought in. From London. That's all I can tell you.' He stood up, necked the rest of the pint and walked away.

'The Reverend?' Carter called.

Yule gave him the finger. Carter watched him go.

One man's Jesus is another man's prophet, and Yule was a

priest of alchemy, collar he wore.

28

Lennymuir

Carter had almost reached the top of the brae of Cramond Glebe when a Mercedes Benz GLS with blacked-out windows passed him, then hit the brakes. A man he recognised from the Reverend's snug got out and held the front passenger door open. Carter's path was blocked, so he took out his phone and started fiddling with it.

'Get in,' instructed the man.

Carter surveyed the street. It was 4 p.m. and quite dark, nobody else was about. The passenger door was closed behind him, and the man climbed into the back seat directly behind him. Jimmy Logan put the Merc into drive and pulled away.

Carter's pulse raced, but outwardly he tried to appear bored. The SUV had come from the direction of the Cramond Inn. Had he been seen talking to Yule? His thoughts brought up names: McKinlay and her 'understanding' with Logan and Mason's Glasgow connections. All very convenient and a bit too coincidental.

'I liked your style last night, Sergeant,' said Logan conversationally. 'Few men can scare the shite out of Carver. But he's seen your likes before, it's what got him his rep. If you ever tire of Nick Mason's crap come and see me.'

'Thanks,' replied Carter tightly. 'I'll pass on that one.'

'Did you get hurt last night?' Logan asked.

'Bruises, that's all.' Only Mason knew he'd taken one in the ribs.

'So, this girl you're lookin' for—'

'I'm looking for the man she was with. You got somebody for me?'

The GLS turned onto Gamekeeper's Road, heading west, out of town. The streetlights were warming up, and a deeper cold was settling in, but the interior of the Merc was soft and warm, even if its owner wasn't.

'I might do, but I won't just give you a name. I don't know you, not the way I know your boss. Now if Cheryl asked, I'd just tell her, reel it off just like that. What's it worth to you, Sergeant?'

'If you're holding back information that can help this case, I'll arrest you.'

Jimmy Logan burst out laughing, encouraging the other man to laugh too. 'What do you think, Justin, should we tell him?' Logan nodded slightly.

Carter felt his head yanked back onto the headrest. Suddenly he couldn't breathe. Something pliable was wrapped around his throat, constricting his breathing. Instinctively, he tried to loosen it. It was a scarf of sorts, but he couldn't get his fingers between it and his neck. Something hard was sown into it, something that was crushing his larynx.

'My car, Sergeant Carter, my rules. I hate disrespect. Understand? What was that? I can't hear you.'

The seat belt held his body firm, and the choker put more pressure on his neck. His vision blurred. Then the choker was released. He grasped at his neck and sucked air in huge gulps, coughing, leaning forward as far as the seat belt would let him. He had no idea where they were going or why they were going there, but he wanted out of the car. He pulled at the door handle, but nothing happened.

'You don't get out until I let you out. Do you want out, Leccy? That's what your friends call you, isn't it? I'm your new friend, and friends do favours for one another, don't they? Call me Big Jim. You've asked me to find out the name of the man who sat beside Alice Deacon in my pub. That's a favour, Leccy, so if you want to know, I want a favour from you too. Quid pro quo. What's it worth, Leccy? A promotion? I'd like to see you promoted. Cheryl was once like you, now look where she is, eh?'

'You're lying,' coughed Carter, regaining some composure. The car had stopped. It was pitch dark on one side of the road and lit up like an airport on the other side. The bright side did indeed have about a dozen Boeing 737s lined up on the apron. This was the Turnhouse side of Edinburgh Airport, used for cargo and VIP flights. He could see the main passenger terminal half a mile away. Razor wire topped chain-link fencing, ten-feet high all around the perimeter. An EasyJet flight sat on the runway two hundred metres away, awaiting ATC clearance. The road ended at unmanned double gates further forward, but the Merc was in the shadows, back from the CCTV cameras.

The passenger door was opened from the outside. Logan's man Justin undid Carter's seatbelt and hauled him out onto the damp concrete. He landed shoulder first.

'I don't lie, I'm a man of my word.' Logan stood over him, placing his foot on Carter's chest. 'Ribs. Don't snap easily but can be painful if bruised. Take some advice, Leccy, because you don't know me. Next time you want a lift, be prepared, eh?'

Both men climbed back into the car and drove off, leaving Carter lying on his back, grimacing in pain, gasping for cold air and coughing. EasyJet spun up the throttle and sprinted down the runway, heading into the west wind. He sat up painfully, the bruising in his ribs competing with the throbbing in his throat. The stone chips from the paved road cut into his backside. He pulled his phone from his pocket, opening up the taxi app. It showed him his location as Lennymuir, outside the city, so he punched his home address in, chose ASAP from the pick-up options and pressed 'book now'.

While he waited, he scrolled to the recorder app and pressed save. Then he listened back to the conversation, wondering just what Jimmy Logan had on Cheryl McKinlay.

29

The Simplicity of Karma

The taxi dropped Carter home just after 6 p.m.

He went straight to the kitchen and noticed a small, slightly crumpled yellow Jiffy bag lying on the kitchen table. There was no stamp or address. Nothing to say it was for him. He tested its weight and texture, turning it over in his hands. It was light and spongy. How did it get there? The house was warm, but to him, it had just become as cold as his wife's grave.

He took a microwave dinner from the freezer and a bottle of beer from the fridge, all the time staring at the Jiffy bag, a bad feeling sitting hard in his stomach. The encounter with Logan played on his mind. Did this package contain a more personal warning from him?

The microwave bell dinged: chicken jalfrezi with pilau rice.

He took his time eating and sipped at the beer. Someone had been in his kitchen. Instinctively he knew it wasn't Logan. The doors had been locked when he got home.

Sometime after 8 p.m., the message he'd waited on arrived.

[2019-01-17:2009] I said it was bollocks at first. It was too coincidental and deep in the past, but then I saw the simplicity of the karma. We was meant to be. Her, me and you.

Carter read the message rapidly. His hands shaking as he held the phone, willing the text to stay on screen so he could grab it. His biggest fear in the next seconds was that the message would be erased before he understood what it meant. The absence of control buttons annoyed him, but he'd guessed that at some point J might allow him a reply, but not tonight. The message bell pinged again, and he dropped the phone in surprise. Carefully he picked it up off the kitchen floor, handling only the casing edges as if any inadvertent touch might cause it to vaporise. A new message had arrived, but the first one was still visible.

[2019-01-17:2014] Not knowing will be your downfall, but I will tell you when the time comes. When you stare at me pleading for your life, you will know then why you have to die.

[2019-01-17:2015] She is the one who truly loves me, she has proved it. My love is vengeance, Carter, so you had better be worth the stinging. Now open Pandora's Bag and weep. J.

Carter found scissors in the kitchen. He was about to cut off the top of the Jiffy bag when he remembered to wear gloves, just in case there was some forensic trace on the outside of the package. He settled for far-too-tight washing-up gloves. He composed himself, aware he was breathing hard. J knew about Kelsa, but this was more than knowing. He spoke as if she was alive and urging him to finish the job.

He snipped the top off the bag and tried to gently shake out the contents onto the table, but whatever was inside wasn't budging. He put a hand in and pulled it out, instantly dropping it onto the table like it was hot.

Carter stood back against the sink, staring at a pair of black knickers.

30

A Spider's Web

They were just black knickers. A pair that could've been worn by any of thousands of women in the country. A minority of his brain cells attempted to convince him they were just a pair of average knickers. His other major organ disagreed because the stink of Calvin's Obsession rose up from them like a witch's brew.

From his place of safety next to the sink, he approached them carefully, like they might take legs and escape. With his hands protected by the yellow gloves that didn't fit, he slowly smoothed out the fabric to assess the knickers accurately. The standard Y shape, but not a thong. Soft but not pure silk, and not the rougher cotton of his own underpants either. Size ten. The label said 'Bodas, London'.

He had to check, was aching to know what else these knickers had to reveal.

His footsteps were heavy on the stairs. He wanted her to know he was coming. She'd be indignant, demanding to know why he was taking this action. Her presence filled this side of the house. He took a deep breath, then entered the bedroom, switching on the big light, half expecting to see her sit up in bed. Her demand for an explanation was ignored. He went straight to the dressing table, next to the window, where her hairbrush, make-up and hairdryer were as she'd left them. He sat on the stool, staring at the man in the mirror.

Right-hand middle drawer. It slid silently outwards. Inside were her day-to-day knickers, white, pink, lemon, blue and black. Still wearing the yellow gloves, he lifted the pink pair; size ten, from Bodas, London. For almost every other man on the planet, this would be damnable proof. He held them up to his face: a much fainter smell of Obsession.

London was one of the cities she travelled to, as a management trainer for a corporate agency. He'd watched her arrive home after work with branded shopping bags but never paid much attention to them. She kept the raunchy underwear in another place and there was clear blue water between these and those; no need to self-harm by checking.

The pink pair went back in the drawer. He picked up her hairbrush and held it up to the light. Tiny filaments danced in the air like prey caught in a spider's web. He ignored her protestations and walked to the door with her hairbrush in hand, giving her no reason.

Flicking the light switch off, he pulled the bedroom door closed and exhaled.

Downstairs in the kitchen, he scrolled through the contacts in his phone, found the number he wanted and tapped on it. While it rang, he eyed the brush, now sealed in a sandwich bag, next to two more containing the Jiffy bag and the knickers. He spoke clearly, outlining what he'd found and what he wanted. The other party consented.

Five minutes later he was driving towards town in the

Smart car, following the usual route that would take him to Fettes Operations Centre.

31

Waiting Room

Rocketman signed him into the Forensic suite.

'I'll have to tag them as evidence,' he said. 'We can't process them without the bar codes. Alice Deacon?'

'Yes.'

'Locus?'

'My home. The hairbrush is for reference.'

'Get some coffee. There's a coffee machine, a fridge with food, microwave, whatever. It'll take thirty minutes at least to do the admin.'

Half an hour, on the dot, and he was back in the office, sitting across from Johnstone.

'We'll check the Jiffy for fingerprints and DNA, probably get a thousand markers including yours, but we have to do it, just in case. I wouldn't put any store by the results. The night shift will run tests on the DNA swabs from the knickers and the hair, but even with our state-of-the-art equipment, it'll take hours. Go home.'

'I'll stay.'

'Leccy, I know its gruesome, but don't let him get to you. We'll catch him. Your hanging around here won't change that.'

'I'm staying.'

'Fine – you can sleep on the couch in the visitor's room if you want. My lead tech knows what she's doing, she'll tell you as soon as she can. I've been here since seven, so I'm going home.' Rocketman stood up and put on his coat.

Carter watched him leave and wondered if he was crossing the Rubicon with this. He pushed back on his fears and kept pushing, learning once more that love was a cruel mistress. Could he live with these dark thoughts and not poison himself? How could he separate professional investigation from personal interest without tearing himself apart? If life seemed simple before, it was because he'd accepted the lie.

Maybe he should hand off this case to someone else.

In need of a distraction, he found an empty room with a computer. He'd take another look at the analysis of devices surrounding Alice's movements; maybe that would keep his darker thoughts at bay. It was 9.30 p.m., and a long night lay ahead. If the worst came, the couch in the visitor's room would serve as his bed of nails.

Even as he logged on to the computer, he could hear Kelsa demanding to know why he was digging up what was dead and buried.

32

Relationships

At 7.30 a.m. the next morning, he was still at FOC Fettes. He had to call DCI McKinlay. She'd be in her car, dodging the traffic pouring into the city from the south. Jammed at Cameron Toll, probably.

Late into the night, he'd necked a few Red Bulls from the vending machine to keep awake, while working the possibilities suggested by the mobile data and avoiding another deep dive into his past. Hours later, the taurine having worn off, he'd rolled himself up in the Crombie and tried to get comfortable on the visitors' couch. It was harder than it looked. By 6 a.m., every joint felt like it would snap if he moved too quickly.

After a shower, he'd felt better. Now he picked up his phone and noticed the SMS nano-app with its pulsing dot. He hadn't heard the ping.

[2019-01-18:0521] I am not who you believe me to be, Carter. I am a ghost inside your head. I can find you anytime, but for you to find me you must go where you've never been. J.

Carter read and re-read it, then grabbed it. What did J mean by *'go where you've never been'*. A minute later he watched it vanish from the screen.

'Where are you?' DCI McKinlay asked, picking up his call.

'I'm at Fettes,' he said, still pondering the latest message. J knew when he'd read the text. Somehow, that felt like a small win for Carter.

'A bit early for Dr Flowers.'

Her comment confirmed that E Division standard operating procedure was alive and kicking. McKinlay had not been told by the brass that Dr Flowers was now a team player. Top jaw forgets bottom jaw and bites off his own head. It wasn't even twenty-four hours since Flowers had told him McKinlay was briefed. He'd thought his boss's lack of reaction was because she had retreated into a mild huff. It was now clear she knew nothing about the elevated status of their new colleague. If he body-swerved the shout, he'd be accused of complicity in the darkest of deeds.

'You've not been briefed, have you?'

'Briefed about what?' The noise of car horns tooting could be heard above the awkward silence on the line. 'I've got an incoming call from Chief Super Goodwin, I have to take it.'

The line broke, and he was free to swim off with the hook stuck in his mouth.

A woman in a white coat approached him. 'Sergeant Carter?'

'Yes.' His pulse leapt a few notches, but not because of her attractiveness.

'I've not seen you around here before,' she said. 'Not that that means anything, I'm usually chained to a thermal cycler machine and kept in the dark. You got ID?'

Carter fished for it. She wanted his corporate pass, not his warrant card.

'What does a thermal cycler do?' he asked, trying to fill an awkward minute.

'It processes PCRs for DNA.' She studied his pass. 'You sure that's you?'

'It's my name underneath,' he replied.

'What case number is it?'

'Is everyone in here like this?' He tried for a smile. 'Alice Deacon,' he said.

'I need the case number. Log on over there,' she pointed to a computer in an empty room. 'Show me the case number and bar code.'

He logged on. Minutes later, the case file was up. She used a hand-held scanner and pointed it at the bar code on the screen. When it beeped, she seemed satisfied.

'OK,' her shoulders relaxed and she smiled, revealing white, even teeth. 'Can't be too careful. A year ago, a journalist blagged his way into Queen Street in Aberdeen and was handed evidence when a colleague assumed his name was the same as a detective from Inverness. She got fired, the journo got arrested, the evidence got published, and the scumbag got off.'

'So, what do you have for me?' Carter asked with trepidation.

'The Jiffy bag has at least a hundred prints, none show for anyone in our database,' she read from her notes, avoiding eye contact.

'And the other . . . items?' he prompted.

'Good quality mitochondrial DNA from the hair on the hairbrush. Female and not on the databases. No fingerprints from the underwear, not good material. The underwear has been washed before, obviously, but not since these cells were deposited. There was trace DNA from one male on the knickers. It needed significant amplification – meaning you hadn't touched them for a while.'

'Me?' Carter was confused.

'Another reason for the ID check, Sergeant Carter: you're a partial match on the database. If you didn't contaminate them at a crime scene – a disciplinary offence – I assumed they must belong to someone close to you. The package was posted to you at home, says the record. The mtDNA from the brush matches the mtDNA on the knickers. My leap-of-faith conclusion is they're your wife's, and you think she's having an affair.'

She now looked him straight in the eye, her expression curious and sceptical. 'We don't normally do this kind of thing for colleagues and using a live case reference is also a—'

'Disciplinary offence,' he finished the sentence for her. 'It's not what you think,' he said quickly, spinning himself up to speed, trying to work out what this news meant, and if it confirmed what he'd hoped earlier. 'My wife is dead.'

Her expression changed slightly. 'I'm sorry, I didn't know.'

'For reasons, you will know, I can't tell you anything about the case, so you'll just have to trust me. Was there anything else?'

'There's one other sequence present on the knickers,' she shrugged her shoulders and put aside her prejudices. 'A good profile of another man, not on our databases.'

33

The Bastard and the Bitch

Having tossed her grenade into the room, Tech Girl turned on her heel and walked off. Carter stood rooted, contemplating his next move. Bishop shafts Pawn Four. Or chuck himself from the roof of Fettes Operations Centre in utter despair? He'd set out to find the truth, knowing there was a strong possibility the knickers were Kelsa's. Of course, it should have been obvious all along. It usually happens, doesn't it? Find happiness, then once you've settled in, the rug is pulled from under and you fracture your skull when you hit the floor.

She'd been seeing someone else.

Grasping at straws, he realised he'd not asked Tech Girl if Kelsa being pregnant might explain this outcome. Perhaps the male DNA could be from a doctor or obstetrician; either might have come into contact with her knickers during a routine check-up. But that was a fantasy born of utter delusion. A doctor who stuffs knickers in a jiffy bag breaks into your home and deposits them on your kitchen table? *'Sorry, found these when I was having a clear-out.'*

And yes, a doctor would have penned a note.

The question drilling into his head was: why now? Knowing he'd never be found out, lover-boy twists the knife in Carter's wound, just for the sake of it. Cruel, possible, but highly improbable. And the next obvious question: how does J know all this? Answer: it can only be him unless he's *'doing it for a friend.'*

The memories he'd been suppressing burst into his mind like fireworks exploding – of the weekend she'd gone to a party – with her girlfriends – apparently – and didn't return until Sunday wearing totally different clothes. At the time, she'd refused to discuss it. She took two baths every day and slept in the spare room. Then shagged him every night for nearly three weeks till he screamed for mercy.

When they did speak, she begged him to leave it be if he loved her. And she knew he did, so he understood why she couldn't speak about it. But he wasn't daft. She'd been assaulted, probably sexually, but she didn't want him tracking down the assailant as a personal mission. It would be too painful to watch.

What had been his options during that raw soap drama? They were married. For other men, marriage might have meant nothing, but he wasn't that kind of man. '*For better, for worse*' implied commitment and he had committed to her without condition. But in the endlessness of time thereafter, they barely spoke a word. She sat on the other sofa in silence, trying to work out – with help from the TV – how she felt about it all. He worked, came home and spent his evenings with the Xbox, or just stared at her. Was it a gamechanger? If so, he had to leave and never return. Simple.

Kelsa was Kelsa. But he was Leccy.

Now, in the full-technicolour of the present, he craved a drink. Not to blot things out, but because it elevated his thoughts and rendered his memory of the drama in sharp contrast. Whisky gave licence to his infamous coldness, his legendary absolute focus on the facts of the case. What was the evidence of Kelsa's infidelity laid bare? A sex-filled pair of knickers, an unknown lover and a buried weekend. He had been a fool to think those missing days had been anything else. Summed up as the bastard and the bitch copulating in a hotel room somewhere far away. He felt slimy.

He returned to the computer – he was still logged on. Tech Girl had said lover-boy had not been convicted of any crime in Scotland because his profile wasn't present on either the Criminal History database or the PFSL DNA database. Carter's heart pulsed blood through the arteries in his neck so hard it was painful. His night had not been totally wasted. He had some names gleaned from the mobile analysis, and just one of them popped up in the CHS database.

He retrieved the profile of Jacky Dodds, with previous for sexual harassment of young women. If J was linked to Carter through Kelsa, how did Alice squeeze herself into their picture? Dodds had been involved, somehow. It was the only lead he had. He pressed print, got a picture, form-card and last known address. It was time to vent some good old-fashioned anger on a Dalry scumbag.

34

Church Hill

A tenement flat on Watson Crescent. Easy staggering distance from Dalry Burial Ground. Carter squeezed the Smart car into a resident's space and settled down to wait. Cars lined the street on both sides. In this part of town, a tenement accommodated eight flats spread over four storeys. On the opposite side of the street similarly-styled flats disappeared in an infinity curve towards Harrison Park, a quarter of a mile away. It was cheap living in the city.

Within fifteen minutes of parking, Carter had succumbed to sleep.

A rap on the window startled him: a traffic warden. He flashed his warrant card at her. She paced off, miffed. His watch confirmed it was after ten o'clock; he'd slept for nearly an hour. He might have missed Dodds coming or going but felt better for the snooze. He got out of the car, sucked in some cold air, then wandered around looking for coffee.

On his way back to the car, having opted for a Red Bull instead, a man passed him on the canal bridge heading south. He was tall and bulky, wearing third-hand clothes, with dishevelled hair and chin stubble that definitely wasn't designer. His skin was sallow from lack of sunlight, but his nose was prominent. Despite his size, there was a vulnerability about his gait. Eye contact was brief, but Carter was awake enough to realise it might be Dodds. Carter kept on walking downhill towards Fountainbridge. After a minute, he stepped up to the door of a flat, hidden from anyone further up the street. He looked at the print-out he'd brought with him. Dodds had bulked out, but it was definitely him; the skin tone, eyes and nose hadn't changed.

Carter started walking back up the slope. He collected his car and minutes later was driving south on Polwarth Crescent. At a mini-roundabout, he turned left onto Granville Terrace, slowing down to peer up Merchiston Avenue. No sign. From here it was straight tarmac to Tolcross. He drove half-way along before spinning a U-turn and gunning the Smart car back the way he'd come. He carried straight on over the mini roundabout onto Polwarth Gardens. Dodds was a few hundred metres further on, at the curve of the road. Carter passed him at speed, drove on for another few hundred metres, and then pirouetted the Smart car into a parking space. As Dodds approached him, he got out and blocked his way.

'Jacky, a word, please.'

'Fuck off copper, I'm clean.' Dodds walked past him.

'Jimmy said I might find you at the drop-in,' Carter nodded towards Polwarth Parish Church. 'He volunteered your help.'

Jacky Dodds looked like he'd been approached by an alien asking for directions.

'Get in,' Carter held open the passenger's door.

Dodds glanced around, then got in. Carter got in the

driver's seat. He started the motor and drove back the way he'd come, heading towards Morningside. 'Thought you might appreciate the warmth.'

'What do you want?' Dodds asked, looking like a large scarecrow packed into a small sack.

'You were in the Reverend last Sunday.' Carter reached into a pocket and took out Alice's photograph. 'Did you see her?'

Dodds glanced at the picture then looked away. 'Naw.'

'Who was she with?'

He stayed silent.

'You fit the suit, Jacky. Height, build and power, know what I mean? You've been building up to this, maybe you're working on a reputation so you can move up a grade.'

'I'm not going back inside.' He started to shake, beads of sweat becoming visible on his face.

'What did you do to her, Jacky? She was an awful mess.'

'I didn't touch her.'

'Who were you drinking with? Nathan Butler was with you, could he corroborate your story?'

'Naw.' Dodds strained at the seat belt. 'I need air, I'm havin' an attack.' He punched the dash and kicked the footwell. 'Small spaces,' he shouted, panic rising in his voice. 'I cannae handle them.' Frantically, he pulled at the door lock, trying to get out.

Carter drove up Morningside Road with the Smart car rocking from side to side. He turned onto Church Hill at the traffic lights, pulled over to the kerb, but kept his finger on the lock button. 'You and Butler walked home together, didn't you? He lives not far from you.'

'Naw, naw. Let me out!' He unplugged the seat belt and tried to stand up but hit his head on the roof lining. Twisting and turning, looking for a way out, he swung his arms in desperation, smacking Carter hard on the nose. Carter's fingers released the lock, letting Dodds burst out of the passenger door. He ran along Church Hill as fast as his big legs would take him.

Carter's face throbbed. He looked in the rear-view mirror and saw blood running from his nose into his mouth, the red stark against his pale skin and shock of white hair. He searched the car fruitlessly for paper or tissues.

'Bastard!' he shouted at nobody.

He jumped out of the car and ran into a coffee shop holding his nose. 'Tissues! Quickly,' he said to the nearest server.

35

Customer Service

Carter sat in the back of the Salt Café nursing a bruised nose with a free latte on the side. Jacky Dodds' reaction to his questions had caught him by surprise. Dodds was long gone, but Carter was intrigued by what he'd said.

He logged into the ICRS app, skimming the latest notes on Alice's case. An interview team was being assembled to doorstep the twenty-eight names he'd requested. DI Mason didn't hang about. The names and addresses were listed in a table, but Jacky Dodds wasn't one of them. He added Dodds to the list there and then – otherwise, Mason and McKinlay would ask for a 'please explain'. He noted names of extra detectives that had been browsing the case. Must be the Major Investigation Team McKinlay was worried about. Keeping themselves informed.

From the list of twenty-eight, he found the address and phone number for Nathan Butler. He noted it down, assigning his warrant number against the record, so no other copper would double-bubble him.

Next, he went into the case evidence tab and scrolled through the lists, finding the items Rocketman had added on his behalf. No stars: they weren't considered important items at the moment. One exclamation mark: the evidence may be inadmissible. He didn't want to open any of the three attachments as there would be an audit trail. He knew what the summary would say, anyway: unmatched DNA profiles of a man and woman, plus possible contamination by DS Carter.

He finished the latte and made to move, then remembered the cotton wool swabs up his nose. He pulled both out and dropped them into the dirty latte glass. Proffering thanks, he promised to return another day and received cheery-byes from the staff as he dashed over Church Hill. The Smart car sat where he'd abandoned it, although he thought he'd left the door open in his rush to stem the blood. When he saw the ticket stapled under a wiper, he knew it was the same traffic warden. Bastard must've enjoyed that. Two in a week; only sixty quid if he paid them early.

Nathan Butler's flat was in Dorset Place, no more than a hundred metres from Jacky Dodds' tenement block, but on the other side of the canal. A nineteen- nineties build, the external rendering of the blocks was dirty white. The repeating square windows reminded Carter of a doocot or a bad upgrade to Saughton Prison. As usual, the street was littered with cars, so he drove around, eventually finding an empty space on Merchiston Avenue, checking first what the parking rules were. He found the meter number and tapped it into the newly installed parking app on his phone. Thirty minutes it warned him; else, financial meltdown would accrue exponentially.

He had to access the blocks from the canal pathway. Besides

the buzzers, Block 4, Flat 2D didn't have Nate Butler's name on it. Instead, Krishna Chellani, Menakadevi JM, Jigar Jobanputra, Bhavesh Mhatre and two others dominated the sub-continental name-fest. He rang the bell anyway. The door opened, revealing a skinny young Indian man with thin black hair and a not quite grown moustache.

'I'm looking for Nathan Butler,' said Carter, showing his warrant card. 'Police.'

The man's eyebrows shot up in alarm before he smiled and held his hand up in the universal 'please wait' sign.

'Can you call someone?' Carter made the sign for a telephone, with index and little fingers extended and held to his ear.

'Yes, yes, please,' the man rummaged, found a mobile phone and dialled a number. A minute of language exchange ensued in a dialect that Carter couldn't even begin to guess at. The man handed him the phone.

'Hello,' said Carter. 'Do you speak English?'

'Indeed, sir, I do. It is my cousin Sivanagaraju, just in from Chennai in Tamil Nadu. Do you know it, sir? A very fine place. He will get a job locally, please do not worry.'

'I'm a police officer. Who are you?'

'Is there a problem, sir, that I can assist you? My name is Krishna, I am the premier customer service manager at the Scottish Gas call centre in Granton. Do you know it, sir?'

'The flat is rented?'

'Of course, sir.'

'Are you the tenant?'

'Of course, sir.'

'Rented from a Mr Nathan Butler?'

'No, absolutely, sir. From New Town Tenant Agency LLP.'

'You don't know anyone called Butler?'

'No, sir.'

'OK, thank you. I apologise for disturbing your cousin's sleep.' He handed the phone back to Sivanagaraju and walked away.

36

Friends and Neighbours

The letting agency was in Stockbridge, a fifteen-minute drive from Dorset Place. A young receptionist sat him down, pending an audience with the senior partner. Giles Smythe looked every inch the big businessman in a small office, wearing a banker's stripe suit, pink shirt and shiny polka-dot tie. He was effusive, offered coffee, tea or water. When these beverages were refused, he resorted to whisky, vodka and gin.

'Dorset Place in Merchiston,' Carter said. 'The address has turned up in an investigation. I'm trying to trace the owner. Currently rented by a Krishna Chellani.'

Smythe picked up his office phone and asked for the file to be sent through.

'Ah, yes. Owned by a company that has six other properties with us. Deptford Management Services. The named landlord is Mr Nathan Butler.'

'Do you have a home address for Mr Butler?'

'Yes, in Ravelston.'

'Have you met him?

'Not personally; the account was opened two years ago by an associate who is no longer with us.'

'Any issues?' Carter went fishing.

'Rents are paid on time. Occasional plumbing and heating issues, but we handle all that on Mr Butler's behalf.'

Carter left with Butler's address; it was no more than ten minutes' drive, but Easter Murray Avenue was a universe away from Dorset Place. Accessed through a narrow gate-way, it boasted affluent detached properties, and manicured driveways populated with expensive cars. BMW, Jaguar and Mercedes, mainly. From what Carter could see driving along the private road's quarter-mile length, the size of front and back gardens was on par with Murrayfield Stadium.

There were no cars in Nathan Butler's driveway, so Carter parked where he liked. The front entrance displayed a high, massively thick double storm door. He rang the large bell push, hearing the jangling coming from inside. After a few minutes, he tried again, eventually concluding that no one was home. Wandering around, Carter realised he couldn't see the back garden, let alone get into it. A double garage was built into one side of the house. The other side had a solid sandstone wall with a locked garden door. High walls separated one property from another, ensuring privacy. Discreet CCTV cameras were set under the eaves. Clearly, these properties could be a target for burglars, given the individual settings and presumed wealth of their owners.

Back in the Smart car, he dialled the number he had been given for Butler. It rang out. No voicemail, so he contented himself by updating ICRS. '*Nathan Butler required to corroborate Jacky Dodds alibi.*'

How would Jacky Dodds know someone like Butler? Carter

wondered if Jimmy Logan had a house like this. Dodds had connections to Logan and was allowed to drink in his pub, but what was Butler to Logan? And Alice? Was she a random, or was she connected to them all? Dodds and Butler were only two out of many people in or around the Reverend that Carter had identified as being close to Alice's phone that night. Why would a man living here, be miles away in a Dalry pub, owned by an Edinburgh boss, if he wasn't connected in some way? He walked to the next driveway where a new model BMW X5 sat beside a battered green Skoda. The storm door was open, so he rang the bell. A woman appeared in silhouette through the inner glass door. She opened it, offering no greeting. A maid, Filipino or Thai. He flashed his warrant card.

'Detective Sergeant Carter, Edinburgh police. Who lives here?'

'Moment,' said the woman, closing the door and disappearing into the depths of the house. After a few minutes, Carter began to feel cold; the afternoon was progressing, dusk was settling in. The temperature was dropping fast. A tall elderly woman appeared, holding herself stiffly, grey hair conservatively styled.

'How can I help you, officer?' she said in a cut-glass accent that reminded Carter of his mother-in-law.

'Next door,' Carter replied. 'Mr Nathan Butler. Do you know much about him?'

'I'm not sure I can say. You could be anybody. Everyone is entitled to privacy, you know.'

'I apologise, madam if you think I'm snooping. Mr Butler may have been an inadvertent witness to a crime. I'd like to eliminate him from the enquiry, but I've been unable to contact him.'

The explanation seemed to satisfy her.

'I don't know a great deal. He lives on his own, works away a lot. He's an executive with some company or other. I've only met him once since he moved here a few years ago. A New Year's party we hosted for the neighbourhood.'

'What did you make of him?' Carter went fishing again.

'Quite entertaining. A big personality that matched his stature. I liked him.'

'Do you have a telephone number for him?'

'No, sorry.'

'Thank you, madam.' Carter turned and walked away, unsurprised that a self-entitled Edinburgh neighbourhood trailed such stench behind it.

37

TGI Friday

He wasn't even back onto Murrayfield Road when the call came in. He took it hands-free.

'Carter?' DI Mason's Glasgow drawl enquired on his whereabouts.

Carter immediately wondered what sin he'd committed to deserve the Inquisition. 'I've been following up on witnesses that were in the Reverend around the same time as Alice.'

'Such as?' Mason inquired.

'Nathan Butler, but he wasn't at home. And Jacky Dodds, bearing previous for sexual assault.'

'I didn't know Jacky Dodds was in the bar. Did Logan give you his name?'

Carter hesitated, not sure if Mason was taking notes intending to brief a higher authority. 'Logan hasn't come through yet with any names. At least, not to me.'

For the first time, Carter could hear background noise through the phone. Mason sounded like he was in a bar. 'What did Dodds say when you questioned him?'

'That she was still there when he left,' said Carter.

'You got a statement?'

'No. He ran off after I cornered him.'

Mason sniggered down the line, seemingly amused at the very idea. He changed the subject.

'We're havin' a wee soiree at Jeanie Deans. Get yourself over here, team bonding session.'

Friday drinks weren't unusual, but not regular enough to forge a culture of in-crowd versus out-crowd. Under present circumstances, Carter would probably have declined, but things had changed. He remembered the outcome of his session with Dr Flowers. The rose-tinted view he'd had of Kelsa as his perfect dead wife was discolouring fast as each revelation took hold. He'd been with her such a short time. Only twenty-two months from first meeting to burial. Months during which, he now acknowledged, he didn't really know anything significant about her life before him. They'd covered the basics: births, dead family (him), living family (her), fee-paying school (her), comprehensive education (him), first-class university (her), third-class university (him). Obvious gaps had appeared in the floorboards that they didn't wish to fill as a couple – exes accounting for the largest of these. But such trivialities had never mattered. Their future together was assured. Therefore, everyone else had been buried in the archive. So much so, that digging them up for discussion over drinks would have felt like tainting the purity of their love. None of his ex-girlfriends were inclined to send their used underwear to him or do anything that suggested rancour for the death of the relationship.

The evening became properly dark and, being a Friday, the roads around town had clogged up with traffic. Getting through Roseburn junction was his first challenge, even in a vehicle as nimble as the Smart car. The junction's traffic lights had a weird sequence, and the narrowing road squeezed everything city-bound into single-file. Throw in pedestrians, parked cars, and lycra-clad cyclistas and progress was near impossible.

A message pinged loudly through the car's speaker. He was wary of the distraction until he saw the name of the sender. He read the message with more than a little satisfaction.

Nearly an hour later he parked in the St Leonard's police car park. If he really wanted to drink to excess, he could get the bus home.

Jeanie Deans was busy. Many early evening diners occupied the restaurant, spilling over into the lounge area, raising the noise level. However, the collection of plain-clothed police had taken over the rear part of the bar. Nick Mason greeted him like a prodigal son.

'I thought you'd given us a body-swerve, Leccy. What'll you have? It's on me.'

'Half of IPA. I'm driving.'

'Course you are,' said Mason. 'Can't have our detectives breaking the law, eh?'

While Mason ordered drinks, Ellen Podolski wandered over and planted a peck on his cheek. 'You bearing up, Leccy?'

'I'm fine, Ellen, really. I'm happy to chat about the usual suspects.'

'And who are they today, Leccy?' said Mason with a grin, handing him the small glass of beer and bringing him into the body of the kirk. Tam Watson nodded his respect; he was deep in conversation with another bobby, but both men were dressed in civvies. DCI McKinlay wasn't around, which might have accounted for Mason's largesse.

Charli Garcia held a glass of Coke, maybe even with vodka in it, chatting away to Dr Flowers who sipped red wine from a balloon glass. The contrast between the two women took his breath away when they both turned to look at him. Garcia's olive skin complemented her dark wavy hair tied back in a loose bun. At the same time, Flowers' blonde tresses tumbled freely around her shoulders, softening her pale English complexion with a broad smile. Ellen stood next to him, chatting aimlessly, although he wasn't listening. He was aware of Joanna Garvie wandering over. Recently divorced and with a child, she was on the market and trying to catch his eye. He was polite but kept his distance.

'Ellen, Jo's got me in her sights,' he whispered. 'But not tonight. Can you just head her off?'

Ellen nodded and whispered, 'It's OK.' She gently guided Jo back towards the Victim Support team, where she'd feel more supported than victimised.

Leccy slid his way off to one side, a little towards the windows where some potted plants offered cover and refuge, glad of the space and not really bothered if no one came to speak. Charli detached herself from Dr Flowers and made her way over.

'Leccy. You need cheering up,' said Nick Mason, appearing suddenly and putting his arm around Carter's shoulder. Carter realised he was drunk. Not yet pished but following the guidebook religiously. Garcia didn't seem phased by Mason's intrusion. She put herself in front of both of them.

'What do you think, Leccy, of our champion Spanish kick-boxer, eh? You kept your secret from us, Miss Garcia. That was unfair, don't you think?'

'Charli,' she said. 'Outside of work and to my friends only.

For you, Constable, OK?'

'A nippy sweetie, eh?' Mason leaned in and whispered in Carter's ear.

Before he could put both feet further in, Tam Watson dragged him away.

'Nick's right though, Charli, it was an impressive display of confidence in the lair of the bear.'

'I heard another Scottish word,' she said, sipping from her glass. 'Sergeant Watson asked if I felt "feart".'

Carter laughed. 'He really asked you that?'

'Yes. He winked, but he didn't tell.'

'Scared,' said Carter. 'The verb is "to be feart".'

'Ha, *no estoy asustada*! I was not feart.'

'I'm off tomorrow,' he said, as an idea came on the spur. 'Let's meet up in town so I can expand your knowledge of Scottish vocabulary.'

38

Alice in Chains

On Saturday morning, Carter woke later than usual. Uniforms would be doorstepping the names on his list today – because it was the weekend – there being more chance the suspects would be home. After showering, he glanced outside. It was dull and damp, with grey clouds threatening rain. Jeans, a T-shirt and a warm jumper under his Crombie seemed appropriate. Perhaps an umbrella. By half-ten, he was sitting in the Kirkgate Café in Liberton having a Scottish breakfast and reading a book on his phone when the call he was expecting arrived. After a few minutes of discussion, he paid and left.

Half an hour later he was sitting on a park bench in the Meadows when a mature woman pushing a Silver Cross coach-built pram approached him. He stood up and kissed his mother-in-law on the cheek.

'How is my beautiful boy?' he said, leaning in to see Nathaniel. His son's eyes were open and radiated blue in the dull grey light.

'He's fine,' said Judith Dunsmuir. 'James told me about the

interdict. With some glee, I might add.'

Carter said nothing.

Judith sighed. 'What a horrible and vindictive man he's become. He turned Kelsa's funeral into a social opportunity to advance his career. Obviously, I didn't tell him that. It would have caused the most enormous row.'

'Can I hold him?' Carter asked, deliberately refusing to engage in the topic.

'Of course, he's your son.'

Carter carefully lifted Nathaniel from the pram. Saliva bubbled at his lips, and for a moment Carter thought that he'd recognised his father, but it was a notion. He cradled him tenderly in his arms. 'Before Kelsa, I'd never really thought I'd ever have a family, but during those final weeks, I was sure I was going to lose him, and I felt numb. Kelsa had made up her mind, so I had to make up mine. We were going to live. And I'd make sure he'd have the best chance in life he could get. Then to have him snatched away—'

'Don't,' said Judith. 'I knew nothing at all of James's scheming in court before Kelsa went into hospital. It was only after the funeral he told me of it. For Kelsa to seek his help, she must have been absolutely desperate. They were gunpowder and spark, the pair of them, but she had the sense not to provoke him – too much, anyway. The boys followed dutifully in their father's footsteps, but she was strong-willed and determined even before she could talk. She was a force of nature; James was always going to lose to her.'

They talked for another hour before it started to rain, so Judith prepared to move. Carter kissed his son and wrapped him up cosily in the pram.

'I'll see you tomorrow,' said Judith. 'James won't notice when I go out with the pram. Women's work,' she tapped her nose.

'Thank you, Jude,' Carter said as he hugged her. He watched her walk across the park then made a call on his phone.

Half-an-hour later he stepped aboard the number 7 bus at the Bernard Terrace stop. Charli was already sitting at a window seat, dressed exactly as she'd been in Jeanie Deans the night before. He sat beside her and pulled out his phone again.

'Why the bus?' she asked him. 'You had a car last night.'

'You can get to anywhere in twenty minutes or so. If I don't need to drive, I'll take the bus.'

'I like buses too. Even if I could afford a car, I'd spend money on something else.'

'Tell me about yourself,' Carter said, making conversation.

'It will cost you many bus fares,' she smiled.

'The highlights will do.'

'Well, I was raised in Rhonda, a village above Marbella.'

'I've never been to Spain.'

'It's a tiny village, very beautiful, but the locals don't trust strangers.'

'Sounds like Gorebridge.'

'Mama was from Manchester. She had a holiday affair with Papa, and I was the result. She died from breast cancer in 2008. I came to the UK in 2012 and got a place with Greater Manchester Police. I put in for a transfer to Edinburgh last year. Is that brief enough for you?'

'Sure, for now.'

'What book are you reading?' she said, watching him swipe the pages on his phone.

'*Plender* by Ted Lewis. Classic noir.'

'What happens?' she asked.

'A psychopath seeks revenge on his long-forgotten school tormentor,' he replied.

'Ha! There should be more books like this. Tell me more.'

'Later, maybe. We're here.'

Inside the Royal Infirmary, they stopped at reception and Carter asked for Dr Murray. Both were given visitor passes.

'Hello again,' Dr Murray greeted Carter. 'You're back. Alice's parents are in the café. Have you spoken to them?'

'No,' said Carter, 'but Ellen in my team spoke to them last week.'

Dr Murray opened the private room. Carter and Garcia went to the side of the bed opposite the monitors. At the same time, Dr Murray glanced at the monitor readouts.

'She's stable again,' she said.

'Again?' Carter picked up.

Alice looked just the same as the first time he'd seen her, nearly a week ago. Her head was still bandaged, face covered in yellow and green bruises, eyes taped shut, and she was hooked up to a couple of IV lines, one in each arm, with a pulse clip attached to her left index finger. He didn't want to think about what was under the bed cover.

'She had a cardiac arrest on Wednesday evening. We lost her briefly but got her back.'

'Should we have been told?' Garcia asked.

'You're not in charge of her treatment, or her recovery. She's my responsibility until she dies, *then* she'll become your responsibility. Remember that Alice is the victim here, she's not just a case number. She had a life and has a family who love her and want her back. Anyway, I'm glad you've come here to see her, that says you're not robo-police, but she'll never be the same again. Have you arrested the arsehole yet?'

'No,' said Carter. 'We haven't got much forensic evidence. There's some technical evidence, but we need a lucky break.'

'What is the diagnosis?' Garcia asked.

'Now all the tests are complete, her short-term prognosis isn't good. Damaged kidneys, spleen and liver, broken ribs, legs, pelvis and a cracked spine, are the main concerns, along with a fractured skull, which caused a severe concussion. We're being careful with how we start the process of bringing her back to consciousness.'

'Is it likely she'll wake soon?' Carter asked. 'If she could tell us who did this to her, it would be a breakthrough.'

'I can't make predictions, but I'm familiar with trauma patients. The heart attack is a pointer like the body is testing itself. She passed, so that's a good thing.'

'Any bad things?' Carter asked.

'Plenty. There will likely be more cardiac episodes. If she gets through them, the survival index will notch up a bit. If she survives, she'll be in a wheelchair for a long time, maybe even for the rest of her life.'

'Thanks, Angela,' said Carter, heading for the door. 'I appreciate everything you're doing. She couldn't be in better hands.'

Once outside the room, Dr Murray closed the door and turned to Carter. 'I trust you to find this sick bastard, Sergeant.'

She walked away, leaving Leccy to watch her go.

'She is very annoyed, yes?' Garcia said.

In the café, it took Carter two attempts to locate Alice's

parents. After they'd introduced themselves, her father gave a motivational speech.

'I'm a good friend of the Chief Constable, and I demand to know what progress you've made in catching this person. If you need more men, I'm sure he'd prioritise my request.'

'George is a retired councillor,' said his wife, proudly. 'He was chair of the Police Committee when it was Lothian and Borders.'

'What do you know about Alice's professional life?' Carter asked them both.

'Very little,' said George. 'Marketing. Brochures and videos, I think. She made a living.'

'Did she ever introduce any clients to you, or mention names?'

'You think someone she worked with tried to kill her?' George's shock was plastered on his face as he choked out the words.

'It's the theory,' said Carter. 'Her diary has regular references to meetings with someone who goes by "J". We don't yet know who that is. What kind of person was she?'

'Very outgoing,' said her mother, smugly. 'We pushed her hard at school, but she thrived on it. She moved out when she went to university and started her own life – something I was keen on. Some people may call it driven or adventurous. The downside was we didn't see much of her, until these last years. You know, she'd matured a bit. I think she thought we might not be around for very much longer and she has no siblings.'

'Does that help, Sergeant?' asked George.

'About her termination,' Carter probed. 'Did you know the father?'

'We don't talk about that,' said Alice's mother stiffly. 'It's not relevant.'

'That's for us to decide,' Carter said.

'Come on, George, it's time for us to go,' she stood up, taking the huff. The old man obeyed.

'If you can think of any reference to "J", please let me know,' said Carter.

'What did you think of that?' asked Garcia once they arrived back at the bus stop towards town.

'Edinburgh is full of Georges. Let's find a bar.'

39

Sweet Happiness

The number 33 took them north-west, towards Cameron Toll, then true north up Dalkeith Road. They alighted at the Grey Horse, a traditional pub a mile south of St Leonard's station, but they had no intention of checking in with Tam Watson. Garcia liked red wine, Spanish Tempranillo. Carter went with Innis & Gunn IPA.

'Are we going on a pub crawl?' she asked.

'When is your next shift?'

'Monday. Day shift.'

'Then we're going on a pub crawl. Where do you live?' He held up his hands. 'Just asking what your experience of Edinburgh's pubs is.'

'Easter Road,' she swallowed a mouthful of wine.

'Leith-ish. The police station is on Queen Charlotte Street,' he said, laughing.

'Call yourself a comedian?'

'What's your local?'

'Middletons.'

After an hour of chatting, they moved on. 'We'll give

the Auld Hoose a miss,' said Carter. 'Too close to home. Southpour on Newington Road is next.'

By 5 p.m. they'd worked their way to Bristo Place. Carter took her into Sandy Bell's, where a music session was in progress.

'I've never heard a violin played like this,' Charli said. 'Papa plays the violin, but he likes Spanish and Italian opera.'

'This is Celtic folk.' Carter whispered into her ear so as not to disturb the players.

They sat in the window seat, looking onto the street, away from the musicians. Ardbeg whisky was poured.

'Tell me about your son,' Charli asked, as the alcohol loosened their inhibitions.

'It's the talk of the steamie, is it?' Carter asked.

'What's "steamie"?' she asked. 'Another Scottish word?'

'A wash house in the green. A place where gossip was rife.'

'Not a nice place, no?'

'It's what happens. Can you keep a secret?' He looked directly at her as if her answer would make a difference to what he was about to reveal.

She stared back at him, with eyes as wide as her ears. 'You don't have a baby son?'

Carter laughed, then got all serious and leaned into the table.

'Nathaniel has been taken from me. The court decided I'm not fit to care for him, so he's living with Kelsa's parents. Her father got a court order.'

'Oh, my God.' She crossed herself. 'Can it be made up? How old is he?'

'Nearly two months.'

Charli reached over the table and grasped his hand in

solidarity. 'What can you do?'

'Well, today, before we went to see Alice, my mother-in-law brought him to the park, and I was able to hold him for an hour. We've agreed more visits, without the old man knowing.'

'This news is great,' she said. 'I will cover for you if you need to spend time with him.' She smiled and then looked around. 'What now? I've had enough of Celtic's fiddling.'

Carter thought, then answered. 'I need someone to make me laugh.'

Carter pushed his way to the front of the queue, flashing his warrant card. Garcia, following behind him, did the same but didn't know why. At the ticket office, Carter recognised the compere.

'Susie, any chance of two compos?'

Two seats left side of the small stage. They sat while the audience streamed into the small venue.

'What is this place?' Garcia asked.

'The Stand,' he said. 'Edinburgh's best comedy club outside of the Festival. I've gigged here before; this is The Saturday Show. A compere and five comedians doing fifteen minutes each.'

The audience settled down. The spotlight came on, and a butch woman with viciously cropped hair and tattoos on her arms assaulted the microphone. She swore.

'Susie McCabe,' Carter whispered into Garcia's ear. 'From Glasgow, a brilliant storyteller in the mould of Billy Connolly, so it'll be close to the bone.'

After her slot, Susie introduced the next comedian.

'She is brilliant,' said Garcia. 'I've never been to Glasgow, are people there like her?'

'Later, look who's coming on now,' said Carter.

Into the spotlight shuffled a tall guy in a T-shirt, wearing dark glasses and swinging a white stick. He stopped at the microphone stand, folded up his stick and started waving it about.

'Jamie MacDonald,' said Carter into Garcia's ear. 'I helped him set up his Fringe performance in George Square in 2016. The theatre he hired held a hundred people, but one night, not a soul showed. We went to the performer's bar and got pished instead; he, his driver and me. He was a banker in the City of London but lost his sight in his thirties. A blind banker is no use to anyone, he'd said, they'd all just laugh at him, so he decided to make money from it. His act is totally non-PC.'

It was after 10 p.m. when they stepped back onto the street.

'That was amazing,' Garcia said. 'But I must go home now.'

Carter had switched his phone on again and looked at it intently. He returned to his relaxed mood.

'What was it, Leccy?'

'Sorry, it's a text message, that's all. Nothing really. Another drink?'

'It's been a good day, we will do it again sometime?'

'Yeah, sure. There's a taxi there if you want it.'

She went to kiss him, but he hugged her instead. 'Thanks, Charli. Really. Do something for me, please?'

She disengaged, got in the taxi and waited for the favour.

'Go to Alice's flat, look for DVDs or a computer. She might have made copies of videos for clients, maybe she has something on J.'

'I am on it,' she nodded before the taxi sped off.

Carter walked west along York Place, then turned left up

the slope of North St David Street. Within twelve minutes he was on the number 11 heading south. The bus was busy, a bit noisy, but it was the weekend, what did he expect? At 11 p.m., he got off at the Braid Burn stop. A ten-minute walk under streetlights took him to what he thought was roughly one hundred and fifty metres from the Dunsmuir mansion.

There were no lights on in the house that he could see, though the ten-foot-high mature hedging prevented him from viewing the ground floor. It didn't matter anyway; he wasn't about to storm the barricades to rescue Nathaniel.

He looked at the picture of his smiling son, who had been texted to him while enjoying himself in the Stand.

40

Keeping Secrets

Sunday morning passed in the haze of a mild hangover, but Carter knew the best way to clear his mind and body of alcohol. He dressed warmly, with a rain jacket and waterproof walking boots, then stood at the bus stop at Malbet Park waiting for the number 31 into town. He jumped off at Newington Road, walked along Salisbury Road, and crossed the A7 onto Holyrood Park Road. From there he began the hill-climb around Arthur's Seat, the two-hundred-and-fifty-metre-high volcanic plug that sat on the eastern edge of the Old Town.

It had always been a favourite walk of his. He'd convinced Kelsa of its benefits, so they did it together at least one weekend a month. At the Hawse, he came off the tarmac and climbed the steep path up to the Radical Road. He was blowing hard; he wasn't fit and knew it. The initial ascent was steep because he was coming at it from the St Leonard's side. Most leisure walkers started outside Holyrood Palace, at Haggis Knowe, where the slope was just a stiff walk.

He stood a moment to get his breath back, nodding at a

couple dressed in colourful scarves, beanies and gloves. He set off clockwise and soon had the Salisbury Crags rising above him. The view was terrific. On his left, the Castle dominated the skyline and he could pick out the dome of the McEwan Hall too. Directly below, it was all residential flats. He tried and failed to pick out St Leonard's police station. There were too many buildings crammed tight together. He reached the Palace of Holyrood and the Scottish Parliament in twenty minutes. But the footpath was badly in need of repair and in places it was downright dangerous. He gazed north towards Calton Hill, quickly picking out Old Calton Burial Ground, where Kelsa had been laid to rest only a week ago. He walked on.

Another half an hour saw him climb the Long Row pathway, which brought him up the last steep section from the south to the peak itself, where two cairns stood, each with Ordnance Survey markers cemented on top. At least fifty others had made it too, all of them scanning the view north to Fife and north-west to the Ochil Hills. On the west side, the hill fell away steeply, promising severe injury to anyone who lost their footing. Carter stayed for ten minutes, letting the wind blow through him, then found his way back down to the Hawse, via the Gutted Haddie onto the tarmac of Queen's Drive. It was after 2 p.m. Time for another appointment with his mother-in-law.

The walk to the Meadows was a skoosh after his climb and he made it in fifteen minutes. The eastern end of the Meadows had the pavilion and children's play park. Even today, with its bitter, brooding coldness, the climbing frames were full of all ages up to teens. Mums kept watch with warm coffee cups, while dads patrolled the area like the mini-me battlefield it could easily become.

Carter saw Judith sitting on a park bench beside the Silver Cross pram. All the other mothers had buggies. He sat down next to her. Nathaniel was awake and he carefully lifted him from the covers.

'I have his bottle here,' Judith said. 'Do you want to feed him?'

'Of course,' he said, taking the bottle from her. Nathaniel guzzled at it.

'He's a strong boy, 'she said. 'Every day, I see him growing. I'm reminded of Kelsa when she was this age.'

'What do you know of her ex-boyfriends?' Carter asked, using the informality of the moment to get Judith talking. 'Before I came along.'

'Not much really. There comes a time in your child's life when it's best not to pry too deeply. She was very much an independent woman. She had to be, in this modern world.'

'Any significant boyfriends that she confided in you about?'

'Forgive me, Lachlan, but didn't you two talk about such things before you decided to marry? Seems to me it would have been best to rattle the skeletons before committing yourself.'

'We didn't. It just seemed— irrelevant. At that time.'

'Passion is a hard master,' Judith said. Carter detected sadness in her words. 'Hugo was the one I thought she was going to marry,' she went on, with some reluctance. 'She was quite young at the time; twenty-two, I think. You might know him if you like rugby, he played for Scotland and became a personality. Hugo Mortimer. James was tickled pink. Then he moved to France. Clermont-Ferrand, I'm sure. That was the beginning of the end of the relationship. I saw a change in her; she began to protect herself. Why do you want to know this now?'

Carter sighed. 'I think she might have been seeing someone else.'

'You were married.' Judith's face revealed just how alien the concept was to her. 'She would never do that. Yes, she was her own woman, and I'm not unaware of how difficult it is these days to be taken seriously, but she would never do that. Never.'

'Did you notice any change in her behaviour after she announced she was pregnant?'

'Of course. Pregnancy does things to a woman; things you men don't understand. She got thinner, which shouldn't have been happening, but I didn't know then she'd stopped eating.'

Silence fell between them. Carter had almost forgotten he was feeding Nathaniel.

'You'll have to burp him,' Judith said, breaking the tension. 'Take this towel and put it over your shoulder. If he's sick, it won't go over your coat. Now, pat him gently on the back.'

Five minutes later, it was all over, and Nathaniel was asleep in his pram again.

'It's time for me to go,' said Judith. 'This conversation has upset me, Lachlan, but I'll keep to our agreement with Nathaniel. One thing I have to know: is this interest you have in her past relationships purely personal?'

'Yes, Jude, it is.' What else could he say?

He watched her push the pram away, but his stress hadn't eased. Judith disappeared from view and he turned away too. Summerhall was over the road, with a reputation for an extensive selection of liquid sedatives.

41

Snog Marry Avoid

Meadowbank Terrace was on the other side of Holyrood Park, a good forty-minute walk from Summerhall. If there was a bus route from Summerhall, he didn't know and was unlikely to use it regularly anyway.

Lesley Holliday instantly burst into tears when she saw who was at her door, falling into his arms and hugging him. 'Oh, Leccy, it's so good to see you,' she blubbed through her sobs. 'Kelsa's father banned us all from attending the funeral. Come in, come in.'

She helped him out of his rain jacket. She directed him to the kitchen and the table there that had accommodated them all, drinking wine and laughing at life's ironies, for more evenings than he could remember. Happy times.

Before they married, this kitchen was a different world for him, inhabited by Lesley, Kelsa and a cohort of thirty-something women. Women for whom men were sheep at market. Gossip was the currency, and Lesley was Kelsa's go-to girl, the long-term girlfriend she confided in when she felt the need. She was the first friend of Kelsa's he'd met, and Lesley instantly loved him for being so besotted with her.

'Jim will be here soon. You'll stay for tea? You can stay the night if you want. Must be lonely for you up there in Liberton.' Lesley stopped speaking and brushed the tears from her eyes.

'I can't stay,' he said, suddenly stumbling over his words. 'But I want to ask you some questions.' The kettle clicked off and the boil died away.

'As a policeman?'

'Something like that, but it's mainly for my peace of mind.'

'What do you mean?' The worry on her face was genuine.

'There are some things about her past I need to understand.'

'Why, what's going on?'

'We met on the first of April 2017,' he ignored her counter-question. 'At the Dome. A few weeks later, she brought me here for a barbie in the back green, so you could interrogate me about my intentions. Just the four of us. The sunshine lasted less than an hour before the rain, so we came inside and sat at this table, drinking wine.'

She continued the ritual of making tea while speaking. 'Yes, I remember. She was radiant, I hadn't seen her like that for a long time. You were so good for her.'

A mug appeared in front of him. She sat opposite.

'Did Hugo Mortimer get the same treatment?' he asked.

'I never met him.' Lesley re-composed herself after the initial shock of the question. 'Kelsa and I weren't that close when Hugo was on her scene, but I was there for her through the aftermath. It was about two years before she was ready to face the world again.'

'What happened?'

'He found a new life in France. He's got kids now.'

They both waited for the other to continue.

'Long after Hugo,' Lesley said eventually, 'Kelsa sat where you're sitting and said she wasn't sure she wanted another relationship. There were six of us around this table, and each of us had had a bad experience. But most weekends we glammed up, got out there and on occasion we got lucky.'

'And before me?'

'She was fussy. She knew the type who'd get the thumbs down. Of course, that didn't stop her having a fling now and again. Girls have needs too.'

Carter studied Lesley carefully. It was clear she was wrestling with something, so he let her take her time.

'Something heavy was going on in 2015. She was coy, and there was fire in her eyes, but then it faded. It started up again, then faded months later. I asked her, but she wouldn't tell. I kept probing. She wanted to confide, but something was holding her back. It was somebody at work, she said, but it seemed very on-off. You know her job meant travel down south, don't you?'

'Yes, training and consulting for senior managers in corporate business and government.'

'I thought she might have been having an affair. She never mentioned names, and frankly, nobody cared all that much as long as she was happy. Whatever it was, it went away. Then you arrived.'

Carter decided to change tack.

'Remember I called you one weekend in March last year?'

'I barely remember yesterday,' Lesley said, dismissively. 'It's a benefit of the wine.'

'She was going out for drinks with you and the girls. She'd

not come home on the Saturday. I called you—'

'Oh, yes, I remember now.'

'Did she confide in you beforehand?'

'No. I thought she was with you. We did our usual George Street run.'

'If you know anything, it might help? You didn't bump into her, or anything—'

'Honestly, Leccy, the first I knew there was a problem was when you called me.'

Carter got up to leave. There was nothing to be gained by badgering a friend.

'Are you saying she was a victim? After Hugo, she grew up. She took responsibility for her life, so don't beat yourself up. Only you know what went on between you. But I know this: she loved you. 2015 was history once she met you.'

At the front door, she hugged and kissed him. 'Don't be a stranger.'

'If anything comes to mind,' he said. 'Call me. Please.'

42

A Magical Place

On London Road, he caught the number 5 going into town. He settled down and almost immediately received a text message. He knew it was from J before he even looked: his heart skipped a beat.

What was next? Not being able to reply was what he found frustrating, even more than the messages being deleted not long after reading. It was like solitary confinement with no parole.

[2019-01-20:2006] Your Baby is such a bad girl but you don't know the half of it. Are you angry or are you playing it cool? The Balvenie is finished. Get another one will you? J.

His temple throbbed as the blood pulsed in his head. He gripped the phone hard. There were only two other passengers on the bus, and he wanted to scream at them, punch them, and keep punching until blood poured from every orifice. Instead, he sat there as the perfect citizen and raged inwardly. Ten minutes later, he alighted the number 5 on

North Bridge and changed to the number 31. The message was erased as soon as he left the bus at Malbet Park.

Reaching home, there were no outward signs that J had been there, and the embers of his anger now burned through his stomach. He had to put the bins out, so went down the side of the house and unlocked the back door. The kitchen was warm, the heating had come on when the temperature dropped. An empty bottle of Balvenie stood on the kitchen worktop. On the drainer, one crystal glass sat upside down. Carter knew that taking it as evidence would prove nothing.

He fired up the kettle. It was nearly 9 p.m. The message preyed on his mind. He was always on edge, expecting something to happen at every turn. But chores had to be done, like washing his clothes, attempting to cook and all the other essential tasks that Kelsa used to take in her stride. Knowing J had been in here just made all these things seem less relevant. He contemplated changing the locks but knew it wouldn't make him feel any safer.

Tea made, Carter stared through the window, through the darkness of the garden, to where the lights of Edinburgh Castle winked at him. Somewhere out there, J was laughing at him. Liberton sat high with a view over the city in all its rambling glory. Kelsa had wanted to know why it had to be this house, with this view, for him.

He'd gone for walks around Gorebridge with Papa Carter, as a boy, listening as the old man rambled on about his days in the coalpits, now landscaped and long gone. A bench had been placed high up the hill from the gas houses, where man and boy sat together gazing out at the Edinburgh skyline, twenty-five miles away. At that distance, in any weather, Arthur's Seat and Castle Rock stood guard. On a breezy spring day, with clouds scudding in and out, it was a magical place. The city basked in the changing sun, breathing in rhythm with the light. The view from his kitchen had once given him comfort, but now it was tainted. Vectoring to a memory, he searched for one that wasn't corrupted by treachery or death.

Standing there, immersed in the moment, gazing out at the twinkling city, and wondering how to deal with J, a sound niggled at him. He plugged himself into the heartbeat of his home. Listening to the washing machine on its cycle, and behind it, the slush of pressurised water, the subtle tick of warming radiators. He pushed himself away from the window, cocking his head, trying to determine the source of the sound that had pricked his senses. Nothing was amiss in the dining room. Walking through the glass doors into the sitting room, he scanned the everyday soft furnishings, table lamps, TV and hi-fi. Was this how he'd left the room this morning? He hadn't paid attention when leaving, but he thought maybe J had sat on the sofa.

Nothing was normal. He scanned the pictures on the walls, of him and her in Las Vegas. On one, something in the bottom corner caught his eye. It was a red emoji sticker. He looked closely; it pointed at the next picture. That one had a red emoji too, and the next one. At the sitting-room door, an emoji pointed up the stairs.

In the front door hallway, on the stairwell, each of the pictures had an emoji pointing upwards.

J was here. In the house. Now. His heart thundered.

There was no security system guarding their home, no visible and audible alarm to check and deter the opportunist thief. They'd relied on triple-locked, deadbolted doors and double-glazed windows, along with the fact of a constant ebb and flow of neighbours, all looking out for each other. He opened a cupboard, half-expecting to find J hiding there. He was losing it.

As he climbed the stairs, her perfume was more potent than usual. Or was that just his elevated senses? He went into the second bathroom first– no running water and no emojis. He checked the smaller of their three bedrooms. It was a mess of his and her stuff that they'd never got around to organising. It was all supposed to go into storage. A tornado could have passed through here, and he wouldn't have known. He stepped back into the upper hallway, gazing around, knowing he was being led.

Her bedroom door was ajar. His heart raced faster; J was here. He grasped the door handle and pushed through warily. His left hand automatically found the light switch, but it was bedside lighting that illuminated the scene.

Her dressing table was set as Carter had left it, but the bedroom had a different look. On each of the framed photographs on the walls, weeping emojis covered Carter's eyes, but not Kelsa's. The bed was rumpled, the duvet had been thrown back, the bedsheet was an untidy mess, like just after sex. Her pillow had a dent in it like she'd slept there. On his side, the shape of a large body was evident in the mattress. The ensuite door was ajar. The unmistakable gurgle of a shower running came from inside.

On the floor of the bedroom lay a single sheer black stocking.

43

Proof of Dominion

J *was* in Carter's home right now. J, the one who'd left the yellow Jiffy bag on the kitchen table days ago. Adrenaline pumped through his body, rippling him with clear and present fear. He approached the ensuite carefully. The noise from the shower competed with the noise of the blood racing in his ears.

J wasn't expecting him to appear. He hadn't anticipated Carter's return home so soon. The bastard had front to be in his home at all, but to be sleeping in her bed, to be defacing his memories so blatantly, he was going to pay for it.

Get a grip on yourself.

Carter grasped the handle of the ensuite door firmly and pushed it open carefully. The sound of running water rose to waterfall proportions. Steam billowed past him into the bedroom, obscuring his vision. He pushed the door open, and boldly stepped in. The cubicle was wrapped in vapour. The tiled walls and mirror trickled water. His shoes caught on the wooden drainers. He reached into the cubicle, found the valve and twisted it closed. The shower stopped instantly.

The mist of water and steam dispersed through the fan, and residual water gurgled into the drain.

It was empty.

Taking two quick steps, he opened the bathroom window. Winter air rushed in to cool the tense atmosphere. The swirling air was bitterly cold but also soothing and reviving. He began to shake and shiver and forced the adrenaline from his body. There would be no release today. J's essence suffocated Carter in every room he'd walked through, in the air he'd breathed, the sights he'd seen and the memories he'd defaced. Yet Carter knew he would have left no forensic trace that would help identify him.

He slumped down onto the pan, defeated.

What had he gotten into, marrying Kelsa before he really knew her? It was all his own fault. It was a challenge, a call to arms, a declaration of war over a woman shared. He should never have let her into his life so quickly, and now, after death, she was lashing her twisted love across his psyche with a cat-o'-nine-tails.

How did J get into his home? No windows were broken. The garage? The external lock was flimsy, but there had been no apparent signs of mechanical manipulation.

Who knew he would be away? Judith, of course, but he discounted her because it was senseless. Charli Garcia on Saturday, but what did she have to gain? He'd been pretty drunk on Saturday night and hadn't checked Kelsa's bedroom when he arrived home, but he would have heard running water.

J's campaign was wearing him down.

For the next ten minutes, he forced himself to think clearly. He made another cup of tea and drank it with shaking hands.

Living in a crime scene? Treat it like a crime scene.

Methodically, he searched the house, re-checking every window and door, confirming none showed signs of forcible entry. In the cleaning basket, he found the yellow gloves, took a plastic food bag from the drawer and climbed the stairs again, warily, as if his enemy was hiding and would leap on him unexpectantly. This was a battle. Text messages first, now physical contact. What next? Maybe one of the earlier deleted messages had offered him a clue and he'd missed it.

Back in her bedroom, Carter sat on the end of the bed, gazing at the stocking. He was back in control: for now. The emojis, the unmade bed, the running shower: all were designed to scare him. To make him feart as Charli Garcia had not been when she confronted Logan's soldiers. On the other hand, he had been feart to come face-to-face with J and privately admitted it. J had proclaimed dominion over him-and-his, and the stocking was absolute proof.

It was Kelsa's; it could not belong to anyone else. He'd seen her put them on in the morning and watched her roll them slowly off her long legs at night. He rummaged through her drawers, pulling out knickers, bras, bodies, tights and stockings. He didn't know how many of everything she'd had but that didn't matter as much as if he found a spare one. After a time, he was certain there were no solos, concluding that the matching stocking – if it existed – must still be with J. Carter left all the underwear on the floor; she could clear it up herself if she were minded.

His thoughts strayed again to Kelsa's missing weekend. Was that where J had acquired the stocking and the knickers? How could he find out? Was it too late now to try?

He took out his phone and photographed the stocking from

multiple angles. Wearing the yellow gloves, he rolled it up, starting at the foot until he reached the thick elasticated top that held it in place at the top of her thigh. As the material came off the floor, and as he pushed it into the clear bag, his phone pinged with another message.

His heart punched out the beats as if the man was standing over him, directing his thoughts.

[2019-01-20: 21:42] Matchmaker, matchmaker, make me a match. Find me a find, catch me a catch. If I give you my number, will you promise to call me, wait till my husband's away. J

44

Shoogly Nails

Before the light broke on the eastern horizon on Monday morning, Carter drove straight to the forensic suite in FOC Fettes. He asked for a private meeting with Rocketman.

'What can I do for you, Leccy?' CTO Johnstone said relatively formally, after arranging a breakfast of coffee and biscuits.

'The evidence I brought in last Thursday,' Carter said. 'I wasn't entirely honest with you.'

'Knickers sent to you in the post, belonging to Alice Deacon.' Rocketman's face resembled a stone wall; solid, impregnable, unforgiving.

'Your tech processed them.'

'Michelle. Knows her stuff.'

'Confirmed that the DNA on the knickers matched the hair DNA—' Carter continued, without waiting for confirmation. 'On my wife Kelsa's hairbrush.'

'Your recently buried wife, Kelsa?'

'Yes.'

'OK,' Rocketman sat back in his chair. 'Let's put aside procedure and disciplinary complications for the moment. Why did you do it?'

'They could have been Alice's—'

'You knew they weren't.' Rocketman was nobody's fool.

'I suspected they weren't but had to prove it.' The confession wasn't healing his soul.

'Confirming your wife had an affair in the process.'

'Yes,' Carter said sheepishly.

'You put Michelle in a difficult position after she'd processed evidence you led us to believe was related to Alice Deacon. I don't like detectives fucking my staff around, so I've made sure she's in the clear. However, your coat's on a shoogly nail, Sergeant. What happens next will decide when it falls to the floor.'

'DCI McKinlay?' Carter asked, beginning to feel the nail loosen.

'My discretion – for now. Your reputation is eroding fast, although I'm intrigued why you'd go to the lengths of sacrificing your career for a dead wife and a dead affair.'

Carter pulled out the clear plastic bag from his pocket and placed it on the table. 'One of Kelsa's stockings. When I returned home last night, this was lying on our bedroom floor. I don't sleep there any more, for obvious reasons.'

'A break-in by your wife's lover?' Rocketman sat forward, intrigued.

'No sign of forced entry.'

'He has a key?'

'I can't think of any other way,' Carter said flatly.

'He could deny it, no evidence of a break-in, etcetera, etcetera,' said Rocketman to himself. 'You believe he's stalking you?'

'Stalking is a criminal offence,' said Carter. Rocketman acknowledged the fact with a nod. 'But I'm more concerned about what else he's trying to prove. You don't know about the text messages.'

'He's been texting you?' Rocketman was stunned. 'Cheryl knows this, I assume?'

'Not just your standard SMS. There is no name. He remotely erases the texts he sends.'

'A puzzle for our Glasgow colleagues,' mused Rocketman.

Carter pushed the bag across the table. 'Can we set up a separate case file?'

'For the stalking? The gift of DCI McKinlay corroborated with Chief Superintendent Goodwin's rubber stamp, I'm afraid. The submitted evidence is one pair of knickers and a single stocking, belonging to your dead wife. Her DNA, your DNA and that of an unknown male, crime of passion clearly established. My apology for being brutal, but what's the crime and who's the criminal? If it were to find the Fiscal's inbox, she'd say "next case please". As it stands.'

'So, what do I do?' said Carter, feeling the ground shifting under his feet. 'There's a new text on my phone, not yet erased.'

Rocketman examined the plastic bag, then looked at the message on Carter's phone.

'Classic cunt, I'd say. The fact he's actually sent this to you means he thinks he's untouchable. The rhyme will have a twisted meaning, and it may or may not mean anything to you or anyone else. What do you think?'

'The matchmaker quote is just a taunt,' said Carter, carefully. 'The text before this one proved he was having an affair with Kelsa, so he's unlikely to give me his number, is he?'

'He might be saying you already have it, so you should call him. I've seen this kind of taunting before, in a case in Arizona, years ago, but never using a mobile phone. Dr Flowers may be your best bet: psychos are her bag.'

'What about the procedure angle?'

'Between you and me for the moment. I'll authorise Michelle to process the stocking, and we'll take it from there, keeping it under Alice's file for now. I think you're right: he's got it in for you. He wants you to suffer emotionally. The longer you don't show any signs of worry, the more anxious he'll get, meaning he'll get bolder and might make a mistake. My advice is to bring all physical items sent by him directly to me, don't respond if he gives you the option and for God's sake, don't tell Cheryl or anyone else about the stocking. Otherwise, we'll both be in the shite.'

'Thank you, sir,' Carter felt genuinely relieved.

'And for what it's worth, the first lines originate from the musical, *Fiddler on the Roof.* Maybe it's a clue.'

45

Leashed

Carter parked the Smart car in the rear car park, accessed through St Leonard's Lane. Tam Watson was in his usual place behind the booking desk.

'You've missed the Monday meeting, Leccy,' he said by way of greeting. 'DCI McKinlay wants to see you, but she's busy right now.'

'I'll be at my desk,' he said.

In the detectives' room, Charli Garcia made eye contact as he sat down.

'Morning, Leccy,' she said breezily. 'Have a good weekend?'

'Morning, Charli,' he replied, aware they were using code.

'I've arranged the statements from the names on your list,' she said.

'Well done.' At least some progress had been made.

'I've made them up based on proximity to the Reverend. Two men saw her in the bar sitting with another man. Both witnesses said they were there with each other, but he was laughing. She had a face like a "soor ploom". They left around eleven-thirty. She was drunk, staggering about.'

'Did these witnesses give you a description of him?'

'Large man, broad-shouldered, six-foot-tall and more, wearing a dark-ish suit and an open-necked white shirt,' she read from her notes. 'Dark cropped hair, clean-shaven. They would recognise him if we made pictures. Another witness outside saw two people staggering along the street. He was too drunk, didn't see what they looked like.'

'Names?' asked Carter.

'John Smith and Teddy Morrison were in the pub. Stewart Allison was on the street.'

'Search our systems, see if we have pictures of Jimmy Logan,' Carter said.

'OK, I'm on it,' Garcia replied.

'If we do, show it to Smith and Morrison and gauge their reaction. Anything of use from the others? Jacky Dodds?'

'His phone rang out, but you'd already made up ICRS,' she replied.

'Dodds fits the description too, he's the same build as Logan, but his hair is reddish-brown. Try his picture on the two witnesses. He's got a profile for sexual assault, but he could be trying to up his game. What about Nathan Butler? Dodds told me he was in the bar too.'

'I spoke to him,' she said.

'You found another number for him?' Carter was surprised.

'Yes. I called the council tax on their emergency line; they gave me a number and a home in Murrayfield. Your queries were in ICRS. I asked about the home and phone number. He said his phone was stolen in the Reverend and thought we were calling because we'd recovered it.'

'Does he think Dodds nicked it?' Carter asked.

'I didn't ask that. Sorry.'

'Did he see anything of Alice?'

'No. He was there for a business meeting. It wasn't regular for him.'

'Late at night? Did he say who he was meeting?'

'No, and I didn't know to ask that either. But the only person I've not spoken to is Joe Moore,' Charli said. 'The phone rings twice then stops. No voicemail. His address is Deptford in London.'

'I've heard Deptford mentioned,' Carter replied, thinking. 'But I can't remember where.'

'I was bored on Sunday afternoon, so I went to Alice's flat to search for videos.'

'Did you find anything?'

'A laptop that has a password. She has a large collection of commercial movies on DVD, but I found DVDs with handwriting. Some are sex.'

Carter gazed at her but said nothing. She picked up on his cue.

'I've scanned it. Made from the internet. She is not in scenes I've seen if that is what you think. I found two DVDs with copies of client projects. I can't tell if any will help us.'

'OK, well done. We have specialist officers who deal with porn. Send those DVDs to them but keep the client DVDs here. I'll have a look at them later. Send the laptop to Gavin Roy's team in Glasgow. Now, read all the case notes in ICRS, review the evidence and tell me what you think. I'm going to see DCI McKinlay.' Carter stood up and put his coat over his arm.

He knocked on DCI McKinlay's office door and went in. 'You wanted to see me, ma'am.'

She didn't ask him to sit, so he stood.

'Where were you this morning, Leccy?'

'I headed straight to FOC Fettes to see if they had any more insights from Alice's evidence, ma'am. We've got her laptop and some DVDs to go through.'

She regarded him with a long stare. 'You could at least have called to say where you were. You know the rules.'

'Sorry, ma'am.'

'Dr Flowers gave us all an update on her new role, as sanctioned by the Chief Super. Pity ye weren't there to hear it, eh?'

'She told me that the Chief—'

McKinlay cut him short with a wave of her hand. 'What's your interest in Jacky Dodds?'

'He was in the bar when Alice was there. His description fits the profile. I've asked DC Garcia to follow up witnesses with his picture.'

McKinlay had more to say. 'Dodds isn't your man.'

'With respect, ma'am.'

'Don't "with respect" me, *Sergeant* Carter.' McKinlay looked like she was going to explode. 'I might spend most of my day pushing paper, but I know what's goin' on out there and who's doin' it. Jesus, he's in his sixties. Dinnae waste your time on him. You have other suspects?'

Carter was about to reply, but McKinlay got her retaliation in first. 'We need to wrap this up, Carter. Alice's parents have called the Chief Super, demanding an arrest. Turns out Paw is also a friend of your father-in-law, amongst other connections, and I can feel the rope being twisted right now. Maybe you're too wrapped up in your wife's death to give it your full attention. I'm seriously considering taking you off duty. Dr Flowers was right, you're not ready yet.'

'Ma'am,' Carter began, but she held up her hand.

'End of the week, Sergeant Carter. Bring me a solid case, or you're back on your own couch. Report to DI Mason every couple of hours. Clear?'

'Very,' he acknowledged.

46

Suspect Suspect

Back in the detectives' room, he went straight to Charli Garcia. 'Have you contacted those witnesses? Shown them Dodds' picture?'

'I've not had time.'

'Priority. I know Dodds was in the Reverend, but I don't know if Logan was in the bar too. Phone me as soon as you've got answers.'

'Where are you going?'

'To eliminate Jacky Dodds from this enquiry.'

Half an hour later, he parked the Smart car on the street outside Dodds' flat. He rang the bell a few times but got no immediate answer. A few minutes later, the entry door opened, and an older woman was caught by surprise when Carter flashed his warrant card in her face. 'Jacky Dodds?'

'What's he done now?' asked the woman.

'Have you seen him since Friday?'

'Oh, I don't know.'

Carter gave her his card. 'Call me, please, if you see him. I'm concerned for his welfare.' He drove the half-mile to

Polwarth Church, where the drop-in was in full swing. He had a chat with the minister, mentioning only that he'd last seen Jacky in a panic running along Church Hill. Reverend Alec Booth wasn't daft.

'I'm guessing you don't know him that well, Sergeant Carter, in a non-professional capacity?'

'No. But a woman was raped in Dalry Burial Ground recently, and it's important we find him. They were in the same bar at the same time.'

'That'll be Jimmy Logan's pub. Jacky is a creature of habit. I've known him for years, but I'm sure he's not your man.'

'That's the second time I've heard that today,' Carter said. 'Mind telling me why?'

'Confidential, I'm afraid, even in the circumstances of rape, but you can take it from me. It wasn't Jacky.'

'How sure are you?'

'As sure as God's love treasures all humanity.'

'Hmm, that sure,' said Carter. 'Thanks, Reverend. How do you know Logan? I wouldn't have thought you and him would be chatting over tea and cake.'

'Mr Logan knows my view of him. He's not on my Christmas card list, although I seem to be on his.'

Carter let it go and was walking towards the church hall's exit door when someone hailed him by name.

'Leccy, ye not stoppin' to chat? It's waarrm in here. The soup's good, and it's free,' the man said, waving his hand for Carter to sit beside him. 'C'mon, Trisha will get you a cuppa, won't ya, ya sexy bitch?'

Carter sat down, assessing the woman standing in front of him with big red hair and a body like a burst sack of turnips. She slammed a mug of tea onto the table in front of Carter.

'Watch your mouth, Duggie McLean, or I'll shove this teapot so far up your arse ye'll be shittin' tea leaves till Easter.'

'She loves it dirty,' he whispered into Carter's ear. 'How's the heid? I'm sorry I clubbed ye, but ye cannae take chances. What ye doin' in here?'

'Lookin' for you,' said Carter seamlessly. 'Remember the guy in the graveyard? Any chance it was Jacky Dodds?'

'Still no' caught him, eh?' Duggie chuckled. 'It wasn't Jacky, I can tell ye that for free. I know him. The way he wanders around. Bent at the shoulders like, and clumsy. Aye, he's powerful. If his mind is set, ye'll no shake him. Aye, it was dark and all, but the boy you're looking for was precise. Knew what he was doin', the way a fox guts a chicken. Know what I mean?'

'Why is everyone so sure it's not Jacky Dodds?' Carter asked.

Duggie got serious, leaning in conspiratorially, his voice a whisper. 'I grew up with Jacky, we were in the same class. He was a bit slow and became a target for the neds. Kept an eye on him, me and some mates. But one day, when he was fifteen, they cornered him in the Braid woods and carved him up. Ming Dalby did it, slimy little cunt. Thought he was a hard man, died in Saughton. Sliced Jacky's sausage and tatties clean off. The doc couldn't stick them back on.'

Carter put his head in his hands.

'He's anxious around women, keeps away from them, then you lot hassle him for shite. He panics.'

'Does he work for Jimmy Logan?'

'Jimmy looks after him, has a wee soft spot for him,' Duggie laughed at his own humour. 'Right, that's enough, I'm no' spillin' all my secrets. Leave Jacky alone.'

Outside the church, Carter's phone rang. It was Charli Garcia.

'Both witnesses say it wasn't Jacky Dodds.'

'I get it, I really do.'

47

More Drawing Boards

Back at St Leonard's, Carter sat with DC Garcia looking through the mobile phone analysis in the detectives' room. Her face was lit up in astonishment.

'You've got an interactive map of all the mobile phones. That's amazing.'

'It's helping,' said Carter. 'But not as much as you might think.'

'What are the limitations?' Garcia was still enthralled.

'The phones must be switched on and need triangulation by at least two masts to determine a location. If the phone is on, but asleep, it won't check in with a mast until there's activity, like a text or call.'

'Any GPS?' she asked.

'We get that from whatever GPS services are enabled on the phone. Mainly Google and Apple.'

'Can you read texts or listen to calls?'

'No, not from this analysis. We'd need an actual phone to read texts and scan the calls list. Listening to live calls is banned.'

'Ha,' she snorted. 'What are we going to make with it?'

'We're going to conference Gavin Roy, the guy who will examine Alice's computer for us. He's our lead forensic computer tech. He pulled the mobile analysis together for me.'

Carter dialled the number. Roy's Glasgow growl leapt from the speaker.

'Leccy. What's your problem?'

'Gavin, I've got Constable Charli Garcia here, she's working with me on the Deacon case.'

'Hi Gavin,' Garcia said. 'The data you sent over is amazing.'

'It's just a pile of shite if you don't know how to interpret it,' he replied. 'What do you need, Leccy?'

'I want to go back to when she arrived at the pub. Can we do that with this data set or do we need a refresh?'

'No refresh,' Roy said. He explained to Carter how to make the adjustments to the program.

'Cool,' said Carter, making the changes.

'I ran it a few times myself at high-speed,' said Roy. 'Ms Deacon has an InterMide account, and it seemed to me many others around her did too. An above-average number. It's just a hunch really. Nothing more to say on the SMS nano-app. I'll call you when I've got something useful.'

Dr Flowers walked into the room. She spotted Carter and Garcia and came over. Carter left Garcia to work the data while he and Flowers sat in an empty meeting pod.

'How was your meeting with the Chief?' Carter asked.

'Oh, you know, the usual corporate political stuff,' she replied casually.

'DCI McKinlay wants a quick win,' Carter said, getting to his point. 'If I don't deliver she'll put me back on bereavement at the end of the week.'

'I've just been the ball in her game of ping-pong with the Chief Super. She'd spent the last few weeks challenging the value of everything I've done. At the same time, the Chief was delighted with the foundation work I've completed for his mental health initiative. Now it's all changed. He wants me gone, and she wants to keep me!'

'Welcome to Police Scotland,' Carter applauded. 'When do you leave?'

'No decision yet. Anything new on the Deacon case?'

'Still haven't got any solid suspects. So, it's back to the drawing board with the mobile data. Charli's going to run that for me.'

He hesitated, not sure how to dance around his predicament or walk off the dance floor. 'There's something I need to talk to you about, related to Alice's case. On Sunday, I discovered my house had been broken into while I was up town.'

'God, Leccy,' Flowers said, shocked. 'What was stolen?'

'It was what was left behind that caused the grief. J is twisting the knife in my back about his affair with my wife.'

48

Call Me Carter

Recounting the truth to a psychologist was only going to show Carter how flawed his character really was. 'The love of my life, whom I thought to be my perfect wife, was a back-stabbing, lying, cheating, devious bitch.'

'Tell me what's happened,' Dr Flowers flipped to psychologist mode.

For the next twenty minutes, he explained the recent spate of texts and the knickers and the stocking, icing the facts with his new-found views on wife and mistress. He laid out what had happened in his home the night before. Once he'd exhausted himself, he felt better. A bitch shared is a bitch halved.

'Rocketman suggested the psychological side is your territory,' Carter said.

'Who's Rocketman?'

'CTO Davey Johnstone, Head of Forensic Science for E Division.'

'What did he say, exactly?'

'Classic over-confident cunt. Quote.'

'Because of the method of delivery of the items of underwear?'

'Yes. And the text messages. Here's last night's communiqué. He's not erased it. I assume he wants me to pass it around. While you've got my phone, look at the photos I took of what he did to the pictures hanging in Kelsa's bedroom.'

After a few minutes, she handed back the phone. 'I've never seen the emoji thing before, but it does fit the mindset of a psychopath. Only your eyes are covered – why not hers too?'

'I don't know.'

'You're investigating Alice Deacon. What's Kelsa's death got to do with her?'

'I used Alice's case files to get Kelsa's knickers tested for DNA,' Carter said. 'Only you, me and Rocketman know that, so keep it quiet.'

'And all this evidence is where?'

'Physical artefacts are in FOC Fettes, including Kelsa's knickers. Other photos, mobile snaps, witness and suspect names, written assessments, facts and conjecture about Alice are documented in ICRS under her case number. You are not to tell DCI McKinlay about the knickers and stocking, otherwise – to quote the bard – "we're all in the shite". All means you too.'

'I don't have access to ICRS,' Flowers said.

He reached across the table, keyed in his credentials and gave her the keyboard. Another thirty minutes passed slowly.

Eventually, Carter needed to hear her assessment. 'What do you think?'

She sat back in her chair. 'It would be easy to jump to conclusions straight away. I may have to do some research, as there's quite a lot around about psychopathic personalities and how they present and what they mean. But I doubt you care about a clinical diagnosis just so I can pigeonhole him between Fred West and Peter Sutcliffe. What you want is a name and address.'

'Yep,' he said, wishing he could strangle the bastard right here and now.

'Don't get your hopes up. J clearly isn't your average bloke getting a wee thrill from an illicit shag now and again. He wants you to suffer from Kelsa's infidelity, but he doesn't want to be discovered too early because that would end his game. He's dangerous. He has trophies, and the reason for keeping trophies is for his personal pleasure and manipulating his victims' relatives. He'll get high by revelling in your pain and angst. You said no crime could be proved, but what about stalking? I'd say the primary objective is to get him off the streets before he does somebody else. He'll likely do it again, whether you ignore him or not.

'But this all started with Alice. Mason is sure I'm linked to J too,' said Carter. 'J is sending the texts, and he's connected to Kelsa, other than being her lover. Look at this text '*but for you to find me you must go where you've never been.*' What does that mean?'

'Is Alice connected to Kelsa in any way?'

'Not that I know of.'

'You've got unknown DNA on Kelsa's knickers. What DNA do you have on Alice's evidence?'

'Nothing. Rocketman thinks he's done this before and has developed procedures.'

'Meaning he's not on Dundee's criminal DNA database. What about England and Wales? Or Northern Ireland?'

'I don't know,' said Carter. 'PNC access hasn't been

requested yet.'

'You sure you don't want to share this news about Kelsa with DCI McKinlay?' Dr Flowers counselled.

'I've broken procedure and could face disciplinary action for using State assets for personal use. Fired without compunction is the most likely outcome. The evidence is categorised under Alice Deacon, and I can't un-categorise it unless he delivers more important items or makes a mistake.'

'So as it stands,' she confirmed, counting on her fingers, 'you have to find him, catch him, make him confess and book him up, all on your own, otherwise eventually, you, me and Rocketman are seriously fucked and will never, ever, work in law enforcement again. Nice one, Leccy.'

'What about this rhyme?' Carter replied to get off the topic of shame and disgrace.

'Classic riddle that means something through your relationship with him, Alice or Kelsa. It could be literal, but most likely it's obscure, designed to make you chase your tail and drive you down rabbit holes. He might even send half a dozen more before it begins to make sense.'

'So we just wait?' Carter thought that was the wrong answer.

'No, we try and work it through, because it might be simpler than it appears. Your notes say that Rocketman said the first line was from "*Fiddler on the Roof*". At first glance, for me anyway, he wants *you* to match the stocking, and the match would be to the stocking you don't have.'

'I've assumed he's got it,' said Carter. 'There was no other solo in Kelsa's drawer.'

'Reasonable assumption,' she replied carefully. 'In which case you can't match it unless he gives it to you. Following this line, he wants you to find it, meaning he once had it, but now he doesn't.'

'It's hidden somewhere?'

'Could be, and the second line might be a clue to the location. "*If I give you my number, will you promise to call me? Wait till my husband's away*".'

'I thought it was a phone number,' said Carter, after ten minutes of kicking other options around and discounting them.

'You have a database full of numbers, could he mean one of those?' Flowers was getting irritated with their lack of progress. 'Or do we go back to the first line and think of another angle?'

'Charli called the twenty-eight phone numbers close enough to Alice in the bar. She spoke to everyone, except a Joe Moore. But following your line, he wants *me* to call him. How would he know it's me calling?'

'Maybe he already has your phone number. He had Kelsa's underwear and possibly a key to your house. What other personal items you don't yet know about? I want to research this, see what comes up.'

'Can you research it here? My user profile has internet access.' Letting Flowers do her own thing unsupervised might take days he didn't have.

'OK,' she said, a bit weary. 'Let's try putting the whole second line into Google, see if there are any references.'

She typed it in and pressed enter.

'Oh my God,' she gasped.

49

Doing the Right Thing

Jacky Dodds was scared and anxious and had been wandering the streets aimlessly for a long time. He couldn't go back home; the cops would arrest him. And his sister would be angry that he'd embarrassed her again. He'd no idea what he'd done this time, but that didn't seem to matter. They always came for him.

The sky darkened. Cold rain fell in big drops. He ignored it, preferring to get soaked than seek shelter. Keeping moving was the only way to stay ahead. He hadn't eaten since Friday when he'd run away from the copper. There was a soup kitchen in the Cowgate, just five minutes away, but they were police informers.

He worried about the woman in the pub. She was no more than a girl, really. She shouldn't have been there. It upset him and made him nervous. Girls teased him because they knew what was wrong about him, and that made it worse. She had stared at him all the time, reading his mind the way girls do. He still had the phone in the pocket of his jacket that wasn't his. When she went to the toilet, he'd had to leave the bar and was to keep the phone on and switch it off once he got home.

The copper had spooked him, asking questions about her. He couldn't remember what he'd said to the copper but knew he hadn't done anything wrong. When Mr Logan came round to his flat, he told him about her. Mr Logan was angry and pushed him about, slapped his face, said he wouldn't be allowed back in the bar until he learned to do the right thing.

Soon after Mr Logan left, while he was still thinking about what 'doing the right thing' meant, Justin turned up. He hated Justin, all the way back to when they were at school together. Justin always picked on him and called him an idiot. Mr Logan could say bad things, but when he calmed down, he'd tell Jacky he was a good man, and he'd look after him. Justin asked him to do things that Mr Logan wanted doing, but Mr Logan never asked him to do those things, so he was confused. Mr Logan said he'd speak to Justin and sort it out, that he'd keep Justin away, but once he did, he'd expect Jacky to stay out of trouble and do what he was told. But Justin didn't stay away.

Justin had said Mr Logan wanted him to do a job, but he didn't want to do any more jobs. Justin punched him in the guts, saying he didn't have balls, that he was a freak, that Mr Logan was angry and would come around to his flat and kill him if he knew what he'd just said. That Mr Logan would shoot him one day when he wasn't expecting it. Mr Logan killed people he didn't like, and the police allowed him to do it.

Without telling Justin or Mr Logan, Jacky had asked his sister how that could be? She said killing people wasn't allowed, he knew that, so why was he asking her about it?

He wanted to know how Mr Logan could shoot someone and not get put in jail, but she said it was complicated and he shouldn't worry about it because it would never happen.

But he did worry about it, and it scared him. He asked Duggie McLean what 'doing the right thing' was. Duggie seemed to know but wouldn't tell, and there was no one else he trusted to ask. When he tried to think about what it might be, he got anxious and tried *not* to think about it. Everyone was after him. They wanted him dead so he wouldn't tell lies about them.

The rain in Newington got heavier, the traffic slowed down, and people on the pavements huddled under umbrellas and tried to find shelter off the street. Cars and buses swished past, splashing water over him as if he wasn't there. Pedestrians didn't look at him, and that made him feel untouchable to ordinary people, just like Batman, his favourite superhero. Cold water dripped off his hair and ran down his face and neck. Batman never felt cold or wet, and today he would fly like Batman. He just had to get up high enough. The Bat-phone in his pocket kept ringing.

He was coming to help him on the previous call to take him off the street before something terrible happened. But that was ten minutes ago when he was walking in circles on the grass around the Queen's Park. Now he passed Surgeons' Hall on South Bridge, heading towards Calton Hill in the New Town. Once there, he could become a superhero. He'd be high enough to fly above the city where nobody could touch him. He'd think straight and work it out. Invisible among the clouds, superheroes always did the right thing.

He took the phone from his pocket and held it to his soaking ear.

'I see you, Jacky.'

Jacky stopped, turned around sharply and looked back the way he'd come. Two people nearly knocked him over, then elbowed past him. 'Fuckwit,' one of them muttered. He couldn't see any people on the street; all he could see was umbrellas.

'Keep walking and listen to me, Jacky. Mr Logan is looking for you. He said he'll kill you now. You understand why, Jacky, don't you?'

'I never touched her. You know that.' He picked up his pace, approaching the Royal Mile, seeing Calton Hill further ahead.

'I'll help you, Jacky. Mr Logan uses you to get what he wants. He's not happy about you speaking to the copper, he knows you'll shop him, that you'll tell them about the girl. He's going to take you out before the copper finds you again. I'll help you escape Jacky, so you'll never have to see him again. Cross the Royal Mile, Jacky, and keep on North Bridge. I'll meet you at the bus stop.'

The rain got heavier, but the walking was more manageable. Jacky felt a burden lift from his shoulders and that made him happy. Cars tooted at each other, buses and lorries argued for space on the busy road, but he kept his eyes on the bus stop. It was just in front of him, a plastic shelter with people crammed inside out of the rain. He got there and squeezed under the canopy, the phone still at his ear.

'Where are you?' said Jacky. 'You're not here.'

'You're on the wrong side of the road, Jacky, do you hear me? I can't wait for you any longer, I have to go now, you've taken too long. You're late, Jacky. I can't protect you from Mr Logan if you can't be trusted to do the right thing. Jacky, you hear me?'

'Don't leave me here.' He began to cry. 'Help me.'

'I'm across the road, in the other bus shelter, Jacky. Do you see it?'

'Aye.'

'Cross now, Jacky – right now. You have to come with me. Mr Logan is getting out of his car. He's coming for you, Jacky. He's got a gun. Quick, across the road. Now.'

Jacky Dodds looked across the street to his right. Twenty metres further down North Bridge, the northbound bus shelter was also crammed full. Cars sped past in both directions. The number 7 bus heading north to Newhaven tooted its horn angrily. It swerved around a Corsa that had stopped suddenly to drop off a passenger.

But he was already halfway across with the phone tight against his ear.

'Bye-bye Jacky baby, don't cha cry no more.'

50

Who the Fuck is Alice?

'What's Elton John got to do with it?' Carter asked.

'It's a song lyric,' Flowers replied. 'From his 1973 double album "*Goodbye Yellow Brick Road*". Side three, track four, "*All the Girls Love Alice*".'

She turned the monitor around so he could see the LCD display. Album art, with a smiling young Elton stepping out of a poster of the yellow brick road, filled half the screen. Underneath was the song title and the lyrics picked out in red: "*If I give you my number / Will you promise to call me? / Wait till my husband's away.*"

'Long before my time.' Carter read through the full lyric. 'I'd never have found that on my own.'

'You're a policeman in the twenty-first century, Leccy. You Google anything you don't know.'

He didn't answer, preferring to consider what this revelation could mean. What did this have to do with Alice's rape? Surely there was more to it?

'So,' Carter voiced his thoughts, hoping Flowers had something to add, 'what's this telling us? That the stocking is linked to Alice, or is there more depth to the lyric? Is there a phone connection? Something on Alice's phone we've missed, perhaps. Should we call all her phone contacts?'

'It's feasible,' said Dr Flowers. 'Have they been followed up?'

'No. I got fixated on the J entry in her diary. Still, there was no obvious J in her contacts. The messages she was receiving weren't from anyone in her contacts list. Still, I've assumed they were from J because they match the format of messages on my phone. Gavin Roy said we'd not find him by email address or phone number, which makes some sense now. Why use a super-sophisticated messaging app but leave your own phone number clear in the contacts?'

'So, J doesn't want you to waste his time chasing ghosts by calling all her numbers,' said Flowers. 'Following that logic would rule out her contacts list.'

'Back to the lyric,' Carter mused. 'If it's not the lyric, but it's the song title, then there's a connection between the stocking and Alice, which means there is a connection between Kelsa and Alice.'

'Make me a match,' Flowers said. 'Are there stockings in Alice's evidence?'

'No, she was wearing tights when she was attacked. We have them.'

'Can you connect any of the evidence you have from Alice with Kelsa?' Dr Flowers asked the question he was thinking. 'Find me a find, catch me a catch.'

Carter was still trying to arrange the pieces of the lyrics in his head.

'He's taunting you.' Dr Flowers said. 'He wants to be caught, but only by you.'

'And how does your psychology training explain that?' he asked, reasonably. 'Why would a rapist want to be caught? He could just hand himself in, save us the bother of chasing him.'

'It's a type of quiz game,' she laid it out. 'But if no one else knows it's a game, how can he prove his prowess at it?'

'Why me?' The question had puzzled him ever since he found the little yellow Jiffy bag lying on his table.

'Kelsa is the obvious answer.' Dr Flowers told him what he suspected but had to hear from her. 'He expects you'll be humiliated and he'll be revelling in your pain. But that won't be enough for him. He's stacking up the levels. Which is why he's entered your house.'

'Is this guy really a psychopath?'

'Be careful, Leccy,' she warned. 'You're stepping over the threshold into the professional minefield of published academic papers on new theories of criminal mental derangement. A holy place where accolades from peers matter more than taking madmen off the streets. We'll never really know until we meet him face to face, but my gut says yes.'

'Why would Kelsa get involved with someone like this?' Carter asked, truly confused.

'Psychopaths are not knuckle-dragging killers; they're engaging, educated and highly sociable people with a low tolerance for the mundane. They're also quick to anger and will tip over easily into extreme violence. She could readily fall for his charms and power.'

'But we were married. Why would she put herself in that position?'

'Maybe it happened before you two were a couple. What do you know about her ex-boyfriends?'

'Jesus Christ, Lisa! Nothing. And you can guess how I feel about that.' *Stupid, for not asking the questions while she was around to account for the answers.*

DI Mason wandered into the detectives' room. Carter invited him into the pod.

'Well,' said Mason, making himself comfortable on a chair in the now very cosy meeting pod. 'Is this our private gang? Cheryl says we're all friends now, so that's good. It's only a matter of time till our rapist realises what he's up against and hands himself in.'

'Don't forget Charli and Ellen,' said Carter. 'They're doing all the hard work.'

'What progress have you made, Sergeant, now that you have to report to me every few hours?'

'Charli is taking a fresh look at the mobile analysis—'

'You're not as smart as you tell us you are, then?'

'There's been a development,' Carter ignored the jibe. 'Charli can call all the contacts on Alice's phone, but I'd rather Ellen did it, so Charli can work with us.'

'What's this development, then?'

'J may have raped another woman, but to be sure we need to look again at the evidence we have for Alice.'

'A new victim?' said Mason. 'Can we interview her?'

'No,' said Carter. 'She's already dead and buried.'

51

Hugo

The hotel was a twenty-minute drive from St Leonard's. They'd all agreed what the next steps should be, which meant decamping the team to FOC Fettes. Rocketman was briefed, he had the resources available to keep the whole event legal. Carter had previously explained to Judith that his time to see Nathaniel meant he might not have much latitude during the working week. She took it in her stride and proposed the Braid Hills Hotel on Comiston Road as a suitable meeting place, south of Morningside and less than a mile from the Dunsmuir residence.

'James always goes to his club after court. I won't see him until later, if at all, so most weeknights I spend on my own. It is not what I imagined the middle-aged years of my life would be. I wasn't prepared for how driven he would become in his desire to sit on the higher benches. He has sacrificed almost everything in pursuit of that goal. He deals with family matters only when he must.'

Carter sat on a comfortable settee in the lounge area of the hotel. At his feet, Nathaniel entertained himself with the secrets of springs on his baby-bouncer-cum-rocker. His eyes were wide open, and bubbles of spit rolled their way down his chin. A waiter arrived and set out some cutlery in front of Carter and popped a small glass of white wine on the table next to Judith.

'I've ordered you some hot food, Lachlan. I know you like beef. You must exist on ready meals and with James being James, inviting you to dinner is out of the question.'

Judith was chatty and filled the void while he munched his way through a delicious medium-rare 10 oz rib-eye steak with hand-cut chips. He ordered a small IPA to wash it down.

'I'm sorry if I was short with you yesterday, Lachlan. Dusting the cobwebs off stressful events has been a chore that our family has never mastered. In the silence of last night, I reminded myself that you are part of our family and entitled to know just what you got yourself into. Of course, in the normal run of life Kelsa would have been here to smooth off the rougher edges so you could digest it in your own time. But she is not, more's the pity.'

Judith wiped a tear from her eye and sat up with purpose. Carter realised that she was willing to drag long-buried secrets into the light for his inspection. Still, as he hadn't prepared the list of questions that detectives are famous for when interviewing mothers-in-law, he started with the only one that came to mind.

'James never really took to me. How did I upset him?'

'He has become myopic as the years have rolled past,' Judith replied in a bitter tone. 'It's hard to believe that he was once the life and soul around these parts in his younger years. The man I now share my life with is not the man I married – but this isn't about me or my choices. When

Kelsa introduced you that first time, James saw only a lowly sergeant in the police force. His prejudices coloured his judgement. He did not consider you as an individual and nor did he contemplate what ambitions in life you might strive for. Conversely, James thought Hugo Mortimer to be the epitome of who he would choose for his daughter to marry. Someone who had a media profile and was feted around town. In truth, Hugo was shallow, grasping and self-absorbed, and cut from the same cloth as James. Maybe that's why they liked one another.'

'I stood in James' court one day, as a witness,' Carter said, 'after I started dating Kelsa. I found him sharp and irritable. My colleagues don't like him either, but that's another story too.'

'James and Kelsa argued over you. He wanted her to stop seeing you. He suggested some names from his chambers and offered to act as a matchmaker. Kelsa was incandescent. It opened up all the old wounds between them.'

'Matchmaker.' The second time he'd heard the word today. But that was a coincidence, surely?

'What did you think of Kelsa when you first met her?' Judith asked. 'I'm intrigued. The Kelsa I knew was inside our four walls, and I never pried into her life outside. Maybe I should have, and maybe I should have been more honest with you too, Lachlan.'

Carter reached down and lifted Nathaniel out of his bouncer and held him in his arms, making eyes and cooing at him. 'She had a big personality,' he said. 'I was drunk on our first meeting, but she approached me. I'll spare you the details. Every time we met, it was like that first time; she gazed at me with an overpowering intensity. I was smitten. It was, for me, love at first sight. I soon learned that she thought the same about me and that shook me to my boots. I mean, I was just an everyday bloke making a living as a policeman. What was it that this incredible woman saw in me?'

'Don't play yourself down, Lachlan,' Judith said. 'You are everything Hugo wasn't. She enchanted you, but she'd learned how to control that side of her personality, to a good degree. When she was much younger, the schoolboys used to stand outside the gate whistling. When she went out, they were like flies. It was her force, but it took her a long time to master it.'

'Lesley Holliday said that Kelsa was devastated when things fell apart with Hugo,' Carter said. 'That it took years for her to ready herself for the world again. That seems a long time. What happened?

'Men don't really understand relationships.' Judith had the hanky ready. 'You seem to just shrug them off and move to the next one as if you're changing a car. When Hugo moved to France, Kelsa expected she would follow. She held onto that dream for quite a while.' The tears slowly trickled down Judith's cheeks, and she wiped them away. 'Even when I knew that Hugo was doing nothing to sustain the relationship, she held on grimly. You have no idea how hard it is for a mother to watch her daughter meltdown and know there's nothing she can do to stop it. Kelsa heard on the radio that Hugo was getting married. He didn't even have the decency to call and warn her before the broadcast. Her confidence shattered into a million little pieces.'

'What happened after that?' Carter felt he had to say something, but he knew there was more to come; a landslide, a tsunami, an earthquake, an asteroid, a void into which she fell. He was only just beginning to understand.

The ping of his phone announced a text message just as Judith dropped her bombshell.

'James got involved.'

52

Under Pressure

'We're looking for a sheer black stocking,' Carter had explained to Rocketman by phone from St Leonard's before he went to meet his mother-in-law for tea.

Protocols had to be observed: requests written, reasons documented, unreasonable questions reasonably answered in the name of governance and compliance and indelible signatures committed to paper, all to get the full inventory of physical artefacts of Alice Deacon's case removed from secure storage and placed in an airtight room deep in the bowels of FOC Fettes.

Carter's head spun after the conversation with Judith in the Braid Hills Hotel. But the ping added some urgency. Nathaniel had fallen asleep in his arms, and he kissed his son's forehead as he tucked him up in his pram without betraying his thoughts to Judith. She began the walk back home, leaving him to ponder the tip of iceberg Kelsa rising up slowly from the depths.

[2019-01-21:1938] I'm the cuckoo in your nest, and you know what cuckoos do. Your only chick has been snuffed out, Carter. Will you die never knowing why she did what she did? J.

He read and re-read the message while standing at the northbound bus stop. Then it vanished from his phone before he could grab it.

'Fuck it. Taxi.'

Just after 8 p.m., he was in the kitchen at FOC Fettes blocking out Mason's Weegie banter. The DI was in a buoyant mood.

'The brass are pushing the boat out to sort the petty emotions of my sergeant, Dr Flowers.' Mason stood on one side of the coffee machine deep underground at Fettes Operations Centre. 'What's his poison?'

'Have you lost anyone close to you, DI Mason?' Dr Flowers countered.

'Aye, but I found them again. It's all a bit touchy-feely, is it not?'

'Why don't you ask him?' said Dr Flowers. 'He's sitting right next to you.'

'In another time and place where the water of life flows, I think I could get him back on track without consulting an incomprehensible textbook that no psychology professional can agree with. Cheryl McKinlay wants regular updates on everyone's progress, so, as part of the team, Lisa, working with me, him, Charli and Ellen, you're accountable too whether you like it or not.'

Waiting in the forensic suite's kitchen, a problem appeared. DCI McKinlay was a senior signatory to the process but was uncontactable. DI Mason stepped in as deputy and signed his nuts off as the accountable officer, should someone grab the items and escape into the night.

Even with signatures, the show wasn't over. Duty scene of crime examiners brought each hermetically sealed bag from the secure storage area, placing them in numbered order on a table in the nominated room. Only then were the detectives allowed to enter: DI Mason, DS Carter, DC Garcia and Dr Flowers noted as interested observers. Rocketman joined them as the DCI-grade officer, and one CSE stood guard at the door. Ellen Podolski had declined the offer of a ringside seat because she was busy with family.

'You're looking for a stocking that matches the one here, in this bag?' said Rocketman, holding it aloft.

'Yes,' Carter confirmed, scanning the thirty clear plastic bags on the table. He had told Rocketman on the phone what they assumed the second lyric meant, and he'd chuckled. 'It had to be Elton John, eh?'

Each bag contained one item: Alice's Samsung phone; white knickers (ripped and soiled); black knickers (Kelsa's, soiled); bra, skirt, top, jacket, handbag, lipstick, compact, brush, nail polish, house keys, tan tights (Alice's, torn); and other items from pockets and hideaways, and, of course, an alien single black stocking (Kelsa's) courtesy of Sergeant Carter (anxious). The silence was palpable, with no one daring to comment on what all could see.

An absence of matching stockings.

'Is this everything?' Carter asked of anyone who might answer. Rocketman looked to his tech guarding the door, who nodded.

'Seems like it, Leccy. We have other physical evidence such as swabs and DNA slides, but this accounts for wearables.'

'Maybe our theory of the rhyme isn't right.' Carter looked to Dr Flowers for reassurance, but she shrugged her shoulders meaninglessly. He was on his own with this one. He thought back to the scene at the bridge where Alice was found. No shoes and the only other item visible her handbag hanging on a tree branch. It hadn't been easy to recover.

'Do we have a copy of the statement Dr Murray gave after she assessed Alice's injuries?'

'Not here, Leccy,' said Mason. 'A transcript will be in ICRS, but the paper will be in storage.'

Rocketman turned to his Tech. 'Can you find it in ICRS, please?'

Tech nodded, 'Yes, sir.'

The written statement signed by Dr Murray appeared on the screen a few minutes later, and Carter found what he was looking for. 'Here it is: "ligature marks around her throat". Do we have a ligature or something that could be used as one?'

Silence in the room confirmed not.

'What about the tights?' Carter asked. 'Were they used to strangle her? Could we tell from cell transfer?'

Tech piped up. 'Sir?' he addressed Rocketman, who nodded.

He read a paragraph displayed on the screen. 'Knickers and tights recovered from the graveyard – DNA and blood of the victim present, no other human organic material found. There's an analysis of the soil and plants, is that important, sir?'

'Not now,' said Rocketman. 'Leccy, tell us.'

'He had the ligature with him. If he kept the ligature after he'd finished with her, how would he get it into evidence so he could text the rhyme? He wouldn't rip off her tights to asphyxiate her, then put them back on. So either he still has the ligature, or it's here somewhere. Her handbag. Is it empty?'

'Yes, sir,' said Tech.

Carter lifted the handbag in its clear cellophane and examined it carefully. The clip was closed for convenience. He opened the zip-lock of the evidence bag and took the handbag out. It was a Louis Vuitton, dark brown with a pink handle and shoulder strap, the distinctive LV logo covering the pure leather, a little scuffed at the corners, not new but serviceable. He opened the clip and looked inside: empty as Tech had said. There was an inner zip on one side, but the pouch was empty. Carter put the bag on the table and stuck his hand inside, running his fingers along the base, trying to lift it away. It was well made and resisted his efforts.

Everyone watched him curiously, like an excruciatingly bad magician trying to pull the non-existent rabbit from the top hat. He turned the bag upside down, with his hand still inside, and pressed the bottom with his other hand.

'Leccy,' said Mason, beginning to feel the atmosphere in the room tighten. 'I don't think it's there. He must still have it.'

'One more minute,' Carter said.

He turned the bag back onto its base and examined the folded edges where the lining met the leather. Otherwise well-stitched, in one place it was slightly loose. He ran his fingers along for six inches or so.

'I feel something inside the lining. But I can't find the opening. Tongs, tweezers – something like that.'

Everyone held their breath. Not wishing to relieve the

pressure that had suddenly taken hold of the air and squeezed, Tech quickly returned with long thin tweezers. Carter slipped them carefully down the inside of the lining and pulled something out.

He dropped a single black stocking onto the table.

53

Tough Love

Between them, Rocketman and his tech processed the stocking. Giving it an inventory tag, Tech packaged it up and took it away. More techs arrived to rescue the remaining items.

Rocketman addressed the assembled group with a tight jaw. 'I apologise.' A twitch appeared at his temple. 'We've uncovered a crucial piece of evidence. I'll open an investigation into how it was missed, but it could be an issue in a trial. The Chief won't be happy. Meantime, we'll get it analysed. I'll let you know the results as soon as possible.' He turned on his heel and walked from the room.

Dr Flowers looked at her watch. 'It's nearly nine. What else can we do tonight?'

On a dreich night in January, the Raeburn bar was virtually empty, so they had their seating choice. A bay window with a decent-sized table and a view of anyone coming in did the job. With put-upon cheer, the waitress delivered two pints of IPA, a large glass of Malbec for Flowers and an equally large glass of Tempranillo for Garcia. Carter voiced the thought he'd spent the last few hours wrangling in his head. 'This formally confirms that J, Alice and Kelsa are connected.'

'You're in this up to your neck, Leccy,' Mason retorted. 'For fuck's sake.'

'Fuck him,' Carter stated. 'Knickers on the table, stockings on the bed, now matched – and likely to have DNA from Alice, Kelsa and an untraceable male. Not a tenuous connection: a fucking mile-long chain of deception.'

'Can't fault your logic there, Leccy,' said Mason. 'But he's planned very far ahead. So much so that Alice's rape wasn't a spontaneous action driven by lustful opportunity.'

Dr Flowers butted in. 'His plan goes way beyond Alice. He planted her handbag in the tree. He's used her as his messenger, and the fact she's suffered life-changing injuries at his hand proves, without doubt, he's psychopathic. He believes he can exert power over anyone. But Alice isn't the only victim here.' Flowers continued to talk to Mason as if making a pitch to keep her job. 'My theory is he was Kelsa's lover sometime in the past.'

'So, maybe he raped Kelsa too,' mused Mason. 'He's got some of her clothing – which I'd say she didn't hand over willingly.'

'We don't know that for sure,' said Carter, necking the remains of his pint. 'There might be a way to find out, but we'd have to agree it's a valid theory and we'd need to set up a case file to log evidence. He might even have murdered her.'

'Steady, Lone Ranger,' said Mason. 'Let's not get carried away. Any "Js" on Kelsa's side of the family?'

'James Dunsmuir,' Carter said. 'While we didn't get on, I

don't see him raping his own daughter out of an abundance of hatred for me.'

The waitress brought another round, in a much less cheerful mood than last time, then Mason picked up where he left off. 'Leccy, I think these relentless text messages and Kelsa's death is blinding your judgement.'

'Don't even think about taking me off this case, Nick,' pleaded Carter, pouring beer down his throat like it was his last. 'Just don't,'

'I think that would be counter-productive, Nick,' said Dr Flowers, with one eye warning Carter to let her make his case. 'He's a bit delicate, but this investigation may be the only thing keeping him going right now. And, when he focuses, he comes up good. Look at tonight: you wanted to close it down, but he kept at it, and he found what we all thought was only a fantasy – now it's evidence.'

'You need to see Kelsa as a victim, Leccy.' Mason didn't give any sign that he agreed with Dr Flowers' assessment. 'She died in childbirth, was it? Unusual these days, I'd say.'

'Anorexia complicated by clinical depression after childbirth,' Dr Flowers clarified.

'And before the birth, before the pregnancy – how was she?'

Carter sat forward with the thousand-yard look on his face, addressing his monologue to Mason. 'We were happy, we'd been married only a few months. For the few months after she knew she was pregnant, she bloomed. Then, in late summer, the shine went out of her. She got progressively more ill. The doctors were concerned about the baby, and they took her into hospital and started force-feeding her. She didn't take it well. That was a difficult time. She held on so she could birth

Nathaniel and love him. I hoped things would change then, that she'd put her energy into living, but – she didn't.'

Charli Garcia reached out and held his arm, tears rolling down her face.

'I am here for you, Leccy, if you need me.'

'It all seems to trace back to that weekend in March when she didn't come home,' he said finally.

'Leccy, it's time you learned to be a cold hard bastard of a copper.' Nick Mason was unsympathetic. 'For her sake if no one else's. J will put *you* in the grave with her at this rate. Lisa can wipe your tears and soothe your brow, but I'll break your fucking head if he walks away while you're contemplating the fluff between your gonads. Now finish that pint because you've got a lot more drinking to do. Service!'

54

Head Fuck

Next morning, the hangover was a belter. After leaving the Raeburn, they had headed into town. Both Dr Flowers and Charli Garcia dropped out quickly. He vaguely remembered seeing them in Hamilton's, but after that, it was mostly a blur. Nick Mason had poured him into a taxi around 1 a.m., almost consigning the evening to history.

When he woke, he knew something else had happened during the night. The reviving hot shower gave him a corner of the jigsaw: he'd texted someone. He dried himself while running through the options. Dr Flowers was his bet, but why? He couldn't remember what he'd said but began to worry it was something inappropriate.

He got dressed in the bedroom but couldn't find his phone; it wasn't on the bedside table, wrapped up in the bedsheets or lying on the floor. He finally found it on the mat at the front door, like it had been posted through his letterbox. He picked it up, unlocked it and started to check his texts when he saw the now-familiar SMS nano-app with its pulsing red dot.

'What's next you conniving bastard?'

[2019-01-22:0416] You're mouthy with the drink, but you're catching up quickly. I'll use your key when I'm thirsty. You'll eat your own words before my vengeance is satisfied. J.

The memory of texting in bed persisted. Slowly the mists rolled back. J had given him a 'reply' button, and they'd texted back and forth exchanging words. Angry words, swear words, words of violence and recrimination, and for him, the vitriol had poured out like a dam bursting. Finally, he was able to answer his tormentor's insults. But even these responses were calculated and drawn from him by J's skill. Carter knew he was being played and had gone along for the ride, full of the confidence that comes from alcohol. But J was preparing the ground and timing of every exchange. His words kept Carter looking backwards, while he set the traps in front for Carter to walk into voluntarily. By the end, all that was visible on his phone was J's damning threat.

J wasn't only stalking him electronically; he was tracking him on the streets. He was on the bus Carter took to work, followed him by taxi, and was sitting in bars watching him drink, listening to his private conversations. He was in the police station looking over his shoulder at the thin file of evidence against him. And at one time, he'd worn Carter's shoes, dressed in his suits and made love every night to his wife.

J was well and truly inside Carter's head, where he'd planned to be all along.

55

Talk is Cheap

Carter caught the 31 bus. Stumbling off it at Rankeillor Street, he walked gingerly to where the road joined St Leonard's Street. He was still over the driving limit and not at his brightest. Tam Watson manned the front desk, as usual.

'Morning, Leccy. You look like the fag end of a great night oot.'

'Always known you were sharp, Tam. Is DI Mason in yet?'

'Nah.'

'DCI McKinlay?'

Tam Watson put his elbows on the desk and motioned for Carter to come closer. 'She's on special leave,' he whispered. 'A week at least, I heard. Someone said she'd crossed swords with Chief Super Goodwin and she's been suspended.' He tapped his nose.

'Right,' said Carter. 'That could be a problem. She's kept the wolf pack at bay. Is Nick taking her place?'

'Nah, someone from the MIT, I think.'

Carter pushed away from the desk and walked tentatively

up the stairs. Police Scotland had been wringing itself out for a long time now, its political masters using oversight of operational matters for their advantage. Allegations of bullying and wrongdoing were rife. It wasn't a surprise that McKinlay had been caught up in shenanigans, not of her liking. Carter just hoped he could stay on the case and wouldn't get swept away in the inevitable purge that was sure to follow.

DC Garcia was waiting for him in the detectives' room.

'Morning, Leccy. This is a wonderful day.'

'You're far too bright, Charli. You should be feeling wabbit like me.'

'What's "wabbit"?' she asked.

'Lethargic, limp, not quite together.'

'Ha,' she nodded. 'These Scottish words are so descriptive.'

He removed and hung up his Crombie, then wandered over to her desk, pulling up a chair beside her. 'What time did you get here this morning?' he asked.

'Six-thirty. When it's quiet, I like it. Look at this.'

Her screen showed a Google map of Dalry with a handful of red dots indicating InterMide mobile phones.

'I eliminated all non-InterMide accounts who spoke with me, and I have here the remainder, including Alice. I reversed time to before she came into the bar. You'd say the accuracy is not reliable. Whatever, she came in the bar together with Joe Moore – whose number rings twice then goes to voicemail. To say he was with her?' she shrugged her shoulders. 'He could have been following her, yet in this time, they are absent from the bar together, then they are present together.'

'Jacky Dodds?' asked Carter.

'Let me check,' she said, racing through the Excel cells at a rate that impressed Carter. Clearly, she was big-data literate. 'He has giffgaff, one of the cheap operators. I'll add him into the play and re-run it.'

They watched the animation as dots moved around. 'Dodds is already in the bar with Nathan Butler when Alice arrives, but both leave about thirty minutes before her.'

'He's walking home with Butler,' Carter said, watching the screen progress. 'We know this, but Dodds said Butler wasn't there. I don't know how Dodds knows someone like Butler and Butler's home is in the opposite direction.'

'Butler's phone was in the bar, but he said it had been stolen.'

'The dots are overlapping,' Carter said.

'So are Alice and Joe Moore.'

'Butler must've been pickpocketed by Dodds, as he said. Either way, Dodds or Butler weren't near Alice during the rape timeframe. That leaves us with Joe Moore. You said you'd not managed to speak to him. Run the play with just him and her.'

She set it up, removed all other phones and ran it. Moore's phone hovered around Alice's phone in the bar, even when the magnification was increased. Once she left the bar, within a few seconds, his phone disappeared.

'What do you think, Leccy?' she asked, with a look that said her mind was certain.

'It's hard to tell if Moore is with her, but he was close before and during the time in the bar. Then no more signal. Dead battery? Maybe. Or he's switched it off deliberately. So, either he's following her, or he's with her, but for me, he's now number one suspect. Track him down, all you can get on him—address, job, birth certificate, wife, driver's licence, passport. You know the score: priority. Bring in Ellen to help if you need to. I want a full profile and picture of him at least, and current whereabouts, as soon as you can. DI Mason will sign off any multi-agency requests.'

Carter stood up and put on the Crombie. 'I'll be out for a wee while, but text me with any news or issues. Have you reviewed the DVDs you took from Alice's flat? What about her laptop?'

'You were to watch the DVDs,' she scolded him. 'It might be important.'

'Damn! I'm sorry, I forgot. Too much on my mind. Ask Ellen to upload them into ICRS when you get a minute? Text me the URL.'

'I am on it,' said DC Garcia, excited that she was now leading a man-hunt. 'One more thing. Another InterMide phone was in the bar that might interest you. It came before Alice and went shortly before her leaving.'

'And who might it belong to?'

'Your Scottish comedian,' Garcia grinned. 'Jimmy Logan.'

56

Legal Difficulties

Forty-five minutes later Carter was sitting uncomfortably in Tommy McGregor's office, staring up at the signed Hibernian football strip hanging on the wall, contemplating Garcia's revelation.

It shouldn't have been surprise-surprise that Logan was in his own bar the night Alice and Moore were there. Back in the pre-history of the investigation, a quid pro quo with Logan would have been out of the question. Now he'd give anything to see Moore sitting across the interview table from him. Almost.

'An interdict is a legal warning to "cease and desist",' McGregor had told Carter by phone the previous day. 'Technically, as the Sheriff has declined to press charges, no sanction can be applied against you, provided you abide by its terms. The interdict will not show on a disclosure search and could stay in effect for years. It's a blunt instrument, but effective nonetheless because the subject can't claim they don't know about it. That's why they're always served by Sheriff's officers.'

'And in my job?' Carter asked, deciding not to complicate matters by telling McGregor he had secret access to Nathaniel. Judith could confess to her husband at any moment.

'I'd consult the Police Scotland HR policy. A detective can't do his job if an interdict prevents him from accessing named property and people. I'd suspect you'll be suspended at least. Might even be accused of bringing the force into disrepute, leading to disciplinary action—'

'I'd be fired,' Carter interrupted, with some resentment.

'Probably.'

'You'd like that, eh? One less copper to hassle your clients.'

There had been an awkward silence on the line after that one landed. But now he was sipping his brief's coffee with no added bitterness. Face to face, McGregor's greeting had been as inscrutable and business-like as ever.

'I'll begin with the easy stuff,' McGregor said as Carter's coffee slipped down smoothly. 'As Nathaniel's father, your rights trump the interdict. On hearing new circumstances, Sheriff Robertson would swat it away.'

'I'd have to appear at court?'

'Not necessary – it's been issued by a Sheriff and has to be annulled by the same Sheriff. But there are two problems we need to discuss first.'

'What might they be?' Carter knew criminal defence lawyers were experts at solving their clients' problems. Even when said client was accosted by police clutching a bloody chib in one hand while standing over his dying victim.

McGregor opened a file on his desk and sat forward on his black leather chair. He removed a single sheet of paper, made sure it faced the right way and slid it across to Carter. 'The scanned copy of Nathaniel's birth certificate, showing it was lodged by Sheriff Dunsmuir a few weeks ago, as he said.'

Carter scanned it. 'OK.'

'The father's entry—'

Carter focused, finding the section. His face turned as white as the paper the certificate was printed on. 'What! Has the old bastard gone mad? I fucking knew it—'

'No visible entry,' McGregor confirmed evenly. 'Technically, that means the father has chosen to remain anonymous. While the interdict is in place, you cannot speak to him about why it is what it is.'

'But you can, can't you? You're my solicitor, you're not bound by the terms of the interdict.'

'Then there's the second problem.'

'What could possibly be worse than this?' Carter said, his mind reeling.

'Technically, you and Kelsa were not married.'

'That can't be,' Carter shook his head in disbelief. 'The marriage registration—'

'Doesn't exist,' McGregor stated with an assurance Carter knew saw him up a dead end. 'No mistake. I've had the registrars of Lothian, West Lothian, Borders and Glasgow searching their systems going back to the date of your Las Vegas trip. Nothing.'

'So—' Carter floundered.

'We can't lift the interdict, for a start,' McGregor said. 'You can't prove you're the father. Normally, when Daddy comes to his senses and seeks to remedy the situation, Mummy can validate his bona fide. The change is made by the registrar, a new certificate is issued, and everyone lives happily ever after. With a dead and buried wife, a DNA test is your only option, and you don't need her family's permission because there is *some* good news.'

Carter had his elbows on his knees, and his hands covering his ears.

'The pictures from Las Vegas prove a ceremony took place and the foreign licence, the witnesses, signatures and all, count as much in Scotland. But without her testimony to validate all of it, including Nathaniel, you're facing a devil of a job'.

McGregor proceeded to the coup de grâce, his poker face giving Carter no quarter.

'Contesting her last wishes will be difficult, take years of court time and require significant upfront funding with no guarantee of success.'

Carter gripped the chair like he'd just been electrocuted.

57

High Octane Strategy

Once outside McGregor's practice in Great Junction Street, Carter hung about, looking for something substantial to grasp. No straws flew past on the wind. Everything he'd thought was certain about his married life had just been shredded by McGregor's mastery of legal procedure. Everyone knew about Kelsa: his grandparents, his mates, his work colleagues. He wore two wedding rings, for fuck's sake. Could it get any worse?

The marriage issue was more common than might be imagined, McGregor had explained. Unfortunately, Carter couldn't fix his problems by legally marrying his legally dead girlfriend again. As that was water under the bridge, a DNA test was the only way to prove paternity. DI Mason's comment in the Raeburn came back to haunt him. Was his judgement being blinded by Kelsa's death? And these revelations about Nathaniel's birth certificate? Could he really go back to the station and carry on investigating as if nothing had changed? Last week, if McGregor had told him what he'd told him today, he'd have said no. Probably.

But Kelsa's dying wish was now entangled in Alice's rape. Sitting at home swearing into the air at his lying, cheating, bitch of a decaying maybe-wife would hardly equip him to start a bright and bubbling future afresh. He turned right at the Great Junction Street crossroads, trudging up Leith Walk towards Princes Street like a condemned man eyeing the approaching gallows. It was warmer today, and he felt sticky underneath his dark Crombie coat, but he needed the air as well as the time to cajole his ducks into a row – so he could shoot them.

Under the weight of his thoughts, he'd been wandering for ten minutes when he glimpsed a dark-haired and well-dressed woman weaving her way through the throng of pedestrians. She was going his way, twenty metres ahead. Something about the way she walked gripped his focus. The heels she wore orchestrated a flounce in her step that swayed through her hips up to her shoulders. She turned her head briefly, and he caught her profile. A slim nose and scarlet lips. It was— but couldn't be. The coat was hanging in her bedroom wardrobe. He broke into a run.

'Kelsa—'

Suddenly, all Edinburgh bore down on him. Couples walking on the pavement holding hands, teenagers and families pushing buggies, singles walking dogs, the injured limping on crutches, cyclists, buskers, old ladies stopping for a gossip, window shoppers, travellers hailing taxis, getting off buses, getting on buses. Everyone was in his way. He lost sight of her. Where was she? He jumped into the road. A bus honked, its slipstream nearly sucking him in. A taxi followed the bus, flashing its lights at him in warning.

It *was* her. He pushed his way frantically onto the pavement again, barging people over. Had she gone into a shop, or turned up a vennel? He looked up and down the street. He climbed onto a bin to survey the big picture but could see no sign of her. He jumped down. A gap in the traffic allowed him to run into the road again and he scanned up and down Leith Walk's wide thoroughfare, looking anxiously across the street, gazing back to where he had come from. Another taxi swerved around him, the cabbie screaming an obscenity through the open window. Wearily, he trudged back onto the pavement and slumped in the door of a kebab shop, holding his head in his hands.

She was gone.

It's time you learned to be a cold, hard bastard of a copper, he heard DI Mason admonish him.

Half an hour later, at the top of Leith Street, feeling a sticky sweat and standing under the statue of Wellington-on-horse, he'd reconnected with reality as others saw it.

The ghost of his dead wife was an apparition only visible to him. He'd also decided to tell no one about these new legal predicaments around his family, including his employer. If confronted with Police Scotland's HR gunslingers' allegations, a promising career would be dead and buried. But if he willingly confessed, throwing himself on their mercy, he'd still bite the bullet.

It was a high-octane strategy, but what else could he do?

His phone rang.

'Where are you, Sergeant Carter?' DCI McKinlay asked suspiciously.

'I'm on my way to examine new evidence in Alice's case,' said Carter, giving nothing away.

'I'm on Rankeillor Street. Call me when you're done.'

He made his way to St Andrew Square, where he caught a westbound tram. Twenty-five minutes later he alighted at Jenner's Depository on Balgreen Road and entered the self-storage centre.

When she'd returned from her missing weekend, Kelsa had stripped off the clothes she wore and soaked herself in a hot bath for hours. Occasionally he heard her crying. Although he'd suppressed his instincts at her insistence, he dealt with her clothes, because she couldn't. He packed them the way he'd been trained and deposited them in their storage unit, out of sight, but always in mind.

He carefully examined them now, photographing each garment with his phone. It was still evident: she would never have willingly worn clothes like these – second-hand with faded high-street labels. So where did she get them? What happened to the clothes she wore on the Friday night? His unspoken fear at the time was a sexual assault, but for her the subject had been closed. He repacked and reset the unit and returned to the tram stop.

The clothes had held a message for him and him alone, one he had been unable to understand at the time because of his highly emotional state. She'd always said reading him was easy. So much of what she communicated was non-verbal. But he had learned that far too late.

Somehow, in those months leading up to Nathaniel's birth, Kelsa made Carter believe her love for him was more vital than ever – even as her mind surrendered her body to the inevitable. Death had been her goal. Now Carter knew she'd prepared for its coming religiously, putting secret arrangements in place for Nathaniel's future and for his future too, all achieved with the help of lawyers. It was feasible to explain to Dunsmuir why no entry in the father's section was appropriate for Nathaniel's birth certificate.

He stared at the pictures on his phone and kept coming to the same conclusion. He sat back and imagined himself in her shoes that night, wearing degrading clothes and crying her eyes out when she was singularly alone in a decrepit hotel room or sterile hospital cubicle. Wondering how to deal with the life-changing fallout of a brutal assault.

She had no future. Her dignity had been wrenched from her violently. She wore no knickers and no stockings.

J had taken those things as trophies.

Along with her favourite leopard-print heels.

58

Goalkeeping in the Playground

At Rankeillor Street, Carter flicked through his phone. McKinlay's number was in his contacts, but he hesitated before letting her know he was here. Their last real conversation had been direct. *'End of the week, Sergeant Carter. Bring me a solid case, or you're back on your couch.'*

It wasn't unknown for senior officers to be removed from post overnight in the current climate, leaving the survivors nervous of a Stalinist HR purge. Rumours of a fresh sacrifice for the Chief Constable's role were rife. Secretly, Carter didn't care who they chained up in the big chair as long as stability followed. Putting geopolitics aside, he hadn't made as much progress as he's hoped. Still a few days before McKinlay's weekend deadline though.

'Ma'am,' he said when DCI McKinlay answered.

'I'm around the corner.'

What was this all about? Clandestine meetings between officers? Was there a schism forming in St Leonard's? If so, which faction had decided they wanted him onside? It reminded him of football in the playground, where he was always at the coo's tail. The boys would line up, and captains would make their choices, the best chosen first. He was a breed apart, the goalkeeper nominated to take the blame for the losing side.

A blue BMW pulled up on the street. The door opened, he got in, and she drove off, not even saying hello. She drove towards the Commonwealth Pool, swinging left at the traffic lights into Holyrood Park. Two minutes later she parked at Holyrood Palace.

Definitely goalkeeper-signing talks.

It was cold outside, and she left the engine running.

'Why were you hounding Jacky?'

'I wasn't—'

'I told you he had nothin' to do with Alice Deacon.'

'I know that now, but—'

'Has Logan been in touch since?'

He hesitated, remembering the conversation in Logan's Mercedes. The phone in *his* pocket now felt like he'd been caught in possession and was about to let another one in.

'Tell me what was said.'

'About what, ma'am?'

'Don't fuck with me Carter,' she raised her voice. 'You were in his Merc.'

'How do you know?'

'He told me.'

So there it was—her confession.

'Said he'd given you a lift. Said Jacky was prime suspect. Said he'd warned you to leave Jacky be. Is that how it went down, Sergeant Carter?'

'He said you and him had an *"understanding"*.'

'He's a manipulative cunt,' she grimaced wryly. 'I told you to report any contact to DI Mason, but you knew better, eh? You were in Cramond with Lenny Yule. Stop fucking me about.'

Carter had no idea who was the bad guy was here, but he definitely felt like he'd conceded too many.

'Yule's a chemist,' she told him. 'He'd worked for McCalman, on and off, until we put McCalman away. Logan's been after his skills ever since. You forgot that all informer contact has to be reported to a senior officer in E Division. MacIntosh followed protocol. You didn't follow my order. Did Logan see you with him?'

'I don't think so. Yule went off towards Granton, on the promenade. Logan stopped me at the top of Cramond Glebe ten minutes later.'

McKinlay went silent, staring out the windscreen at Arthur's Seat rising steeply above them.

'Can I trust you, Leccy?' she asked calmly. 'Do I have your loyalty?'

His keeper's gloves still fitted. 'Of course, ma'am.'

'Logan's on the warpath. He's got connections on the High Street and at Holyrood. There's a train of thought saying he's got a finger in the pie of nasty stuff goin' on in the Police Authority. If it's true, it makes him a very dangerous man. He'll get young guns like you to compromise yourself for information, so he can chuck a carcass to the wolves when he needs out. Know what I'm saying?'

'Maybe this will clear your mind, ma'am,' Carter reached into his pocket and offered up the ball.

They sat in silence while the recording was played back.

'I have a question,' Carter asked afterwards. 'About your

relationship.'

Cheryl McKinlay sighed, letting the leather car seat take the strain of her long experience. 'We go back, Logan and me – Jacky too. We were all at school in the seventies, different years though. Do you know why I was so sure Jacky didn't rape the woman?'

'Duggie McLean told me.'

Her eyes softened, then the tears flowed. 'You get about, Leccy. You're a good copper, but you're too trusting. Duggie was in our gang. After the incident, Jacky was in the hospital for months, and when he got out, he was different. The police were blamed for lettin' it happen, so they roughed up Dalby's crew and charged them. Dalby got five years, and the others got three each. Dalby got chibbed in Saughton, and the prison hospital doggedly followed procedure till he died of blood loss. Logan wasn't much more than a gadge then, but he knew that confronting the police was a loser's charter. He took over Dalby's crew and built them up to what they are today. Justin Greig – the cunt that strangled you in Logan's car – was the one that held Jacky down.'

She wiped the tears away and took a deep breath while Carter waited, knowing there was more to come. 'Logan looked after Jacky. I'll give him that. Whether he felt sorry for him or was lookin' for leverage over me, I don't know, but he kept him close. Jacky trusted him.'

McKinlay went quiet, staring out of the car but not seeing anything. Carter said nothing while she built herself up to speaking again.

'What's on the recordin' is Logan trying to convince you I'm bent because he had Jacky onside.' Her voice broke. 'I'm sure Jacky told him what happened in the Reverend. But we can't bring Jacky in now, because he's dead.'

'What?' Carter was shocked. 'How?'

'He was run over by a bus on North Bridge yesterday,' Cheryl McKinlay's grief overflowed. 'And I think you, Sergeant Carter, drove him to suicide.'

Carter looked out the window of the BMW, staring across the car park. It had started to rain, big drops exploding on the windscreen like artillery shells without being wiped away.

'You're not suspended,' Carter said with insight. 'You're bereaved. Jacky was your brother.'

59

Helplessness

McKinlay dropped Carter off at Rankeillor Street, close enough to walk to St Leonard's station, but far enough away that the gossips wouldn't have wares to peddle.

'I'm sorry I said you drove him to suicide,' she apologised, 'but this is personal Leccy. After he ran away from you, did you ever catch up with him again? Or speak to him on the phone?'

'No ma'am, his phone rang out.'

'Jacky was easily led, but I know there must have been more to it than that. I just know Justin Greig's fingerprints are on it, the slimy bastard.'

The BMW sped off, leaving Carter wondering. He was still wondering when he passed the desk with a catch-you-later wave to Tam Watson, so he wouldn't be tempted to engage in conversation. He went straight to Charli Garcia in the detectives' room, pulling up a chair next to her.

'You've spoken with the boss, yes?' she said when he sat down.

'You two in the thick of it?' Carter asked.

'A family member died unexpectedly,' Charli said. 'She wouldn't speak more. Ellen told me a man killed by a bus on North Bridge was related to her.'

'It was Jacky Dodds. I tried to talk with him a few days ago, but he got upset and ran off. Call Ellen and ask if we can have read-access to the case notes for the accident.'

A few minutes later, Garcia brought up notes from ICRS and read out the main points.

'Early evening, dark, wet and cold. A car cut in front of the bus to drop off a passenger. The driver braked to avoid a crash. He didn't see Dodds, was angry at the Corsa driver. Corsa driver didn't see Jacky at all. The CSE said Dodds died instantly under the front wheels.'

Carter filled in the blanks. 'McKinlay thought I'd driven him to suicide.'

'Is she in deep sorrow?' Garcia asked.

'I was just shaking the tree, to see what fell out,' Carter said ruefully. 'Maybe I shook it too hard. His clothes will be at the mortuary in Cowgate, right? Did he have a phone on him?'

Garcia consulted the ICRS notes. 'No.'

'Eye-witness statements from passengers on the bus, or those in the shelter?'

'In the shelter, three. Then bus driver and the Corsa driver,' said Garcia. 'Ellen read the statements. They are consistent. One *hombre*, to be tracked, went quickly into the road, and helped pull him out of the way. The driver came out of the bus, Dodds was underneath the wheel. *Muerto*. The driver, he will be in counselling for a long time.'

'CSE is saying the driver's side,' Carter pondered again at

ICRS. 'He came from the other side of the road.'

'Is this important?' Garcia asked.

'The Samaritan in the north-side shelter?'

'What are your thoughts, Leccy?'

'A key witness in our case has gone under a bus. Coincidence?'

'No,' Garcia voiced his thoughts.

'Call Ellen.' Carter stood up. 'We're taking Jacky's case. I'm going to speak to DI Mason.'

Twenty minutes later DI Mason had squared away the internal priorities and secured a marked car with a uniformed driver. Mason in the passenger seat; Carter, Garcia and Ellen Podolski in the back. They drove through the netherworld of Cowgate to examine Jacky Dodds' clothing at the mortuary, then signed out his house keys.

Mason parked the car in Watson Crescent. The flat was on the second storey of four and opened quickly. A long hallway had two bedrooms and a bathroom running off it, and at the end, a kitchen on one side and the lounge on the other.

'I'll take the main bed,' said Mason. 'Leccy, you take the lounge. Ellen, the bathroom. Charli, the other bedroom.'

The lounge was a mess of newspapers and DVDs, mainly kids' programmes, but Batman and the Marvel superheroes were prominent. Dirty plates were strewn across the floor. There was a two-bar electric fire in the fireplace, and opposite that a window looked onto Watson Crescent. A decrepit chair faced an old-style cathode-ray TV, the remote sitting on the arm, and a sofa offered evidence someone had sat there, an imprint on the cushion. Not Cheryl McKinlay, he thought; she would have cleaned up. Next to the chair, covering the floor, were sheaves of A4 copy paper, with crude schoolboy drawings in blue pen.

'This bedroom is made up. No sign of use.' Garcia came into the lounge and stopped at the door. She surveyed the sitting room. 'What a fucking mess.'

'Check the kitchen, will you,' Carter asked.

'What are we looking for?' Garcia responded.

'A phone, a computer. I don't know. Connections to Jimmy Logan, Justin Greig or Alice Deacon. Maybe even Nate Butler.'

Nick Mason came through. 'His bedroom looks like the lounge too.' He saw the pile of A4 sheets on the floor. 'There are more drawings and writings next door. I think he was scared of Justin Greig.'

Carter and Mason went into the bedroom, where Mason showed Carter sheet after sheet of confusing drawings. Of women screaming, crying, covering their eyes, ears and mouth. Names Carter knew and names he did not: *Mr Logan, Mr Butler, Alec, Eddie, Joe, Ting, Ming, Slicer, Cheryl, Duggie*. More drawings of men, some crossed out, like crude attempts to erase them—a man holding a knife bigger than him. Rev Booth featured prominently. Other men and women, with no names, bolts in their heads, one with a big blade cleaving his head in two. *Justin, Justin, Justin, Justin*. More stick men seemingly punching themselves in the head, some cutting themselves between the legs. And more and yet more and *Justin, Justin, Justin* scored out. A woman hanging from a noose.

'Justin Greig had it in for him,' said Carter. 'Should I read anything into these other known names? Logan gets a "*mister*", so does Butler. I think this could be a job for Lisa. Nick, I'd get the CSEs in here as soon as possible.'

'This is mental,' Mason agreed. 'We'll have to keep Cheryl

away from here.'

Podolski and Garcia joined them.

'The bathroom is clean,' said Podolski. 'This place looks like my teenage son's bedroom.'

'The *Cucina* has the same mess as here,' Charli said. 'There is hard blood on a big knife and on the counter. A phone is charging. It is open, and it's from giffgaff.'

'That's Jacky's phone,' said Carter. 'But where's the phone he stole from Nate Butler?'

60

Greetings

'The guy who tried to save Jacky Dodds,' Carter said to DC Garcia once they were back at the station. 'He's the key, he must've seen it all unfolding in front of him. I've got a hunch who he is and why he was there. Contact the scenes of crime manager at Fettes. They should have downloaded the bus video to ICRS. When the CSEs have finished here tell them to send copies of all of Jacky's writing to Dr Flowers, along with copies of the drawings.'

'I am on it,' she said.

'Keep Ellen involved, share the workload. How's Joe Moore's profile coming along?'

'No driving licence, a home in London, bank account, cards, bills, certificate of birth, not married—'

'Has he got a passport? It would have a photo.'

'I'll check the Passport Agency. Metropolitan officers are coming to the house today. DI Mason authorised requests for the PNC and Home Office National DNA Database. If he's been a criminal, we'll know soon.'

'Does he have a job? His bank will give us a source of funds.'

Satisfied that the plates were spinning, Carter headed for the door. 'I have to talk to DI Mason, and there's something else I need to do.'

An hour later, he unlocked the door of his home. A red envelope was lying on the floor, stamped and posted locally. It was a card.

The picture on the front was of a walker at the top of a hill gazing at the view. 'Arthur's Seat, Edinburgh' was the caption. Inside was a handwritten list of names.

John Stape, Lowell Baldwin, Joe Moore, Ben Weston, Tom Waterhouse, The Narrator

Underneath the names, J was prominent, but it was *'Joe Moore'* that caught his attention. His heart skipped a beat. He'd received another card like this. He went into the sitting room and rummaged through the cards on the mantle and side tables. Its black dahlia motif stood out from the others. He compared the names in the two cards. They didn't match, but the signature did.

The letter J itself was large, like a calligraphic signature, with sweeping serifs rendered in black ink. What he'd first assumed was a card from Kelsa's colleagues was something else entirely. Had he missed a vital clue?

Suddenly Carter slumped on the sofa. He was exhausted. This simple-but-complex greeting card had diverted him from his purpose in coming home. He should he get the laptop out and do what he came here to do. He relaxed for a few moments, closed his eyes and tried to reboot his mind.

Ten minutes later, he woke with a start and got himself

together. In the garage, he opened the safe, removed Kelsa's MacBook, her iPhone, the cables and the envelope her father had given him, with its instruction to '*Open only when you understand*'.

One last compare of the handwriting confirmed that, no, it definitely wasn't Kelsa who had sent the cards. But did he now 'understand', as her words written on the envelope demanded? He understood that there was more to her death than met the eye. He understood that she had made arrangements to keep their son safe. She had left clues for him that suggested she had been assaulted that weekend in March, and, of more importance now, his understanding of this letter's content had improved.

He extracted the sheet of paper. The number was the code to unlock her phone. The other clues required more thought.

8 2 6 4 2 8 9 5
Licence to thrill, M
Zip up a dress, Joe

He lifted her iPhone and pressed the power button: discharged. He tried the MacBook: as dead as a cunning wife. He plugged them in to charge.

His own laptop was charged and ready for that something else he promised he'd do. He logged into his laptop, opened ICRS and sat down to find the video files Ellen Podolski had uploaded from the DVDs in Alice's flat.

He scanned a list of more than a hundred files, all with company names and dates. Alice had been a busy girl. He spotted a known company name: *InterMide*, the European telecoms giant, and the prominent network in the phone analysis. He opened the first file. It was a corporate video of an InterMide product launch, with speakers and an audience sitting in rows in a corporate theatre. Some others stood at the sides. The commentary was boring and the camera angles changed regularly to keep viewers from falling asleep. After five minutes, he knew he didn't have time for all this. There were ninety-nine more videos to view.

Before he stopped the video, a woman in a pale blue dress walked into the shot and back out again. He shot forwards like he'd been stabbed up the arse. Scrubbing the video backwards, he replayed it again and again. He couldn't see her face, but the dress was hanging upstairs. The timecode read May 2016 – nearly a year before they had met. He scrubbed forwards at four times the speed until the end. She wasn't presenting, but she was moving around the edge of the shots, occasionally stopping, engaging with colleagues. He closed the file.

There were three other InterMide files, the newest dated October 2018. He played that video sitting on the edge of his seat, watching it on fast-forward. With no sign of her, he breathed a sigh of relief and switched out of ICRS.

Alice and Kelsa. Did they know each other? What about J?

'Where are you?' he asked as soon as Dr Flowers picked up.

'I'm fine, thanks for asking.'

'I've got jobs for you while you're waiting for the papers from Jacky Dodds' flat.'

'What papers?'

'Dodds is dead. I think I know why and who killed him. Papers in his flat contain scribbles and names. I've asked Charli to make copies, so you can take a look, see if you can make sense of them. But before that, I want you to look at some other stuff I'll bring over to you. I want your professional opinion.'

'What stuff?'

'Taunts, maybe—'

'He's contacted you again?'

'Rocketman said that if I didn't react, his taunts would get extreme. He's resorted to sending me greeting cards.'

61

Listening Devices

Prestonfield House claimed to be the most fabulous, most baroque, most luxurious hotel in Edinburgh. As Carter drove down the long drive with bare trees lining either side, none of its lavishness peeked through the branches. Its whitewashed façade gave no hint of its reputed glamour. Dr Flowers waited on the steps of the entrance. He parked the Smart car and joined her.

'Close your eyes,' she said. 'Otherwise, the opulence in here will severely overload your working-class sensitivity. Just follow me, it's quiet this evening.'

The flocked paper of rich maroon-on-gold set the tone in the Yellow Room. A sizeable ornate fireplace with real logs burning provided additional ambience, not that it was needed. They sat in a corner away from the door, on a brown leather Chesterfield sofa with a marble coffee table in front of them.

Carter played his cards, describing the state of Jacky's flat to Flowers, what writings the papers contained, before filling her in on Cheryl McKinlay's relationship with Dodds, his teenage castration and his association with Jimmy Logan.

'I've just looked at some of Alice's professional work for InterMide,' Carter went on as his eyes adjusted to the low lighting. 'Marketing and video production. Proving she might have known Kelsa. They were both freelancers, and both had InterMide phones. The company connection could be what binds them.'

'Can you prove it?'

'Not yet. But there's more.' Carter laid his conclusions on the table. 'Jacky Dodds knew who Alice was with at the Reverend, and when J discovered I was looking for Dodds, Jacky had to go.'

'And these greeting cards?' Flowers asked him, reading the hand-written names. 'You think they're a message, not a list of colleagues?'

'J knows things I don't know. Suppose it's an initial of a name. In that case, it could be Joe Moore, Jimmy Logan, Justin Greig . . . or it could be someone else entirely, with or without an InterMide mobile account.'

'Why would any of *them* send you cards like this?'

'Taunting. Maybe a list of future victims, I don't know.'

'And you think there are connections between all the names on the cards?'

'If it's not obvious, try Googling them,' Carter said mischievously. 'As a starter for ten, Moore's name is on the most recent card. He's our number one suspect, and he has an InterMide phone.'

'And what are you going to do while I try and work this out?'

'Flush out some rabbits.'

The Reverend bar on Dalry Road was Jimmy Logan's preference for quiet business meetings during the week. This Tuesday night, the regulars were in place for the Scottish Professional Football League post-winter restart. Pie-and-pint deals and a few pence off drams offered encouragement. It was any pub in an unfashionable part of town tourists never saw.

Just after 8 p.m., a bright young couple entered and ambled up to the bar. They glanced around. She spotted a free table. Her man went to the bar, scanning the taps as he approached.

'What'll it be?' Jake Malone asked.

'Pint of Deuchars and a vodka coke. Absolut, if you have it.'

'Seven-fifty,' said Jake, serving the drinks. 'Do I know you?'

'Fraser Thomson. That's my wife, Debbie.' Debbie waved. 'Want to see my ID?'

Jake shook his head, dispensed change of a tenner and began serving other customers.

Fraser sat beside his wife, watching the TV. Rangers at home to Dundee. He kept one eye on the game and the other on the punters. She took her phone out and fiddled with it. The bar gradually got busier, and men moved about, getting animated as the game ebbed and flowed, but nobody bothered them. At half-time, they finished their drinks and left. 'Bye,' Fraser called towards Jake.

Carter, Garcia and Nick Mason sat in their unmarked Astra in the Lidl car park and watched the couple appear on the street. They turned down a side lane, disappearing from view. Fifty metres away from the Astra, a dark-coloured Mercedes four-by-four was parked. After a few minutes, the radio crackled, and Fraser Thomson gave them a sitrep of the pub.

'The snug was closed, but lit. Two men outside the snug.

Tattoos, one with a snake running up his neck.' Carter and Mason looked at each other. 'Also, two blokes strategically placed at the entrance. Malone is behind the bar.'

'Did they snap you?' Carter asked.

'Fairly sure they did when we left. There was a group at the bar shouting, and I saw some phones come out. There's no obvious CCTV.'

'Jimmy won't like it on home turf,' Mason said. 'Too risky for his private meetings.' He switched the Airwave radio to broadcast. 'Ready? Uniforms in two minutes from . . . now.'

The trio got out of the car. One minute later, they entered the pub and stood just inside the doors. Jake Malone spotted them.

'Mr Mason. You're becoming a regular.'

Carter turned to the two doormen who'd started to rise from their seats. 'Sit down, lads, nothing to get excited about.'

Garcia sauntered toward the snug, where she could be seen but wouldn't be a threat. Everyone was watching the detectives. Most knew the result of the fight the week before and weren't keen for a replay. The group of five men that Fraser thought had snapped pictures began to split up and move away from each other.

The door from the street opened, letting in two uniforms, followed by more. At the back of the bar, where the kitchen and toilets were, four PCs appeared. The Dobermen stood up. One rapped on the glass of the snug door. Carter ambled towards it, keeping his distance from Garcia. Three PCs trailed him.

The snug door opened; Justin Greig's head appeared. 'What?' he asked.

Carter was only feet away. 'Step out please, Mr Greig. I'm Detective Sergeant Carter, you know me.' Carter closed the snug door behind Greig and held up his identification card. 'We're going to take you into the kitchen for a few moments. Stay calm.'

The cops guided Greig through the narrow passageway. He sneered but said nothing. The cook wasn't sure what to do so kept back. Other uniforms guarded the exit door leading from the kitchen to an open back green and a close.

Carter told Greig to sit on a chair.

'What's this about, copper? I haven't done nothin'.'

Carter ignored him and turned away while the uniforms held Greig tight.

In the bar, the snug door was open again. Carter joined Nick Mason who sat inside, opposite Jimmy Logan. Logan's face was thunderous. Two other men in the snug wearing business suits looked agitated.

'Mr Logan, we'd like to ask you questions about the rape and attempted murder of Alice Deacon,' Mason said calmly. 'Also, we have questions about Jacky Dodds' death, a man you knew well. You are not being charged at this time but are helping us with enquiries. I'm happy to ask my questions in here, for the two gentlemen to listen to and digest at their leisure. However, you might find our interview rooms at St Leonard's more accommodating.'

Logan scowled and stood up. 'I'm calling my lawyer, Mason.'

'Good. I promise not to listen.'

62

Brief Relationship

Logan and Greig travelled in separate vans on the journey to St Leonard's. Once inside the station were deposited in individual interview rooms. The two businessmen from the snug received similar treatment. Tam Watson took their particulars, then everyone was left alone to contemplate past sins while drinking police tea.

Carter and Mason debriefed the uniformed PCs and stood them down: job done and no casualties. While Mason updated DCI McKinlay by phone, Carter got the lowdown from Tam Watson on the unwanted catch.

'Murray McCormack, Labour MSP at Holyrood. Has a private home in Grange. His pal is Willie Taylor, a weel-kent face around the Labour trenches in the City Chambers on the High Street. Lives in a council house in Trinity.'

'Has transport been arranged to take them home?' Carter asked.

'Yes.'

'I heard the car has a puncture. Make sure it's sorted, Tam.'

'Sure, Leccy. Sure,' Tam Watson smiled. 'I'm on it.

Interview Six and Seven.'

In Interview Six, Murray McCormack sat on a hard chair with his head in his hands. He was forty-one but looked older. From the observation room, Carter wondered what was weighing him down. He entered Interview Six and McCormack instantly switched to outrage mode.

'How dare you detain me here. I demand to go home.'

'Transport is being arranged,' Carter informed him. 'We weren't expecting visitors – you are not part of our enquiry, sir.' He sat down opposite McCormack. 'However, if you can establish your relationship with Mr Logan and why you were in the bar, it will speed things up.'

'I was having a drink with one of my constituents. That's not a crime, is it?'

'How well do you know Mr Logan?'

'As a constituent. He asks for my help from time to time.'

'Did you give him the benefit of your advice on Sunday, thirteenth of January, sir?'

McCormack's eyes bored into Carter's. 'I'm not sure, Sergeant. I'd have to check my diary.'

'Mr Logan is not easily forgotten, I'd think.'

'Quite,' said McCormack.

'If you could confirm tonight, sir.' Carter stood up, letting the chair scrape on the hard floor. 'In the meantime, I'd appreciate it if you would not share the information I've asked for with anyone else. I'll check when we'll have a car ready for you.' Carter gave McCormack his card, left the room and closed the door.

He repeated the exercise with Councillor Taylor in Interview Seven, then walked back into Tam Watson's den. 'That puncture sorted Tam?'

'Aye.'

'Take them home. Tell the constables to warn them not to speak to anyone, including each other, until they've given me the information I've asked for.'

Thirty minutes later, Carter and Mason were sitting drinking a mild dose of sheep's pish with Garcia when Tam Watson buzzed them. 'The briefs are ready for the interviews, gentlemen. Interview Four and Five. What's the tag team?'

'I'll take Logan,' said Mason. 'Leccy will take Greig.'

As they walked down the stairs to the interview rooms, Carter asked DC Garcia, 'Any update on the witness to Dodds' accident?'

'No,' she said. 'Maybe tomorrow.'

'Justin Greig helped castrate Dodds when he was in his teens. Dodds was scared of him, so I'm going to lean in hard. Take my cues, but mostly just listen. If anything significant occurs to you, we can take a break.'

Walking into the interview room, Carter immediately locked eyes with Tommy McGregor sitting beside Justin Greig.

Garcia sat down, but Carter pulled her arm. 'This interview can't proceed.'

Carter returned to the observation room while Garcia interrupted Mason.

'Conflict of interest,' Carter said once Mason came back in the room.

'Tommy McGregor is Justin Greig's solicitor. McGregor is also handling a personal case for me.'

Mason nodded to Garcia. 'Get us another coffee, Charli. This is going to be a long night.' After she'd gone, Mason held Carter in a firm stare. 'Jesus Christ, Leccy, why didn't you tell me?'

Carter gazed at his senior officer in defiance, but he knew he wouldn't get away with a right to silence on this point. 'Everybody thinks I'm caring for Nathaniel, but I'm not. It's a long story, a private one, and one I won't go into right now. I have to step back from questioning Greig, or McGregor will need to recuse himself. I'm betting he won't.'

'Let's get both briefs in another room, see what we can do,' Mason sighed.

'Mitch is my partner,' said McGregor, once they'd all sat down. 'There's just two of us. We have paralegals but no one else with court experience. We've represented Mr Logan in business deals, and I can tell you he will not agree to us stepping back.'

'Have you asked him?' said Mason.

'What do you think?' said McGregor with a tight smile. 'I wasn't aware Police Scotland had so few detectives they couldn't allocate another. You could release my clients, and we sort it out tomorrow?'

Mason grimaced, the muscles in his jaw betraying his anger. 'Back in,' he said to the two lawyers. 'I'll fix it.'

Mason ran his fingers through his hair once they were alone again. 'We go with the plan. Garcia replaces you. The duty DC will handle the equipment. I'll take Logan on his own. He's not being charged with anything, but we'll video it as usual.'

Mason left as Charli Garcia arrived with coffee. Carter sipped the full-strength sheep's pish from his cup. Charli had some experience interviewing suspects, but did she have the nous to run on the edge and know when to take a chance?

63

Stretched Loyalties

Charli Garcia walked into the interview nervously, knowing what Carter wanted from Greig, but not sure she could get it.

'Start with Dodds,' Carter had said to her, briefing her on the best approach to take before the interview began. 'You're familiar with the scene in Dodds' flat. Greig might be the man who saw Jacky run across the road. If he was, take a break, and we'll reset the interview. I'll be here in the observation room.'

'You tell me to remember too much, I'll forget everything.'

'No worries, just two things: if Greig was on North Bridge, that means he's the prime suspect for Dodds death. The other is Alice.'

The duty DC flicked the switches, ran the tapes and briefly squeezed Garcia's hand under the table. After introductions, Charli opened the folder in front of her and got straight to business.

'Where were you yesterday at five-twenty-five in the evening?'

Greig sat back and folded his arms. 'I was in the Blue Thistle pub in Hunter Square all afternoon.'

The duty DC leaned in and whispered in Garcia's ear.

'Mr Greig, what is your relationship with Jimmy Logan?' Garcia asked, her face blank.

'I'm an employee.'

'Is the Blue Thistle one of Mr Logan's pubs?'

'Yes.'

'What is your job?'

'Head of Operations,' he grinned. 'I hire and fire, do deals, buy stock and allow him to concentrate on strategy.'

'Jacky Dodds. He is an employee?'

'You're kiddin', right?' Greig sneered. 'He's a punter.'

'You have known him a long time, yes?'

Greig sniggered and held out his hands. 'What is this? A fuckin' history test?'

Tommy McGregor intervened, 'Please be specific, constable, we haven't got all night.'

Garcia felt herself redden, but she recovered quickly. Addressing Greig, she rephrased the question. 'You knew him from school?'

'So what?'

'You met Jacky Dodds yesterday on North Bridge, didn't you? You scared him so much he ran across the road to get away from you. He was killed by a bus. That's murder by proxy. We have CCTV of a man of your description pushing him under the wheels.'

The smugness vanished from Greig's face.

McGregor informed his client, 'When a deliberate killing is caused by indirect actions of the murderer. Or a third party orders the murderer to kill. Are you charging my client with proxy murder, constable?'

'Witnesses have provided statements. Mr Dodds was distressed.' She opened a Manila folder, extracted a clear cellophane pouch with an evidence tag on it and pushed it across the table. 'One paper lifted from Mr Dodds' home. We collected many more. Your name is there, Justin, many times. As you see, your name is more than others. On this drawing?' she pointed to an image of a man slicing another's testicles off. 'You cut Jacky Dodds and saw prison. You hated him, didn't you? You tortured and assaulted him, and since then, you have forced him into crimes for your boss, Mr Jimmy Logan. Is this how you treat your customers?'

'But I never left the Blue Thistle until after closing,' Greig pleaded.

'This is impressive, but it's all circumstantial,' McGregor filled in before Greig, who was now looking anxious. 'Do you have any evidence that my client actually killed Jacky Dodds on instructions from Mr Logan? That's where you're going with this, isn't it?'

'The spin goes many ways, Justin, but you have admitted being a proxy for Mr Logan.' Garcia kept directing her comments to Greig. 'Allegations are being made to Mr Logan next door. Do you think he'll clear you from blame when he hears you are here singing a canary?'

Her confidence was growing. 'Charges are not made at this time, Mr McGregor, but Justin is a suspect. It would be in his interest to cooperate. However, I have undeniable evidence on other matters and would like Justin's statement on them.'

'Maybe,' said Greig, not waiting for McGregor's intervention.

Garcia picked up a photograph from her folder and showed

it to Greig. 'On the night of thirteenth of January, Alice Deacon was in the Reverend bar, owned and run by Mr Logan. You too were present.'

Greig looked at the picture and shrugged his shoulders. 'I can't remember everyone who comes through the door.'

'Before leaving the Reverend, photographs were made of her.'

Greig smiled at DC Garcia and glanced arrogantly at Tommy McGregor.

'You got me,' he said immediately.

'I want those photographs. Mr Logan was there also that night, yes?'

Greig looked at McGregor, who shrugged. 'It's a reasonable question.'

It took a while for Greig to consider, and as time went on, it became even more evident what a crucial question it was. 'Yes, he was.'

64

A Friendly Chat

Looking on from the observation room, Carter was pleased. Garcia had snookered Justin Greig, and he hadn't seen it coming. Things were going less well for Nick Mason. Logan was an auld heid and didn't roll over easily; he denied knowledge of Jacky Dodds' death. When asked if he was in the Reverend bar the night Alice was there, he said he wasn't, but couldn't recall his whereabouts.

While Carter had been watching both interviews, Murray McCormack had called back. He hadn't seen Logan on thirteenth January and, before that, hadn't seen him since thirteenth December 2018.

Carter turned to the constable in the room. 'Interrupt DI Mason, please, then ask Tam Watson to check the meeting schedule for Scottish Police Authority meetings from last year and get me a list of the members.'

Nick Mason appeared a minute later. 'Not having much luck, Leccy, he's a hard bastard to crack.'

'Greig has confirmed a photo was taken of Alice in the Reverend and we're to get it tonight. Greig also said Logan was in the bar and we already know his phone was, so he likely has multiple phones. Ask him for a list of his numbers. Murray McCormack, the MSP, was one of the guys in the snug, and he's confirmed Logan wasn't with him the night Alice was raped, so Logan is still a suspect.'

'You going to release Greig now?'

'Yes. Charli will follow him; he's not getting a lift home, like McCormack. She'll call Cheryl once she knows where he's heading, then they'll pick him up for a wee chat off the record. I'll bet Cheryl's ready to tear his fucking head off.'

After twenty more minutes, Logan was a bit less assured. Nick Mason was a skilled questioner and changed his angle of attack regularly. Mitch-the-Brief kept trying to intervene, claiming Mason was fishing. Still, Logan had a reason for the multiple phones and finally gave a location for the night, an Indian restaurant on Nicholson Street, along with remembering the names of a string of people who'd corroborate his alibi.

A constable entered the observation room and handed Carter a list. Before Christmas, the last Scottish Police Authority meeting was held on thirteenth December in Pacific Quay, Glasgow, discussing Complaints and Conduct. None of the SPA Board members were politicians.

He'd hand it off to DCI McKinlay, who'd decide the next course of action.

There was that damned ping again. The pulsing red dot invited him to open the message. The interviews were over anyway.

[2019-01-22:2259] She told me about you so blame her for it. Didn't take me long to piece it together, after that. You were a

screamer, Carter, you just wouldn't stop howling. J.

A red light blinked on the observation room's internal phone: Tam Watson at the front desk.

'Leccy, we've got the photos you wanted. Charli wouldn't return Mr Greig's phone until he showed us your suspect. Might be able to reduce the crime rate in town if we had that phone, eh?'

Moments later, the three policemen were huddled around the printer as the paper came out. Charli had already submitted the photos as evidence into Alice Deacon's file.

'Who is it, Leccy?' asked Tam.

Carter studied the image intently. Alice was on the left of the shot, her face a doll-like mask. Drinks sat on the table in front of them – a tall slim glass with ice and lemon in a dark liquid, probably vodka coke, and a half-consumed pint of IPA. The man beside Alice dominated the border of the picture. Broad-shouldered, a powerful chest, his legs open in a virile display of manspreading, hands on his knees. He looked like he'd punched weights in the past, but not so many now. He wore a dark suit over an open-necked white shirt and displayed aggression in his manner, in the way he sat forward, like a puma in a tree ready to pounce.

Carter shuddered, the feeling racing up his spine as he stared at the man who was threatening to kill him and who might have raped his wife. The gaze coming back at him was face-on, looking straight to camera, knowing full well he was being photographed and caring not. Like a sniper taking aim, the half-sneer, half-smile targeted Carter, as if he knew precisely who would receive his .50-caliber bullet.

'It's Joe Moore,' Carter replied to Tam Watson. 'Looking a

bit older than his passport photo.'

A flashback from the drunken conversation he'd had with J last night came to mind.

'I'm coming for you, Carter. Don't waste my time.'

65

Game of Numbers

Carter arrived home just before midnight, totally shattered. It had been a long day. Joe Moore's arrogant face had seared itself in his mind and left an ugly feeling in his gut.

He'd married Moore's ex-girlfriend: so what? We're all someone's needs and dreams, aren't we? But it didn't add up either. Every ex- isn't a psycho. He didn't need Dr Flowers to tell him that Moore's justifications were a psychopathic response; excuses to himself to validate violence. Thugs like Justin Greig weren't much different. They were mouthy but didn't go to the extremes that Moore would. Violence wasn't Carter's choice of debate either. His warrant was mightier than their sword.

Moore was a different league – as it was plain to see in his face and body language. He had the arrogance of someone who'd killed for fun. Why would Kelsa be drawn to him? Would Alice swoon for the same reason? That was definitely Dr Flowers' turf. Regardless of deeper motive, Moore had Carter in his sights. Many of J's texts hinted at reason without coming right out and saying it. But what was it?

Carter slumped on the sofa with a midnight beer since Moore had finished his whisky. If Kelsa really had known Moore, he knew where to start looking. Kelsa's iPhone and MacBook were charged and ready. He switched the iPhone on and, while he waited for it to boot, grabbed another beer and retrieved the envelope with the printed codes.

8 2 6 4 2 8 9 5
Licence to thrill, M
Zip up a dress, Joe

He was sure the numbers were the passcode for her phone, and maybe a password for the computer accounted for the second clue. But what about the third?

He tapped in the numbers and got immediate access to her phone. Quickly, he changed her security details to his own. InterMide was the mobile operator, the same as for Alice's phone. But that was no coincidence now. He thought about her riddles. Things important to them but to no one else? He was sure that was the track. But they'd have to wait.

He scanned her contacts: no *Joe Moore* under M or J. He scrolled past names he knew, friends and family, and many people he didn't know, but one name made him sit up.

Nathan Butler.

Filed under N instead of B. There was no phone number, no email address and no other detail. Carter picked up his own phone and logged in to ICRS. Butler had a green flag set on his record, meaning his home address and phone number had been corroborated. The evidence was a bill from InterMide, but it wasn't for the number of the phone that Jacky Dodds allegedly stole.

InterMide.

Carter became animated. He got up from the sofa and paced the room, punching the air.

'Yes, yes!' he shouted to no one. This was the break he needed: InterMide. He searched for the identification documents Charli Garcia had collected on Joe Moore, found his mobile bill and opened the document. *InterMide.* Next, he returned to the Excel mobile analysis. He filtered it to show only InterMide numbers, getting hits on fifteen names out of the twenty-eight.

Of the fifteen: Moore, Butler, Alice, Greig and Logan had InterMide accounts. On a whim, he changed the filter to give him all the InterMide accounts in the analysis, even if they'd been discounted earlier. It threw up some surprises.

Kelsa's rugby-playing ex-boyfriend was caught in the net along with another '*weel kent face*'. But the analysis put them in orbit of the Reverend a week before Alice's rape. On the night Kelsa died in hospital. Coincidence? He thought not. Carter immediately dialled Mortimer's number. France was one hour ahead. It went to voicemail.

He grabbed another beer. The alcohol sharpened his thinking. He opened and played the InterMide video again and watched Kelsa walk through the shot. This time he looked at the people she stopped and spoke to. One man on the edge of the frame might have been Moore, but the video resolution was too fuzzy. He checked the other three InterMide videos and was left clutching at straws.

He picked up Kelsa's iPhone, rechecking her contacts. No entry for Mortimer under H or M. Could Gavin Roy discover when Butler's contact record was added to Kelsa's phone?

There were no calls or texts associated with it.

Kelsa had WhatsApp on her phone, mostly for family. There were messages from her mother Judith, her brothers, aunties and friends. His own WhatsApp messages appeared too, but none resolved to Butler or Moore.

He scanned the other apps on her phone and recognised the icon for the SMS nano-app. This was a breakthrough. He opened the app. The newest message was dated on the day Kelsa died, 4 January 2019.

[2018-12-09:1509] So, it's a boy.
[2018-12-15:2154] Nathaniel. A good name.
[2018-12-21:2205] You will do the right thing now.
[2018-12-29:2108] You know how important this is.
[2019-01-02:2231] Not long now, you will do it.
[2019-01-03:2302] You can't do it without me.

[2019-01-04:0215] I'm here. Soon be over.

Carter had expected to find messages as part of Moore's sick plan, but these didn't make sense. He read them and re-read them. What was it that was important? What could she not do without him?

Carter had last seen his wife on the night of 3rd January, in a private room, and she had resembled a corpse. There was nothing more the doctors could do, they said; it was down to her desire to live or die. The skin on her face had sunk into her skull. Her body was concealed by blankets, and he could barely look at her. She was not the woman he'd known and loved, she'd become something else entirely, and he'd left the room as soon as he could, tears streaming down his face.

Yet Moore seemed to have been in the hospital on the night Kelsa died.

Kelsa could not have responded to Moore's messages. Carter didn't even know where her phone had been kept during that time. Her personal effects were handed over days later.

Scrolling through the groups of texts, he was struck by the significant time gaps between them. Was there no reason to communicate at those times, or had Moore deliberately preserved only the messages he wanted Carter to read? It was a virtual desert before she'd been admitted to hospital in October 2018, when there was a flurry of disinterested texts from him and, apparently, no replies from her. Scrolling back further, Carter hoped to discover how she had fallen into Moore's clutches.

Messages around the weekend in March that she'd gone missing were sparse, other than to confirm what Carter already knew: she had willingly gone on a night out with Moore. The first text was from him, and she replied six minutes later.

[2018-03-16:1922] I'm on my way.
[2018-03-16:1928] Meet you at the station, babes.

The next set of texts were from February 2018, but the tone was different.

[2018-02-27:1532] Let's have one last night together.
[2018-02-27:1856] It's not happening.
[2018-02-27:1903] I never got to wish you all the best for your

new life with Hubby.
[2018-02-27:1910] I'm sorry, but that's the way of it.
[2018-02-27:1913] You don't get it. We're having a night out.
[2018-02-27:1917] No, I'm married now. I've moved on.
[2018-02-27:1922] You'll do it because I say so.

[2018-02-27:1930] Don't threaten me, I'll go to the police.
[2018-02-27:1934] Will Hubby arrest me? I'd like him to try. I'll tell him the things he doesn't know about you and your dysfunctional family. All the dirt you've shared with me.
[2018-02-27:1940] Stop it.
[2018-02-27:1946] You'll come. Otherwise Hubby will suffer.
[2018-02-27:1951] You wouldn't dare.
[2018-02-27:2002] Don't push me. I know where you live, I know your routine. I know his routine.
[2018-02-27:2010] Stop it, you're scaring me.
[2018-02-27:2014] You'll come home one evening, he'll be in bed, seemingly asleep. Not a mark on him. Heart attack probably. Happens all the time. Some people, they just die.
[2018-02-27:2030] I'm so sorry for what you went through as a child, you know that. But I can't help you. You should see someone professionally.
[2018-02-27:2048] I'd be a different man if it wasn't for him. I'd have had a normal life. But then, I wouldn't have met you, would I?
[2018-02-27:2100] He's done nothing to you. It wasn't his fault; he was just a child too.
[2018-02-27:2120] There're things you don't know about me. What I've done, what I've seen, what I'm capable of. If I'm backed into a corner. Let's talk.

There was a gap of hours in the timeline. Carter assumed they were talking on the phone.

[2018-02-27:2341] OK, OK. This one time.
[2018-02-28:1646] You're doing the right thing. For us to celebrate what we had. Hubby will never know unless I tell him. Leave it with me.

Carter threw her phone across the room. His breathing came fast and deep like he'd just been through fifteen rounds of boxing.

'I'll break your fucking teeth, you arrogant prick. You'll bleed from every fucking orifice when I'm done with you, then we'll see how fucking good you really are.'

From where it lay against the skirting board, Kelsa's phone pinged. It was a ping Carter knew well.

This time it was a picture of the outside of his house. The date and time proved it was taken only fifteen minutes ago. He leapt to his feet, the beer bottle fell to the floor, and he paced the room, chewing on his anger like a hungry lion, stoking his desire for vengeance. He opened the front door and screamed into the dark street.

'You want me, Moore? Come and have a go if you think you're hard enough, ya prick.'

He stepped outside, pulled the door shut behind him and began roaming the estate.

66

Pick a Card

Carter arrived at St Leonard's at 7 a.m. the next morning feeling exhausted. The ever-present Tam Watson said a cheery good morning.

'A wee celebration after last night's success, Leccy?'

'Not now, Tam.' He climbed the stairs leadenly, not waiting to hear his older colleague's sworn statement.

'Any news?' he asked of anyone upon entering the detectives' room.

Charli Garcia was already at her desk, typing away.

'Not yet,' she replied. 'I'm expecting the profile result from the unidentified DNA at ten. Also, I'm expecting Moore's finance report from his bank.'

'You've seen his picture?' Carter asked. 'It's in ICRS. Check if he was ever in the military. Also, call InterMide and ask if he is, or was, an employee. Is DI Mason in yet?'

'No.'

He went to the coffee machine and pressed the button marked 'Recycled Sheep Pish', then added extra sugar. It couldn't make him feel any worse.

'When is Dr Flowers due in?'

'I am not your personal secretary, Leccy,' Garcia admonished him.

He phoned Dr Flowers, who answered on the third ring. 'I'm on my way, be there in five minutes.'

'You're bringing the greeting cards?'

'Of course.'

By 7.30 a.m., the three of them were settled in a meeting room.

He explained about the messages he'd found on Kelsa's phone. 'I'll submit them as evidence. Gavin Roy can see what he can make of them. Tell me about the cards.'

Dr Flowers brought Garcia up to speed. 'Two greeting cards sent about a week apart. The first was a sympathy card, assumed by Leccy to be from Kelsa's work colleagues. The second card came in yesterday, and he brought them both to me. What's very clear is that Sergeant Carter doesn't watch soaps.'

Dr Flowers slid the cards across the table. Garcia studied them then asked what Flowers had concluded.

'To a soap addict, it'd be simple, but I had to dig for most of them. Ken Barlow is a character in *Corrie*. His wife died in an episode. Sam Dingle's wife died in *Emmerdale*. In *River City*, Raymond Henderson's wife died shortly after their wedding. *Brookside* had an episode where Jonathan Gordon-Davies' wife was electrocuted. Roy Johnson beat his wife to death in *Corrie*. There are no Google references to a Stan Butler in the UK soaps anywhere.'

'By association, should we assume his wife died too?' Garcia said.

'So did mine,' said Carter. 'So what?'

'I've gathered Joe Moore's life artefacts, birth certificate and other things,' Garcia said. 'He was born in 1982. His mother's name was Corina. His father's name was George.'

'Did Moore's mother die when he was young?' Dr Flowers started to get excited. 'It's a classic marker of a psychopath, no female role model around to counter an overbearing father. Can you find a death certificate, Charli?'

'It will go on Leccy's wish list.'

'What about the other card?' Carter asked.

'Similar kind of thing,' said Dr Flowers. 'More complex, though. Obviously, Joe Moore is one of the names, but I've been stuck on "*The Narrator*". I can't resolve it to soaps. I'm not sure what the genre might be.'

'"Fight Club".' Garcia's eyes lit up. 'A favourite movie of mine. The Narrator is played by Brad Pitt, but he is also Tyler Durden and takes on other identities throughout the story. It's supposed to be a film exploring dissociative identity disorder. Incidentally, in the book of the movie, The Narrator is occasionally known as Joe.'

'Fucking hell,' Carter spat. 'Why can't Moore just say, "My name's Joe and I like to kill people?" It would be so much easier.'

'I've never seen that movie,' Dr Flowers said, a little shamefacedly, considering its theme. 'But I'll watch it. The other people named in the card were soap characters who assumed other identities to hide their real character. Either after committing murder or before they planned to commit murder. So it makes sense now.'

'What do these cards tell us about Moore?' Carter queried. 'Does he have a psychological identity problem? Or is it more than that?'

Dr Flowers felt the question was for her. 'He might have multiple disorders; there's nothing in the DSM handbook that says a person can only suffer a single disorder. He's clearly psychopathic, but that hypothesis doesn't exclude DID or any other condition. He might be "simply" using another name to confuse. Charli has his ID documents, and that would be a lot of effort to go to just to use another name.'

'I've got something else,' Carter said. 'Last night, I got upset reading these texts on Kelsa's phone, and I ran out of the house half expecting to catch Moore staring through my windows. I didn't find him in the housing estate, but he was around.'

'How do you know?' Garcia asked.

Carter reached into his jacket pocket and pulled out a cellophane sleeve with a sheet of paper in it. He laid it on the table and smoothed it out. It was a photocopy of a faded newspaper article from London's *Evening Standard*, dated 21 June 1989. There was no picture, only text and a headline, *DEPTFORD FAMILY TRAGEDY*.

'I didn't lock the door behind me. This was lying on my kitchen table when I returned from my sweep of the development. I'll summarise. "After watching his mother Eileen die in Lewisham Hospital of injuries sustained in a car crash in Scotland, Stan Butler took his son home. That night, suffering incredible grief, Stan Butler shot himself with a pistol, leaving his son Nathan, an orphan."

Dr Flowers stared at him, and Charli Garcia's mouth fell open.

'Deptford has been mentioned before.' Carter remembered. 'Nathan Butler's property rental company has Deptford in its name.'

'Oh my God,' muttered Dr Flowers, finally. 'Why would Joe Moore leave a reference to Nathan Butler in your home?'

'I don't know,' Carter said. 'Why would Moore send cards with these confusing names in the first place?'

'That one's easy,' said Dr Flowers.

Charli Garcia finished her sentence. 'He didn't send the cards.'

67

Secret Squirrel

'Any more theories?' Carter looked around the room.

Dr Flowers and Charli Garcia both shook their heads.

'Why are you so sure Moore didn't send the cards?' Carter asked.

'Too subtle,' said Dr Flowers. 'Not much fun either. He seems to come and go at yours as he likes, so why waste a stamp?'

'It's a *mujer,*' said Garcia. 'A woman. A man wouldn't do this, it is too delicate. The script is expertly drawn. She is showing you the path. She is bringing you to come to it on your terms. She is in the background, guiding. You must take all the credit.'

'So there's a woman out there who knows him. An ex-wife?' Carter said.

Both women shrugged their shoulders.

'A survivor, I'd say,' said Dr Flowers.

'So he has done it before,' Carter stated again. 'As Rocket-man said.'

'Oh yes,' said Dr Flowers. 'But that's not news. We won't find her until she's ready to come out. She has to know she's safe.' Dr Flowers turned to Garcia. 'Charli, do you mind? There's something private I have to say to DS Carter.'

Garcia stared at both of them like she knew they were lovers and had been asked to protect the secret.

'It's not what you think,' Dr Flowers said, knowingly. Garcia left the meeting room, closed the door and went back to her desk.

Dr Flowers wasted no time. 'Go and see your grandparents – the Carters. Right now.'

'Why?'

'Jesus, Leccy, you're so bloody infuriating. This is all about you, can't you see that? You've spent thirty years ignoring your past. Did you seriously think you could live your whole life without knowing who your real mum and dad were? Have you ever even been to their graves?'

'This isn't the time to start salvaging my soul, Petal.'

'Look at me,' she said tightly. 'You should speak to your grandparents about the car accident. It's important.'

He gazed at her curiously. He'd enjoyed the banter in the office at Fettes, a million years ago last week. She'd gotten under his skin, and he liked her for it. Now her green eyes were on fire. Her lips were set like concrete, and her ponytail was orchestrating everything like a maestro.

Her words sank in. He remembered what she'd said, on the third session in Fettes, or maybe the fourth. The one where he'd wiped all her stuff off the desk, while she sat in her swivel chair daring him to slap her and blow his career to smithereens.

'How do *you* know what happened to them?'

'I don't, but the whole fucking world has moved on in thirty years. Out of eight billion people, you're steadfastly holding out. Even now, when he's been shoving it down your throat, you still won't accept it. You've spent so long denying them you can't see the danger you're in. I've looked at the texts you grabbed. He said you were a screamer. The past, Leccy – somewhere you've never been. He remembers it, can't you understand that? Deptford and Nathan Butler. You need to hear about the accident from your grandparents, and when you do, all of this will make sense. A warped sense, but it will be a light-bulb moment, I'm sure.'

Still, he sat there, refusing the invitation.

'Your gran and papa have waited for thirty years for this,' she continued to try and persuade him. 'Don't deny them any longer. They haven't got time and will want to go in peace.' Her fiery green eyes glistened, she was nearly in tears, and by refusing to look at her, he was playing down her insight.

'OK.' He stood up. 'Will you come with me? You're an expert in these things.'

She shook her head. 'You don't need an expert. Just be their only son.'

68

Ancient History

The Smart car knew the route. Much of the traffic was heading into the city, so Carter wasn't held up at the usual trouble spots. It was a blue-sky day, bright and bitter with a watery sun that promised better days ahead if only you could hang on in there. He turned off the A7 south and began the shallow climb up Hunterfield at a sedate twenty-five miles per hour, loitering through Arniston, past Newbyres Park where the Rangers played. There was no Brexit-ish hard border between the communities, but the locals knew where the line was.

He turned left into Newbyres Row, technically a lane that separated the back green from the row of cottages. Extensions and patios now encroached onto it, leaving just enough room to park your bike. Gran's patio had seen many winters. It needed power-washing, a job for him. The pots, urns and barrels that overflowed with flowers in the short summer were looking dreich.

'Gran?' he called softly, opening the back door.

'Lachlan? It's you? What's goin' on? It's only just past ten.'

A fearful look covered her face as she entered the kitchen from the extension. Her peenie was tied around her waist, and her baffies were worn, causing her to shuffle over the linoleum. 'I'll call your papa, he'll want to see ye.' She put the kettle on and found her phone while he toured the house, as he always did, just to check nothing had changed.

'He's havin' his breakfast at the club,' she said. 'He'll be around the now. Tell me before he gets here – what's happened? How's ma bonny wee boy?'

He'd been thinking on the drive over. Best to start with news of Nathaniel. Not good, but not bad either. Men going down the pit and not coming up was really bad; all else was shades of good. He explained about the lawyer, about James Dunsmuir's determination to bring Nathaniel up as his own and how Nathaniel was well cared for by Judith. He told his gran about the interdict but kept Tommy McGregor's revelations out of it. She wouldn't understand.

The Las Vegas ceremony had solved a pressing problem: where to hold a wedding celebration and who to invite. They hadn't foreseen the unintended consequences of the future when the idea to get married surfaced on their first night in Joe's seafood restaurant on Las Vegas Boulevard. The Dunsmuirs and the Carters were pure oil and water: the Sheriff wouldn't countenance anything less than a society wedding, and Deek Carter would've marched out of a venue like Prestonfield House in disgust.

The back door let Deek Carter enter his own house. At one time a man equal in size to his grandson, he was now a full head smaller, quite a bit leaner, but matched Leccy in the hair colour department. His hand was once a steel vice with rivets for fingers, but now Carter shook his hand lightly like it was delicate crystal covered in thin paper.

'Faither,' he said.

'Aye,' the old man acknowledged homage. Deek glanced at his wife of sixty-five years to see what was troubling her. Tears filled her eyes.

'It's Nathaniel. The Sheriff has taken him.'

'Aye, well, we'll see aboot that.' The miner spoke with his fists, even now. Deek Carter straightened his back, preparing for war.

'It's in hand,' said his grandson.

Deek looked up at Leccy and knew there was more. In the over-warm extension, the two men sat down opposite each other. 'Tell me about Mum and Dad,' said Carter quietly.

'What's happened?' Deek asked fearfully. 'Why now?'

'A ghost.'

He nodded as if he'd been expecting that very answer and now it was given. Gran put more tea and biscuits on the low coffee table and sat down next to her husband.

'One of yer colleagues was here a few days ago,' said Deek. 'Fishin'. Inspector Mason. Glasgow lad. Said ye was up for an Inspector's ticket. Wanted to know yer background, skeletons, that sort of thing. 'Course, I said ye was the perfect boy.'

Carter was wrong-footed by this news but kept calm. 'What else did he ask?'

'He asked if any of yer mates had names beginning with J,' Deek replied. 'I pointed him at Jimmy Wilson. I hope yer no' in trouble, Lachlan?'

'It's fine,' Carter said, unsure whether Mason was flying solo, or whether the rest of the team knew about this. 'Tell me about the accident.'

'It was Burns Night, 1989,' Deek said with care like he'd been practising it for thirty years. 'We had a do at the Club an' all, so you'd been taken to your granny in North Berwick.'

'What were things like between you and the McKenzies?'

'We didn't see much of them. North Berwick is no' exactly next door, but your da' didn't say anything was wrong. We all of us were at your Christening an' your birthdays, so we got along fine.'

'But after the accident?'

'Things changed. Aye. Well, ye know some of it. I would call them; they'd put the phone down. Tried quite a bit for the first few years, but they never spoke and wouldn't answer the door. Grief probably: she was a braw girl, your mum. Ye know what families are like; maybe they blamed Dan. Eventually, we got on with it. Tried again when ye were older.'

'The accident – where did it happen?'

Deek looked at him thoughtfully. 'This what yer man was really here about?'

'I can't say too much. There's an open case, can't be any leaks. You understand?'

'We're no' daft,' Deek snorted. 'How come the crash has come up after thirty years? The polis investigated at the time. Do you no' have case files you can look up?'

'It's not a lending library. And you were involved. Close up.'

'What about the ghost?' Deek persisted.

'Someone going by the name of J.'

'I don't understand,' his gran said, 'about this ghost.'

'Somebody who was there, Sarah,' Deek explained, squeezing her hand gently, comforting her. 'It happened the morning after, at the Dirleton junction to Drem. Your mum was drivin' the Astra, Dan was in the passenger's seat. You were strapped into yer seat in the back, and that's what saved you. Polis said she was doin' sixty. Heading home after picking you up.'

'Where was home?' Carter saw tears in his gran's eyes again. It never occurred that he'd had another home, and suddenly it hit him how little he knew about his early life. His memories were shards, but he could never connect them together. Flowers was right, he was incomplete.

'Portobello, a flat around Abercorn Park,' Gran said. 'It was lovely.'

Deek picked up the story again, now that he knew the urgency. 'The other car pulled out suddenly from the Drem junction, and yer mum ploughed into them. She had right of way. Polis said the Astra corkscrewed, landed on its roof thirty yards beyond the junction crumpled against a tree. Dan and Caroline—' Deek paused, tears suddenly present, remembering when the police came to him, man to man, as it was then, with no Victim Support. 'They died instantly.

'When the ambulance arrived, ye were screaming but didn't have a single cut or bruise. You were kept in the Sick Kids hospital at Sciennes for two weeks. You screamed all day and night, and they thought ye had internal injuries. Even once ye were home with us, it was months before the screaming an' crying stopped. You just clung to us all the time.'

Deek wiped the tears away. 'We just got on wi' things. You seemed fine when ye started school. We hoped you'd forgotten about it.'

J's text now made sense. He and J had both been in the children's hospital.

'What about the other family?'

'We didn't know for a long time, a year or more. The local polis came to the door with a detective from Edinburgh. Rutherford, his name was. Said the other driver had been over the limit, even though it was the next mornin'. She and her husband had been transferred back to London. They'd had serious injuries too'.

'And that was it?'

'No' really. The detective said they'd both died months later. Complications from their injuries, he said, so it was a real tragedy all around.'

'What about the boy?'

'I dinnae know. There was a fatal accident enquiry in Edinburgh, but it took years to arrange and by then— I went some days. Once I heard the description of injuries suffered to Dan and Caroline, I couldn't face goin' back.'

'What was the other family called?'

'Butler.'

'And the boy's name?'

'Nobody ever mentioned him.'

69

Bungalow Country

His grandparents wanted to know how he was coping since Kelsa's death. He promised he'd come and see them soon and talk.

Driving back to the city, he called DC Garcia. 'Any news?'

'Moore's finances are complicated,' she replied. 'HMRC confirmed he pays tax through a personal service company and Companies House shows his company makes a profit. He's a customer with NatWest Bank and has multiple accounts. Source of funds is the Isle of Man. The IoM Bank provided evidence for NatWest's funding sources requirement, but they have no visibility of any overseas sources.'

'He's legit?' Carter asked.

'Yes, but the NatWest man says he has "*a bad smell*". Nothing can be proved without reasons to follow the money to the "*steamie*",' she said.

'Money laundering?'

'The last deposit was on the third of January, for fifty thousand pounds.'

'What about his address? You said the Met was checking it

out.'

'I was spinning for a while, but eventually, the name of a retired sergeant was given. He knew the area and the people. Said it was once his place. After redevelopment, the address doesn't exist. A family once lived there, there was a fire, and the house got destroyed. He's going to dig deeper.'

'Moore's using a non-existent address,' Carter whistled, 'and gets his money from off-shore accounts. What did your NatWest man say about the address?'

'Paperless statements. Said customer's homes are not checked unless they flit around. His InterMide account uses the same non-existent address.'

'Good work, Charli. Is DI Mason in yet?'

'Yes.'

'If you need help to get other details, ask him.'

Carter killed the call. He was back inside the city boundary but didn't want to return to the station just yet, so he dialled another number.

'Leccy,' Cheryl McKinlay answered. 'You collared J yet?'

'Can I pick your brains?'

'Thanks for your help with Justin Greig, by the way. He's now on the snitch fast-track. I'm considering askin' Financial Crime to investigate Edinburgh City Council. I think there's an expenses scandal just waitin' to pounce onto the stage.'

'Councillor Taylor has his hand in the till?'

'Aye, something like that. It'll keep Logan's gas at a peep too.'

'A detective in the eighties. Name of Rutherford.'

'Inspector Rutherford?' McKinlay's tone told him he had to explain.

'He spoke to my faither years ago, about the car crash that killed my parents. I'm curious why a detective from Edinburgh got involved with a car accident in East Lothian.'

'What's the relevance to Alice an' Jacky?'

'Was Nick Mason authorised to visit my grandparents?'

The sudden low background hum from McKinlay's phone confirmed it was.

'Rocketman and I have cleared up the shambles of your wife's underwear,' McKinlay retorted. 'And its relevance to the Deacon case. Once the scope of the facts were revealed, I let Nick loose to probe your background. Tactfully.'

'Why wasn't I told?' Carter asked, feeling bruised.

'Why wasn't I told about your dirty washing?' McKinlay raised his bruising to a slash.

'What's the conclusion?' Carter played poker face.

'Nick's in his kennel. With instructions to sit, as long as you keep bringing your inner copper to work. There's more to Kelsa than you think, eh? Rutherford?'

'DI Rutherford might have information he doesn't know is important.'

'Stuart Rutherford was Drugs Squad,' she said. 'Why?'

'You'll have to trust me,' Carter played his ace.

'Do I have a choice?' She gave him Rutherford's last known address. 'Be nice to an auld man.'

Squeezed between Blackhall and Davidson's Mains, Vivian Terrace crouched in bungalow country. Number 87 boasted a high hedge and mature trees to keep the bairns from tearing up the daisies. Whitewashed render, white door, white facings. Two white-painted dormer windows in the black slate roof completed the look of the panda-eyed retirement home. Carter wondered if the hedge got sprayed white too. Only in summer though.

The ring of the black doorbell was answered by a white-haired old woman. She was thin with wrinkles and grey with fatigue, like she was training for death.

'He's retired you know,' she said. 'Some tea?'

Carter declined.

Stuart Rutherford glanced up from where he sat in the bright conservatory. His view over a manicured lawn was blocked by the broadsheet newspaper he then began to fold. He had a thick head of black hair and a chiselled jaw below hedgerow eyebrows. He didn't look seventy-something; more like still-shagging-his-younger-mistress age.

'Sergeant Lachlan Carter. Cheryl McKinlay said I'd find you here.'

Rutherford completed the folding of his paper. 'Mary, a wee pot of tea?' He offered Carter a seat. 'You a cold case man?'

'No, and yes,' said Carter. 'Car smash at Dirleton. 1989.'

'Aye,' Rutherford mused.

'Why were you involved? North Berwick uniform handled the wreckage.'

'What's your interest?'

'The case I'm on,' said Carter. 'Woman drugged, raped and attempted murder. You ever come across Jimmy Logan?'

'Aye,' Rutherford sat back in his chair. 'You're shite at the poker, Sergeant Carter. Drugs don't mature like old whisky.'

Carter said nothing.

'What else, Sergeant? The link to the accident.'

It was Texas hold 'em, and Carter felt his heart dance to the rhythm of the deal. Rutherford wouldn't have told Deek and

Sarah; it would be an unnecessary wound. Local polis would be in the dark too.

Had his dad been selling drugs?

70

Tea's Up

Carter held his breath. Rutherford's experience interviewing druggies still gave him an advantage. 'Your family? Thirty years ago, you'd have been—'

'Three.'

'The car you were in was the—?'

'Astra.'

Now it was settled, Rutherford began to talk.

'We got involved after the casualties were removed. Traffic had started the clean-up. They wanted the road open again, then had to close it until we'd finished. There was a kid's safety seat in the Astra. One in the Cavalier too.'

'Why were you brought in?'

'Cocaine and heroin found in both cars. Initially, we thought separate packages in separate cars. Traffic gave us the speeds and trajectories, and eventually, we worked out what happened. It came down to luggage. The suitcase in the Astra was coated with brown and white powder, on the outside only. A holdall in the Cavalier contained a mix of both drugs. It was unzipped, and the cellophane encasing the drugs must've got torn on the zipper when the car flipped over. Somehow, the Astra got contaminated with powder from the Cavalier. The wind was blowing in the right direction.'

'What else?' Carter asked.

'The Sick Kids hospital called us about drugs covering two boys brought in from the accident.'

'And the Butlers?' Carter asked.

'She was over the alcohol limit,' Rutherford recounted. 'And wasn't wearing a seat belt. She was in a coma all the time she was here. He was conscious, had head and facial injuries, a broken wrist and a broken leg. He claimed he didn't know what was in the bag. Said he was asked to deliver it by a man he didn't know to a man he didn't know. After his release from hospital, he was charged with possession with intent to supply and bailed to appear. Never did.'

'You checked up on him, though, didn't you?'

'The Met knew Stan Butler as someone with form. He was suspected as a distributor and had connections with the Yardies. The price of a toke went up around Leith a few weeks after the accident.'

'You're poker-faced now, DI Rutherford.' Carter was relieved.

'She died later, in London. Back then the scuttle going around said Stan copped it soon after. His Jamaican pals got him.'

'Jesus,' Carter shook his head in disbelief.

The conservatory door opened. Mary Rutherford nudged herself through the doorway, holding a tray with teapot, cups, milk and sugar. 'Tea's up, boys.'

Rutherford opened up his paper and sipped at his fresh tea.

'Why did this one stick all these years?' Carter asked, getting up to leave. 'You must've seen it worse.'

'The kiddies car seats. Now I know what became of you both.'

Outside in the Smart car, Carter analysed this new information. A puzzle remained, despite him now knowing the graphic facts of the 1989 accident. Nathan Butler had never initiated contact in thirty years, but Carter was confident Butler knew all about him. He lived in Edinburgh, his name was on Kelsa's phone, and he was in the Reverend bar on the same night Alice was raped by Joe Moore, as evidenced by the phone data. What were the odds of all these data points being coincidental? Possible, but the threads of silk making the connections still only amounted to a hunch.

The Butler-is-Moore angle meant Carter had to track down all the same data points for Butler to compare against Moore's. The odds weren't even. Was he chasing one man or two? A fragment of one of J's texts came into his mind. *'I'm not who you believe me to be'*. Or something like that.

Jacky Dodds had been the key witness. He'd known about the connections between Logan's mob, Alice, Butler and Moore. Did Justin Greig know of Dodds' connection with Butler? If so, then Greig knew Butler and may have something on him that could bring Logan into the frame. More than ever, Dodds' death looked deliberate.

But Kelsa had more information for him.

He drove home to Liberton and picked up Kelsa's phone and MacBook. Back on the road, he called DCI McKinlay again, offering her a summary of his conversation with Rutherford without giving too much detail. He told her his thoughts on Greig and Dodds, and it fired her up, as he hoped it would.

She said she'd handle it, but she wasn't daft either.

'And what's your next move, Leccy? While I'm running around like a bare-arsed DC chasin' down your leads?'

'I'm heading to Glasgow, ma'am, to ask a favour of Gavin Roy in OCD. There's more data on these mobile phones than we think.'

The Cybercrime Investigation team worked out of Helen Street in Glasgow, ninety minutes' thinking time away. He closed the call before she could respond, hoping she would allow him the space to compute it all. He didn't need more distractions.

71

Distractions

Carter's hands-free phone rang as he joined the M8 motorway at Hermiston Gait.

'Lachlan?' queried a familiar, but concerned voice through his phone.

'Hi, Jude?' Carter replied, immediately concerned for Nathaniel.

'We had a break-in overnight. I think. Nathaniel is completely fine. Some strange things have happened in his nursery though – his cot has been moved, and he's acquired a new teddy bear.'

Carter drove onto the hard shoulder and stopped the car. What he was hearing didn't make sense. Jude wasn't flighty and usually took everything in her stride. 'Have you called the police?'

'That's why I'm calling you,' she replied. 'What should I do?'

'What evidence of a break-in? Broken glass, a busted lock, that kind of thing?'

'Should I look outside? I'm afraid I'm not familiar with

this kind of thing. I thought of calling 999 then felt I should speak to you first.'

'You said *"overnight"*. It's afternoon now, have you only just discovered it?'

'Amanda, our nursery nurse, spoke to me twenty minutes ago. She thought I'd rearranged things in the nursery and assumed I'd bought the teddy. I hadn't, and neither had she. I asked the other staff; they know nothing. James is working, and I don't want to alarm him as he will think it's your doing, and he might do something stupid.'

Like call the police and accuse Carter of breaching the interdict.

'OK,' he said. 'I'll send someone round. Just leave everything as it is.'

He dialled another number. 'Ellen? Are you on Victim Support, or are you helping Charli?'

'I'm helping Charli, but as you've called – we're pulling threads together to update Nick. He'll tell you later, official-like, but the unknown DNA in Kelsa's underwear matches a profile in England for three rapes and another three unproven killings. Why are you calling?'

'As soon as you're finished there,' he said, 'go to my mother-in-law's house.' He gave her the address. 'There's been a break-in.'

'I'm not a PC, Leccy.'

'Ellen, please. My son is there, and I don't think this is a random crime. Know what I mean?'

There was silence for a moment.

'Will I take backup?'

'Call me as soon as you can.'

Moore or Butler? Butler would take time to track down, to

flesh out. As it stood, Butler's connections were to Carter and Jacky Dodds. Moore made sense, if only for the J tag. Moore was dangerous, maybe Butler wasn't. Carter's memory of the early, erased, text messages was scant. Could both men be using the J pseudonym independently? A partnership of sorts.

If it was one man using two identities, it wouldn't matter who he prioritised. But if it was two men and he chased the wrong one, somebody else could get hurt. He was zooming past Harthill when the next text landed. Attempting to read it at eighty miles per hour wasn't a good idea.

He was considering his options when his phone rang, causing his heart to skip a beat. 'Number withheld' appeared on-screen. Was J trying to distract him while driving? Hoping he'd die in a motorway pile-up?

'Hello?' he said warily.

'Sergeant Carter?' static on the line gave the caller a time-shifted feel. 'It's Hugo Mortimer. You called me last night.'

'Yes,' Carter replied. 'I don't have much time, so I'd appreciate your clarity. You were in Edinburgh on the fourth of January. Mind telling me why?'

'A meeting at Murrayfield. Providing intelligence on French rugby players likely to face Scotland in Paris.'

'When did you return home?'

'I caught the Saturday morning flight to Paris.'

'You were in the Reverend bar on Friday, late evening.'

There was a pause on the line, a breath taken. One that told Carter he'd touched a nerve.

'A catch-up with old friends,' Mortimer said, tightly.

'Jimmy Logan?'

'What's this about?'

'The Reverend is an easy stroll from Murrayfield. I'm guessing you and your mates went there after games?'

'So what?'

'Laid on free hospitality, did he?'

'Look, Sergeant, what's your point.'

'I think you know, Hugo,' Carter said. He let the slight static on the line reinforce the tension. 'Logan has many friends; like Jacky Dodds, Nathan Butler and Joe Moore. Some of his friends have Jennyr reputations to protect. You must've met many of them, during hospitality.'

'I have to go, Sergeant, I have other meetings.' Carter heard that breath again.

'Quid pro quo,' Carter said.

'Goodbye, Sergeant.' Mortimer's voice faded.

'James Dunsmuir.'

The line stayed open, but Mortimer didn't speak for long seconds.

'I don't know what you're talking about.'

'She's dead, Hugo. But you already know, don't you?'

72

Tracking Your Tears

Helen Street was on the south side of the River Clyde, within coin-throwing distance of Ibrox Park, home of Glasgow Rangers FC, Nick Mason's avowed team. To someone from Edinburgh, Planet Glasgow was an alien universe.

Sitting in the car park, Carter read J's message that had come in before he'd spoke to Mortimer. No reply button was offered.

[2019-01-23:1517] Paw and Maw well? Could go anytime heart just stops. Unlike the wee man. Next generation has good genes. He didn't even have a teddy to remind him of his da. J.

He texted his grandfather's mobile.

The ghost may be in your area. Be careful and lock the doors. Dial 999 if concerned. L.

He dialled Ellen's number, hoping to catch her while she was still at his in-laws'.

'Do they have an alarm system or CCTV?' he asked.

'An alarm system,' he heard Jude reply to Ellen's relay. 'No CCTV.'

'Tell her to call the company; he's bypassed it somehow. Send me a picture of the teddy.'

Carter had never met Gavin Roy before, but he fitted the type. Dark hair with a double chin, he was a man who over-exercised his fingers and carried his forty-five years' bulk like the child he never wanted. He escorted Carter through the corridors of a basement to the Cybercrimes area. Carter was aware he was one notch above civilian here.

'You're no' what I imagined,' said Roy, staring at Carter's hair. 'Is that a syrup?'

'One hundred per cent pure terminal,' Carter replied, well aware of Glaswegians' reputation for straight-talking. The comedy scene in Glasgow was a force of nature. 'You've no idea what I went through to get this look.'

Roy had multiple computer monitors in his office. Next to them, he'd placed a machine that Carter had never seen before.

'Hardware encryption cracker,' said Roy tapping it proudly. 'Designed by GCHQ and better than the Kiosks for cracking phones.'

'Will we need that today?' Carter asked without irony. 'I've got the code to open her phone.'

'Ah, maybe not, then,' Roy blushed. 'Kelsa's your wife, right? You think she was attacked by the same guy who did Alice Deacon?'

'Right.'

'Exact dates?'

'Sixteenth to eighteenth of March 2018.' Carter handed over her iPhone.

Roy plugged it into the encryption cracker with a cable, then turned his attention to the computer screen. 'Apart from her tracking data, is there anythin' you want off the phone?'

'She has the same SMS nano-app system installed that's on Alice's phone, and I want to know when some contact names were added.'

'Let's start with the contacts.'

'Nathan Butler and Hugo Mortimer.'

Roy tapped the keys, and a stream of contacts appeared, some with pictures and many, like Butler and Mortimer, without. 'The metadata is dated June 2016,' said Roy. 'But it's the same for many others too. Nothing before that date. It's a bad import from an older phone. The actual creation date has been overwritten.'

Carter nodded – it had been a long shot anyway. 'I want to know where she went that weekend.'

'OK. DCI Jim Geddes wants a word – on the second floor. On your way back get us a coffee from the canteen. This will take a wee while to set up and run.'

Carter found his way. The station was busy with people running around with purpose, although it was hard to tell what was urgent. Helen Street was also the base for Organised Crime and Terrorism, so people didn't chat in corridors. Jim Geddes' office had a closed door, and Carter knocked before entering.

'Sergeant Carter, E Division, sir. You wanted to see me?'

The man sitting in the chair looked to be in his late thirties, wearing a confident smile and a nondescript blue suit. The jacket hung on a stand, and he was behind his desk in shirt-sleeves. The computer beside him purred like a favoured cat. Geddes extended his hand across the desk, and Carter shook it. 'Coffee?'

'No thanks, sir, I have a mission for Gavin on the way back.'

'DCI McKinlay speaks highly of you, Sergeant, and even Nick Mason had a good word. Only the one though. Nick showed me the ropes before he moved across to the dark side, like.'

'Thank you, sir.'

'I know you're busy. Gavin briefed me about the app on a phone.'

Geddes pushed a bound folder across the table. 'Official Secrets Act. Just sign it.'

Carter signed.

'Project Fulcrum,' said Geddes. 'Intelligence-led design and development of an ultra-secure text messaging app. All police forces in the country are stakeholders, including military, MI5, MI6, Foreign Office, blah, blah. Design is GCHQ, the app build and beta service are provided by mobile operators. Seeing it appear in an active criminal investigation is a shock. Gavin says InterMide. No one else knows about the leak yet, and I hoped you might enlighten us.'

'A suspect, but no real evidence yet,' Carter said.

'Name?'

'Joe Moore. His profile is filling out. I think he may be ex-army – just by his picture – but we know little else right now.'

'Any connection to InterMide?'

'We're waiting on an answer to that question.'

'Do you need help? I won't ram-raid your investigation,

but if there's a leak from InterMide I have to be told.'

'I'll bear that in mind.' Carter could almost feel DCI McKinlay's breath on his neck.

'Cheryl and Nick both said you keep things close. Don't bite off more than you can chew, Leccy, we're all on the same side. I can ask my military colleagues on the steering group. A *quid pro quo*, you understand. The wheels of administration can be slow.'

Carter was worried about Geddes' choice of Latin. 'When would you have answers?'

'Tomorrow morning, latest. Keep your channels open though.' Geddes stood up and extended his hand. Carter reciprocated. 'Better get that coffee for Gavin, before he gets cold.'

Back in the office with two coffees, Carter was met by a Glasgow map on the screen with a flashing red dot. InterMide.

'That red dot is the location of your wife's phone on the sixteenth of March.' Roy said. 'Starting at the Hilton in Anderston. I'm sure you're not interested in how she got there. I'll run it forward – where was she supposed to be?'

'A night out in Edinburgh.'

'The Hydro in Finnieston is where she went. Kings of Leon gig at the Hydro then bars in the city centre, and back to the Hilton – at one-twenty-seven a.m.'

The red dot moved across the city. Carter had a front-row seat for an animated performance he didn't care for. 'She was drugged and raped,' he told Roy.

'After six a.m. she's movin' – inside the hotel. Then suddenly at speed across the city to the Royal Infirmary. A taxi to A & E, I'd guess. She's there a long time. I checked while you were away, no complaint was lodged by her at that time or since.'

'She didn't want police involvement,' Carter said tightly, controlling his emotions. 'She knew what had happened, and she knew why. The only person she wanted seeing this was me. Can we do counter-tracking of Moore with this data?'

'Nope, but you've got his phone number an' IMSI code from the Excel analysis I gave you, so ask your boss for authorisation. InterMide will provide us with a tracking feed for the timeframe when Kelsa was here. We can overlay that on Google Maps to help you prove it was him.'

'Anything else on Kelsa's phone?'

'We've got procedures. I'll let you know.'

73

By Royal Appointment

He parked at the Hilton Hotel in Anderston, close to the River Clyde. After the usual pleasantries, the manager gave Carter the facts. Moore had booked the room in his own name, even used 'Mr & Mrs Joe Moore' on the registration, pre-paying, so Mrs Moore didn't have to endure the tedious chore of checking out. The credit card matched the number NatWest had provided. Carter's phone acquired a new picture of a cuddly teddy bear. It had red, emoji-like eyes, confirming the break-in theory as truth. J was piling on the pressure.

He drove to the Royal Infirmary in Townhead. A collection of Victorian and new-build buildings smeared across a large campus with all the delicacy of a Glasgow Oyster and brown sauce. After encountering some dead ends, he finally happened on A & E from the inside. Front-line staff triaged him, concluding he was only mentally scarred. They pointed him at Admissions and Transfer, who would answer his questions in between soothing trollied patients.

Moira, a Glasgow girl, offered to be his go-to woman once

the formalities of warrant cards and authorisations were sorted out.

'Kelsa Carter or Dunsmuir. 17th of March 2018.' Carter didn't need to look it up.

'Got her,' said Moira, pleased with herself. 'Admitted at just before six-thirty in the morning.'

'Doctor's notes?' Carter asked.

'She'd been battered. Wasn't giving anything away. Bruising to the arms, breasts and abdomen. More bruises and cuts under her hair. Blood in her urine. Doctor AJ Nicholls assessed her and wrote it up during and after. Vagina and anus showed bruising but not tearing. She allowed blood tests. They provided alcohol, measurable traces of scopolamine hydrobromide and various drugs. AJ concluded she'd been date-raped and noted that most of her bruising would be invisible when wearing clothes. He says here that suggests intent.'

'She couldn't fight back?' Carter replied evenly as if he held no emotions one way or the other. 'Was any DNA taken from her at the time?'

'She declined police involvement at the time. Do you know who did it to her?' Moira asked. 'Has she decided to press charges now?'

'We have a suspect, but you know how difficult rape can be to convict.'

'We see hundreds of women like her every year. The arseholes in this town are sick, they need a punchbag – especially if Celtic lose. I couldn't put up with it.'

'You're not married?' Carter asked, trying to keep it casual.

'Twice divorced. Better off with someone who cares. You know – someone who swings my way.'

'Understandable,' Carter said neutrally. 'The clothing she wore when she came in?'

'The women don't want them back. There are charity shops in the entrance mall. They take the clothes and send them away for cleaning.'

'Do you have a note of what she was wearing?'

Moira returned to the computer. 'Yes. Mustard-coloured coat, leopard-print dress, black bra and knickers.'

'Tights or stockings? Shoes?' Carter asked.

'Not recorded on here. Are you sure you're taking this seriously enough? The girl deserves justice, and the problem is you lot think it's not a real crime, so the dicks get off.'

Carter almost laughed but knew Moira wouldn't understand.

'Trust me, I'm taking it seriously.'

'When will I see this scumbag at the High Court, do you think?'

'As I said, these things are complicated, and if there's no DNA, it's much harder. She was from Edinburgh. A loving, caring girl, married with a young family.'

'You talk about her in the past. Has she topped herself?'

Carter wanted to scream, but he sighed instead.

'Moira, please – where are these charity shops? You've been a great help.'

'Back out the way you came in, then turn left. Follow the wheelies.'

'Thanks. Email copies of the doctor's report and the list of clothing to me.' He gave her an email address and walked away.

Five minutes later he was in a public sector entrance mall. On his left was a Rape Crisis shop and, across from it, Chest

Heart & Stroke. An older woman behind the counter in Rape Crisis remembered the leopard-print dress. 'It was lovely. Too expensive for here. It got sent to the distribution centre. They'd clean it up and send it somewhere else.'

'A mustard-coloured coat?'

'Yes, that went to the distribution centre too.'

'Leopard-print shoes? Matching the dress?'

'No, not that I remember. We get a lot of shoes, but a pair like that would stand out. Sorry.'

'Don't worry,' said Carter. 'I think I know who has them.'

74

Stretched Loyalties

Driving home, the M8 was busy with cars crawling nose-to-tail. Carter's phone nestled on the passenger's seat like a secret lover. He kept glancing at it, demanding a confession. Moore had been in his home more than once. That took nerve – unless he always knew where Carter was. Carter would have to prove Moore had access to mobile phone tracking services and the secret text messaging technology and was using it for his own ends, all of which would be difficult. The app was designed for stealth, for one thing. What help the UK intelligence community would provide to civilian police was another. Moore could easily dodge a shared suite in one of Her Majesty's Hiltons if the spooks wanted to bury their embarrassment.

Moore's bleeding-edge tech had kept him miles ahead of Carter, so it was time to crank up the ante and use Moore's own technology against him. It didn't sit comfortably with him, but swallowing his anger was essential to avenge Kelsa's death.

The phone rang. He swallowed.

'Leccy,' Nick Mason's voice boomed through the car's stereo speakers. 'Where are you?'

'I'm on the M8. But you probably know that already.'

'National DNA Database confirmed the profiles we submitted to them are on the wanted list down south. It's the profile of an unidentified serial rapist, and there's the possibility of murder too. He doesn't like women, so you need to catch him ASAP before the brass have your nuts for earrings.'

'You just calling to gloat?'

'Have you followed up on Nathan Butler?'

'Charli was doing it. You know, delegation. The skills all senior officers pretend to have.'

'He'll be sitting in your house right now, Leccy. Drinking your Balvenie.'

Been there, done that, Carter almost said. Instead, he asked, 'How was North Berwick?'

Outside the Smart car, traffic on the motorway was easing, speeding up to fifteen miles per hour, passing the Dakota Hotel at Eurocentral.

'A sunny day. But cold by the sea.' Carter could hear the tension in Mason's voice.

'Cheryl and me are sorted,' Carter said. 'Do you want to be sorted out too?'

Mason could be a knob at times, and Carter always rose to the fly, angered by these jousts when Mason was digging at him. Mason would keep going only until a higher authority gagged him.

'Can't do it, Leccy. Privacy concerns.'

'So, Nathan Butler?' Carter decided to keep his powder dry. Vengeance was best served cold.

'DC Garcia followed up on Moore's address,' Mason laid it out. 'Her retired Met officer is a good find, wish we had people like that. The property doesn't exist now—'

'This isn't news.'

'That's true, but the house *was* once rented by Butler's family. Now, why do you think Joe Moore would use that address for his bank accounts?'

'Because they're brothers?'

'Tut-tut, Leccy. This is good detective work, not a shot in the dark.'

'Get on with it.' Carter accelerated, passing Newhouse, leaving the Glasgow conurbation in his rear-view. He sighed in relief.

'Another family was living there when the fire was set, but the house was empty at the time. Butler was detained on suspicion of arson but was released for lack of evidence. Butler was an adolescent back then, an angry teenager fighting the system, lashing out at everyone, and was on local plod's radar. Met Man tracked down their old headteacher. Seems Butler and Moore were thick as thieves back then. Both left school at sixteen, but after that, the headmaster never saw them again.

'Butler lives here in Edinburgh. Why haven't you brought him in for questioning? Bet ya he's in touch with his old school mate? We know both were in the Reverend bar at the time, so you better have a good reason to be kicking tyres in Glasgow when you should be arresting rapists in Edinburgh.'

'Kelsa was raped by Moore, the weekend she went missing in March,' Carter kicked back. 'Glasgow Hilton is emailing me a copy of the reservation Moore made in his own name. The Royal Infirmary treated her for rape, and the A & E doctor's report will be in ICRS shortly. It confirms she had traces of scoop in her blood. She was a victim.'

'What did Geddes want?' Mason's question confirmed he and Geddes had form. 'He's Organised Crime and Terrorism, what's his interest in a scummy Edinburgh rapist?'

'Ask him yourself, Inspector. He seems to know you very well.'

'If you're withholding information from senior officers, that's misconduct. But don't worry, I'll help you get a premium place outside a McDonald's with a paper cup for your change.'

'Geddes offered to find out if Moore is ex-Army.'

'Garcia's on that lead though.'

'He said he has contacts. We'll know tomorrow morning.'

Mason was silent for a moment; Carter could hear the cogs grinding. 'It's not his gig,' Mason replied. 'Apart from having you in his pocket, what does he have to gain? He's only interested in his own success. He's not one for long-term snitches. You're holding back, Sergeant.'

Mason's monologue had given Carter time to think. 'He's investigating InterMide. Said there was a leak or something but wouldn't elaborate.'

The car passed Harthill Services at full speed. Halfway home.

'InterMide is circumstantial to this investigation, isn't it?'

'Alice and Kelsa both had phones on InterMide contracts. Butler, Moore and Logan's crew have them too. Jacky Dodds was on giffgaff.' He nearly said there was no other link but stopped himself just in time.

'Come straight to the station, Sergeant Carter,' DI Mason said formally. 'We need more from you.'

The call ended, leaving Carter with only one option.

75

Slings and Arrows

A maid let Carter in a side door and took him to a cosy room where Judith sat waiting. She'd arranged tea and a selection of hot finger foods. He hadn't realised how hungry he'd been. Nathaniel was in his baby bouncer, asleep.

After disposing of DI Mason's call, Carter had called Judith and given her enough of an explanation to tell her he had news.

'James won't be home until late. He prefers being at his club; like-minds and social networking he calls it.'

'I spoke to Hugo,' Carter said, hoping he'd remember what he planned to say. 'By coincidence, he appeared in a case I'm investigating.' He glanced up and met Jude's eyes. 'He was aware Kelsa had died.'

'No one here told him,' Judith said tightly, while Carter munched his way through the food. 'Once he ditched Kelsa, he was no longer welcome in this house.'

'I need to speak in confidence, Jude. About Kelsa.'

'So, your questions in the park were not as innocent—'

'I can't pretend her life didn't happen.' Carter didn't want to lose the trust they'd built up.

Judith's face projected the betrayal she felt in her heart.

'You said that you'd forgotten I was family,' he said. 'This is a family matter.'

'Go on,' she said reluctantly.

'Kelsa's name has appeared in an investigation. Obviously, she's not around, so I was asked—'

'In what way has her name appeared, Lachlan? I will not have my family's reputation sullied.'

He'd run through the choices in the car. Now he was ready to pull back the curtain.

'A woman has been raped and is in a coma in hospital. She worked for InterMide. Kelsa, who also worked for InterMide, appeared in a corporate video the rape victim made for the company in 2016. A friend of Kelsa's – Lesley – mentioned she thought Kelsa was having an affair with someone around that time. Probably someone she worked with.'

'She was brought up correctly, to cherish the values we hold dearly. I can't believe she would wantonly split a man from his wife and family. Do you know this for sure, Lachlan? You must be truthful with me.'

'I don't know. But it's possible.'

'Do you have the name of the man?'

'I can't say, Jude, it's confidential.'

'But you believe he is the rapist?' Judith was aghast. She sat, staring at Carter as if he was the Devil's advocate. Eventually, she lowered her head, and Carter heard sobs. 'One's family is sacrosanct. We believe that nothing can contaminate the home. Still, we have to allow our children to be corrupted in a terrible world outside. James—' She stopped herself.

'What about James?' Carter pressed, drinking cold tea. 'What does he know?

'He won't talk of these things and forbids me to mention them.'

'So, she *was* having an affair?' Carter kept his composure. 'How did you know?'

'She wouldn't confide in me, of course, but she was a very non-verbal woman. I knew something had been going on when she stopped eating and went back into therapy.'

'She'd been in therapy?'

'Yes, after Hugo's very public French marriage,' said Judith matter-of-factly. 'She spent nearly two years at the Priory in Southampton being treated for disorders, self-harm and clinical depression. James arranged it. He said Hugo paid some of the fees. Is Hugo involved in this crime?'

'He's a distraction.'

'What is going on here, Lachlan?'

'I could ask you the same question, Jude. Kelsa's behaviour last summer totally astounded me. She went from being happy with life to craving death in a heartbeat, and you are only now telling me she had a recurring illness. I watched her die in total disbelief, but you knew she was vulnerable.'

'Lachlan, please, don't do this to me, and don't do this to yourself. Nobody takes pills for anorexia. Maybe there was something in her makeup, she was possibly predisposed to resort to extreme measures when she couldn't cope with the slings and arrows of life.'

Carter lifted a sleeping Nathaniel from his bouncer. He walked to the window overlooking the back garden, to gather his thoughts. He was sure there was more to it than that.

'When was the first time, Jude?'

'She was about ten. I took her to a private clinic; she was cutting herself.'

'So, what was her trigger last year?'

'I don't know,' said Judith, with tears running down her face.

'The break-in was meant to scare us,' Carter said, rocking his sleeping son in his arms. 'And it's all to do with the teddy. Get rid of it.'

76

Crumbled Empires

Outside it was a typical Edinburgh winter's night, damp and chilly. Not a soul was on the street. A standard, everyday text came in from Gavin Roy.

We've downloaded all the content and will review. Phone couriered to St Leonard's for 8 a.m.

Carter arrived at St Leonard's just after 7 p.m. The detectives' room was empty, except for Charli Garcia. 'War Cabinet,' she said, 'with DCI McKinlay. We've been waiting for you.'

McKinlay and Mason sat together behind a table. Surrounding them, electronic whiteboards displayed relevant information on the Deacon case, including Alice's picture with Moore beside her, taken in the Reverend. Carter still felt that grin was directed at him. There was no picture of Kelsa yet. He'd be asked to provide one soon.

Dr Flowers sat on his side of the table, on the left. Charli Garcia and Ellen Podolski sat on the right, leaving an empty chair in the middle for him. The atmosphere was electric.

Carter sat down.

McKinlay turned up the current. 'The Chief wants the MIT to take over; he thinks I've lost control. I've given you too much latitude, Leccy, and not enough support. That's the official line.'

'You gave me to the end of the week,' he replied. 'It's Wednesday, I've got a few days yet.'

'Don't be a smart arse, Leccy,' Cheryl McKinlay spoke with weariness in her voice. 'You've been running this investigation like it's your personal right. Have you disclosed everything you know to DI Mason? Is ICRS up to date?'

He glanced across at Charli and Ellen, who both nodded slightly. 'With the exception of the information about Kelsa that I found out today,' he said. 'It should be updated shortly.'

'This discussion isn't about Charli or Ellen's performance, it's about yours.' McKinlay was exasperated. 'I don't appreciate having to justify my operational procedures to senior officers and then have you scatter them to the winds. My assessment of this case is that you've missed a significant suspect. Nathan Butler. I believe DI Mason has shared our thoughts with you.'

'Incontrovertibly.'

McKinlay sighed. 'Do you have a plan of action?'

'Of course, ma'am.'

'Share it with us, please.'

For the next thirty minutes, Carter outlined his thoughts and plans.

'Do you know where he is now?' McKinlay asked after he'd finished.

'No, but I know where he'll be in two hours.'

'You'll want rent-a-mob to make sure you get him?'

'Too visible. He'll case the place, and if he sees riot vans, he'll melt away. Better with just us.'

'I'll not be going,' said McKinlay. 'I'm an auld wifie for this kinda thing. DI Mason will fill my sturdy boots.'

'Right. Well, I'd better be on my way or none of this will happen.' Carter turned to Dr Flowers and Ellen Podolski, 'You two OK with this? Not exactly the kind of fieldwork you're used to.'

'I might be in my forties with three kids, Leccy,' Ellen replied, 'but victims sometimes have to kick back.'

'What about you, Lisa?'

Dr Flowers gave him a look that crumbled empires.

'See you all soon, then.'

77

Pattered Pish

For the second time that day, the Smart car climbed the high road into Midlothian mining fields. Carter parked at the Gorebridge Bowling Club and entered by the side door. It seemed an entirely logical thing for Moore to track his phone, once the concept landed in his head, taxied to the gate and shut down its engines. It required skills, a laptop computer and a gaggle of servers buried deep in a data centre. Once those possibilities were accepted, likelihood about–turned from impossible to probable. Moore could harvest all the numbers he needed from Kelsa's phone because he'd presented it to her as his gift and she didn't care to look in its mouth. Moore had tracked every step she took, every move she made, even when she wasn't with him.

Carter wasn't an InterMide account holder, but that didn't matter because – as Gavin Roy had told him – all the operators exchanged public account data. Suppose Moore had the right credentials in the company? They could enable him to harvest the unique IMEI and IMSI codes on any phone in the country by running a lookup on the InterMide servers.

If he commanded the servers to track Carter's phone and then scrape the location data gathered into a file, he'd get data points spat out onto a Google map when he wanted it. Simples.

The margin of accuracy? About the size of a Smart car.

Until the Champions League football return in a few weeks, Wednesday was comedy night at the bowling club. It moved to Mondays after that. After finishing the conversation with DI Mason that they'd begun while still on the M8 from Glasgow, Carter had called the club secretary.

They were delighted to host him. 'You're on third the night, Leccy,' wheezed the stage manager, as Carter checked in and prepared his off-the-cuff material. 'We've already lined up another compere. You'll likely know her. Miss Chris.'

Carter glanced at a thirty-something woman sheltering in the shadows. He didn't know her but nodded respect. Attractive, possessed of a bull-dozer figure and wearing a long blonde wig with a red Santa hat on top, she looked like she could handle herself in the rough and tumble. They'd know soon enough. Controversy was the way to go for him tonight; wind the audience up and take it from there.

At 9.30 p.m. exactly he took the stage.

'Ladies and Drunkards, give it up for a good old Gorebridge boy, Leeeccy Caaarter!'

'Spankin',' Carter said into the handheld mic as the local crowd cheered and whooped. 'Spankin'.' The spotlight picked him out on the darkened stage. 'Brexit. What the fuck's goin' on there, then? Mother Theresa – May not, May will, May won't, May can't. We'll have a people's vote, here, tonight, Mother T. Raise your right hand for Leave or your left hand for Remain.'

Half the audience stuck up both hands, the other half sniggered. 'Looks unanimous to me,' Carter said. 'If we really want to leave Europe this quickly, all Mother T has to do is give the job to Alex McLeish. We'll be out before half-time.'

That got a much deeper laugh.

'Forget the UK and EU,' Carter marched his way across the stage, pointing to people in the audience. 'I think the nice folks in Arniston have been holding back the Great Scottish town of Gorebridge for far too long. I propose to invoke Article 50 and tell them to fuck right off without a deal. We'll have a hard border across the Rangers park, with no backstop, and we'll impose tariffs down the middle of the railway station platform. If they want to catch the train to Edinburgh, they'll have to pay double.'

Somebody threw a half-pint glass onto the stage. It shattered and sprayed dirty lager over his trousers.

'Ladies, calm yourselves. This isn't the Strangers' Bar in Westminster.' He walked away from the lager to the other side of the stage and waited. 'It's a little-known fact that Jeremy Corbyn's parents were stoned when they christened him. I mean, their names were Toby and Miranda Smith.' That got a snigger or two – the village was solidly SNP.

'Have you watched PMQs recently? Mother T gives Corbyn really patronising looks when he's getting all puffy over the Despatch box. The contempt on her face is thicker than her Cabinet. "You're not big in the trouser department, Jer, are you? You debate like a goldfish, and your contribution to British political history will be a mere footnote unless you VOTE FOR THE FUCKING DEAL."'

He paced the stage, back and forth. Some of the audience were laughing, but not all. It was like they were waiting for something else to happen. Nick Mason was standing at the bar, one elbow on the counter, nursing a drink. Carter couldn't see his face.

Charli Garcia sat on his far right. She wasn't smiling either; it was torture, right enough. Dr Flowers and Ellen Podolski sat close together. Out in the darkness, all eyes were on him. Waiting for the heat to come on. He about-turned and began his next lap of the stage.

'Just when it couldn't get any worse for Mother T, President of the United States and the next King of Scotland, Donald J. Trump, slithers into the debate.' Carter swept back his hair and cocked his chin. In the middle of the stage, he turned to face his audience. 'She asked me for advice, folks,' he held up his left hand at breast height, making an 'O' shape with his thumb and forefinger. 'I mean, who wouldn't. Trump told her – sincerely – that she should read his wonderful book – *The Art of the Deal* – available in all great bookstores, people. You heard it straight from Trump. I'm telling you, and Trump never lies.'

That got a longer laugh; his Trump impersonation was good. He gazed out into the audience. Was Moore here? If not, it was going to be a long and tortuous fifteen minutes.

'Listen to me, folks. I said to her – this is the truth, Trump never lies – I said to her – Theresa – how do you spell your name, by the way – is that an H in there? Theresa – Theresa – forget Stephen Barclay, he's a goose. Trump wouldn't let him shine his hair – and Trump has got great hair. To Make Britain Great Again, I'll lend you Don Junior – for a great price – he's a great negotiator – he was taught by the best.'

Carter made a Trump gurn and held it. 'Showtime, folks.'

The house lights came up suddenly. Carter leapt off the

stage and pushed his way into the throng of people. At the same time, Nick Mason abandoned the bar and swooped in from behind the audience. A man rose up from his chair, of more substantial build than those around him. Carter could see the surprise on Moore's face, but Moore recovered quickly. Two men next to him collapsed, screaming and holding their faces. Chairs skittered across the wooden floor. Men and women panicked and charged for the exits, thinking it was a gang fight. Some were pushed down to the floor, becoming trapped in the melee, barged and kicked by others climbing over them. High-pitched screams infected the audience as more blood and alcohol was spilt on the floor.

Dr Flowers positioned herself at an exit, beside Ellen Podolski. Charli Garcia and Nick Mason tried to keep Moore in view.

Mason came in from behind and laid his hand on Moore's shoulder. Instantly, without turning his head, Moore's elbow caught Mason's ribs hard and knocked him off-balance. Moore turned and nutted him in the face, then kicked his legs out from under him as he stumbled. Mason crashed to the floor and groaned.

Carter was a few metres from him but was blocked by bodies.

'It's over Moore, we've got you.' He clawed his way through the panicked audience.

'Think so, Carter?' Moore laughed, then moved away at a march, taking advantage of the chaos. Garcia appeared in front of him and threw a Muay Thai roundhouse kick up towards the side of his face. He parried the blow with his left arm, grabbed her right leg in flight and wrenched it counter-rotational at the knee. She screamed in pain and collapsed on the dirty floor.

Flowers and Podolski barred Moore's way at an exit. He stopped and grinned at them.

'It's all fucking birds these days.'

Reinforcement appeared from the stage wearing a Santa hat. Miss Chris tagged up with Flowers and Podolski at the door.

'If you think you're hard enough big man—'

Moore punched Miss Chris full in the face before she'd finished her sentence. The club's foundations shook when she hit the floor. Flowers stood her ground, but Moore grabbed her by her blonde ponytail and launched her over a table.

Ellen decided she should let him leave. Stepping over Miss Chris, Moore disappeared through the door.

When Carter finally got outside, Moore had gone. The bowling green grass was winter long and crowded with crying women and stunned men. He grabbed a girl by the arm. 'The big guy, did he pass you? Did you see him?'

'Don't touch me.' She recognised him in the dim outside lighting. 'This is all your fault.' Her boyfriend began to take an interest, but Carter rushed through the gate that led into the car park. It too was full of shocked and bewildered people. Beyond the car park was Hunter Square, with plenty of escape options: lanes, side streets and vennels. To his left, the road climbed up Bonnybank Road. Main Street was fifty metres away, all downhill.

His phone pinged.

[2019-01-23:2209] Nice, Carter, very nice, but not nice enough. You've hurt a lot of people. I don't think you'll get invited back

anytime soon. The railway station in 5 mins. J.

Carter ran the two-hundred-metre length of Main Street, careful not to tumble down the steep hill. The road swung left and down over the railway bridge, past the station some four hundred metres further. He saw no sign of Moore. At the corner of the bridge, he rested past a narrow vennel, breathing hard, hands on his knees.

Strong arms pulled him inside the narrow passageway, pinballing him hard off its stone walls. A knee found his crotch, and he cried out in pain as Moore pressured his balls and squeezed his throat at the same time. Carter felt his head twist up and around, so his right cheek scraped off the rough sandstone. Moore punched him under the ribs with his right fist.

'It's no' your time, Carter, so you'll live tonight. But listen well.' His mouth was up against Carter's left ear. 'You're a dead man, an' I'll take you when I'm ready. She played you. Told me fuckin' you was tame, an' you was soft in the head, as well as the trousers. But you're special, Carter, 'cos no man shares my girl. You die when I tell you to die. Got it?'

Carter felt his earlobe being bitten hard but couldn't scream because of the compression on his throat. As the pressure came off his balls, he relaxed, but it was the wrong thing to do. Moore's knee smacked him hard in the testicles, twice. He crumpled onto the ancient slabs in agony, throwing up whatever was in his stomach.

'By the way, your patter's pish.'

The kick to his face smashed his skull against the wall, and he blacked out.

78

Walking Wounded

Carter woke up on a trolley and tried to get off it. A monitor squealed, alerting NHS reinforcements, who arrived in surgical green.

'Take it easy,' one of the cavalry said, gently pushing him backwards.

'What's going on?' Carter looked around. His sight was blurry, but he could hear Nick Mason's Glasgow slur and Lisa Flowers' clipped tones talking, along with those of others he didn't recognise.

'You're in A & E. Do you know what that is?'

'I'm fine,' he said. 'What's happened?'

'Carter, don't be more of a clown than you've been.' Nick Mason sat on a seat against a puce-coloured wall and began to take shape through Carter's fuzzy eyes. Beside Mason, Dr Flowers seemed subdued. As Carter's eyes adjusted to working again, he was able to see her bruised face, red eyes and dishevelled hair.

'What happened to you?' he asked.

'He asked me to get out of his way. I didn't, so he threw

me over a table. I was lucky, better than Charli. At least Ellen was able to drive home.'

The memory jolted him back into focus, causing him to sit up too quickly. His head spun as the blood drained off and he crashed back onto the trolley. The monitor whined its annoyance but was silenced.

'You've been sedated, Mr Carter,' said a man dressed in green, wearing glasses. 'Don't get up. You might have a fracture in your skull, so the only place you're going tonight is radiology.'

'Moore has vanished,' Mason informed him. 'Someone called 999. The village was quickly awash with paramedics and ambulances, and you were found lying unconscious on the street. It's made the late TV news too. The boss is incandescent.'

'What did he do to you?' Carter asked. 'I didn't see it. Or maybe I did.'

'A Glesca kiss,' Mason replied. 'Broke my nose again. The docs here reset it. Again.'

'And Charli?'

'Sore head, possible wrecked knee,' Dr Flowers said. 'She's having an MRI scan now. Her neck brace is cautionary. She won't be training at the gym for a while.'

Carter turned his head slowly towards the nurse who was adjusting his drip. 'What's so bad with me that I'm drugged up?'

'Well . . .' she started to list his ailments. 'There's potential short-term memory loss. Your left earlobe has been bitten off. Your skull may be cracked – and your testicles are traumatised,' she said. 'Give it three months at least before you try to use them again.'

'Can I walk?'

'Stand up slowly with support. No running and definitely no wanking.'

'Any bad news?'

'Bruised ribs under your left arm and battered kidneys, too. There might be more internal organ damage, so you're staying here for twenty-four hours at least. A bed's coming free, we need this trolley for serious cases.'

'Seriously?'

'You'll live. Many don't.'

'There's a car waiting for us.' Nick Mason stood up. 'Any update you want me to give to the boss? Apart from the stunning success of your meticulously planned sting? The inquiry will ream you for not having troops on standby, in case the audience rioted at your shitty punchlines.'

'He turned up though, so it proves he's tracking me.'

'We'll be meeting our new colleagues from the MIT later today, no doubt. Not you though, Leccy, you'll officially be on sick leave. C'mon.' Dr Flowers and DI Mason got up and walked away.

'Lisa,' Carter called her. 'A minute?'

Lisa Flowers turned back and came to his trolley. The nurse had abandoned him for a moment. 'Thanks for coming tonight. If I'd thought this would happen—'

She laid a hand on his bare arm. 'I learned something tonight.' Her eyes moistened, and she wiped away the beginnings of tears. 'I'd always thought I was a big girl. I'd sat across the table with psychos like Moore and never flinched. But tonight, when he confronted me, ready for violence, I realised I was in a cage with a bear. He could've killed me anytime he wanted. I've got massive respect for you and

Nick, for fronting up. With hindsight, you should've taken McKinlay's advice and brought reinforcements.'

'He'd have spotted them early and not shown up. We've taken a kicking tonight, but we've learned he's real. Not a ghost.'

'I'm worried about Charli,' said Dr Flowers.

'You don't win kickboxing gold without injuries and set-backs.' Carter's eyes were glassy, but he couldn't feel any pain. 'We've got Moore in our sights. It's a matter of time now.'

'You're still going after him, aren't you?' she said with a tremor in her voice.

'I don't have a choice. You said it yourself, this is all about me. And Kelsa.'

'Did he say anything when he attacked you?'

'Nothing that helps us find him again.'

'Remember, he wants you to be angry, to lose the plot, so he keeps control.'

'He's a scumbag, Lisa. He might be bigger, and he thinks he's smarter, but he's still a scumbag.' Carter lost his train of thought for a few seconds, then it came back. 'When this is over – and it'll be over soon – we'll have a drink together to celebrate.'

She smiled, ignoring the tears trickling down her face. She leaned over the trolley and kissed him on the forehead as a brace of A & E nurses came striding down the corridor.

'Time for your scan, Mr Carter. Let's see what's inside that thick skull.'

'Do something for me, Lisa,' he said as they wheeled him away. 'Go back to Gorebridge and get my car.'

'Then what?'

'Bring it here.'
'You can't drive.'
'But you can.'

79

Reset and Recovery

Sometime later, Carter woke. He felt disorientated all over again and tried to sit up. A monitor complained about this unregulated movement with a high-pitched blast. Instantly, it was silenced. A hand was placed on his bare chest, pushing him back safely onto the bed. The touch was cool and soft.

'It's OK,' a soothing female voice said. 'You're fine. You're in hospital. You asked to see me, remember?'

Carter turned to the direction of the voice, struggling to connect memory with sight. A woman with long mousey hair tumbling over her shoulders stood beside his bed wearing a stethoscope around her neck. A light blue open-necked blouse revealed cleavage that stirred a sensation in Carter's bruised testicles. The flat shoes she wore were perfectly designed to conceal her approach to unsuspecting patients.

'Apparently, I didn't make that much of an impression on you, Sergeant Carter, but your imprint is on me. Nurse Donaldson told me where to find you. Don't worry if you don't remember, it'll be the drugs.'

Like two pieces of string that just wouldn't touch, Carter's memory still couldn't connect with—

'Angela Murray,' she put him out of his misery. 'A doctor of this parish.'

The fuzziness cleared, and the connections clicked. 'Alice Deacon.'

'Our mutual friend. You came off worst in a fight with Joe Moore, the rapist.'

'You're wasted here,' Carter mumbled. 'There's a career as a stage mind-reader calling.'

'I spoke to your colleague in the waiting room, Dr Flowers. She gave me the highlights.'

'How is she?'

'Resting. The waiting room isn't designed for a good night's sleep.'

'Alice—'

Murray smiled. 'As she was, but the signs are good. The brain is an amazing organ, and it'll bring her back when it feels she's ready.'

'Speech?'

'You're full of it, as I remember. Must be a giddy night out when you're buying the drinks. To answer your eloquent question, I won't know until she reboots. There's nothing obvious to prevent her from speaking again, assuming she can remember what happened.'

'As long as she remembers.'

A nurse approached them, carrying a mobile phone. 'Your phone keeps buzzing,' she aimed the device towards Carter. 'Seeing as you're awake.'

Carter took the phone, silenced the buzz and started reading.

'How is he?' Dr Murray asked the nurse for her opinion.

'He'll live – no conclusion on the skull fracture, watching brief recommended. Bruised kidneys will make pissing fun. Other than that, and the pain in his bollocks, only the drugs are keeping him from entertaining the dead.'

Carter came back to the party. 'Nurse, can you ask Dr Flowers to come through?'

'Duty calls,' said Dr Murray. 'Behave yourself, DS Carter, if that is your first name.'

'Lachlan, and only on a Sunday before church. Leccy to everyone else.'

'Don't be a stranger, Leccy.' She walked out of the ward just as Dr Flowers came in and gave her second look. The nurse returned to her station.

'What time is it?' Carter asked.

Dr Flowers looked exhausted. 'Four, give or take. I need to go to bed.'

'Not now, Petal. You have the car? Find my clothes, we're leaving.'

'Where are we going at this time of night?'

'Princes Street Gardens.'

80

Trainspotting

Before they got in the car, Carter deviated to the gents' toilets.

'I need to check the plumbing,' he said. 'Two minutes.'

'Fuck, fuck—' The stream of piss was like hot iron filings and crushed glass heated to melting point. He grabbed the piping of the urinal to stop himself fainting. Slowly, the pain receded with the flow, but he knew it would be back. Washing his hands, he observed that the man in the mirror had genuinely been in the wars. He took a deep breath and looked closer. His cheeks were puffy like a boxer's, and his face was covered in cuts and bruises. His left eye was bloodshot, adding colour contrast to the steel-grey iris. A plaster crossed his nose for a reason he couldn't recall. Only his white hair was fashionable, but it needed a wash. He angled his head to check out the torn earlobe, but it was wrapped in a thin dressing like the rugby players use on TV. It throbbed, and it would remind him of Moore for the rest of his life.

'Why are we here?' Dr Flowers asked him, twenty minutes later.

'I don't know,' Carter replied to her reasonable question. They'd approached the city from the south, along Potterrow, past the McEwan Hall. Now they rumbled along George IV Bridge. There was no traffic in the chill of early morning. Lawnmarket and the Mound were next, then down onto Princes Street where he commanded her to stop. He extracted himself from the Smart car like a farmer lambing a sheep and hobbled across to the West Garden gates. They were locked and chained. Getting into the car was like putting the lamb back in.

'Drive to the next set of gates,' he pointed along the totally deserted avenue of Princes Street.

'I'll check them,' Dr Flowers said. 'Otherwise, it'll be daylight before we're finished.'

Five minutes later they sat in the car staring at the final set of black-painted gates on King Stables Road at the West End of Princes Street. The timeless monolith of Edinburgh Castle Rock towered above them. The gardens were in darkness, and all the gates were locked.

'So, what drove you to leave your warm hospital bed and drive all the way into town?' she queried.

'He told me to come here.'

'Joe Moore texted you?' There was shock in her tone and fear in her face. 'As himself, or as "J"?'

'As "J". He knows now that we can track him. Look.'

She read the message on Carter's phone.

[2019-01-24:0405] Princes Street Gardens. The consequence of your rash attempt to interfere with my plan of vengeance. You

didn't take me seriously, so there's a price to pay. J.

'Are we tracking him?'

'Well, I thought we'd take him down at the club,' Carter replied, regretfully. 'So I haven't asked DCI McKinlay for permission for tracking yet – it requires top brass approval. But it's unlikely he'll be using that same phone and SIM anymore.'

'What now?'

'Call the police.'

On cue, a strobing neon-blue light pinballed off the buildings at the Grassmarket end of King Stables Road. A police van rounded the corner at speed, heading straight for the Smart car.

'That's impressive,' said Dr Flowers.

Carter said nothing. The van stopped a few feet away but kept its headlights on full beam, dazzling them. Uniformed police tumbled from the van and rushed to the locked gates. One PC came to the driver's side of the Smart car and tapped on the window. Dr Flowers pressed the window button.

'What you two up to, then?' said PC, casting his eyes around to see if the occupants' clothing was loose. 'You'll have to move, there's a police incident.'

Carter reached into his jacket pocket and flashed his card. 'This is Dr Lisa Flowers, a police psychologist. We were ordered to come here. What do you know?'

'Sir,' PC said, changing his tone. 'British Transport Police. We're securing the scene from this end. The City Council was supposed to open the gate. We don't usually call the 'tecs till it's official.'

Another set of headlights appeared behind them. A man in

plainclothes got out of his car, walked to the gate, unlocked it, returned to his car and drove off. The PCs started blocking off the road and wrapping crime scene tape around the open metal gates.

'It'll be a woman,' Carter said.

'Can we drive in?' Dr Flowers attempted to secure an advantage. 'The Sergeant here has a disability.'

PC nodded. Dr Flowers drove through the gates and negotiated the narrow road at crawling speed. She passed a bridge that spanned the railway cutting, but kept right, where the road narrowed to a pathway. She parked tight on the right, leaving space for other vehicles.

Carter eased himself carefully out of the car.

'You alright there, big man?' called a uniform, seeing Carter's struggle. 'We've got a stick if you need it. Left the wheelie back at the depot, mind.'

'Was that a guess?' Dr Flowers asked quietly. Behind them the coppers had spread out, loosely searching, delaying the moment when they'd find a body.

'Probability says it's a woman. These guys are not Police Scotland, but Bilston Glen will be aware of what's going on.'

On their left was narrow-mesh metal fencing, designed to stop climbers accessing the railway cutting that ran past Castle Rock. Partway down the tarmac slope was a substantial wrought iron gate, locked by a heavy padlock and chain.

'Do any of you have a key to this gate?' Carter called to the coppers. A PC came running up and showed him the key. 'Network Rail property, this is. Can't let you through without authorisation.'

'Have you called the locals?' Carter asked.

'Our sergeant is in Waverley Station coordinating with

your lot, and we were to meet up in the middle. Power's off; standard procedure for a jumper. Going to be chaos this morning if there's a body. TV and journos will be over us like the pox.'

'Who reported it?'

'Driver of the one-sixteen to Aberdeen. He's stuck in the tunnel.'

'Talk to your Sarge, find out who the senior officer is and tell him I want to come through with Dr Flowers.'

PC stepped away to radio the request.

'It doesn't look feasible for someone to jump from the castle onto the tracks,' Dr Flowers said, looking up above herself. 'I think they'd fall well short.'

'It's high enough, I suppose. The castle is closed though.'

PC returned. 'Inspector Peter Conway from St Leonard's. Says he knows you but wants to know why you're here.'

Within seconds the order came back.

81

Pictures of Lily

Walking for Carter was uncomfortable. The two cricket balls between his legs were chafing. He had to stop regularly as dagger-like pains shot through his testicles at the slightest stumble. On the castle side of the railway, a public walkway snaked up the hill towards Castle Esplanade, but access via this gate was only ever meant for railway engineers.

A hundred metres ahead was another bridge. Arc lighting illuminated the scene. On their left, another gate was open, allowing direct access to the rail tracks. A large white tent appeared, spanning all four rail tracks leading from the station. White-suited CSEs were walking around, safety boards covered the rails. A man wearing the peaked cap and checker-board design came to meet them.

'Passing my arse, Leccy,' said Inspector Peter Conway.

Carter introduced Dr Flowers. 'What's the story, sir?'

'I'm guessing,' said Conway, 'you'll know more than we do. A woman has jumped from the bridge and been decapitated by the west-bound Aberdeen LNER train. What's happened to you? You look like you've been in a fight.'

'That's a reasonable description,' Carter replied.

'Why are you here?' Conway demanded but was interrupted by a shout from the crime scene manager, standing further along the rails.

'A suicide note.' CSM held a cellophane sheet in a gloved hand. He walked along the boards with a young man's confidence. 'Addressed to Sergeant Leccy Carter, E Division.'

'Who just happens to be here,' Conway said.

'Less than two weeks ago,' Carter said, 'another woman was thrown off a footbridge in Dalry. She's in a coma in hospital. An hour ago, when I was in hospital with these injuries, I received a text from the killer. I was to come here.'

'So this isn't suicide.' Conway said.

'Nope. Can I open the note?'

CSM slit the envelope along its edge then handed him a single sheet of paper.

36874521

Bye-bye Lily baby, don't cha cry no more.

'Have you found her phone?' Carter asked the CSM whose badge said, Norrie McLean. He held out the paper for Dr Flowers to read. She hesitated.

'Who else do you need down here, Leccy?' asked Conway.

'Nick Mason. He'll just be settling into his bed.' Carter smiled.

CSM McLean helped Carter walk along the wooden boards. Inside the tent, a photographer and four CSE's, all wearing facemasks, were busy. The metallic smell of human blood caught in his throat, even before he saw the remains. He put on a facemask.

The torso was being carefully attended to by a female crime scene examiner. The head lay a few metres closer to the bridge. Carter couldn't see the face and wasn't sure he wanted to, but he knew she deserved the dignity of recognition. Death by ScotRail was always savagely brutal.

He shuffled over until he could see more. The steel wheels had mangled her, and all he could see of a human face was bloody, matted, dark hair. He turned back to the torso. Her left arm was severed just below the elbow, and her left leg had been severed at the shin. The right leg had lost its foot just above the ankle, but otherwise, the torso was intact. The pathologist would confirm her exact height, weight and age. Still, he couldn't help noticing the sleeveless dress, drenched in blood but otherwise showing patches of white and teal. His breathing got shorter as his heart raced. He turned to the CSM McLean, and both men went outside, grateful for the snell breeze.

'Shoes?' Carter asked.

'Not that we've found,' said McLean, pulling down his white hood to reveal blonde hair.

'Other outer clothing? Coat, scarf, gloves?'

'Not yet. Might be under the train.'

'She's been raped and drugged. He's taken her shoes, and possibly her knickers too.'

'How do you know?' McLean asked.

'He's done it twice before that I'm certain of. This is a murder scene. He's thrown her off this bridge deliberately. Did she have a Louis Vuitton bag?'

'Yes, the note was in it.'

'What else?'

'Usual stuff – purse, makeup, lipstick, tissues. Also, two phones and a small box with glasses and alcohol.'

Carter shuffled off towards the crime scene examiner processing the LV bag, noticing Dr Flowers walking along the boards.

'Do you really want to see her, Lisa?' he warned, then spoke to the CSE, 'Purse? A driving licence?'

'Yes,' the man said. He opened the LV purse with gloved hands. 'Lily Sutherland. An address in Trinity.'

'Scan it into ICRS as soon as. The box?'

'Two shot glasses, miniatures of Talisker whisky. Fingerprints only on one glass.'

'He'll have cleaned his away. This code will open one of the phones.'

Carter keyed the code from the note into the first device, a gold iPhone. It opened, and he quickly found the SMS nano-app, with its pulsing red dot. He tapped.

[2019-01-24:0123] I've decided it's your time, Carter. Today is your last day on earth, so use it well. I will tell you where you should be and when you should be there. Alone. J

The message vanished before he'd a chance to grab it. Dr Flowers appeared, face grey, green eyes dulled.

'Are you OK, Lisa?'

She didn't reply.

'Let's get up top, leave the experts to their jobs.'

'You have to stop him, Leccy,' she said fearfully.

They turned to walk along the boards, and she took his arm, helping him, steadying him, steadying herself. Peter Conway was where they'd left him, issuing directives and maintaining control of his locus.

'Sir,' said Carter. 'The garden gates are all locked, so he's come from the castle area.' Carter pointed towards the dark hulk of the Esplanade slope. 'Maybe someone saw them. They had drinks beforehand; it was a ritual execution. We'll find she's been raped somewhere around there. Ask the train driver if he saw anyone on the bridge.'

'Nick Mason is on his way, Leccy,' Conway confirmed.

'He can fill you in. Dr Flowers is not well.'

They slowly retreated the way they'd come, back to his car. 'I don't want to bump into Nick just yet,' Carter said to Flowers. 'I need some sleep before we face the team tomorrow.'

'Come to Prestonfield with me, will you?' She asked. 'I can't be alone tonight with him out there. Please.'

82

Major Investigation Trauma

Sleep on the couch was fitful but necessary. Carter couldn't quite shake off the images he'd seen on the railway tracks, and the painkillers for his injuries didn't render his dreams less stark. Lisa Flowers had cried herself to sleep.

At 7 a.m. he gave rest up and caught the number 31 bus. It dropped him at Rankeillor Street ten minutes later.

His phone rang. 'Morning, Gavin,' he answered.

'There's a video on your wife's phone that's password protected. We tried to crack it overnight, but it was taking too long. One of my team read some metadata telling us it was saved on the seventeenth of March 2018, timestamp 03:47:43. No other vids are passworded. Thought you should know.'

'Right, OK, thanks.'

The detectives' room was full of people he didn't recognise. DC Garcia was at her desk with her right leg in a grey plastic support.

'Morning, Leccy,' she said quietly. 'Who are these people? No one will speak to me.'

'The Major Investigation Team, I guess,' he said, still distracted by Gavin Roy's call.

'Why are so many more *personas* needed to review the evidence and make the strategy?' she said. 'We were going just fine. The boss and Mason are upstairs.'

Carter limped up to the next floor, knocked on DI Mason's door and entered. It was empty. He went up another level, knocked on DCI McKinlay's door, heard the 'come in' and complied. Three people in the tight office stared at him critically.

'Sergeant Carter,' McKinlay said breezily, 'is SIO on this case.' She wasn't speaking to Carter. 'He's closest to the detail.'

A forty-something woman in a formal skirt-suit stood up. 'I'm DCI Karen Jacobson from the Major Investigation Team,' she introduced herself and reached to shake Carter's hand. 'I'm here to support you in apprehending this suspect. DCI McKinlay called us in, as you know, and DI Mason here has just finished updating us on Lily Sutherland's death this morning. Quite a gruesome scene for our scenes of crime experts. Counselling is being extended to them now.'

'Go back to base,' Carter spoke directly to DCI Jacobson. 'We can handle it. Nick, me, Charli, Ellen and the boss. Dr Flowers too.'

'It's her programme, of course—' Jacobson let the sentence roll away.

'He left a message for me on Lily's phone,' Carter addressed DCI McKinlay. 'He wants to meet me later today. Alone. It was erased as soon as I read it.'

'What's your take on the investigation?' asked Jacobson, ignoring Carter's statement in favour of her own question.

'What's critical, in your view?'

'He wants me to die.'

'How do you know this?' Jacobson seemed confused by the brevity of Carter's assessment.

'We need Dr Flowers' experience,' Carter said. 'Without it, I'm a dead man.'

'Sergeant. How can I help you?' Jacobson tried again. 'I have officers at my disposal, experienced in all aspects of running a major investigation. I'm not taking this case away from you.'

'Ma'am,' Carter said, addressing DCI McKinlay again. 'Can you authorise a real-time tracking plot on Joe Moore's phones? Urgently, please. InterMide will have all his numbers.'

McKinlay looked towards DCI Jacobson. Jacobson nodded and answered. 'Starting when, Sergeant, and for how long? Our arrangements with the mobile operators require twenty-four hours' notice unless the Chief Constable believes there's an imperative. It'll need a justification paper, with three signatures: DCI McKinlay, me and you. You'll draft it, of course.'

'You can draft it before you go back home, but I need that tracking up and running before midday. The tracking stays in place until somebody dies.'

'What is more important than drafting this request, Sergeant?' Jacobson asked again.

'My life.' Carter left the room.

83

JFDI

The custody desk was empty. *He'll be having his tea*, Carter thought, plunging into the ground floor rooms, usually the exclusive enclave of the uniformed bobbies. 'Tam! Jesus Christ, where are you?'

'Try the garden,' said a uniform, referring to the underground cell complex. 'He'll be tending the plants.'

Carter limped downstairs like a three-legged donkey failing to outrun the vet, nearly crashing into the veteran copper as he came up the stairs.

'Has a package arrived this morning from Helen Street?'

'Aye.' He found the box and put it on the desk.

Carter tore the plastic sheath and took out Kelsa's phone.

'I need a car to take me home. I can't drive.'

'Cheryl will have to authorise it. There's a form to fill out,' he said haughtily.

'She's busy, but she told me I could have whatever I needed. There's going to be another killing,' he looked at his watch, 'any time before midnight – unless Moore is arrested.'

'Hmm.' Tam wasn't convinced a human life weighed

equally with the unauthorised use of a police vehicle.

'For fuck's sake,' said Carter, losing the plot. 'What's happened to your spirit of Just Fucking Do It?'

'Corporate accountability,' Tam said. 'My nuts are on the line if the cost isn't justified.'

'My nuts have been in the line of fire recently, and I have the swellings to prove it.' Carter replied, hand on his zip. 'Want to see?'

Tam Watson deflated. 'Naw, well, but– I heard what happened. I'll see what I can do. By the way, don't mention JFDI to anyone from Corporate; it's a sacking offence these days.'

Carter dialled Dr Flowers' number while he stared at Kelsa's phone. He needed to get home, but Lisa had his car. 'When can you get down here?' he said. 'I need your help.'

There was a slight hesitation on the line that Carter instantly picked up. 'What's happened?'

'My contract has been terminated. The Chief called me twenty minutes ago. I'm packing now, got a plane at half ten this morning. I'm sorry, Leccy.'

'Unpack. The only place you're going is with me. Bring my car – we've got a video to watch.' He killed the call and limped his way up four flights of stairs. At McKinlay's office, he didn't knock. The three inspectors were precisely where he'd left them.

'Ma'am,' he said interrupting. 'With respect, what the fuck is going on? Dr Flowers' insight is vital to help us catch Moore. She understands his behaviour.'

DCI Jacobson jumped in before McKinlay could answer. 'She is not an operational resource, Sergeant. She has implemented the counselling initiative that she was engaged to do. Her job is finished: it's as simple as that. We must control costs.'

'Arrange a TV slot to find Joe Moore,' he spoke directly to Jacobson. 'And while you're appealing to the public, you can justify the murders of women in this town as an operational efficiency. Tell us if the public agrees with your approach.' Carter was incandescent. 'You need to take a good look at yourself, Inspector.'

Jacobson was speechless.

'Ma'am,' Carter addressed McKinlay again. 'You agreed Dr Flowers could work with me on this case, so she has your operational authorisation. We're this close to catching Moore, and when we do, we'll need someone in the interview room who has sat in front of psychopaths and made them weep.'

A thin smile flashed across DCI McKinlay's face. Carter knew he'd won. All that remained was the theatre and Jacobson hadn't read her lines.

'Karen,' said McKinlay, 'the remit of the MIT on this case is crucial. You have extensive experience in managing complex cases, and I welcome your judgement. I also welcome the new minds you're bringing to the table. All of them good police officers; just what we need to ensure the case files have no gaps and all leads are accounted for and watertight. Putting this case before the Fiscal is a vital task. That is why I suggested your team could help. Are we agreed?'

'Yes, of course, but—'

'Do your officers have any experience interviewing suspects with complex mental disorders? Narcissism, bipolar, sociopathy, or DID?'

'Not that I'm aware of, but I can request—'

'I believe Dr Flowers added a profile assessment into ICRS on the personality type we're dealing with here that has greatly influenced the direction of the investigation. You are familiar with that assessment?'

'Well—'

'I'm going to call the Chief Superintendent now. Will you support my request for Dr Flowers' contract to be extended for, say, a couple of weeks? In light of the evidence of her efforts so far. I'm sure he's not entirely familiar with her work in this regard. Still, we can convince him of his role in bringing a vicious killer to justice with your support. Yes?'

Jacobson paused. 'Of course.'

McKinlay nodded. 'Carry on, Sergeant.'

84

Murder by Proxy

Ten minutes later, a horn sounded on St Leonard's Street. Carter squeezed himself into the passenger's seat of his own car, preferring it to Tam Watson's option. Another dose of Dicloflex dulled the inflammation in his nuts but kept him sharp.

'What's happening this morning?' Dr Flowers asked.

'The MIT have found something to do. They're going to appeal to the public for sightings of Moore, and McKinlay has agreed your contract extension.'

As they pulled into the drive at his home, Carter's phone rang again.

'Sergeant Carter,' Rocketman greeted him. 'Sad news about this latest victim, it's still total chaos at Waverley Station. Lily's remains were taken to Cowgate mortuary about an hour ago. The post-mortem is scheduled for midday, though I can't see there is any doubt over cause of death.'

'We need to confirm a few things, though,' Carter said, putting the phone on speaker so Dr Flowers could listen. 'Was she drugged, was she raped, and how did she get onto the tracks? Was she lying on the tracks when the train ran over her or was she pushed, like Alice, as the train went underneath the bridge?'

'We know she had a phone in her bag that held a message meant for Leccy,' added Dr Flowers. 'Moore has likely set all this up. But it's still possible she put herself in front of the train.'

'A new case file has been set up for L Sutherland,' Rocketman replied. 'We have swabs and samples, and the team is working on it now. Do you want her bloodwork prioritised, Leccy?'

'Yes, sir.'

'The rape assessment will have to wait until after the PM. You can be there yourself, of course.'

'I have Kelsa's phone. Gavin Roy downloaded all the content and has tracked her locations covering the whole weekend she went missing. She was treated for a date-rape drug in Glasgow's Royal Infirmary. She was a victim too.'

Dr Flowers put her hand on his arm. Rocketman spoke up through the speaker, 'I'm sorry we doubted you, Leccy.'

'It clears up a mystery,' he said flatly. 'I have to die because Kelsa dumped him for me. She was the first, then Alice, now Lily, and he's got reasons to keep going unless I stop him. He's been careful and has made sure he can't be directly implicated in any of these crimes. Kelsa's death: circumstantial. Alice: attempted suicide. Lily: also maybe-suicide. Jacky Dodds: maybe-accident. Four coincidences, each hard to prove individually. Or all of them are murder by proxy and orchestrated by Moore. It might not even be Moore.'

'So, what next, Leccy?' Rocketman asked.

'Kelsa's phone. There's something on it that could turn this pure speculation into hard fact.'

85

Crimewatch

'Thanks for staying with me last night, Leccy. But why am I here?' The Dr Flowers Carter knew was back. 'What do you need from me?'

'I want your opinions, your support and your prowess at unpicking rhymes.'

They went inside Carter's home, and Dr Flowers immediately noticed the emojis stuck on the pictures hanging in the stairwell.

'There are more upstairs,' he said. 'Check them out while I get things ready. Coffee or tea?'

'Lady Grey if you have it; otherwise, your local sheep's pish instant will do.'

Ten minutes later, she was back, and he was ready with two cups of coffee.

'Emojis are used in social media chats to let the reader know the sender's mood,' she said, sipping the hot coffee. 'Obviously, in a chat setting, they're innocuous, and he's chosen these emojis because of their harmlessness. He's turned something innocent into a vile warning. He'll have found this stunt hilarious. He's saying you don't exist. By placing emojis over your eyes, he's obliterating you.'

'He broke into my mother-in-law's home on Wednesday and left a teddy bear in Nathaniel's cot. The bear had emoji eyes. I told Jude to get rid of it.'

'Really?' Dr Flowers said in awe. 'That was brave of him.'

Carter shook his head. 'He's trying to tell me that no one in my family is safe. He has skills, Lisa. Skills that ordinary people don't possess.'

'Yesterday, he could have killed you and been done with it,' she mused. 'But he didn't. In his mind, the situation was too dangerous. It was unplanned and he wasn't in control. The fact that you designed it and it nearly came off probably unnerved him. I wonder if Lily's death was planned for later, but once he knew you were going to Gorebridge, he judged he could have fun with you. He must've got back into town in a rush and brought his plans forward. But in doing so, he's exposed a weakness. Unfortunately for her, she had to die so he could reboot his controlling personality. I've just thought of something. If he's visited Nathaniel, what's to stop him visiting your grandparents?'

'Jesus, Lisa. No. You want me to use them as bait? You're sick.' Carter stood up to make a call to them. 'Have a look at these rhymes instead.'

She heard his muffled words through the closed kitchen door. After a few minutes, he slumped back down on the sofa. On the coffee table was Kelsa's phone, laptop and the single sheet of paper.

'They're fine – nothing unusual. I told them to go away for a week, so they're going to Ayr. They're terrified.'

'The number means what?' Flowers looked at the codes on

the paper.

'The passcode for her phone. I can't get into her laptop. I'm assuming she wanted to conceal the obvious and she didn't want just anyone getting access.'

'OK,' Dr Flowers said. '"*Licence to thrill, M*" must be a play on James Bond's "licence to kill". Did she and you have a love of Bond movies?'

'When we married in Las Vegas, I wore a tuxedo and she dressed as Tiffany Case in "*Diamonds are Forever*". The witnesses came as extras from the movie.'

'Right. M was Bond's boss, so is there a link to McKinlay?'

'Kelsa only met McKinlay once, but I talked about her, sometimes.'

'You need a licence to get married in Las Vegas,' Flowers said.

'I've got the marriage licence in the safe.' Moments later, he came back with the document. 'It's got a serial number on it. I'll try it on her computer.'

It didn't work.

'Try the video password on her phone,' Dr Flowers said.

It worked.

Carter switched on his TV and cast the video on to it.

'Are you sure you want me here, Leccy? She's gone to a lot of trouble to make sure no one can watch this by accident.'

'The date and time put it when she was in the hotel with Moore,' Carter said, 'according to Gavin's assessment. It could be the evidence we need, and you're a credible witness. If you don't do it, I'd have to ask Mason.'

Lisa Flowers considered the implications for a moment, swallowed the rest of her coffee and said, 'I need to go to the loo first. When I come back, tell me if it is what you think it is.'

86

Boxed Set

'Well?' Flowers asked.

Carter nodded.

'Before we go any further,' she said, distancing herself from him on a cushioned chair, 'I have to declare my reluctance, but feel I must do this. I've only ever come face to face with men like Moore after they've been through the prison system. With years and decades stretching ahead of them in secure facilities, they find different ways to cope, knowing they'll never taste freedom again. Art, writing or religion, one way or another, eventually they want to speak about their crimes.'

'Making peace?' Carter asked.

Flowers nodded. 'But there's one per cent of the one per cent that is just evil.'

'And Moore is in that percentile?'

'In Gorebridge, he looked at me like I was food. What I thought was fieldwork clearly isn't. I'm conflicted between advancing my career in psychology and exposing my feelings of being a woman in a world dominated by malevolent male power. Sitting here, I feel like live prey. But I'm determined not to be a victim by proxy either.'

'You don't have to do this, Lisa, I'll ask Nick—'

'Don't treat me like the little woman who can't make up her mind, Leccy. I'm not asking for your permission. I can, and will make my own choice, but I have to be comfortable with who I'll be afterwards.'

'The female of the species—'

'Don't patronise me, *Sergeant* Carter. Lily didn't have the choice I now have, and that's before we know anything about her life and who she was. Kelsa made this choice to save you, so don't you ever forget it.'

'I'll shut up, will I?'

'Rape changes women's lives. The justice system denies them true legitimacy. Alice might see Moore brought to justice, but Kelsa and Lily never will, so I'm privileged to be able to speak to it on their behalf. Press the damn button.'

Two hours later, they sat in stunned silence, gathering their thoughts. Dr Flowers' face was wet with tears. Carter was stupefied, and his eyes were red too.

Kelsa had endured a brutal and violent attack that had left her unconscious. Somehow, she had hidden her phone in a position that recorded every single second of her ordeal. Yet Moore seemed unaware of its existence.

Instinctively, Carter knew this wasn't the first time this had happened to her. She had known what was coming, and she wanted him to see it as a detective, not as a husband. In the final ten minutes of the video, Moore had abandoned her to fate, she had regained consciousness, and her disturbed face appeared on camera.

Kelsa looked directly to camera, and he felt a shiver run up his back. He was glad of Dr Flowers' presence because it gave him reason to keep himself together.

'I don't know what to do now, Lachlan.' Kelsa spoke through tears. 'I don't know when you'll get to see this recording, or if it will be lost or destroyed. Whatever circumstances you are in, you must know that I love you with all I have. I didn't want this to happen. I regret not talking about my past, but I couldn't take the chance of you walking away if I told you about him. Anybody would, he's a maniac, and he blames you for the things that happened to him when he was young.

'Once I realised how deeply you loved me, it became utterly impossible for me to recall those past experiences. Had you known and left me, I would have fallen into my pit of darkness again. Except, this time, I wouldn't have come back, because no one could be better for me than you, my darling.

'Years before we met when I first got involved with him, I thought I could help him. He wasn't the only one who'd experienced a horrendous childhood, and so, innocently, I saw us as kindred spirits. But his demons are terribly violent, and eventually I couldn't take any more. I left him. I don't know what you might have discovered about him before seeing this, but he contacted me again when he heard we were together. He became jealous and made threats to me and described what he would do to you. We met so I could calm him down. He wanted to try again, promising to control himself, that things between us would be different. I explained you were the one for me. He asked, and stupidly I told him about you, how you became an orphan and who you were now. But he wouldn't let it go and kept badgering me. I worried he would do something, so when you and I went to Las Vegas, I thought getting married there and then would do it. He would finally leave me alone to get on with my new life with you.

‘But he didn't, and now, after this, I know he will never, ever, leave me alone. Our future is so unclear, Lachlan, yet it's so precious to me. I won't tell you what has happened here when I get home, and I think things will be awkward between us for a long time. But if you love me as much as I believe you do, you'll understand.

‘If you don't, I have only one other choice.’

87

Post-mortem

'Are you OK?' Dr Flowers asked. 'More coffee?'

'No,' he said, glancing at his watch and avoiding answering her reasonable question.

'Come on,' he stood up from the couch, 'let's sort ourselves out and go to Cowgate. We'll catch the business end of Lily's post-mortem.'

They made the drive in silence. When they arrived, Nick Mason was in the viewing gallery watching the activity. His face was grim. This wasn't the time for west-coast gallows humour.

'Is it over yet?' Carter asked.

'Death by train, as we know, but it wasn't going fast. The driver said he was only doing fifteen miles per hour.'

'Did he see her on the tracks? Surely even a long train can stop quickly from that speed?'

'She wasn't on the tracks,' said Mason, tight-lipped. 'As the train passed under the bridge, she fell in front of him.'

'Feet first or head first?'

'I don't think that question was asked.' Mason looked at

Carter. 'Is it important?'

'Coming up to the bridge, did the driver see anyone on it?'

'He was watching the signals, and it was dark. Said he's never seen anyone on that bridge. The gardens side of the bridge has a padlocked gate, only Network Rail has the key. Someone could've climbed over it though.'

'All the public gates to the gardens from the city were locked as they are every night,' Carter said. 'On the castle side of that bridge, there's no gate. Can I speak to the pathologist?'

'Fill your boots,' said Mason.

Carter pressed the button for the microphone. 'Professor, it's Sergeant Carter here, we've met once before.'

'Yes, Sergeant,' replied the pathologist. 'What would you like to know?'

'I think the victim was deliberately drugged, sometime before going over the footbridge parapet. Are you familiar with Scoop?'

'We'll have to wait for toxicology to confirm it, I'm afraid,' she said. 'But yes, it's one of the date-rape drugs. Potency can vary because it's manufactured in unofficial labs. Your own techs have access to known signatures, so I can't comment on where it might've come from.'

'But the effect of a large dose on a woman of Lily's size and weight? How far could she walk unaided, over, say, a steepish hill, and rough ground? Coming down from Castle Esplanade, for example?'

'Leading the witness, Sergeant? Scopolamine is taken up quickly by the body, one reason for its date-rape success. I'd say not very far if she was on her own, and on ground like that, she'd quickly lose her senses. She'd probably tumble down the slope. And before you ask, there was no evidence of a fall, no dirt, earth, grass. Nothing like that.'

'What about the soles of her feet?'

'Both feet were severed by the train, but we have them, of course. She was wearing stockings, not tights; they were ripped off and wrapped themselves around the wheels of the train. Her soles were clean, no dirt embedded in the skin, which would be the case if she walked or stumbled barefoot down a hill, even with stockings on. What's your point, caller?'

'She was carried down the hill, I think. He gave her more Scoop on the bridge, and they were on the bridge for a while. I think she was out of it when he took her shoes off. If she landed feet first, wouldn't the angle of the cuts made by the wheels present a different scenario than if she landed head first? One could be suicide, the other murder. Do you know how she landed, Professor?'

Carter looked at Mason as if he was about to say something more. Then the pathologist answered.

'Yes, head first, legs pointing west, in the direction of travel of the train.'

88

Surveillance

Outside the mortuary, in the dank subterranean underworld of Cowgate, Dr Flowers got into the driver's side of Carter's car. From the passenger's seat, Carter took a call from Gavin Roy in Glasgow. He put it on speaker.

'Leccy,' said Roy, 'I'm confused. You're tracking two mobile phones that have just arrived here by courier. And the tracking plot for the phone registered to Joe Moore isn't picking up a signal. It must be switched off.'

'The two phones were found in a victim's handbag,' said Carter. 'I'm fairly sure why his phone is there, and if that's confirmed, it will solve another mystery.'

'For real-time tracking, we're commanded to set up round-the-clock surveillance, with oversight from one of Jim Geddes' crew. If there's no action, he might shut it down and snap on the latex gloves for a wee chat with you.'

'Put me through to him, will you?' Carter asked.

'Sergeant Carter, I wondered when you'd call,' Geddes said cheerfully. 'Thought you'd be dying to know what I've got on your suspected rapist.'

'Add killer to the suspected crimes, sir.'

'I won't detain you if you need to accost him now.'

'The information you have may be important.'

'The details we have might never be heard in court. Joe Moore is ex-Special Boat Service. Known in the trade as *"the lads from Poole"*.'

Carter looked across at Dr Flowers. Flowers glanced back, the fear in her eyes communicating what they both felt.

'He was a soldier with an outstanding operational record in Afghanistan and elsewhere. A photo will be in your inbox in a moment. He's multilingual in Farsi, Pashto and Arabic and was a sniper and telecoms specialist in the field. He was discharged from service in 2010 when he was questioned about the death of a woman in Bournemouth who fell from a bridge and was killed by a train.'

Dr Flowers nodded but kept her eyes on the road. Carter listened, his insides churning, not sure if he should be afraid or elated.

'The locals couldn't pin anything on him,' Geddes continued, reading from notes, Carter assumed. 'However, something had also happened in Helmand, involving a woman and her brothers. All three were Taliban, so the Service decided he should leave. Although much of his active duty record is sealed, InterMide put him forward as their lead to work with MI6 a few years ago. His involvement in developing the messaging nano-app and other secret applications has been crucial, so this is a bit of an embarrassment for the Services. They're keen to help if you need it.'

'When did he join the Army?' Carter asked.

'SBS is affiliated to the Navy, not Army. He was twenty

when he joined the Marines in 2004,' Geddes confirmed. 'I'll email you his record before the SBS, but there's nothing to see from 2005 to 2010.'

When they finished the call, Carter opened email on his phone and found the message within a minute. A picture of a younger and leaner Joe Moore smiled for the camera. The sneer he'd displayed when sitting next to Alice was already there, though not quite as pronounced. Carter scanned Moore's service record and administrative notes and spotted something. Immediately, he posted the photo and record into ICRS, adding a note for immediate follow-up, assigned to DC Garcia.

He dialled the office number for St Leonard's and spoke to her.

'Hi Leccy, how are you feeling?'

'Much the same as you, I suspect. How's the knee?'

'Sore.'

'Did you follow up with InterMide on Joe Moore?'

'I'm expecting a call back at any time.'

'I've added his force's record to ICRS. Spot the home address.'

There was a delay while Garcia located the record. She came back on the phone, 'It's the same one used for his bank accounts.'

'Have you or anyone else talked to his parents? George and Corina, if I remember.'

'I haven't, I'm not sure about our retired Met copper though.'

'Track the parents down and if your man can't find them, tell him to go to the local hatch, match and dispatch. Call me as soon as you know.'

89

Miss Hetty

At St Leonard's, Tam Watson had a message for Carter. 'Cheryl McKinlay wants to see you.'

Dr Flowers helped him climb the stairs. 'You're like an old man, Leccy.'

'It's coming together, Lisa. We're nearly there,' he said. 'I hope this isn't more grief from Jacobson.'

The scene in McKinlay's office was like the opening of *Groundhog Day*. McKinlay and Mason sitting behind the desk, and a few empty chairs on the visitor's side. In between McKinlay and Mason was a woman of McKinlay's age. A folder sat on the desk in front of her. She wore thick round glasses and a look that could shatter planets on sight. Somewhat confused, Dr Flowers helped Carter to a chair.

'Sergeant Carter,' McKinlay began. 'We have an HR issue regarding your non-disclosure of key information, affecting your ability to do your job to the fullest extent. Miss Hetty, here,' McKinlay indicated the woman, 'is present to take notes and to ensure I stick to the script.'

'Ma'am?' Carter queried, sitting up straighter.

'From time to time, we review various databases and lists, all in the name of governance and compliance. Operational officers can not be put in positions where they may be open to compromise. Specialist companies conduct searches on our behalf. If they find anything of concern, they notify Miss Hetty's colleagues in Human Resources. HR then approach me to fill in any blanks. An example may be when a criminal offers an inducement in return for an officer turning a blind eye to certain illegal activities. In such circumstances, loss of trust between colleagues results in a dysfunctional team. Compromised officers have no place in my team. Is there anything you'd like to say before I continue, Sergeant?'

Carter looked at Dr Flowers, but he had to ask.

'Were you told about this, Lisa?'

'No – How would I know what she's talking about?' Dr Flowers complained. 'Have you been taking kickbacks from criminals?'

'No,' he almost shouted. His worst nightmare was here, and the potential outcome would put him back to where he'd been nearly two weeks ago.

'Is this a disciplinary meeting, ma'am?' he asked, playing for time. 'Has DCI Jacobson made a complaint against me?'

'No,' McKinlay said, flatly. 'This meeting is about gathering facts from officers in possession of those facts. There may be mitigating circumstances to be aired. However, unless the truth comes out at the earliest opportunity, it's difficult to determine the range of outcomes. Do you understand, Sergeant?'

'If the facts emerged, would it affect my role in the cases I'm running?' Carter knew the answer.

'As SIO of the Deacon case, it would directly impact your

role and would likely result in DCI Jacobson's MIT taking over the investigation.'

'Meaning Moore will be free to attack other women.'

'Get it off your chest, Lachlan,' urged McKinlay. 'And hang the consequences.'

Even now, his instinct told him he should say nothing, that somehow, he could keep it quiet and get back to chasing Joe Moore before he killed again. He knew that wasn't going to happen.

'It's all about Nathaniel,' he said, putting his head in his hands.

'The interdict,' clarified McKinlay. 'You felt you could keep it quiet until you worked something out, or until your solicitor convinced your father-in-law to lift it?'

'Yes,' he conceded.

'Had you come to me earlier with this, we could have found a solution. But it's too late. You need time to reflect, Sergeant Carter. I've given you too much rope. First of all, you need to fix things at home, and once that's resolved, we'll reconvene this panel to determine what your future is.'

'What does that mean?' Carter asked.

'From this moment, Sergeant Carter,' said DCI McKinlay without emotion, 'you are indefinitely suspended from duty.'

90

Cracking Up

Dr Flowers drove him home in silence. Carter invited her in; it was his turn to not want to be alone. In the kitchen, the kettle boiled and instant coffee was made. She sat at the kitchen table, he propped himself against a worktop, sipping from the hot mug.

'This is a fucking disaster,' Carter said after a long silence. 'I'll take my chances with the panel, but Moore is going to get away.'

'Others will pick it up,' Dr Flowers replied. 'DCI Jacobson—'

Carter threw his coffee mug hard against the far wall. The violence of its demise into smithereens caused Dr Flowers to flinch.

'Jacobson is an arse,' Carter shouted, venting his pent-up anger. 'The force is full of jobsworths like her. Pen-pushers, risk reviewers, compliance officers—'

'McKinlay will take over.' Flowers glanced at the far wall as rivers of coffee trickled down the plasterboard like dirty blood.

'She's too old.' Carter started pacing the kitchen. 'Mason might be able to deal with Moore but look what happened in the club. He was on the floor in seconds. I'm a fool, I should have told her about the interdict.' He punched the nearest wall and left a big dent in the plaster.

'You know this isn't all about the force, Leccy,' she said. 'You've just watched your wife being raped on video.'

'Not now,' he said tightly. 'This isn't the time.'

'It is time.' She wouldn't let it go. 'Deal with it, Leccy.'

'Fuck her, and fuck you,' he shouted. 'She's got what she really wanted. She's dead. She's checked out and abandoned me to deal with it. She planned all this, even her own rape, for fuck's sake. Who does that, eh? Now she's fucking with my head because she knew he'd come for me but didn't care enough to give me warning.'

'That's unfair, Leccy. OK, she said it herself, she initially thought Moore was a kindred spirit, but once she realised what she'd gotten into, she bailed. She didn't *ask* to be raped. But she went through with it because she felt she had no other choice. She had to protect you and her marriage.'

'Nathaniel is not my son.' Tears began to show in his eyes. 'I know it, I just know it.'

'You don't know it,' Dr Flowers said, calmly.

He turned away from her and faced the wall, so she couldn't see the tears. 'But do I really want to know? The birth certificate clearly states that I am not his father. She instructed Dunsmuir to leave that entry blank.'

'Was that why she wanted to die?' she asked him quietly. 'She couldn't deal with the consequences for her marriage if her son had a rapist for a father?'

'I've always known he wasn't mine; I just wouldn't admit

it.'

Dr Flowers heard. This was the core of his pain. It all came down to this. Nathaniel wasn't his blood.

'A DNA test will bring closure,' she advised him. 'You can't move on until you know.'

'And if it proves he's not of me, then what? I couldn't go back to work. I'd be a laughing stock. "There's Lachlan Carter. His wife had an affair and pretended the boy was his." What about my vocation then, Petal? I'd be better off buddying-up with Duggie McLean on the street, or maybe I'd fill Jacky Dodds' role as the resident freak.'

'Don't beat yourself up, it's not your style,' Flowers said dismissively. 'What can I do? This interdict, how can it be lifted?'

Carter pulled himself together. Practical things, actions, not emotions, were what he needed. 'Tommy McGregor has to approach Dunsmuir, see if he can persuade him to see sense. Now I'm benched, I'll see McGregor about it tomorrow.'

'What was next on the list to catch Moore? Will Mason or Jacobson pick up the threads from ICRS?'

'Yes, if they can. Mason and Charli Garcia could get things to move quickly.'

'OK,' said Dr Flowers, standing up. 'It's time for me to go. You won't do anything stupid, will you?' She gazed into his eyes, searching for deeper signs of his vulnerability. 'I'll stay with you tonight if you want?'

'When have I ever done anything stupid?'

After she'd gone, Carter sat on the sofa and looked at Kelsa's MacBook. Dr Flowers had shown him the way, and the last puzzle was easy. *Zip up a dress, Joe.* The zip code and address of Joe's seafood restaurant in Las Vegas. It took him a couple of tries to get the number combo right, then he was in.

Now what? Logic told him there was something on the laptop for him. It didn't take him long to find. A folder called 'Joe's Seafood' held two videos. The titles said, 'For Lachlan' and 'For Mother'.

His video was dated September 2018, and when he played it, Kelsa appeared on camera. She looked healthy – if skinny – but troubled.

'*Hello, my love,*' she said with a weak smile. '*We made it to now. If you don't know what I'm talking about, my password clue has been far too easy, and you should first watch the video that's on my phone.*' She spoke the password to him.

'*After watching it, you'll have questions. You're a detective, a good one, and you'll get justice for me, I know you will. What did you get yourself into and just who am I, your wife? I love the sound of those words – "I am your wife" – because I always believed in the fairy-tale ending of a wedding. Through the dark days of childhood, the fairy tale kept me sane. The magical end of the story was achievable only for adults, and, oh, how I wished to be an adult. Once I was grown up, everything that went before would be scrubbed clean. True love would establish itself forever— such childish dreams. Real life was very different, but you, my love, re-lit my magical flame.*

'*I was sent to boarding school in England as a teenager. I knew why, of course, but knowing doesn't excuse it. I was called a rebel, and rebels must be rehabilitated. The reprogramming worked, and I was allowed back into the family home in time for university. I was on track I got instructed quite a lot in those days, and regularly. After all, I couldn't sully the family name.*

'Do you know about Hugo? Ask Daddy if you don't, he can tell you what a controlling bastard Hugo was. Well, it takes one to know one. Hugo had high-society plans for me. As an escort. Yes, my love, he put me to work. It was back to rehab for me when I punctured his ego with one of my stilettos. I've often wondered what Hugo's family really knows about him. My truth could blow their lives apart, but his children are innocent.

'But what you really want to know is: what will happen to us now? Hugo introduced me to Joe. But Hugo was a pussycat by comparison. Joe promised me once that he'd deal with Hugo, but Hugo tumbled down Joe's priority list after I dumped him. More rehab for me, for a similar but different reason. After I'd gone through all that, I thought the dark days were over – the memories of Joe faded into the background, and you burst into my present. Life turned good, and we got married.

'Joe had other ideas when he found out you and I were serious, and that was when he told me things. First of all, Joe died of meningitis when he was eighteen.'

91

Leading the Witness

'I'm sitting on our bed, explaining things, but you're not here. You're at work, locking up criminals and keeping people safe. You don't yet know of Joe Moore but you soon will, unfortunately, and it's all my fault. He has a well-honed skill of extracting information from people under the guise of conversation, and in my praise of you, I said too much. However, I have not said enough, and you are wondering how a dead man can carry out such crimes. It's simple when you know his name is really Nathan Butler. He will come for you now, and later he'll come for me. He has what he wants from me for now, and I genuinely have no idea what he will do next. I hope by the time you see this video, it's not too late.

'You accepted my silence about that weekend in March, and I often wonder what has gone through your mind since then. You're not stupid, but because of our love, you are letting me deal with it in the only way I know. Thank you, and I apologise now for everything that may happen in our futures. It is all of my doing.

'I have spent so much time working through the options. I've

concluded there's only one option that gives me control of my life. Had I taken this path a long time ago, you would not now be in this hellish predicament, but you are, and it is for me to resolve it for both of us. I've put plans are in motion as I speak to you now.'

Carter watched as she reached out to him. She held her hand on the screen and said nothing. He touched the screen and said nothing in reply. When she took her hand away, tears were in her eyes.

'Father has been instrumental, and he has good reasons. He will carry out my wishes, but he is not privy to my thoughts and feelings. He will have to deal with the consequences in his own way, as will Mother, although she knows nothing. As for our unborn son – I asked the doctors for the sex – against your wishes, my darling, but by the time you watch this, you will know him. His welfare is everything, but for me, there are still many weeks until his birth. I wrestle with my demons every day, and those demons will ultimately determine my fate.'

Carter needed a drink after she'd finished speaking. The Balvenie was the ideal tonic, so he went to the local off-licence and bought another bottle. The first glass didn't touch the sides.

Kelsa was baffling when she was alive, but in death, she was enigmatic. For every 'why' answered, more questions popped up. Led by Butler-once-Moore, his wife was orchestrating her moves from beyond the grave.

As if a page had turned, his phone reminded him he had an important appointment.

[2019-01-24:2117] Go to Arthur's Seat, below the cairns on the west side. Midnight. Don't bring your friends to the funeral, and

don't be late because Death is always on time. J.

He had time for another drink. There was another video to watch.

92

Sheep Heid

A burden had been lifted, and he actually felt lighter. Things he'd dared not consider were now thinkable. Finally, it made sense to a simple man – in a warped, twisted and knotted way. At least he now knew why she wanted to die, but he felt weak at the strength, courage and willpower it must have taken to see it through. Maybe she'd tasted death's breath in another place and had left a promise. This time, as the end came, she knew she could make it.

With time on his hands, he attempted a login on ICRS through his own laptop, hoping the tidal wave of suspension processes hadn't yet reached the technological far-shore of departmental usernames. It hadn't, and he was in. He located the CCTV video taken from the bus that had killed Jacky Dodds. Charli Garcia had taken a punt on it when she put it to Justin Greig; she hadn't actually seen it then. There were multiple camera angles. From the driver's cab, he saw Dodds running in front of the bus and from the front door he saw the Samaritan converging on Dodds. He scrubbed both clips back and forwards until he was satisfied it was premeditated.

He dressed warmly in hiking boots, caught the late bus into town, alighted at Bernard Terrace, and headed up the hill. He'd shovelled more painkillers down his throat, chasing them with more whisky. He needed to be alert and careful. His dongles couldn't take another ringing.

Hillwalking on Arthur's Seat required decent fitness during daylight, but it took on an aspect of danger at night. Suicides off the Salisbury Crags were common. It took forty-five minutes of painful scrambling until the lights of the city were presented before him. Conditions on the hill were damp and slippery, winter grass with mist obscuring the cairns at the very top.

He had prepared. He'd texted Flowers, telling her where he was going and why. If he didn't check in by half-past midnight, she was to call Nick Mason.

'This isn't clever, Leccy,' Dr Flowers had warned. 'You're suspended and injured. You should be in bed.'

'I'm following your advice,' he replied. 'I'll ask him what he remembers about the 1989 accident.'

'I didn't advise you to throw yourself headlong at a killer, in a martyr's vengeance for the death of your parents and wife.'

He was on a slope of wild grassland on the northwest side of the hill. Once there had been a hill fort here, and in places, the ridged walls provided meagre cover. Even though the visibility was down to twenty-five metres, he'd still see Butler coming from any direction, except directly behind. Carter crouched down, hands in the pockets of his weather jacket, and took a 360-degree survey. His watch said 00.05 a.m. and the time agreed for the rendezvous was midnight. He felt something on the dampness, a breath, and turned to face it.

'Nathan,' Carter said in anticipation, watching a shadow eerily emerge from the mist. He was tall – over six feet – and broad-shouldered, moving with the trained step of an experienced soldier negotiating a minefield. Carter pressed his finger on the phone in his pocket, sending his planned text.

'You took your time getting here,' Butler replied in an accent bred in London's East End, dipped in Scots and roasted in Arabia.

'You could've finished me at Gorebridge.'

'Better this way.'

'I've known about you both for a while.' Carter maintained his distance as Butler edged closer.

'Not until it was in your face. You're quite stupid, really.'

'You pushed Jacky Dodds under the bus,' Carter laid it out. 'Captured on video. Pretty dumb for a so-called smart soldier.'

'I didn't touch 'im, Carter.' Butler kept reducing the distance between them. They began edging upwards, towards the summit and the cairns.

'You didn't know the buses have cameras, did you?' Carter said, aware only a few metres separated him from death. 'The Bournemouth girl, she wasn't the first, was she?'

'Some girls go all wobbly at heights.'

'Why use Joe's identity?'

'You've no idea, Carter, what life was like then. We was mates, he was all I could trust after Da was—'

Carter interrupted him. 'We have his death certificate.'

'I was seven when your car smashed our motor,' Butler edged closer. 'You was lucky, too young to know your Ma and Da, but I 'ave memories. After Ma died, the Yardies came. Da's head exploded when I shot 'im. If they'd given *'im* the gun, he'd have done me nae bother. I still see him some nights. You really 'ave no fuckin' idea.'

'Joe helped you join the Forces.'

'Got the Jamaicans off my back. Joe's a true mate, never breathes a word to anyone.'

'Tell me about Kelsa.'

'Let's 'ave a drink, Leccy. Old mates, chattin' about our women. The Sheep Heid is just over the 'ill.'

Carter couldn't see how to get off the hill without Butler cornering him. He pulled out his phone. 'I'm calling it in.'

'For fuck's sake, Carter, you're really a stupid cunt,' Butler laughed. He pulled out a device half the size of a mobile phone from his pocket and waved it at Carter. 'Been blocking your phone since I got 'ere. Military issue lifesaver. Stopped the ragheads from blowin' us up. Your pals in Cybercrime think I'm watchin' Strictly.'

'And Kelsa?'

'Couldn't make it tonight, has to be somewhere. You're desperate to know, aren't you? Let's pick a stone around 'ere where you'll fall and smash your skull while gazing over the city at night.'

Carter glanced at his watch: 00.35 a.m. 'If I don't text soon, uniforms will be here in minutes.'

'You're flyin' solo, Carter. Nobody knows you're 'ere, that's how stupid you are. Anyway, I've gotten out of tighter scrapes than this.'

Butler sprang at him with the agility of a puma. Carter dodged downhill, following the path he'd climbed up. Butler was faster and stronger and soon caught up. Carter sidestepped, ducked, evaded and spun, turning back up the slope, the adrenaline suppressing the pain in his testicles and helping him push on. Going uphill, Butler was cumbersome, allowing Carter to put metres between them. Carter climbed the rocks towards the cairns, emerging on the steeper and dangerous city side.

Breathing hard as he scrambled, he lost his footing. Slipping and tumbling the city lights beckoned, then his head took a glancing blow on a sharp rock.

His eyes went woozy. Above him, a dark shape loomed.

Butler was about to kill him.

93

Home Run

He came to consciousness slowly, shivering, acutely aware of the cold. His head throbbed. Disorientated, a flurry of rain flashed across his face, and the smell of damp earth brought him back. Voices sailed on the wind. Cautiously, he clawed up the steep hill, every muscle complained – it was nearly too much, but somehow life drove him on. At the top, he saw multiple flashlights swaying, dancing and searching. Everywhere except where he was.

Pulling himself upright on the northern cairn, the sight before him was a miracle: a company of uniformed police officers. Then he remembered Butler's phone jammer. He struggled to keep his feet, using the cairn to steady himself. 'I could do with a medic,' he shouted to no one in particular. The lights converged on him as he stumbled down the rocky pathway, inches from death by extinct volcano.

Tam Watson emerged from the darkness, shining his light in the direction of the voice. 'Jesus. Leccy, what the fuck? You're bleeding, that's a bad cut on your head.'

'Is Mason here? Or Dr Flowers?' Carter casually asked the man who knew everything.

'Nick's here.' Tam Watson began tending his wound.

'Butler?'

'Is unconscious over there,' Tam pointed towards the Haunch. 'Nick says he's not Joe Moore. I dinnae understand, Leccy.'

'They're one and the same man, Tam,' Carter groaned. 'Tell Nick to cuff him before he recovers, or he'll scatter your boys over the hill like skittles.'

Tam motioned at two constables to get their cuffs out. 'Why are you here, Leccy?'

'I thought I could bring him in on my own.'

'You're a real twat,' Tam shook his head in disbelief while wrapping an elastic bandage tightly around Carter's head. Nick Mason appeared beside them.

'You can thank Flowers,' Mason said without compassion. 'She called me straight away, didn't wait for your daft deadline. The boss rounded up everyone we had. Even the Glen doesn't know about this wee soiree, yet. What the fuck were you thinking?'

'He wanted to meet up here. He raped my wife. If he raped your wife, you'd do the same.'

Mason ignored the protest. 'Charli got the birth and death certificates for Moore. Meningitis for Joe at eighteen. Then InterMide HR identified Joe Moore's picture as Nathan Butler, a senior executive who runs their Special Projects Division.'

'I knew that,' Carter said.

'How come?'

'I talk to the dead.'

'Did Butler hit you with his baseball bat?' Mason asked.

'No, I slipped and fell. He was about to crush my head with a rock.'

'So how did you manage to club him and drag him over there?'

94

Capture

Twelve hours later, Carter felt revived. He'd slept soundly at home, had had a relaxing breakfast and had taken congratulatory phone calls on his arrest from people he didn't know. Nobody called to revoke his indefinite suspension.

His head ached. He removed the bandage to check the wound on his forehead. It looked cool, but not quite the Harry Potter lightning bolt. He needed painkillers, so climbed into the Smart car and drove to Cameron Toll shopping centre. He wandered around the mall aimlessly, unsure, drained. Butler dominated his thoughts but was denied the critical activity of interviewing him. Who was leading the questions, and what approach were they taking?

He hoped it was Mason. He'd watched his DI skilfully twist and turn Jimmy Logan earlier in the week. McKinlay wouldn't get involved with the actual face-to-face but would offer guidance according to the evidence against him.

At 2 p.m. she finally called him.

'I heard about your escapade last night, Leccy. Why did you

follow through with Butler alone when you'd already been suspended from duty?'

'It was him and me,' Carter replied. 'Those were his conditions when he sent the message. I felt that maybe, somehow, I could bring him in.'

'You didn't inform me of this development at our meeting yesterday,' she said. Carter could hear the weariness in her voice when she challenged him about his ways of working.

'I did. During the discussion with DCI Jacobson,' he replied. 'Are you going to suspend me again?'

'DCI Jacobson questioned Butler this morning, but he hasn't said a word. Won't even confirm his name. He refuses to engage. His brief says his client will not cooperate unless you are the interviewing officer. So I've spent the morning saving your rump from the spit-roasting it deserves. The seniors all want you sacked, but now we have a problem they can't solve. The Chief Super is in a murderous mood but has agreed to lift your suspension temporarily. Get down here.'

Thirty minutes later, Carter stood in the observation room for Interviews One and Two, watching Nathan Butler awaiting his lawyer's return. Dr Flowers, DI Mason and DCI McKinlay were present.

'This bastard killed Jacky.' McKinlay kept it tight. 'You'd better not let him off the hook. You've to call this number before you go in,' she said, handing him a note.

'Understood, ma'am. Dr Flowers here will keep me straight.'

'Aye, right,' McKinlay said. 'I'll be upstairs. Nick will keep me informed.' She patted the lanky Detective Inspector on the shoulder and walked out of the room.

'I'll give Sergeant Carter and Dr Flowers a break in a while,'

Nick Mason said to her disappearing back. 'Charli Garcia will partner me.'

The interview began at 3 p.m. Dr Flowers operated the solid-state voice recorder for show, knowing multiple video cameras and dangling microphones in the room recorded second source material.

The contrast between Nathan Butler and his lawyer, Dominic Love, was stark. Carter suspected it was planned. Love wore a grey suit with a striped tie in two shades of pink, over a bright blue shirt, but it was the shock of ginger dreadlocks that marked him out as a special brief. Butler wore a black T-shirt and black jeans. His chin was on his chest, eyes closed, his arms folded. The epitome of a man finally defeated. Carter didn't buy it.

Butler spoke when Carter entered the room. 'Mate.'

'For the record please.' Carter spoke. 'Confirm name, address and age.'

'Sergeant Joe Moore, number 1520936.' He maintained his non-threatening manner.

'Joe Moore died a long time ago. Your name is Nathan Butler, you're thirty-five and live at The Limes, Easter Murray Avenue, Edinburgh. A huge house for a wee shite like you.'

'Sergeant, my client answered your question,' Love interjected with a Glenrothes accent, straight from Dougray Scott's housing scheme. 'There's no need for insults.'

'Tell me about your relationship with—' Carter paused as if choosing from a long list. 'Jacky Dodds.' This was Butler's weak point. 'You used Jacky to cover your tracks as Nathan, while Joe raped Alice for fun.'

Carter had been briefed by Geddes' friend that Moore had

twice been captured in the field, suffered torture, and escaped his captors both times. He was resourceful. Carter knew he didn't have the skills to get him to do anything he didn't want. 'He won't use the befriending techniques he might have used in the battlefield scenario,' said the Friend. 'It's a negotiation. Freedom is what he wants, so if you can offer him that, he might respond.'

'How am I going to do that?'

'Use your imagination,' Friend had said.

'When will you ask the questions, Sergeant?' Love said. 'We're waiting.'

'A double act, you two are,' Carter responded. 'When shown pictures, Nathan, four witnesses, identified you as the man closest to Jacky at the bus stop. And the CCTV from the bus shows you up close. Jacky was your problem, Nathan. I spooked him, and you lost him. In the Reverend, Jacky took your phone to lay a trail away from Alice, on your instructions, leaving us to chase Joe across town. But you left it too late to get the phone back. He'd gone walkabout, and the phone was dark. You found him once he lit it up, desperate for help. You knew we would discover the call you'd made to your own phone, but Jacky would be silenced by then. Dropping the phone into Lily's bag was spur-of-the-moment. You weren't thorough enough; as evidence, it confirmed you and Joe were the same person. Had you dumped it in a drain, we'd still have found it.'

'Ah,' said Love. 'Evidence. I wondered when we'd get to that. Do you have any worth discussing? My client attempted to save Mr Dodds' life at the bus stop – the witnesses were clear about that. Can we move on to something substantial, or cut to the credits and leave?'

'Alice Deacon,' Dr Flowers said. 'You raped her and pushed her off the footbridge. What drives you to kill, Nathan?'

Nobody replied to the question for a minute.

'My client has authorised me to answer on his behalf,' Love clarified finally. 'My client had been in a relationship with Miss Deacon, and sex was consensual, but she suffered from mental health issues.'

'Let's take a walk,' Carter said, scrutinising Butler's body language. 'Revisiting the scene of a crime can induce a grief-ridden confession. Shall we go to the bridge, Nathan? I'm willing. Are you?'

Butler stretched himself and regarded his watch, as if late for a meeting.

'Lily Sutherland,' Flowers took her turn. 'Raped, drugged, pushed off a bridge in front of a moving train. Bit of a pattern forming there.'

'My client ended his relationship with Miss Sutherland the day before,' Love said, expressionless. 'Clearly, she was fragile and distraught and took her own life. My client was at home sleeping and, unfortunately for him, he has no witness to attest to his slumber.'

'Kelsa Dunsmuir—'

'Ancient history, Sergeant Carter,' Love smiled smugly.

'Maybe for you.' Carter wanted to punch him and keep punching till he choked on his dreadlocks.

'Since her marriage – to you, Sergeant – my client hasn't seen or spoken to Mrs Carter. I expect you to be objective about this. My client's freedom is at stake.'

'Not seen her, eh, Nathan?' Carter grabbed the opportunity. 'What about the messages on her phone? We have them recorded as evidence of contact. Your advisor is lying, you know that. You haven't told him the truth.'

Butler still didn't react. At this pace, Carter would achieve nothing. Butler had been charged with assaulting a police officer, to get his DNA for comparison with the profiles from the National DNA Database. Love had complained about the charge and claimed it represented a fishing expedition. In a few hours or so Butler could be released, unless a judge was compelled to extend his time in custody based on more substantial fare.

It was tag time.

'Kings of Leon, Nathan. Great live band, aren't they?'

Dr Flowers stopped the recording, and they both left the room.

95

Sniper, Sniper

'Does that slothful stretch mean he's interested in your proposition, Leccy? Go to the bridge?' Dr Flowers asked as soon as they were in the observation room. 'DCI McKinlay won't agree to that, would she?'

'He's reacted to the possibility,' Carter replied. 'Nick, you can try the bad cop routine and see how far you get.'

'Brilliant handover, Leccy,' Mason said sarcastically. 'Where am I supposed to go with it?'

'Use some imagination.'

They climbed the stairs leaden-footed. 'Where did that experience land on your weeping psycho chart?' Carter asked her.

'He's in battlefield mode,' she replied. 'He doesn't care about the women; he's focused on you. You could try for shared experiences, things you both have in common. The accident— and Kelsa. You said he got all angry on the hill when you mentioned the things in his past. Maybe it's an angle?'

'Leading him to confess in tears?' Carter doubted it.

At the custody desk, Tam Watson beckoned them.

'Leccy, a woman's here asking for you. She's in office G Four.'

'It's not a good time, Tam.'

'She witnessed your fight last night.'

Carter stopped, stunned. He'd not seen anyone else on the hill. He found G Four, knocked, and went in. 'I'm Sergeant Carter, this is Dr—'

'Lisa Flowers,' said the woman sitting at a table. She was slim and well dressed, thirty-something, her black hair cut in a bob. The white blouse was open at the neck, revealing a silver St Christopher pendant on a chain. She smiled at them with anxious blue eyes.

'Jodie Reynolds,' she introduced herself hesitantly.

'How can we help, Miss Reynolds?' Carter sat across from her, missing the cue.

''I sent the greeting cards to your home.'

Carter and Flowers shared a glance.

'I know he's here,' Jodie's tone was uneasy and guarded. 'TV said a thirty-five-year-old man had been arrested.'

'Charged with assaulting a police officer.' Carter played for time. 'What do you know about him?'

'I want to make a statement.' She said, blue eyes glancing anxiously between them.

Flowers looked at Carter and, seeing no dissent, took the lead. 'He raped you too, didn't he?'

She nodded delicately. 'I had the baseball bat,' she said. 'He was going to kill you.'

Carter acknowledged the fact with a nod.

'Kelsa and I were good friends during my InterMide days.

I followed him to the hill. I knew you'd go it alone because that's how you are. But, trust me, you don't know Nathan like I do.'

Carter's thoughts were spinning. 'I'm missing a few pieces of your jigsaw, Jodie. Greeting cards, baseball bats—?'

'Surveillance, tracking, listening, following, researching, planning, wishing, hoping. All at him and anyone who crosses his path. I have other pieces, Lachlan. I was at Kelsa's funeral too. He kicked you into her grave.

Carter's face didn't reveal his confusion, but he felt he'd gained a lever.

'Why post the cards? Call the station, it would have been easier.'

'At InterMide,' she looked only at Carter, 'we shared the same telecoms skills – wired, wireless and satellite communications. Nathan had had the benefit of military training. Handling kit I never knew existed. He trained me up, taught me everything. We were soul mates till I tasted his particular brand of vodka.' Her voice turned bitter. 'He changed my life. After he attacked me, I was broken for years. When I'd recovered, I made a pact of vengeance, to see him dead or locked up for life.'

'You've been tracking me,' Carter said. 'You know Dr Flowers through her association with me.'

'To answer your question, Lachlan, snail-mail is hard to intercept, and I do things my way, it keeps me alive. You're the only policeman that's come anywhere close to knowing how he operates. You'll save lives, Lachlan, but you need protection because you're a bit of a wild card.'

'The vodka?' asked Carter. 'He spikes drinks with it.'

'Yes, Scoop is his favourite, and I know the sources of his

drugs. He occasionally hummed "*Bye-bye baby*" at work, but it took me some time to work out what he meant.'

'It's his signature.' Dr Flowers had kept quiet, but now she needed to know something. 'Does he know you're stalking him?'

'After he violated me, I was angry and suicidal – most of his trialists take the suicide way out, leaving him free to move on. But my rage fed my desire for vengeance. My early attempts at hacking him were amateur. I left digital DNA everywhere. I had to up my game. Since I've moved companies, I've learned more. Tracking his whereabouts has become my life, my obsession, my safety net.

'He told me once about an operation in Iraq. "*To kill a sniper, you must become a sniper.*"

'I heeded his advice. Last night, he never saw me coming.'

'Right,' said Carter, feeling more confident about things. 'Make your statement please—dates, places, times and what he did to you. Keep the stalking out of it, be the tearful victim for a while. Can you do that?'

'Of course,' she said. 'But there's something else. You have to get inside his house.'

96

Fallacious Logic

Tam Watson stuck his head through the door. 'Case conference, Leccy. McKinlay's office.'

'Find the duty DC, Tam. Jodie wants to make a statement about our friend. Jodie, stay close, I'll need more from you.'

'I'll cut to the charges,' said McKinlay. 'Rocketman has confirmed that Butler's DNA matches the profiles provided by the National DNA Database from down south. Also, the DNA in Kelsa's case too, but I'm guessing you know that already. The Fiscal wants to review the evidence supporting. So, the eye of the tiger is on you, Leccy – did Butler kill Jacky, and can you prove it away beyond doubt?'

'Yes, we have CCTV from the bus, Jacky had Butler's phone and Butler dumped it in Lily's bag.'

'Murder? Or culpable homicide?'

'Murder.'

'Did he murder Kelsa and can we prove he murdered Lily?'

'Kelsa died ten months later, but murder is feasible, with the right QC. We have clear evidence of Kelsa's aggravated rape. But Lily—'

'So, Jacky is the lead case,' McKinlay said, cutting him off. 'For these other cases in England, the balance of probability is on our side, but that counts for fuck all in front of a judge, especially if it's your father-in-law. Anything else?'

'Jodie Reynolds. He raped her some years ago.'

'That's no fuckin' use to us now.'

'She's downstairs, making a statement.'

McKinlay's demeanour changed instantly. 'Do you know about this development, Nick?'

'News to me,' Mason stared furiously at Carter.

McKinlay took a deep breath. 'So, murder on Jacky, rape on Kelsa and rape on this Reynolds woman. Aggravation will take it up to thirty years at least. We'll add Lily to the sheet when full forensics are available. If Alice wakes and ID's him—'

'Meaning fifteen to eighteen as punishment, before release,' Dr Flowers jumped in with both feet. 'Providing someone in my profession believes he's reformed.'

'Sergeant Carter, I want you to know, so far, you've done a good job. Nick, you have my authority to charge this bastard with murder and Section One rape. Make sure the charges stick with the Fiscal.'

Twenty minutes later, Nick Mason entered the interview room with Carter following. Both detectives wore solemn looks. Butler was chatting to Dominic Love, and both had plastic cups of coffee in their hands. Carter hoped Butler was drinking the full-strength, unrecycled sheep's pish.

'Officers,' Love began his objection, 'I hope you're here with good news and Mr Butler can be released to go about his business.'

Carter operated the recorder and noted the date, time and those present. Butler stretched his powerful back, looked at his watch and resumed the position he'd maintained throughout the interview: bent forward, chin on his chest, arms folded.

Mason sat across from Butler and read out the charges.

'Nathan Butler, you are charged with the murder of Jacky Dodds, on North Bridge, Edinburgh on twenty-first January 2019, and second, with the aggravated rape of Kelsa Dunsmuir Carter, at the Glasgow Hilton Hotel, on seventeenth March 2018, and third, with the aggravated rape of Jodie Reynolds in Dumfries on thirty-first August 2012. You are not required to say anything, but anything you do say will be submitted as evidence. Do you understand the charges?'

When Mason had mentioned Jodie Reynolds, Butler lifted his head, stared at him, and then glared at Carter. Carter's face said *gotcha*. Butler dropped his head again, glanced at his watch and spoke for the first time in the interview. 'What now?'

'Nathan, I'll handle this,' said Love. 'We'll petition for bail immediately.'

'You know that's futile, sir,' said Mason. 'Your client will be remanded in custody until trial.'

'How long will that be?' asked Butler as if such an outcome was impossible in his mind.

'Nine months to a year.'

Butler exploded into action. His chair tumbled backwards as he rose, catching everyone in the room by surprise. Mason reacted instinctively, rising up to face Butler. Butler sidestepped the lanky DI's move and thumped Mason's shoulder hard with a straight arm. Mason pirouetted and stumbled. In one move Butler pulled Mason into a reverse bearhug and kicked his standing leg away. The detective dropped backwards. Butler held him up under his chin by wrapping his arms tight around Mason's throat. Butler stretched Mason's neck and back and his windpipe closed as his own bodyweight choked him. He began to panic.

'Enough,' Butler shouted. 'If I'm not out of 'ere now, hundreds of innocent people will die.'

'What are you talking about?' Carter had watched Butler's move in shock and awe. This wasn't in the script. Fear had infected Dominic Love, and he shrank himself under the table. As the DI's legs skittered and trashed around the floor, Butler pivoted Mason with a knee in his back.

'A hostage is strapped to a suicide vest in the city.' Butler shouted. 'If I don't stop it by ten tonight, the whole place goes *boom*.'

97

False Dilemma

Carter pressed the panic button on the wall. Seconds later, six uniformed PCs burst into the room. Tam Watson followed moments later. Butler released Mason and raised his arms in surrender. Mason collapsed onto the floor, gasping and coughing, before slowly getting back to his feet. He made for Butler before the PCs pulled him back.

'Nick,' said Tam Watson. 'Get out of here.'

Butler retrieved his chair and sat down. He spoke to Love, who was still under the table. 'Your services are no longer required, Dom.'

Clutching his briefcase, Love scrabbled away.

Butler slouched in the chair and pressed home his advantage. He smiled up at Carter, who'd stood when Mason was in the bearhug.

'Sorry about that, but I hate bad news. I'll have another coffee while I wait. Maybe some freshly ground Colombian beans, if you 'ave them. A flat white. If not, milk and two sugars in the instant and a proper cup. I must insist.'

Carter sat down, not really sure what to do. Butler pressed his lead.

'Sergeant Carter. To business. The blood of hundreds of people will be on your hands.'

'You're bluffing,' Carter played for time.

'On your head.' Butler smiled up at the PCs in the room.

'Where is she?'

'Yeah,' Butler looked at his watch. 'Four hours and fifty-two minutes. Better talk to your boss, sonny.'

'What do you want, Nathan?'

'What do *you* want, Leccy?'

'To put you away.'

'I know the code. Where she is. My terms.'

'You'll disappear,' Carter said.

'You should be evacuating homes,' Butler smiled. 'I'll tell you where. Run along now.'

In the observation room, Nick Mason was rubbing his throat. Cheryl McKinlay looked worried.

'I heard,' she addressed Carter. 'It could be a bluff, but we can't take the risk. We'll mobilise the emergency services, but that's Chief Super Goodwin's call. Go back in, Leccy, and tell him yes. Tam's boys can take him to the cells while we organise.'

'I could call the people who called me earlier, they seemed to know about his capabilities.'

'Are they military?' McKinlay asked.

'They didn't say, but you'll need Bomb Disposal too, won't you?'

'An army escort; good thinking. See what else you can get out of them.' McKinlay left the room.

'You OK, Nick?' Carter asked, concerned.

'He's a cunt.' Mason didn't like losing fights.

'He's above our pay grade,' Carter said, not wanting to wind Mason up.

'You respect him?'

'He killed my wife, but we need bigger guns. I'll go back in, you stay here.'

Carter sat opposite Butler, staring at him. Butler smiled. After a few minutes rutting contest, during which neither man spoke, Carter turned to Tam Watson.

'Prepare his cell, he's going back inside while we check this out.'

'For how long?' Butler asked.

'What type of vest?' Carter replied.

'Would you know? I could tell you anything.'

'Somebody will know. Your credibility is at stake.'

Butler laughed uproariously. 'Hell, yeah. You're listening to the wrong people.'

'It's an IED,' Carter tried again.

'You've seen one, 'ave you? IEDs that toss Jackals in the air like confetti at a weddin'? This one has a phone and three kilos of Semtex, held together by a bedsheet and some cord. Improvised. Explosive. Divisive. Probably bring the flats down, 'cos building standards are shite these days. Think Grenfell, with more collateral.'

Carter believed him.

'Nathan,' said Carter. 'Where?'

'Western Harbour,' Butler stated without emotion. 'Four hours, twenty minutes and change, Carter. This isnae a movie where the hero switches off the timer with seconds to boom. Under ten minutes, I'm no' goin' near it.'

Carter signalled for Tam Watson's boys to cuff Butler and move him out. Before the door to the interview room closed, Carter heard him humming.

'*Bye-bye Jenny baby, don't cha cry no more.*'

98

Blast Radius

'Could be worse,' Cheryl McKinlay said when Carter updated the MIT a few minutes later. 'Merchiston or Newington would resemble Syria if it went off there. I'll brief the Chief Super; we've got emergency plans for this.'

After she left the room, Carter found a quiet corner and called the number on his phone's '*recent*' list. Geddes' friend.

'Sergeant Carter. You're calling to chat,' said a clipped English voice.

'Could he build an IED?'

'Should I turn on the news?'

'Not yet.'

'I told you he was resourceful.'

'But the materials—?'

'When he raped your wife, when he wooed Miss Deacon into ending her own life, he planned forward.'

'How do you know about Kelsa?' Carter's blood boiled. Was this just a game? Had these people been aware of what Butler was doing all along? 'Could you have prevented all this?'

'He's not a priority, and the queue is long. We'll help where we can, of course.'

'You vetted Joe Moore but didn't find Nathan Butler. You Oxbridge types are supposedly uber-intelligent. No?'

There was silence for a few seconds. 'Got that one off your chest now?'

'Tell me you track explosives, maintain an inventory of who's got what?'

'We're not B&Q. Is there something you want from me?'

'Is he bluffing?'

'You'd be foolish to think so. Explosives have a shelf life, the mixture degrades, cartridges get written off. There's wiggle room. As I said, he's resourceful.'

'So, why's he on the outside? He's an asset in your wars. On the public streets, he's a feral gorilla.'

'Attracted the wrong kind of attention, rumours of double-dipping, collateral damage and more. Rather an unknown unknown, then a known unknown. We informed the Met at the time of his leaving. Maybe you should talk to them.'

The line went dead.

With forty-five minutes to go, Carter stood inside a Police command centre on wasteland outside the forecourt of the Asda supermarket on Sandpiper Drive in Newhaven. A G4S prison security van hovered fifty metres away. Beyond the estimated blast radius, the inner cordon ran from the Red Car Park at Ocean Terminal, north along the A901 for two kilometres, all the way to Newhaven Harbour. The residential towers on Western Harbour Drive were empty. During the evacuation that had occupied the last few hours, Butler's hostage identified as Jenny Jones had not been discovered.

The Army were present, not just for bomb disposal, but

for sheer manpower. An outer cordon had been created too. All houses and businesses between the Ocean Terminal entertainment complex and the pubs and restaurants at the Shore at Leith were evacuated. Roughly ten thousand people displaced some bedding down in local schools.

The official reason was a WW2 bomb dredged up west of Newhaven Lighthouse. The absence of dredgers and heavy lifting equipment didn't seem to register with the locals, and everyone moved out without complaint. The Police Press Centre at Trinity Primary School dispensed information to news crews on the five-hundred-kilogram SC bomb dropped in July 1940, when the Luftwaffe attacked Granton. TV crews weren't allowed closer than the sea wall at Granton Harbour, another three kilometres west.

They were cutting it fine. The plan was for Butler to go in, accompanied by a team of bomb disposal soldiers. As Carter had reminded everyone in the MIT team, Butler said it was a simple timer, and he knew the code to unlock the phone. Nobody really believed it.

The first smell of something going wrong came when Butler wouldn't sign up to the plan.

'I'm not goin' anywhere with fuckin' pongos.'

The clock ticked down, and Butler hung tight. With thirty minutes to go, he proposed the solution. 'Me and Carter, no one else. You can wire 'im up if you want.'

'You don't need to do this, Leccy,' Dr Flowers said.

'It's all about me, that's what you said, isn't it? I don't have a choice, do I?'

'He'll kill you.'

'Is Jodie here?' Carter replied. 'I could do with her insight.'

'She bolted after signing her statement. Once she heard

the kerfuffle at the station.'

They tried to put a blast protection suit on Carter, but he refused because it was so heavy. Everything he knew about Butler told him he needed mobility. Instead, it was a wire, a radio and a hand-held GPS locator.

'I'm taking my phone too.'

Now Butler stood beside him, handcuffed. The guards unlocked the rigid cuff on Butler's left wrist and were about to open the right cuff when Carter stopped them. He held out his own left wrist. The guards hesitated.

'Do it,' he said. 'Don't waste time. He won't like me dragging him around.'

DCI McKinlay nodded. 'A running commentary, Leccy.'

'Well, here we are, Sergeant,' Butler smiled tightly, gazing down at Carter. 'Aren't you the clever boy?'

They got in the back of a police car. Another uniform got in the front passenger seat. 'Where to?' he said.

'The far side,' said Butler.

The car accelerated west along Sandpiper Road, turned right and disappeared into Western Harbour View.

Twenty minutes to *boom*.

99

Cuffed

The police car scurried to safety, leaving Carter and Butler on rough ground beside the blustery Forth Estuary. The wind skimmed in from the east, escorting staccato bursts of freezing rain. The absence of human activity oozing from the high towers was eerie. No music, no laughter, no arguments. Occasional house lights had been left on in a rush to leave. Some cars had been abandoned. Above them, in the darkness, a helicopter circled, picking them out in its spotlight.

'Lose the chopper,' Butler said. 'Otherwise, I'll strap you to her.'

Carter called it in.

'So, what now, Nathan?' Carter tried for brothers in arms.

'Let's go,' Butler said. They walked between the towers and the bushes, turning down a service road, Carter giving a running commentary into his mic the whole way. Reaching an underground car park, Butler punched a code into the wall-mounted digital pad. The electric shutter rolled up. Cars were parked in some of the spaces, but it wasn't full. Butler pulled him towards a set of red double doors that allowed service access.

'Keep up, Carter. If you're dragging, I'll cut your arm off.'

Carter had lost signal contact with the command post. 'Hello?'

'They can't hear you,' Butler said. 'We're under four feet of steel-reinforced concrete. The car park is a weak Faraday cage; it disturbs low-power radio frequencies. The builders installed repeaters down here so the residents could use their phones, but kids keep breaking them. Funny, eh?'

The electric shutter hit the floor with a metallic bang, sealing them in.

They reached the service unit with its red doors.

'Take the wire off, Carter, and lose the GPS. Unlock the cuffs.'

'I don't have a key.'

With his free hand, Butler reached around the side of the concrete wall and felt for the keysafe. He punched in the code, removed the key and unlocked the red doors.

'What are you doing?' Carter now knew he'd been set up and Butler had him cornered. How was he going to get out of this?

'Givin' you a second chance to open the cuffs before you force me to kill you.' Butler now held the biggest hunting knife Carter had ever seen; a shiny steel blade with a deadly serrated edge designed for slicing up big game. He came in close and pressed the point of the knife against Carter's neck, under his good ear. He spoke quietly and quickly, confidence honed by years on the battlefield.

'The skin protecting your jugular vein 'ere is two millimetres thick, no more. Beneath it are the triangles, the muscles that keep your head up. Next to the ear, they're also two millimetres thick. Below them is the vein and artery.'

Carter couldn't argue.

'The point goes in six millimetres, no more.' There was joy in his voice, this, after all, was his profession. 'Once I pull out the point, a thin spray of your blood will paint those cars. Seven-and-a-half minutes later, you're dead. No pain, so the ragheads told me, just a peaceful but inevitable death. If you don't 'ave the key, I'll cut your arm off below the elbow. You'll survive, but the screaming—?'

Carter handed him the key. Butler transferred the knife to his cuffed hand and unlocked the cuff. Once free, he dragged Carter towards a car and kicked the plastic cover off the towing eye. Carter resisted and, with his free hand, took his phone from his pocket.

'That won't save you,' Butler said.

'Kelsa,' Carter replied with trepidation. No rescue party would be coming for him.

Butler smiled like he was indulging a child. 'You're too trusting to be a copper. We was to be married. I was to be fixed, and so was she. Kindred spirits, we was. When you came along, I promised to take you out. She begged me not to but knew I would, so we made a pact.'

'A pact?'

'That she would die to save you,' Butler smirked. 'But she couldn't go through with it, so I must 'ave my blood.'

Carter couldn't quite believe what he'd heard, and Butler made no attempt to grab him and cuff him to the car. He just stood over him, waiting, a knowing smile spreading across his face. 'All the time in the world, Leccy.'

'She'd die for me. But— you're saying she's alive?'

'I've tracked every move you made since Las Vegas. You saw the messages on her phone when she was in hospital. Then there's the interdict keepin' you away from Dunsmuir's home. She was inside when you was drunk outside. She *gave* me the knickers, and the stockings, and the key to your house. All she could talk about was us bein' together again.'

'You're lying,' Carter reacted angrily. Butler knew things he couldn't know unless Kelsa had told him. 'You couldn't have seen her in hospital. I was there most days. I didn't know then that you'd raped her, but she knew you'd hound her forever. She wanted me to promise I'd care for Nathaniel. The doctor called later to say she'd gone. She was so thin.'

'How was it you made detective?' Butler said. 'Before all that, she went to court to secure custody of our boy with the family, and you didn't even know. After you'd left the hospital at night, I'd come in, and we'd refine the plan. She'd been through the whole Anorexia thing many times. She controlled *it*. It didn't control her.

'On her last night, I gave her Scoop and DMT. It slowed her vitals right down. It fooled the doctors, and Kelsa's doctors was expecting death. Once she was in the mortuary, I revived her and switched bodies with another. Swapped the toe tags too.'

'I don't – I can't believe that.' Carter's thoughts were a maelstrom. 'There're processes, procedures, checks and balances in a mortuary. There are door locks, for fuck's sake.'

'You never saw her lying in the parlour because the old man didn't want anyone near her. He and me has an arrangement, and he has reasons to stick to it.'

Once more, it seemed everything Carter had thought was true was a lie. Was Kelsa really in the grave? As a police officer with probable cause, an exhumation would resolve it. What would her family agree to that? No, and he knew why.

'I was there,' Butler sniggered, relaxing on the bonnet of a car while Carter lay on the concrete. 'Dunsmuir invited me to the funeral. Kelsa told him you wasn't to be allowed. But I knew you'd come. It was so funny, everybody crying over a corpse that wasn't her.'

Carter held out his phone, pressed play on the video and turned it around so Butler could see. 'Look at this. The Hilton, inside the bedroom of Mr and Mrs Moore. You're raping her. This isn't consensual sex. Look at it – she's screaming at you to stop, to leave her alone. You're kicking her, punching her, banging her head off the walls.'

'Loved it rough, she did. Was addicted to being knocked about, always came back for more of daddy's cock. She liked the girls too, we had a foursome once, two blondes—'

'Shut up, you arsehole.'

'You're weak, Carter, you're mentally screwed. Your understandin' was blighted by grief. You never cared about what happened in 1989 until I shoved it in your face. Total coincidence that we were in the same accident and shared the same woman. A coincidence that will see my vengeance satisfied tonight. You're the worst kind of son a mother could 'ave. You've denied your old folks the release they've earned, so you're 'avin' a binary choice tonight because you can't be trusted to do the right thing on your own.'

'Where is she?'

'Once I've sorted you, I'm goin' to her. She's far away from her family. It'll be just her and me.'

The knife came into play again, and shortly Carter found himself cuffed to a black Mercedes. Butler smashed Carter's phone on the concrete floor with the knife's hilt, then went to the access cupboard and returned with a hip flask.

'She pleaded I wasn't to kill you, but she's not here. If you like the look of Death when you meet him, just say yes.'

He checked his watch. 'Ten minutes. Jenny's in a rental flat and I'll pin the address on your corpse.'

With Carter lying cuffed on the concrete floor, Butler stepped inside his legs and kicked him hard in the testicles. Carter screamed with the agony. Butler crouched and forced Carter's mouth open further, pouring the contents of the flask down his throat. He coughed and choked, but the pressure reflex in his abdomen made him swallow all of the dark liquid.

'Never tried vodka coke on a bloke. Die or live, Carter, your choice.'

Within seconds Carter's eyes rolled back into his head, and he lay supine on the concrete, experiencing the beginning of a kaleidoscopic nightmare. His head lolled to one side. He saw Kelsa standing in the car park, only metres away from him, wearing the clothes she'd worn on Leith Walk. He reached for her.

She sang to him. '*Bye-bye Leccy baby, don't cha cry no more.*'

100

Inner Space

Lachlan Carter's world blurred into a high-speed, time-warped, slow-motion movie of his last moments on earth. Detectives, paramedics, doctors, soldiers, ambulance crew all vied for his attention. Deep inside, he didn't know why they were prodding, probing and poking him, literally and verbally. It was over. The crabs that had been chewing through his brain had retreated. They'd been beaten back by the seals, and as long as both stayed apart, the battle in his head wouldn't start up again, and he could just peacefully let go. A shadow stood beside him, anticipating.

'I can't find a pulse,' someone shouted. 'Get him to the Western General now.'

Jolts, bangs, slams, oxygen. Sways, shouts, rips, injection. Bleeps, horns, blues, twos. Harder jolts, louder bangs, brighter lights, inner darkness. A feeling of his insides being sucked out of his body. Rapid tom-tom thumps on his chest.

Electrical whining, winding up, screaming, louder, louder, louder. Long beeps. 'Stand clear, everyone.'

Boom.

Dr Lisa Flowers sat on a hard chair in the soulless waiting room. Nick Mason was on the phone, pacing up and down like a nervous first-time father. Finally, he ended the call.

'Well,' she asked anxiously. 'What's happening?'

'They're on their way from Ayr. They'll be here in ninety minutes.'

A man in a green smock entered and identified himself as an A & E nurse. 'You're his parents?' he asked, raising an eyebrow.

'Jesus,' Nick Mason said. 'Just tell us.' He made the universal survival sign: thumb up, thumb down.

'He's back with us.'

'Grandparents are on their way. Maw an' Paw are deid,' Mason informed the man.

'The rest of the diagnosis can wait till they get here,' the nurse said, disappearing.

'Any news on Nathan Butler's whereabouts?' Dr Flowers asked Mason anxiously because there wasn't any other topic they could discuss – now that the question of life had been resolved.

'Vanished. We need Carter to tell us what went down in the car park before he was drugged. The hip flask was on the floor, and he had the note in hand when we got in, giving Jenny's true location.'

'Well after the deadline, though.' Dr Flowers wasn't happy about any of it.

'Too risky,' Mason defended the approach. 'Once contact was lost, the Chief Super was convinced damage limitation was the only option.'

'Still, Leccy will be pleased his colleagues moved heaven and earth to rescue him.' Flowers said, sarcastically.

Mason ignored the bait. 'Jenny was in Merchiston, and there was no bomb. She's badly dehydrated but is otherwise OK. We'll hear her story once she's recovered.'

'How will you catch him again?'

'A nationwide campaign on TV and radio, pictures in all the papers, ports and airports alerted, increased searches of vehicles leaving the country. A fugitive can stay in hiding for two or three days, maybe a week, but eventually the milk will turn sour. Somebody will shop him. You don't look convinced, Lisa. You think he's got special psycho-powers?'

'You've continually underestimated him,' she retorted. 'He planned all of this, knowing you couldn't dismiss the bomb threat as a hoax. He'd planned his escape from custody before you'd even caught him. Realistically, when will you give up?'

'Never.'

'He'll be drinking with Lord Lucan in a few days, I'm sure,' she said.

'Aye, and he's deid too,' said Mason, emphatically.

Deek and Sarah Carter were shown into the waiting room. After the introductions, Nick Mason gave them a summary of what the police knew. The nurse entered the room again, and the Carters agreed that the police should hear everything he had to say.

'Can we see him?' Deek Carter asked.

'He's in intensive care and won't be going anywhere today. I'm sorry.'

'Will he die?' Sarah asked fearfully. 'Deek, what are we going to do?'

'The drug slowed his heartbeat down and caused much of his brain to shut down too,' the nurse said. 'When heartbeat and brain function fall to these levels, God casts the dice, and the mix of chemicals in his body decides what happens. He died on the table, but we brought him back with adrenaline.'

'I'm sure Cheryl will allow him a day's sick leave once she hears that,' said Mason.

'It's down to him now,' said the nurse.

The door to the waiting room opened, and a woman walked in and identified herself. 'Angela Murray, orthopaedic trauma, RiE.' She nodded to the nurse then turned to Lisa Flowers and Nick Mason. 'I've seen you two before. I heard about the incident on TV. They said a policeman had been taken to hospital, so I bet my consulting exam score it was Leccy.'

'You know him?' the nurse asked.

'We've been sparring over a patient of mine, who's now recovering consciousness. Leccy wanted to know when she re-joined the living.'

'Mr Carter is sedated at the moment.'

'Is it the same drug Alice was given? Ironically, she's awakened from it, and he's now under it.' Dr Murray turned to the nurse again. 'Can we see him?'

'Well – we don't usually—'

'I'll keep them under control.'

'How is Alice?' Dr Flowers asked. 'Can she remember anything? Can she speak?'

'She is speaking words, but she can't hold a conversation.'

'Can I send a couple of constables to question her?' Nick Mason asked. 'We only need to know if Butler was the one who raped her.'

'I'll let you know in a day or two, Inspector.'

Five minutes later, they were at Carter's bedside. Around him, five other patients received similar treatment: monitors, wires, oxygen, IVs and hot and cold running nurses. Leccy Carter lay with his head back, eyes closed and taped, propped up with pillows supporting his neck and shoulders, like the other patients. Unlike them, he had no traction wires and no stookies.

To Deek and Sarah, the distinction between Lachlan, the grandson, and Daniel, the son, was long blurred; they'd never been given a choice to see Daniel fight for his life.

'Oh, Deek,' Sarah said, tears flowing. 'He doesn't look good.'

'What's the prognosis, Sister?' Deek asked the oldest of the nurses beside him.

'It's touch and go right now. It'll be another day or two before we'll know for sure.'

101

Heels and Toes

Thirty-six hours later, Deek Carter arrived at the Western General to collect his grandson. Carter walked out unaided and got in the car. 'How're you feeling, son?'

'Fine, Faither, just fine,' Carter said. In truth, his physical wounds would heal, but the man who walked out of hospital wasn't the same man who'd walked away cuffed to a killer.

'Your gran is keen to look after ye, so don't disappoint her, eh?'

'Can I use your phone? Mine got broken.'

'Aye.' The older man handed it over.

'Drive to Murrayfield, Faither, Easter Murray Avenue.'

'What's there, son?'

'The ghost house.'

Twenty minutes later they pulled up next to a couple of uniformed coppers. Carter identified himself. 'Is Nick Mason here?'

'No, Sarge. They were all here yesterday. Crime scene examiners only today.'

'Faither, I can't take you in. I won't be long.'

He identified himself to the lead CSE, was given gloves, shoe covers and a mask.

'Has anything been removed from the house?'

'Not yet, I'm waiting for the nod from your lot.'

'Who's in charge?'

'DCI McKinlay.'

'Anything you consider interesting? You know the suspect and what he's alleged to have done?'

'The back room, right-hand side. Big picture window, floor to ceiling glass. Curved, like a rare first-generation New Town property. Your man had class.'

The double doors that defied him a week ago now invited him in. The hallway was as large as his sitting-room in Liberton and led to the kitchen at the back. The flooring was an intricate, symmetrical parquet design of polished hardwood laid decades ago, in keeping with the exterior design. Butler had bought the place, not built it. Carter assumed someone was tracing where the funds came from. He glanced in the downstairs rooms: modern upgrade, but not the sleek monochrome minimalist look that many moneyed houses chose to adopt.

The kitchen was as up to date as he expected. There were additional rooms for garden, utilities and a shower-cum-toilet. Outside, the gardens were in winter hibernation, but looked after and tended – not by its owner, he assumed. There would be time for a more in-depth look into the house later. Butler wouldn't return here, and that meant the police had unfettered access.

The staircase off the hallway featured a balustrade made from the same wood as the floor. It had a runner with a

180-degree curve, halfway up. Gran's house, in Gorebridge, had a stair runner, with two ninety-degree curves, one at the bottom and one at the top. Nowhere near as grand as this one, and he wondered if there was a sinuous connection to Butler's family home in Deptford. He smiled as he climbed the stairs, careful of the pain between his legs, remembering how he used to slide down the runner on his bum, much to his gran's annoyance.

The room the CSE highlighted was easy to find. It offered a fabulous view over the rugby stadium and the city in the foreground and then onwards to the Pentland Hills in the background, twenty miles away. But it was the other contents of the room that got Carter's attention. A leather-covered armchair occupied the centre of the room; next to it was a side table. On the room's right-hand side, a bar and gantry were sunk into the wall and stocked with various whiskies, vodkas, rums, and more. He scanned the brands and distilleries; Butler's preference was islands and lowlands: smoke, peat and lightness, and this again revealed them as men of difference, not concurrence.

On the left-hand side of the room was a built-in hi-fi. The CSE had opened a set of concealed wooden doors that folded back the whole length of the room, from the back wall to the window, revealing another sunken alcove. Lighting inside the recess, from top, sides and bottom, could be manipulated to pick out cherished items. The lowest shelving held shoes, lots of shoes, two rows high. Women's dress shoes, all neatly set in their own places, all polished like new. Carter counted twenty pairs for twenty women. In the centre of the top row, a pair of leopard-print shoes with four-inch heels stood out from the rest on a raised plinth.

Kelsa's.

102

Private Enterprise

Carter eased himself down the stairs into the isolation tent, where he divested himself of the shoe covers, mask and gloves. He oozed into the car beside Deek and gave him directions into town. On the way, he made a call on Deek's phone.

'Any luck with Alice?' he asked his superior officer.

'I'm fine, thanks,' replied DI Mason. 'Glad you've recovered. Now we've been polite, why the fuck are you working? You're on sick leave.'

'I've been discharged,' Carter said. 'Faither offered to be my chauffeur for the day.'

'Alice has ID'd Butler. DC Garcia showed her the picture from the Reverend, but she knew him as Moore.'

'Kelsa's shoes.' There was a change in Carter's tone, a focused tightness.

'Oh, you've been to his house? Where would we be now, if only you hadn't marked him as a dead end?'

'Have you matched names of women to the pairs yet?' Trying to keep Mason on track could be hard work.

'It's work in progress.'

'Alice and Jodie will be two, Lily a third,' said Carter. 'Seventeen women we know nothing about. We'll need to track them down. I'll start with Alice once I've got a new phone and replaced the SIM.'

'Give us all the new number when you get it,' Mason said.

'It's the same number I used to have.'

'He'll be able to track you again.'

'He'll know I'm back and he'll know I'm coming for him.'

'I'll bet he's shittin' himself right now,' Mason said. 'Wondering where his next drink is coming from.'

'Things have changed, Nick. Jodie said something to Flowers and me about Butler when she came into the station. I've signed up for sniper training at the local college.'

'You're still the same pish-talker, Carter.'

'Where is Dr Flowers, anyway?' Carter asked.

'Contract terminated. Again. Now Butler has gone, she's got nobody to weep with. As a bonus, we need the money saved to pay for your private medical care, even if it was NHS staff doing all the caring. That's how private enterprise works, I'm told. Fucked if I understand it.' Mason rang off.

Faither drove his grandson back to the Royal Infirmary and sat in the café. Dr Murray escorted Carter to Alice's room. She was awake, but her blue eyes were subdued by drugs. Her face was full of red, grey and yellow blotches, and the monitors remained connected and monitoring.

'She's doing really well. Memory is still a bit dodgy, but it's coming back,' said Dr Murray happily. Alice looked at Angela hazily, but in the look, Carter saw something more. Devotion perhaps, love maybe, appreciation certainly.

'Her physical injuries are another story, though,' Dr Murray continued the review. 'A wheelchair for a long time and lots of physiotherapy. After that, who knows what medibots could do.'

'Are you, Sergeant Carter?' Alice spoke directly to him. 'Angela says you've been tracking down Joe, although his real name was— I've forgotten.'

'Nathan Butler,' Carter filled in one blank. 'Can I show you a picture of some shoes and can you tell me if yours are there?' He took out his new Samsung phone, opened the ICRS app and showed her the pictures.

'Wow, so many pairs – I wasn't first; I knew that. I've made up what's left of my mind – if I don't like you, you can fuck off,' she smiled. 'The green stilettos with the ankle straps. He liked me to wear them on dates.'

'How long had you been seeing him?' Carter let the question hang.

'I knew him from InterMide, but he was seeing someone else for a long time.'

'Kelsa Dunsmuir?' Carter asked.

'She was a contractor too.'

'When did you start dating him?'

'Christmas – 2017.'

'Did he ever speak to you about Kelsa?'

'That's how I knew.'

'What?'

'She was special, and I wasn't.'

'What do you remember? The bridge?'

'The drinking was always the start. He'd give me vodka coke sometimes to spice things up, but that night it was rocket fuel. He had a thing about suicide. When I'd had enough of him, he'd said there was only one way out.'

'So you knew?'

'Twice before – but I'd bottled it.'

'Did you jump?'

'After sex on the tomb, I remember being carried, then the noise of traffic and I knew where I was. He put me down and punched and kicked me, told me it was my time. A stocking – he choked me with it. Then I was flying. That's all I remember.'

'You landed on top of an ambulance and slid off. It ran over you.'

'Really?' she said. 'Have you arrested him?'

'He's escaped,' Carter said, disappointed. 'But you're safe.'

'She needs to rest,' Dr Murray said. 'This has all been very stressful.'

In Dr Murray's face, Leccy saw a deeper look. She held his gaze and, for the first time, he really took her in. They turned to leave Alice.

'Who is Kelsa?' Dr Murray asked as they walked, smiling at his hesitation, misreading it, but prepared to give him the benefit of the doubt.

'It's a long story,' he said. 'Longer than even I know.'

'You can buy me a few drinks before we get to the end of it, then.'

'Yes,' Leccy said. 'I will.'

103

A Cupboardful of Skeletons

'Lachlan, why are you out of hospital. One of your colleagues informed me you'd been drugged.'

Carter's mother-in-law had an eye for detail. He'd called her from the station and confirmed the arrangement. After sending Faither home, he arrived at the mansion on Hermitage Drive in a police car, knowing the Sheriff would still be at his club.

'What on earth have you been up to?' Judith asked while ringing the service bell. 'I'll arrange some tea.'

Her private sitting room overlooked the back gardens, but tonight the curtains were closed, the heating was on, and it was about to get much colder inside. It was just the two of them. Nathaniel was asleep in his cot upstairs. She sat in a comfortable chair. He made himself comfortable on the sofa.

'Kelsa may still be alive.' He watched for her reaction.

'Lachlan, how can you say that?' she stared at him. 'It's hurtful, and it's in poor taste.'

The door opened, the maid came in. She served tea and cake and cut the atmosphere with a knife. Once she left, Carter sipped his tea and sliced his accusations into easily digestible bites.

'Nathan Butler was the mysterious boyfriend in between Hugo Mortimer and me. He has a psychopathic alter ego called Joe Moore who revels in raping and murdering women. Kelsa was his victim last March, and it was one reason why she wanted to take her life.'

'I don't really want to hear this,' Judith said angrily. 'But you're not giving me a choice, are you? You're going to ram it down my throat and to hell with the consequences.'

'I've suffered the consequences, and you do have a choice, Jude.' Carter put a USB stick on the coffee table where she could see it. 'You can watch and hear it from her own lips. Butler is real, and hours ago, he killed me too. If it hadn't been for the doctors, you'd have no choice other than to watch a video left to you by a dead man.'

'I'm sorry, Lachlan.' She sobbed into her hands.

'Answer me, truthfully,' he said. 'Were you a party to this conspiracy?'

'What conspiracy? What are you talking about?'

'Yes or no.'

'Lachlan, you're not making sense. I don't understand.'

Carter got up and stood over her. 'Judith Dunsmuir, I am detaining you under caution—'

'Are you out of your mind? No, no, a thousand times no.' Judith was shaking, a hand across her chest. 'I feel faint.'

Carter poured her some fresh tea and sat down.

'I'm sorry, Jude, but I had to know if you were involved.'

'Involved with what, Lachlan?'

'The conspiracy to murder Kelsa while she was in hospital after she gave birth. Butler agreed to do the murder. Others were along for the ride, too.'

'How is that possible?'

'Kelsa made videos last year before going into hospital. One was of her actual rape by Butler in March. There is no value in watching it. She saved a video on her laptop in September, for my eyes only, before going into hospital. In it, she was cagey and resorted to hints because she knew I didn't know the full family background, and I didn't know what had happened to her as a child. The third video on the laptop was for you, and a digital copy is now on that USB stick. Kelsa knew I'd watch it because she knew the family would cover up its secrets like it's covered up everything else.'

'Is this a police investigation?'

'According to Kelsa's testimony, witnessed by a lawyer, James first raped her aged eight. He continued the abuse until her teenage years. Then Mortimer took over until her twenties when he saw profit in her. She was caught in a circular net of abuse and couldn't get out. She thought she'd found her hero in Joe Moore, but he ultimately wanted her for himself. Nathan Butler was Moore's public face, and he has committed at least twenty rapes and murders.'

Judith had turned pale at the revelations. 'What am I supposed to do with this information?'

'Two nights ago, Butler told me she wasn't dead. But you would've seen her body before it went to the mortuary.'

There was a pause.

'James wouldn't allow me to see her.'

'The police have a duty to exhume if they believe she's been murdered, but the family can challenge in court. It won't happen quickly, and she's not going anywhere soon. Meantime, watch her testimony. DC Ellen Podolski will stay here with you. She's outside in a police car. Stay out of sight when James arrives, I'll detain him and take him to St Leonard's.'

Carter left her sipping cold tea and looking at the USB stick in absolute horror.

104

Epilogue

Judith Dunsmuir sat precisely where she'd been sitting when Carter had left her, two weeks previously. But everything around her had changed. Surveyors, estate agents and workmen had the run of the place, leaving her at the centre of a black hole of professional activity. She wore a stunned look, and Carter wondered if she was on sedatives. He sat on the couch, reached over and squeezed her hand. She'd lost weight since he'd last seen her. Her eyes were red and the skin of her face and neck, once radiant with health, had sagged.

'I'm going to live with my sister in Perth for a while. I cannot bear to be here any longer, Lachlan. For forty-five years, this house was my foundation. But as I slept upstairs, it was rotting from the core. I never knew, and I never thought to enquire, and for that self-deception, I am as guilty as him. She was a troubled child, but this abomination has shattered my self-belief. I doubt I will ever recover.'

'James is under remand,' Carter said. 'He's segregated in Saughton for his own safety. A psychologist and two detectives interview him every day. He's not giving in easily. We have evidence he paid Butler fifty-thousand pounds on the third of January, via a lawyer called Dominic Love. He took out a loan against your home on the thirtieth of December. On the fourth of January, in the Reverend bar in Dalry, Mortimer gave him a cheque for twenty-six thousand euros, which James deposited in his bank the next day.'

Judith put her hands to her mouth. 'How do you know this?'

'Bankers never lie about their clients. Throughout, I'd spent too much time looking at who *was* in the Reverend, when I should have been looking for who *wasn't*. Mortimer and Butler were present on the fourth. So was James, or so his mobile phone implied so I needed eye-witness confirmation. An informer who works in the Reverend said James was the man in the snug when shown his picture. As part of their conspiracy, I was to die too. Mortimer has fled. He's abandoned his family in France, and there's a European arrest warrant out for him. One out for Butler too.'

'A few days after you were last here,' Judith said, reeling from the latest news, 'Robert Stenhouse, our family lawyer, came to see me. He was a long-time friend of James. Robert handled Nathaniel's residency order on Kelsa's behalf. He refused to be involved with the interdict against you, because, by then, he'd witnessed Kelsa's testimony and couldn't bear to be in the same room as James.'

'About Nathaniel—' Carter began to speak, but she cut him off.

'Robert gave me an envelope. A private letter from Kelsa, most of which I'd prefer not to share if you understand. She dictated it to Robert in hospital after giving birth. She believed Nathaniel was Butler's son and that it was unfair of her to expect you to raise the child of a rapist and murderer. She said you knew her feelings.'

'I'd always wanted a son,' Carter spoke quietly. 'I don't really know why, something to do with not having my own parents, I guess. I wanted to name him Daniel, after my dad, but she wouldn't hear of it. She was adamant about the names, said I would understand one day. I understand now. Nathaniel and James were the two of the three men she hated most in the world. She handed me the biggest clue ever, and I totally missed it.

'You are Nathaniel's grandmother, so I'd like you to care for him. I won't contest the residency order. This situation isn't his fault, so he shouldn't suffer for the mistakes of his family. But I can't be the father he's going to need.'

Judith stood up and walked to a chest of drawers nearby. 'Do you really believe she's alive, Lachlan?'

'No, I don't.'

'I've spent much time thinking about the implications of exhumation. If it's not her, she won't want to be found. Maybe by you, but not by any of us. I'd rather leave things as they are.' She came back from the chest with an envelope and handed it to him. 'Robert had an envelope for you too.'

Written in Kelsa's scrawl were the words:

'Wherever you go, I will be there.'

The flap was sealed with a kiss of her scarlet lips. He hugged his mother-in-law and walked out.

'Goodbye, Jude.'

That same evening, the light dallied higher in the sky. Spring was winning its annual battle for dominance, although it would be months yet before the sun warmed Leccy's back. The entrance gate to Old Calton Burial Ground was chained and locked with a heavy padlock. Eighteenth-century technology, designed to prevent illegal burials had worked well – there hadn't been one for more than one-hundred-and-fifty years – so Carter found one of the other ways through its defences.

This dusky evening, it wasn't raining like it had been at her burial, but the air was bitterly cold. He pulled the collar of his Crombie coat around his neck and ambled around the sacred site, gazing out to the lights of the Old Town and the Castle on his right. On his left, Arthur's Seat brooded in the gloaming, a reminder not to take liberties again. He walked down the gravel path to her grave and stood before it. Her headstone wasn't yet installed, but the flowers had succumbed to the wintery weather. At the spot where he'd prayed only weeks ago, he took out the DNA profile graph that had been sealed inside Kelsa's envelope. On the reverse were three little words.

Pick better names.

'Well, babes, if I believe your ex-fiancé, I'm not talking to you at all. But if you are there, I know that you died knowing of our beautiful boy. I hope it made you as happy as it makes me. You knocked the rough edges off me while you lived. But you tore me to shreds in death, and I'll take a long time for me to recover from you. Our newly named son, Daniel Caroline Kelsa Carter, will grow up knowing how extraordinary his mother really was.'

His phone pinged, not the ardent tone of an incoming threat from J, but a softer and quieter, read-me-at-your-leisure type of ping. Angie Murray was a Facebook Messenger addict and must be calling him to a pub. He looked at the message.

'*One day, I'll come for the boy.*'

'Aye, right,' Leccy straightened his strong Carter back and spat his words high into the frigid darkness. 'We'll see about that.'

Detective Sergeant Lachlan Carter marched away from the grave, climbed over the wall of the burial ground and vanished into the vibrant city of Edinburgh.

The End of *A Wife Worth Dying For*

105

Story Notes

I'm touching up these notes in February 2021, and Covid-19 measures on web pages do their best to obscure critical story detail readers might want to query as fact or fiction. Researching on the ground is restricted too, as it feels insensitive to ask trivial questions on points of fact when people are dying with the virus.

The messaging app used by Nathan Butler/Joe Moore does not exist, as far as I know. No one in Government would confirm either way. In my profession, I have spent decades working on the Internet of things, and I genuinely believe untraceable forms of communication for espionage are as likely to exist today as they were in their Cold War heydays. Like a virus, it wouldn't take much for such an app to jump into civilian mobile phones.

The Reverend bar on Dalry Road, Edinburgh is a figment of my imagination.

I've taken literary licence with the functions of Police Scotland's Fettes office block. Although it has extensive grounds and warehouse-style structures, by default, Police

Scotland don't publicly comment on operational matters. The SoCO acronym for Scene of Crime Officers, well-used by crime writers over decades, has now been confined to criminal history in Scotland. Scene Examiner (SE) is the official title. However, I've stretched it to CSE to be in step with Crime Scene Manager (CSM).

For those readers not familiar with Scotland, it has its own legal system, distinct from the English system, but there is cross-over of the Lex in solemn matters. Legal marriage in Scotland is simpler and easier than in England. If Scots couples choose to marry abroad, they cannot "sign the register" when they return home. Instead, they can voluntarily add their marriage to the Book of Scottish Connections held by the Registrar General in Edinburgh.

The conversation between Leccy and his lawyer, Tommy McGregor, about Nathaniel's birth certificate is accurate at the time of writing.

All other flaws are mine alone.

106

Acknowledgements

Writing a novel is mostly a solitary undertaking, but a writer needs help along the way to the title's birth. So, in no particular order:

The author C. M. Taylor mentored me during the final stages of drafting and helped me keep focus on the story.

Many thanks also, to all the editors, book doctors, agents and publishers that Harry Bingham, CEO of Jericho Writers summoned to the stage at the numerous Festivals of Writing I attended in York. I wasn't the brightest of students, but enough mud stuck to the wall.

Thanks to "Big Jim" for his honest review of an early revision of the story – and for his insight of the Scots legal system. Afterward, I embarked on a re-write which eventually surfaced the story you have just read. I commend to tender writers the benefits of beta-readers as a method of shaking the deadwood from your gnarly tree well before publication.

Thanks to my editor, Abby Parsons, for her skill, dedication and points of order when my prose got a bit too colloquial.

Thanks also to Cherie Chapman for her wonderful cover design.

Snippets from two song lyrics appear at a critical point in the story.

All the Girls Love Alice, ©copyright Elton John and Bernie Taupin, from the 1973 vinyl double album *Goodbye Yellow Brick Road*. Awaiting permission.

Matchmaker Matchmaker, by Sheldon Harnick and Lewis Bock Jerrold. ©Jerry Bock Enterprises, Trio Music Co., INC. From the 1964 musical *Fiddler on the Roof*. Awaiting permission.

Finally, to the unsung heroes who supported me through long days and longer nights. To Ruth, who encouraged me with motivation, love and coffee from the furthest reaches of the garden.

To my daughters, Sarah Hughes and Kirsty Wilson, for just being there, for helping me not talk about writing stories during the dark days of pandemic – and at all other times.

To dogs, Angus, Betsy and Sam, and to cats JB (now deceased) and Jeff all of whom can't write and only care about where their next ball is coming from. This title is dedicated to my grandchildren, Boyd and Lexi Hughes, who are too young to read the story anyway.

Wilson B, February 2021.

Edinburgh

About the Author

I live in Edinburgh, Scotland and have been writing novels for the past nine years.

You can connect with me on:

- https://wilsonsmillie.com
- https://twitter.com/WilsonSmillie
- https://www.facebook.com/wilson.smillie

Also by Wilson B Smillie

A Wife Worth Dying For

Want to explore more of Leccy's world in Edinburgh?

Great! Leccy has a quiz waiting for you to play. Answer one hundred questions set across four levels from dead-easy to infuriatingly difficult.

Test yourself: see how much you really know about Scotland's favourite Detective, his life, his investigation and get yourself to the top of the leaderboard!

Sign up at https://wilsonsmillie.com.

Read the story and start quizzing.

Printed in Great Britain
by Amazon